HIDEOUT

OTHER BOOKS BY KATHLEEN GEORGE

FICTION

The Odds

Afterimage

Fallen

Taken

The Man in the Buick

NONFICTION

Winter's Tales: Reflections on the Novelistic Stage

Playwriting: The First Workshop

Rhythm in Drama

HIDEOUT

KATHLEEN GEORGE

MINOTAUR BOOKS
A THOMAS DUNNE BOOK
NEW YORK

This is a work of fiction. All of the characters, organizations, and events portrayed in this novel are either products of the author's imagination or are used fictitiously.

A THOMAS DUNNE BOOK FOR MINOTAUR BOOKS.
An imprint of St. Martin's Publishing Group.

HIDEOUT. Copyright © 2011 by Kathleen George. All rights reserved. Printed in the United States of America. For information, address St. Martin's Press, 175 Fifth Avenue, New York, N.Y. 10010.

www.thomasdunnebooks.com
www.minotaurbooks.com

Library of Congress Cataloging-in-Publication Data
George, Kathleen, 1943–
Hideout / Kathleen George.—1st ed.
p. cm.
"A Thomas Dunne book."
Summary: "The new book in Kathleen George's stunning Pittsburgh-set police procedural series begins when a young mother dies in a hit-and-run accident caused by two young brothers. Desperate and afraid, Jack and Ryan Rutter flee to Sugar Lake, the summer community where they vacationed as children. As Detectives Colleen Greer and Richard Christie search for the brothers, Jack and Ryan create a terrifying hostage situation. As fast-paced and brilliantly plotted as the book that earned her an Edgar' nomination, Hideout is a riveting police procedural like no other"—provided by publisher.
ISBN 978-0-312-56913-6
1. Police—Pennsylvania—Pittsburgh—Fiction. 2. Traffic fatalities—Fiction. 3. Hit-and-run drivers—Fiction. 4. Brothers—Fiction. 5. Fugitives from justice—Fiction. 6. Hostages—Fiction. 7. Pittsburgh (Pa.)—Fiction. I. Title.
PS3557.E487H53 201
OCT 2011
813'.54—dc22

2011009132

First Edition: August 2011

10 9 8 7 6 5 4 3 2 1

m(31)

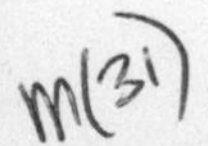

For Hilary

ACKNOWLEDGMENTS

AS ALWAYS I WOULD LIKE TO THANK the many police who have helped me, notably Chief Michael Phillips of the Cochranton Borough Police, and especially retired Commander Ronald B. Freeman of the Pittsburgh Police. When I needed drug information, consultants at Alpha House and Addiction No More were patient and invaluable sources. Sheryl Dawson of Sugar Lake and Stacey Hoey and Grace Motzing of Cochranton gave me a sense of place. Inga Meier at the University of Pittsburgh helped with research. And certainly inspiration came to me from two remarkable women—Alice Provensen and Adlin Loud.

I am blessed to have loving siblings, friends I can rely on, and a supportive atmosphere at the University of Pittsburgh. My most profound thanks go to my husband, Hilary Masters, who is a marvel of wisdom and generosity.

HIDEOUT

ONE

SATURDAY

COMMANDER CHRISTIE SLAPPED DOWN a file folder and got up to look out his office door. It was late on a Saturday in early May and there was nothing going on in Homicide. Some of his detectives were relieved about the slack; others were restless. The few who were in were slogging through paperwork.

It was long past time to go home; he'd put in his shift, set a good example and all that. He left his door open and went back to his desk, as if chaining himself to it might keep up the spirit of his troops.

He wanted to talk to his kids so he dialed his ex's house. Catherine was just answering, saying, "Oh, it's you," when he noticed a flutter of activity outside his door. "Kids aren't here," Catherine added.

He tried to see what was happening on the floor. "How come they're both out?" he asked. It was six thirty. Where would they both go?

"It's a crime?"

"No."

"Because I have a date. Shock you?"

"No. No, I'm glad." While he watched his two detectives—phone, physical movement—he tried to picture Catherine on a date, still battling so much anger. "The kids are where?"

"At my friend's house."

"Have a good time."

She didn't answer.

He said, "Take care," and hung up.

Paul Mertz and Irina Alexandratos were fetching their jackets, but Alexandratos was on the phone again as Christie hurried over to them.

"What is it? You got something?"

"We just got a 911. Kid on a sidewalk," Mertz said hopefully, buttoning his sport coat. "Caller said he looks dead. Probably crack, so we can get there in case—" His raised eyebrows finished the thought. *You got crack, you got a potential killer,* Mertz always said. It was more or less true. The crack addicts were the worst.

Alexandratos had a hand up to silence him.

"She's on with the ambulance," Mertz told Christie.

Alexandratos's face fell as she hung up. "Nah, he's still alive," she said glumly. "Ah, well." She wagged her head and looked at her deskful of memos and other junk waiting for her attention. "Commander? We'd like to go to the hospital, you know, in case there was any intention or in case he doesn't make it."

Christie nodded. It might be something. He hoped the tide was turning and there'd be cases to get their teeth into. Dolan and Greer were due at midnight. Murders didn't happen on an even schedule. You either had four of them or none. "I'm going home," Christie told them. "Watch crime on TV."

JACK RUTTER, DRIVING THE RED TRUCK, had looked for his brother in the usual places. The base house where Ryan bought his rocks looked different today, curtains opened. Jack drove around the corner to East Ohio, where he immediately saw the flashing lights of a police ambulance. He thought, Oh, no, please no. People were standing around. Shit, shit, shit, he breathed. Then he saw through the gaggle of onlookers that his brother's friend Chester was down on the pavement. Ryan was alive at least, squatting next to Chester in front of an empty barbershop with the windows papered over. Jack put the truck in a NO PARKING space with the motor still running and leapt out and went over to his brother. Two baby-faced medics were trying to talk to Chester, turning him slightly. Chester was big, 250 pounds or more.

"What'd he take?" one of them asked Ryan.

"I don't know."

"Come on, talk. You want to be responsible for killing him?"

"Crack, I think."

Jack moved over to Ryan and squatted down beside him.

"We're getting a heartbeat," one medic said to the other, who was clapping an oxygen mask on Chester. "His name?" the guy asked Ryan.

"Chester Saunders."

"Address?"

"I don't know."

Jack was trying to get Ryan to stand up when the one EMT man took a call.

They could hear a woman asking, "He's still alive?"

"Yeah. Barely." The medic hung up. "Some detective on the prowl," he said.

Ryan couldn't stand up at first. He was usually jacked up high after he'd smoked, but he was stunned, scared. Jack lifted him and he slid up the wall. "Come on, man. You got to get out of here."

One of the medics looked hard at Ryan. "What's *your* name?"

"Ryan Brown."

Brown wasn't their last name.

"He smoked it?"

"Yeah."

The EMT men swept Chester onto a stretcher and into the ambulance as Jack dragged his brother away from the wall and toward the truck. The people who were hanging around moved aside to let them through.

Ryan moaned. "He might die."

"I know," Jack said. "But we gotta go." The EMT, hardly older than Jack and Ryan, slammed the door of the ambulance and the driver took off as Jack guided his brother toward the corner. "I left the motor running. Hurry. You can't hang out here."

Two dressed-up people holding hands stopped walking to watch Jack helping Ryan into the passenger seat of the truck. Jack said, "What are you looking at? Keep to your own business." Ryan took a mock swing in their direction through the window of the truck.

Jack drove away from the scene toward a place on Western where he wanted to buy food so they'd have it later when Ryan was able to eat. He kept looking behind him in the rearview mirror. No police were following them.

"Chester is my friend . . ."

"I know. You feel okay?"

"I feel sick."

Ryan was the older of the two brothers. There was a point in their childhoods when Ryan took care of Jack. Now it was the other way around most days. "What were you doing on East Ohio?" Jack asked, meaning in front of the barbershop with the FOR SALE sign.

"The other place, the basement place, is being watched."

The open curtains. That was it. "So you went like, what, ten feet away?"

"Morgan figured how to get in the back way to the barbershop.

He's meeting people there until he can find somewhere else. You think Chester's going to make it? He did the chicken."

The chicken was bad. That was the flapping around before everything stopped. "He's going to make it."

"I opened the front door and dragged him out and made some guy with a phone call the ambulance."

"How'd you drag big old Chester?"

"Some other guy helped."

"Who?"

"I don't know who he was. He helped and then he booked."

"Where was Morgan during this?"

"He got out the back way."

Jack parked the truck and took a deep breath. All day today he had thought about getting away from this scene, even if it meant getting away from Ryan. "You are real bad messed up. This has to end."

"I know."

"Where'd you get the money to pay Morgan?"

"Up the hill. Turned out some lady was home." Chester and Ryan had been laughing about roughing up some old lady. They said they'd leave Jack out of it because he was a pussy and you had to be very persuasive with the old ladies.

"You hurt her?"

"No," Ryan said vaguely as if not quite sure.

Jack finally went into the shop. He watched out the window to be sure his brother stayed put while he ordered a couple of pieces of pizza and a large cup of coffee. As soon as he put the order in, he returned to the truck with the coffee and leaned in the passenger window. Ryan was drumming on his thighs. The coffee was boiling hot.

"You okay?" Jack said.

"Just chilling."

They both laughed a little, thinking of the same thing—one of

Chester's stories. Chester once broke into someone's house, ate their food, drank their wine, popped their prescriptions, then curled up on the sofa and went to sleep. Owner came home, ran out, called the police, the police came. None of it woke Chester. The police had to shake him awake. According to Chester, the police said something like, "Hey, buddy, what're you doing here?" And Chester gave them a nice big smile and said, "Oh. Just chillin'." Afterward, the police kept imitating him, joking and laughing. "He was just chillin'." Even the owner of the house found it funny and didn't press charges.

Chester was big, sly, always playing, and Ryan admired him.

"Let's go up to Tanya's," Ryan said now.

Chester's girlfriend had an apartment she'd let them stay in a couple of times when Chester wheedled her into it and they gave up a couple of dollars for the pleasure of sleeping on her floor.

When he figured the pizza slices were ready, Jack went back inside and paid. It felt fantastic to have money in his pocket. He vowed not to tell Ryan how he got it.

"Not hungry," Ryan said as Jack got in the truck and handed over the box. Ryan put the cardboard box on the floor.

Jack drove up the hill to the clump of bushes where they parked the truck at night and he finished up his coffee. He wondered if Ryan could be a different person if he got away from here, away from Chester and Morgan and the lot of them.

Ryan felt in his pockets for a pack of cigarettes, as if he'd finally remembered what he wanted. Finding a crumpled pack, he scooped out a bent one and lit up. Suddenly his eyes came alive. "Hey. How'd you pay for the pizza? Hey, where the fuck *were* you all day?"

"Just driving. Mostly. Got a little money."

"No shit." Ryan blew out a large bellows of smoke and punched him on the arm, too hard. "Good, good. You finally *did* something."

Jack looked out the window into a cluster of wild bushes. Night hadn't completely fallen yet. He'd actually taken Chester's advice about finding a summer place to break into where they could hole up for a while. And he'd found one. Or more accurately remembered one at Sugar Lake and found it again. He hadn't broken in, but he'd thought about going there on his own, just to live for a while. It was two hours away. He couldn't figure out how to get there without the truck, and if he took the truck, Ryan would be angry.

That was only one of the things he did today.

But Ryan was all attention now. "How'd you get the money?"

That was another story.

"Took it?"

"Yeah." A lie.

"Where?"

"A house. Way out. Rural."

"No shit. Anybody home?"

He hesitated. "Yeah."

"And what? Who?"

"Some old lady."

"Chester says the old ones are the best."

A patter of sound began on the truck's roof and the windshield. Ryan sighed. "Fucking rain." He started to shiver. He looked back at the bed of the truck, where they usually slept.

The dashboard clock said it was after nine. Just dark.

They waited for a while. The rain kept coming down, not hard, but hard enough to keep them out of the bed of the truck.

Jack started up the engine. "Maybe Mum'll put us up."

Ryan had called their mother every name in the book and then asked her for money. Even though he hated her, he'd probably be able to get around her. They hadn't seen her for over a year. "I hate the bitch."

It was ten thirty when they drove up to Perrysville and then to Defoe Street to their mother's place. They tried the doors of her place, back and front. Both doors were locked. They banged on the back door, hard. A window went up in the second floor of the house next door. A man's voice said, "Go away. You're disturbing the peace. Your mother's gone."

"How would you know?"

"I've seen you two banging on the door before. You're talking about the red-haired woman? She's gone. She moved."

"Where?"

"How the hell would I know? She moved."

"Let's get out of here," Jack said. He hauled Ryan to the truck. They went too fast down the hill, Ryan shouting that he wanted cigarettes and he wanted to go to Bippy's and get some booze. "And I want to go see about Chester."

ADDIE WARD LUGS PRIMER AND SANDPAPER and a couple of scrapers from her mudroom to her living room windows so she'll have to *face them* tomorrow morning when she must attack the rotting windowsills, must.

She thinks back to earlier today, the odd boy who came by wanting work. She'd been trying to make herself *do* things, but not succeeding very well. Something was wrong, a flutter in her heart. She'd had a terrible dream last night—of her own death. She felt it. She was in the dream-film and out of it at the same time, so that she *saw* herself dying, but she also *felt* the sensation of lying down, feeling panic, feeling everything stopping. In a couple of weeks she has a birthday, eighty-three, and if she learned anything at all during the forty years she worked in a doctor's office, it was what a dangerous age eighty-three is. That's when it falls apart—that's when a person faces illness or death. Car mechanics can say, "In ten thousand miles, you'll need new brakes." Doctors are afraid to use that language, but if they were honest, they'd say, "Make it past eighty-three and you're probably good for a while." Also, if doctors were honest, they'd say, "Tiptoe for about a month before your birthday, any birthday." Because people tended to die (at whatever age they died) about a month before the year turned. There were mysteries still to be solved; the body had its own secret calendars.

This morning she'd wakened and she couldn't shake off the dream. She had a whole list of things she wanted to do—everything from shingle the roof to drive into town for groceries—but she threw up her hands. Time to pause. She couldn't quite go to an emergency room to report she'd had a bad dream last night.

Then the boy came by.

If I konk out, she told herself, at least someone is here. He can call 911. Maybe he knows CPR.

She had a Gary Cooper movie on TV. *The Fountainhead*. She could remember seeing it with Archer, oh such a long time ago.

And when the boy came to the door, her first thought was, he seemed odd. Guilty and mumbly. She had her hearing aid in, but she also had the television up loud. She had to concentrate to hear him.

"Need your grass cut?" He had a bit of an accent. The "cut" ended in a glottal stop. So he was English or something.

"How much?"

"I'm not expensive." Yes, there it was again, the *t* in the back of the throat.

"I can do it myself, tomorrow maybe."

"You? It's . . . a lot."

"I was about to fix the roof," she added almost defiantly. "I can still do things."

"I can fix your roof."

She looked at him skeptically. He'd pulled his truck around back as if he planned to stay. He cast his eyes about her house and yard.

"Whatever you usually pay," he said.

"Go ahead, then, on the yard." She had grave doubts that he could do CPR or layer shingles.

He moved off to her garage, a barnlike shed that she'd left open, and took out her power mower. He looked at it as if he didn't know what to do with it. She'd been up here since mid-April to get the lettuces and flowers and vegetables in and thriving. She hoped he wouldn't ruin them.

But she decided not to be afraid. She let him work all day. She taught him how to do the roof and then . . . she'd seen how skinny he was, how he inhaled the iced tea and water and anything she gave him, so, in the long run, she fed him dinner, too. It was a dinner made out of nothing, made out of magic. A frozen fish Tom Jensen had given her last summer. Some grits. A rind of cheese. Vegetables she had frozen for soup that she mucked up with a lot of oil and onion. She found a loaf of bread in the freezer and baked it. The boy said it might be the best meal he ever had. Well, she'd done that for him.

The windowsills are raw. She'll have splinters for sure. Tomorrow. Tomorrow.

THE GUARD AT EMERGENCY is a middle-aged man with a shaved head. He looks like he could put both of them down with one arm. He studies their faces, makes them go twice through the scanner, and examines with apparent suspicion all they have taken out of their pockets. Jack tries to make eye contact. Ryan doesn't even try to be civil. Finally the guard nods them through.

The harried intake clerk inside looks up and begins typing. "Name?"

"We're just here to see about our friend."

He examines them briefly. "Friend's name."

"Chester Saunders."

"Just came in?"

"Tonight."

The clerk clicks at a few keys. "No," he says. "No."

"What?"

"Can't see him. I'm sorry."

"What the fuck . . . ?"

"Orders. It's in the computer."

"Is he dead?"

The man smirks. "Alive, but he's being sent somewhere."

"Where?"

"Confidential. I can't give that out."

"Come on, man. We got the whole way up here—"

"Family only. There are rules. And you have to quit harassing me."

"Just tell us where he's going to be."

"I'm not allowed to give out that information."

"He's our friend."

"I'm sorry. There are privacy laws."

Ryan says, "This is a fucking fascist prison."

"Hey. Let's go." Jack nudges Ryan along to the exit.

They shuffle out and take their time walking down the steep hill to where the truck is parked. It could rain again. "I want to sleep at Tanya's. Maybe he's there and that's all bullshit. Hey, how much money you have?"

"Almost fifty."

"Let me see." Ryan takes the bills, saying, "I'll hold it."

It's getting on to midnight when Tanya opens the door. Her eyes widen in anger. "I don't want you guys coming around here anymore. You know? Just go away." She's tall, thin and lanky, but she wears heeled shoes with her cargo pants and T-shirt. Her hair is processed straight and bowl-like so that she looks like an upside-down exclamation point. Her face shows stress, upset.

"We came to tell you where Chester is," Ryan says. "Unless he's here."

"I know where he is. He's going to get serious rehab. You stay away from him, you hear. He almost didn't make it. You're a terrible influence on him."

"It kind of goes the other way around," Jack says irritably.

But Ryan is laughing, now lighting up another cigarette. "What are you, some angel all of a sudden? He's my best friend. He's—"

She hesitates for a moment, softens it looks like, and then slams the door.

They stand there for a while. Ryan kicks the door once. Then he slumps off toward the truck, gets in the driver's side, barks, "Gimme the keys," and practically starts driving before Jack can get the passenger door the whole way open.

"Where you going now?" Jack asks.

"Morgan. And Bippy's. I need a smoke and you could use some booze."

They drive too fast up the hill and over a couple of streets. Jack doesn't care anymore to try to stop Ryan. He's tired of working so hard; he just wants a couple of quarts of booze; he just wants to be.

ALEXANDRATOS AND MERTZ HAVE HAD TO cool their heels for a long time. They even went down to the Park House after a while to watch TV and have a few. Then, finally, they were allowed to see this Chester Saunders.

He was a really chubby kid, according to the chart, twenty-one years old and 270 pounds. He smiled at them.

"Any chance anybody did this to you on purpose? Do you have any enemies in the trade?" Alexandratos asked him.

"I don't tend to have enemies," Chester said. He appeared to find the question amusing. "I like people, they like me."

"Very Christian," Mertz said. "What about the kid with you? Helping you. Who was he?"

"Just some kid. Hangs around me."

"You deal to him? He deal to you?"

"Nah. He likes my stories. Like a little kid. He likes stories."

"How bad is he hooked?"

"I don't know. I don't know him that well."

"You going to get yourself clean?" Alexandratos tried.

"Gonna try."

"You're looking pretty healthy. We almost lost you." She tried to sound concerned.

She and Mertz left the hospital, looking at their watches. Pretty much time for them to sign off after an evening of waiting. It was work of a sort.

ADDIE USES A HUNDRED-WATT BULB in her bedside lamp for reading. She wishes she could sleep. But there's something pleasant, wonderful, about this middle-of-the-night wakefulness. Outside her open window—stars visible, animal and insect life getting on with it, the cool breeze coming in.

She plunges into the book again, not sure if she's read this section before.

She can't concentrate. She's pretty much got her heartbeat under control, but she can't help thinking about the damned birthday. And other things. Tom Jensen. He's coming in a week or so. His house is just up the road. If her heart gets wonky on her, she can call on him anytime, day or night. On the other hand, there are complications.

Tom Jensen fell in love with Addie many years ago. There were the whispered how-are-yous in the kitchen and the inevitable eye contact. It was both unsettling and exciting. Then they'd had one night of folly fifty years ago when she came up to Sugar Lake early to do the planting and he followed. A chill in the air, a lot of wine, a slough in the marriage, and she'd let him hold her. And that led to more. They'd made love. The next day she woke up horrified at herself and sorry for what she'd done. Tom was not sorry. He wanted her to leave Archer. He said he was ready to leave Marian. She took long and painful stock. She loved Archer. The Jensens were their *friends*. Their children were friends. They all met at Sugar Lake every summer. We can't throw our lives away, she told him. And she prevailed. The whispered how-are-yous stopped. They settled back into friendship.

But Marian died last year and Tom . . . is floating. He thinks he's in love with her again. He won't say it, but she can hear it in his voice.

After marking her place in the novel with a clean tissue, she goes down to the kitchen, where she puts a little water in the electric teakettle. The boy, Jack, who worked yesterday, passing through the house, touched it, pulled out the wire to be sure it actually was electric.

"I'll bet you've seen one of them before," she said. "Haven't you?"

"Um. Yeah. When I was little."

In England, she guessed. He sounded English. "They're a great invention. Don't you think?"

"Yeah."

Not a talker.

She pours herself a cup of tea and listens to the sounds of the night.

THREE IN THE MORNING. Ryan is driving and it's bad, bad. He's wired up high and playing at the accent game. Sometimes they play at being Irish or Australian: *Mates* become *mites* and all that.

Jack keeps shouting, "Slow down. Let's stop. Let's stop for the night."

Ryan jabbers, "That was amazing shit, mite. Amazing amazing shit."

The road is spinning; Jack feels sick from the booze and the way Ryan is driving; he looks at the three paltry dollar bills in his hand, all that's left from his day of work. Ryan makes a funny warbling sound and starts screeching the truck to a stop, swerving in ways that make Jack's head spin, too. They're going to end up in jail if he can't stop him. "Pull over."

"Pull over where, fooking bloody wimp?"

"Up the hill. The usual." Jack tries to lean over to see the gas gauge, but the movement makes him sick.

"Get your head out of my lap, you asshole cocksucker."

They swat at each other hard. "More like you you're talking about."

The whiskey bottle in the back is empty, rolling around, making noise. Jack reaches around to the floor behind him to reposition the bottle. "Slow down. I really feel shitty. I feel sick."

"Yeah." Ryan swerves again, just for the heck of it. "Looka that."

Jack twists up to see out the front window in the empty streets a bit of movement two blocks down—a girl walking through the park. She steps rapidly, trying not to look about, braving the night.

"Scare the bitch." Ryan accelerates, yelling, "Monster coming, baby. Just like you thought!" The traffic light turns red, but he keeps going.

"Don't," Jack yells.

"Give her a good one."

She looks at the light, red, thinking she has time, moves forward, changes her mind.

Jack says, "Stop, turn the wheel." He grabs at the wheel, but Ryan swerves, pulling away from him.

It's just a sound at first. But then the girl is flying, up, up, and to their left.

"Oh, man."

"Oh, my God," Jack says.

Ryan keeps going as if there are no brakes on the truck. Somewhere to Jack's right, in his peripheral vision, is a man running toward the accident.

"It'll be okay."

"You hit—"

"Don't," says Ryan. "Don't say anything."

They move through glaring streetlights until Ryan stops at a traffic light near the post office, where a few other cars appear.

When the light turns green, Ryan says, "Don't ever talk about it."

Jack can't think what to do. He claps a hand over his own mouth to keep himself from yelling. The running man will call an ambulance and maybe get the girl fixed up.

No, they killed her; it's all over for her and it's all over for them; they're on the run.

Nobody in the other cars seems to look their way. Ryan obeys the lights now but moves on and on, then loops around and starts back toward North Avenue. Just when Jack thinks Ryan is going to take the truck to where they park it at night, Ryan says helplessly, "I don't know where to go."

Jack is startled by the tone. "Pull over. I'll drive."

Ryan obeys—which in itself is different.

Once he's behind the wheel, Jack concentrates on being stone cold sober. He concentrates on the road. Everything looks a little unreal.

For a long time, neither one says anything or puts on the radio or the CD player. Jack keeps remembering the sound the woman's body made and he keeps seeing her flying through the air.

"You know where you're going?"

"Yeah." He gets on the highway going north. Ryan doesn't question him. The silence continues.

When they pass the Wexford exit, Ryan mutters dreamily, "Posh, i'nit? Wexford." And when they pass the Cranberry exit, Ryan says it again: "Posh." A yellow Hummer comes alongside them, passes them as if to make the point. "Tell you one thing. I plan to be rich someday."

He's out of his head. Just . . . out of his head.

Their headlights carve out manicured rolling hillsides fringed with trees in bud.

Jack drives for a long time, willing himself the whole time to be steady. They pass one exit after another. Finally, they're in a section of old farms with the buildings, mostly barns and sheds, close to the road. Then a sign for the Harmony Historic District—Amish types. Zelienople . . . clumps of trees like bouquets . . . Portersville exit.

There is still not light in the sky, but there are clean roads and bright road lights illuminating every sign, as if to give them high importance—Slippery Rock University. Grove City College. Westminster College.

"Smart fookers live up this way," Ryan observes.

Another college. Thiel. One of their mother's husbands taught there. Neil. That joker. Neil from Thiel. They remember him all right. Neil was how they ended up in Sugar Lake the first time, ten years ago.

"I think I know where you're taking me," says Ryan.

"Maybe you do."

The first dead deer they pass lies on its back. When they pass a second dead deer, lying on its side, Ryan says, out of the blue, "The guy who helped me, you know, turned Chester on his side. He said that was better. It's called recovery position." After a moment, he says, "I'm going to say we hit a deer. If anybody ever asks."

That old man running toward the accident . . . it happened so fast . . . he couldn't have seen the license plate, Jack is sure.

Crawford County line.

Then with admiration: "You came up yesterday, right?"

"Yeah."

"And?"

"Jensen's place is empty."

"Man, that's brilliant."

"It's lucky. We're going to stay there."

"But the money you got—it wasn't old lady Jensen?"

"That was . . . down on the road somewhere. I don't exactly remember."

"How can you not remember?"

"I just don't."

After he'd circled the place yesterday, squeamish about breaking in, Jack drove down the road and tried another place, hoping for easy entry. He knocked first and a gray-haired woman came to the door. It turned out the woman, Addie, let him have a couple of jobs around the place. When he didn't know how to do things, she was patient. All the while he thought he'd finally figure out what to steal, but the afternoon kept progressing and she kept being friendly, showed him where the gas went and where the oil went in the mower, talked about this and that—even when she cut flowers she explained how she cut filler to make a bouquet look good. She taught him how to do roofing. He did roofing.

She was different. Living up here alone with all that work to do. She had an old station wagon in the garage—it had to be thirty years old. Gearshift up in front of your face. He said, "Funny you keep that old thing in a garage."

She said, "Don't talk ill of that old thing. It's done me well."

He thought, Maybe she doesn't have much.

And he ended up working. And not disliking it. Tell that to Ryan or Chester and he'll never live it down.

They pass dead trees, houses close to the road, barns and sheds in decay. Then suddenly fields of dairy cows, the black-and-white kind. With barns for silage—like in children's picture books—the scene is beautiful and peaceful.

They pass churches and cemeteries, and then they're in the little town, Cochranton. The town holds a small movie theater that might or might not be still operating; coin laundry; car repair; insurance; convenience store; gas station; market. That's about it. The basics. Also the French Creek Café and a pizza shop.

Jack gets on the road to Sugar Lake when there is just the hint of light coming into the sky.

DETECTIVE COLLEEN GREER, ON NIGHT DUTY, got there when the ambulance did.

The young woman was dead. She was a tiny figure, slight. The men kneeling over her looked up and said there was no hope whatsoever.

Colleen had trouble looking. She was not quite a rookie anymore but still one of the newer detectives on the force. Her colleagues didn't give her much guff these days; she'd proved herself on the last couple of cases.

There was blood in the long streaming black hair; the woman's face was so badly damaged it was clear the injuries would have made her life difficult had she lived. From the way she was hit by the car and the impact of her fall against a tree, there must have been significant internal bleeding, too.

She turned to the patrol cop on the scene. Peters. "Who is she?"

He produced a purse. "Everything's in here. Name is Joanna Navarro. She has an ID for working at Allegheny General."

Nurse? Wrong outfit. Doctor? Quality of the nail polish and soft flats seemed wrong.

"Doing?"

"Cafeteria staff."

Colleen nodded.

"Could have been on her way from work or to work. Or maybe she was just out for the night having a good time."

Colleen could tell from the clothes, the shoes, and the handbag that it wasn't about having a good time. To work, she guessed. Maybe the early staff that prepares the breakfasts. "Let me see." She nodded toward the wallet, and when he handed it over, she went through it quickly at first. There was still money in it. No driver's license. Where the hell was Dolan? He was partnering her, but he was always off on his own these days. "Call the hospital for me. When you get them, ask what her shift was. Then . . . then put me on. Where did the handbag fall?"

"About there." He pointed to a spot on the road ten feet from the body. "The old man who called in the hit-and-run picked it up from the road, so we can't be totally sure."

She continued to study the wallet. Hospital ID. Children's pictures. Yeah, little kids. "Let me see the handbag."

The cop handed it over.

Everything neat. Makeup in a little case. Larger hospital ID on a badge. Checkbook with neat writing. She looked at the pictures of the little kids again, two of them, a boy and a girl, toothy, eager, not beautiful. "Shit."

"Yeah. It's bad."

"Where's the witness?"

"He's somewhere close. He's a vagrant. He's okay, though. Sensible."

"I don't see him. Where is he?"

"I . . . don't see him either. He was crying. I told him to go take care of himself. I'd already got the particulars."

"Find him. I want to see him myself."

"Yes, Detective."

Colleen left a second message for Artie Dolan. He was Christie's former partner and probably Christie's favorite detective, a neat muscular man, small and always immaculately dressed. Up from the black ghetto and interesting, often whimsical, always entertaining. Dolan was one of the detectives who hated to be idle. He'd been acting on info he got that a guy who might know something about an old shooting hung out in a block on the upper North Side in the nights.

But she wanted him with her now. She'd never done a case like this, a vehicular homicide. There was measuring to be done here—skid marks and what looked like broken headlight glass, the placement of the body—to determine the speed of the vehicle. She'd called the accident investigations unit to do the measuring and the math, though it wasn't going to require a lot of science to figure out that the maniac who killed Joanna Navarro had been going much too fast—sixty or seventy on a city street.

Still, Dolan should be here.

"I can't find the witness. The guy. Oliver Moore." The cop who'd come back to her swallowed hard. He was red-faced. "I asked him a lot of questions."

"Tell me what you have."

"Truck came down the hill, ran a light, going very fast. Victim was crossing the street. Truck ran right at her, swerved away, then back. Then it kept going. Gray truck. She got hit hard. She was thrown against that tree. The witness, Moore, tried to see if she was breathing. He ran to the street for help. Finally got somebody to call 911 on a cell."

This was pretty much what Colleen had heard from the 911 call. "That's it?"

"Right."

"And we have the APB out on the gray truck?"

"Yes."

"Nobody else around?"

"No."

"I still want this witness. Find him."

Her phone rang. It was Dolan, saying, "I'm on my way. You got a good one, girl."

"Traffic unit is nowhere in sight yet," she said. "Sunday morning, nobody moves. There's headlight glass. That'll help."

"Be right there."

Ten feet away, Joanna Navarro lay beyond help. The battered woman's limbs were folded in and she had landed a bit on her side, so she looked almost fetal. Colleen hoped the death itself was sudden and without consciousness or pain. If you didn't know better, if you caught the position from a distance, you might think the victim had wanted to take a long nap and was so tired, she didn't care where she did it.

TWO

SUNDAY

THE SUN EDGED INTO THE SKY just as the topography flattened out and the sky became large, almost western.

"Your old lady where you got the money—tell me about her."

"I got all she had."

"Where's her place?" Ryan's eyes narrowed.

"Some small lane on the way. I don't know if I could find it again."

The rough dirt road made them slow down a little. When they passed the driveway to Addie's place, Jack was careful not to cast his eyes toward it. "Remember," he said quietly, "we used to take our swimming and fishing stuff and go down to the lake." He and Ryan floated around the lake on tires—they'd never had a vacation before or after. It was the best time they ever had, but they had to leave after four days because the owner, Jensen, kicked them out.

"I hated that old guy. Jensen."

Jack turned off the dirt road to a narrow car path, completely unfinished. Before them was the white wooden house Jensen owned. "We didn't hate his house. Remember?"

Jack forced the truck around the side of the place where weeds had come up high and where there were a couple of planks of wood they had to drive over.

Once they were parked in back where nobody could see the truck, Ryan began to shake. "It's really cold," he said.

It wasn't. But Jack said, "Yeah. Yeah, it is."

They slid out of the truck, walked around to the front of it, and looked at the driver's side. One smashed headlight, a dented front fender, and a smear of human being. Neither one of them said anything. They moved away in tandem from the truck. Jack leaned against a tree and caught his breath. He could hear Ryan gagging. He walked thirty yards or so into the woods, sucking in clean air, and somehow didn't throw up. He turned back to see Ryan getting rough with the back door, pushing and shaking it. "Going to have to break a window," Ryan said. But he went at the door again hard, this time with his shoulder, and the door gave.

A slice of sunlight played on the floor just inside the door, lighting their way in.

They stood inside the kitchen. The house had a smoky smell from fires burned when the place was last used. It looked familiar, much the same as it had years ago. There was the big long kitchen table that looked like something from a movie with medieval knights in armor eating and tossing meat over their shoulders to the dogs.

"Remember eating here?" Jack asked.

Two walls were lined with wooden cupboards of old dark wood. Ryan started opening cupboard doors.

"Bowls. Glasses. Couple of cans of soup," Ryan reported.

Jack moved to a low cabinet. He found a large metal container with a lid on and pictures of farm people tilling fields painted on the side. He pried it open. It was practically empty, but there were three tiny packages. "In here is crackers, spaghetti, and, let's see, beans." Little bits of each. Unfortunately *very* little bits.

"Beans . . ." Ryan scowled. "Beans."

"Well, there's the soup like you said. You're going to want to eat sometime later today."

They moved into the living room. They appeared in a mirror near the door—two look-alikes, fake leather jackets, T-shirts, jeans, tousled hair. Their mother said they got decent chins but that their noses put them on the wrong side of the tracks. She used to tell them the fancy people got those big nosey noses, all bone, like Prince Charles.

They weren't much in the mood to look at themselves. They studied the room instead. Some saggy sofas, a chess set on its own table, the usual end tables.

"Phone."

It was pretty ancient looking, gray and large, awkward. Ryan lifted the receiver and tried pushing buttons. "It's dead."

"Shut off."

"Right. No dial tone, nothing. Let's look at the upstairs." They moved cautiously up the stairs to the bedrooms.

Three bedrooms. Beds with bedspreads and blankets. Clean sheets put away in the drawers.

And there was a bathroom with a shower and some leftover soap and shampoo from when somebody was here last.

Jack tried the bathroom faucet, but nothing came out. Water. They'd have to have water. Suddenly everything in him collapsed. He'd gotten Ryan this far and he could do no more. He stumbled to the bedroom with the twin beds, climbed onto one on top of the spread and pulled a wool blanket from the foot of the bed over him.

Ryan stood beside him. "You can sleep?"

He was almost asleep already. He didn't answer. He could hear Ryan go to another room and come back. Soon he heard the sounds of a creaking mattress. Bowl of soup, he thought. Crackers. Shower if we can get the water going. And beyond that, he couldn't think.

DOWN THE ROAD, HALF A MILE AWAY, Addie was walking her grounds with a cup of coffee in hand. There were a few clumps of grass where the boy hadn't gone over things a second time. She'd have to catch up with them. She'd warned him about watching out for her lettuces in a border in front and for the vegetable garden out back. Lord knew what the roof looked like. She'd brought him a glass of water, then a jug of mixed iced tea, and she'd sat him down on the steps to show him what to do next. He didn't believe she knew how to do roofing. She liked surprising people. She did drawings for him, illustrations, where the big nails went, how to put the glue on. Then she held the ladder for him. At least he wasn't wearing flip-flops. She'd go up to the roof sometime, see what he did. The downspout she let him paint didn't look too bad, though there were drips on the grass at the bottom.

She went back indoors and had a second cup of coffee. Cereal would have to be it. She kept not getting to the store. The meal she made last night used about the last of what she had in dinner makings. She still had oatmeal and a few other odds and ends.

She was halfway through the oatmeal when her phone rang—a sweet ring, not too loud, so she knew before answering that it was her daughter, Linda. Phones *did* ring differently depending on who was calling.

"Just checking on you," her daughter said.

"Oh . . . I'm fine."

"I don't know how you do it. I want people around me all the time."

People got more dependent with each generation. Addie and Linda had traded stories about kids on their cells—*What are you doing? Oh, nothing, just talking to you. Did you hear from Jeff? Yeah, me too.* Baboons grooming each other. Sound strokes.

"Is anybody else up at Sugar yet?"

"No. Nobody has come by."

Just then a truck drove into the yard to give her the lie. "Never mind. I think Frank McCauley just drove up. Let me look." A forty-something fit lumberjack of a man got down from the cab of his truck. "Yes, it's Frank."

"Anybody ready for company? Anybody got some coffee brewing?" he called.

Addie stood at the front door where Frank was approaching. "Yes!" Her laugh rippled up. "Oh, yes! Only I didn't really get dressed yet, I didn't do my hair."

Frank peered through the screen. "Sexy! That just out of bed look."

"Oh!" She made a face, playful shock. She was well covered in a robe that was like a wraparound dress. Old loafers because she'd been out in the dew. She straightened her hair with her fingers. Then she remembered the phone. "I have to go," she told Linda.

"Such a flirt," Linda said affectionately.

Addie was pleased that Frank had come up to Sugar Lake early, too. "How about a bowl of oatmeal?" she asked him.

"Sounds wonderful."

"I don't have a lot of milk, but I have brown sugar and raisins."

"That's perfect. You need me to make a food run for you?"

"Oh, no. I'm going later today. I need my baking things. I'd make you cornbread if I had the ingredients."

"Cornbread!"

"Next time you come by. For sure."

"I'm going to miss you." His face got sad. He paused long enough for her to get the hint that he had bad news. "We're . . . I came by to tell you we're selling."

"Oh, no. Oh, I'm . . . oh, dear."

"I'm sorry to say it. The fact is, we don't get here enough and we have a kid going to school. We could maybe get two years' tuition out of the place. You know how high it is? Parents get college-poor."

"Oh, I do know. It's terrible. But have you thought about—we love our old places, but—what if you rented?"

He hugged her around the shoulders, squeezed, kissed her cheek. "We calculated all that. It wasn't quite enough. Well, maybe if we put in a swimming pool or a hot tub and gussied it up, but it isn't that kind of a place now."

"I like it the way it is."

"We do, too. We do, too. So, I cleaned it up as well as I could yesterday and . . . I let the Realtor put out the signs. She'll be bringing people by to see it. I can't say it isn't a jolt, seeing those signs. But I wanted to be the one to tell you."

"Where will you be while it's selling?"

"Back home. I came by to see if there was anything I could do for you. Looks like you cut your grass."

"I . . . hired somebody."

"Oh, hell, I wish I'd come by earlier. Who did it?"

"A boy who's going around doing work. Could you—if you could look at the roof, see what sort of a job he did on it?"

"Gladly."

They got out the ladder. She held it for him as she had held it yesterday. It was more worrisome to watch someone else climb than to do it herself.

Frank McCauley stayed up there awhile. She could hear some noises as he moved around. Then he came back down. "Good job. Not great, but definitely not terrible. It ought to hold you. Who's the worker?"

"A drifter. A kid."

"You be careful."

"Oh, I'm fine. My daughter worries about me. She wants to build an apartment onto her house for me. She thinks I should sell the Pittsburgh house and this one and come live with her. I don't know how many ways to tell her no."

"At least she cares."

"Oh. Oh, I'd better get your cereal started. Here I am, talking. Let me—" She started for the house, and he went to the garage to put the ladder away. Oh, she felt such a sadness that Frank McCauley was leaving.

DOLAN AND GREER AND THE TRAFFIC UNIT had measured the marks at the accident site, taken samples, and had the body carried away. They had driven to the Foster Square apartments and rung a bell and roused a woman of about fifty, Celia Navarro, who said she was the mother of Joanna and that she lived with her daughter and her grandkids. Colleen made a note that the woman had the same last name as her daughter.

"Is there a husband? Is she married?"

"She was," the woman said bitterly.

Colleen said, "May we sit down?" Dolan stood at the door. "I'm afraid I have bad news for you."

"She isn't sick?"

"Please sit. This is going to be difficult to understand." Finally the woman sat, and then Colleen did.

"She's in trouble with the Immigration?"

If only. Surely preferable.

"Is . . . about her job?"

"No, nothing like that."

Colleen waited the requisite ten-count to allow Joanna Navarro's mother to understand. Then she said, "There's been an accident. A hit-and-run."

"Oh, my God. Is she hurt?"

This time Colleen only made it through a five-count. "I'm afraid there was nothing anybody could do."

"Are you—? What—?"

"There was nothing anybody could do," she repeated. "It happened very quickly."

The mother shouted in Spanish and wept and asked many times if it was so. Colleen sat helplessly, trying to comfort the woman. Dolan moved in to Celia after a while; he stooped and took her hands. He had a steadying effect on her. As he held on to her, he began to ask a few questions. The woman gave answers as if by getting them right, by appealing to this other person who held her hands, this man with big sympathetic brown eyes, she could change what Colleen had said to her.

"Do you work, too?" he asked.

"We both have work at hospital cafeteria."

"Allegheny? Both of you?"

"Yes. But different times. They give us different times so—because to be with the children."

"How did your daughter feel about work?"

"Very good work. She like. Everything good there."

"She had friends?"

"Yes."

"Any enemies?"

"Oh, no. Just happy to meet families who come for a sick person, and she like the doctors."

"Who was she dating?"

Navarro shook her head. "Nobody for long time."

"Nobody?" Dolan appeared to be incredulous.

"There is a doctor works there that . . . maybe something will happen soon. I think Joanna likes . . ."

"You know his name?"

"No." She seemed distressed that she couldn't think of it.

"You don't know his name?"

"I'm sorry. He does . . ." She pantomimed cutting. "Operation."

"Okay. What about the man she was married to? How much contact?"

"We never see him again. He live in New Mexico with new wife."

"She gets phone calls from him?"

"Sometime. Not too much."

"How about money? Does he provide money?"

"No! No, nothing from him. He was—"

"Was he violent?"

"No, just never come home. The lawyer call him a . . . a derelict father." She said the words carefully.

Dolan shook his head as if he'd never heard of such a terrible thing. "Could you get me his address and contact information?"

"She have it somewhere."

"Thank you. When did you last see him in the city?"

"Long time. Once he come to see his kids."

"When was that?"

"They were . . . little then." She used her hand to indicate the height of two- and three-year-olds.

A tiny sound caught their attention. Dolan stopped asking questions. A girl of four or five stood in the frame of the doorway into the living room, clutching her pajamas away from her as if she'd wet them. Colleen couldn't tell whether the child had or was simply trying to get her grandmother's attention. The girl looked crossly at the strangers in the living room. "I need you to see something in my room," she said. "And I'm hungry."

"You can take care of the children. We'll be back in two or three hours," Colleen said. "We'll know more then."

"We have to miss mass?" Celia asked.

"Yes. Yes, you will. Do you have friends you could call? To come sit with you? Make some coffee for you, just to help out?"

"Good idea," Dolan said to Celia Navarro. "Call your friends. We insist."

The woman nodded.

All the way back to Headquarters, Colleen silently berated herself for not suggesting the woman go to mass. Our Lady Queen of Peace had several services. She could have *driven* her.

Eight o'clock was the time for their night shift to end, but neither she nor Dolan was likely to get home until late today.

Could have been intentional, she thought. Somebody drove straight into the woman. Husband or a boyfriend? The idea sickened her.

Their commander, Christie, was at his desk with a cup of coffee and part of the morning paper. They poked their heads into his office.

"Hit-and-run, I heard," he said. "Anything on it?"

"It's ugly," Dolan said. "Nice, hardworking mother. Probably an illegal."

"Do we need to mess with that?"

"Not so far as I'm concerned. She's got enough trouble."

"What do you need from me?"

"Nothing," Dolan said. "We're on it. Greer was there first. She's got it in order."

"Why so quiet?" Christie asked her.

"Patrolman lost our witness. I have him looking for the guy. Careless. *He* was, not me. It makes me irritable, I guess. And I need breakfast. I'm getting a hunger headache."

Dolan laughed. "There's my girl."

Christie stood. "There's more to be got from the witness?"

"Maybe."

"Let's pop over to Lindo's. You two can catch me up while we eat."

She loved Lindo's greasy breakfasts; she adored her commander; but work called. "I want to get over to the hospital to talk to some of the people who knew her. I can eat a hospital breakfast over there."

Christie said, "Sure. Good idea. We can all go over there."

RYAN LAY UNDER A BLANKET, SHIVERING. He wanted to be up, going through cabinets and drawers more thoroughly, but he couldn't stop the shakes and he thought he was going to throw up again. He looked over at Jack, who was sleeping. His thoughts kept whirling. What would Chester say? *Be cool. Don't look back.* He got up and found another blanket in one of the bureau drawers and he spread it on his bed. It was funny that neither of them had taken the bigger bed in the other room. He took it as a sign that they didn't know how to grab the good things in life. Ryan intended to change that soon. His teeth chattered. His smokes last night were cut with something strong. Something in the up category. Every time a bird chirped outside, his heart raced.

This was the very bed he'd slept in ten years ago, and that was why he and Jack had gravitated to this room now.

He could hear again the argument that had happened downstairs in the living room. The old man told their mother they'd ruined his place. Said this and that looked broken or burnt—dishes and coffeepots. Told them he wanted them to leave before their two weeks were up. Their mother called him a stupid fucking uptight old geezer. She wanted Neil to yell insults at the old guy, but instead Neil Schlager started packing his bags. "It's okay," Neil said, "we'll just leave."

"Are you fucking kidding me?" their mother said. "You want us to leave the place *and* let him have our money? I want the whole fee back. I'm not leaving here without the whole thing." She stared at Jensen. "Thinks he's something. Thinks we're nothing. Can't you tell?"

Shaking, Jensen handed over the rent check he'd never cashed. "Just go," he said.

"He couldn't be in more of a hurry," their mother said. "Hurts him to look at us."

Huddled under the covers, Ryan puts a hand on his chest—yes, his heartbeat is too fast. Brakes on, he tells himself, but he can't slow it down. His heart is like a car with the brakes failing.

That stupid woman. There was something wrong with her the way she couldn't decide what to do. Maybe she wanted it. To stop. Bam. You wouldn't think a body would make that kind of sound, hollow, like thunking a drum.

He can't get warm. He gets out of bed and searches in the clothes closet for a third blanket. He doesn't find one but spies, way in back, a space heater. He drags it out and plugs it in. Good news. The electricity in the place is working. Heat cranks out, dusty smelling.

This heater was probably here for years before his family rented. He can still see the old guy's worried face, the sickly-type wife sitting in the car the whole time, while the old guy looked at them as if he pitied them.

Same owners, he can tell.

The sun fully up, birds chattering, heater sending out waves of warmth, and him waiting for some sound from Jack, Ryan finally falls asleep.

SHE'S SANDING THE DOWNSTAIRS WINDOWSILLS, coffee mug beside her.

When her phone rings, she knows.

"Coming up early," he says.

"Oh. When?"

"Couple of days. Nothing to stop me. Well, there *are* things that *could* stop me, but my daughters can take care of them." His voice is his old voice, almost young.

She tells him about the boy who did the roof. And Frank McCauley.

"You sound great," he says.

"Tom, don't get . . ."

"What?"

"You know."

"Addie, I'm dying to see you."

"I don't want you to get ideas."

"Hmm," he says. There's an awkward moment of silence. And then he makes her talk about her garden. What she'll be cooking.

GROUPS OF WORKERS HAVE GATHERED at cafeteria tables, eating, drinking coffee, complaining about this and that. By reading uniforms—nurse, doctor, tech staff, cafeteria staff—Colleen identifies those she most wants to question. And the good news is there is only one person in the cafeteria who appears to be a member of a patient's family. This is good. It's still early. It's Sunday. The timing is perfect for turning the place into a police inquisition area. Who was Joanna in love with? Who will know the answer to that?

She's persuaded Christie and Dolan to grab only a quick carbohydrate to tide them over and to do a real breakfast later. "Ten minutes max," she says, and she hears that she sounds like a martinet, ordering her superiors around, no less. She butters her scone and dunks it in the coffee. It comes up dripping. "Pretend you don't see me. I'm at home, eating it the way I like."

Dolan dunks his muffin.

Christie, in sloe-eyed delight at his big pretzel doughnut, dunks and brings a sopping piece to his mouth. "I'm going to help you question the workers. What do you want?" he asks, both testing her as a junior detective and at the same time acknowledging that she's the primary on the case.

"Name, position at the hospital, driver's license, make of car driven to work, knowledge of Joanna, *who* she was interested in, and after they answer all that, who they know who drives a gray pickup," she says.

"Sounds about right," Dolan drawls.

They finish up their pastries and walk over to the group she has identified as kitchen staff. She makes her announcement. She's witnessed this reaction before—shoulders drop, hands clap over mouths. *Oh no. Oh, my God.* They are stunned, and when they can speak, they have the usual questions: *Are you sure it was Joanna? How did it happen? What happened? When?*

"We're sure. I'm so sorry."

With her hand she splits them up into three groups, explaining the police need to talk to them individually. "Commander Christie is helping us out on this one. You know him. You've seen him on the news."

Several people nod simultaneously.

Christie smiles in that way he has that says, *I don't do it for the limelight,* which isn't exactly true. He's not averse to being famous.

"You've probably also seen my partner, Detective Dolan. I'm Detective Greer."

They take over a couple of tables.

She finds out in minutes from an older woman, whose accent claims her as a good old Pittsburgh Southsider, that Joanna was romantically interested in an anesthesiologist.

"Not a surgeon? Her mother mentioned a surgeon."

"No. Definitely Dr. Jason Oakes. He was always friendly to her when he came in; she thought they might go out sometime."

"They never did?"

"Not that I know of."

"He was interested in her?"

"I thought he was just friendly. You know, maybe she was setting herself up for a big disappointment."

"Is he here?"

"He will be. Seems like he always comes in for something on Sundays. He does emergencies."

Colleen looks at her watch. She calls the hospital switchboard and asks to have him paged.

When the three detectives gather to pool their information, Christie offers, "Jason Oakes—is who she was interested in."

"I got that, too."

Dolan looks irritable. "My people didn't know beans."

"Anybody drive a gray truck by any chance?"

"Smart enough not to admit it," Dolan says. "I'm going to head out to the parking lot and have a quick look. Maybe find the permits guy and see what's registered."

It isn't going to be anybody here, Colleen thinks sadly. It could be a hit-and-run that never gets solved. Lucky her, getting primary on the only homicide case there is and ending up looking bad.

"I'm going back to the office," Christie announces.

"Walk you out, Boss," Dolan says. He takes a few steps back to Colleen. "What—maybe half an hour meet back here?" He waves at the cafeteria steam tables. "Or we could go somewhere else."

"Lindo's," she says. Though it's changed, as restaurants do. Still, there's the breakfast they call the one-armed bandit.

"Okay with me," he says.

About five minutes later Jason Oakes comes in. He's a handsome fellow. Dark hair, beautiful face, faltering smile.

"Police, did you say?"

"Yes. Detective Greer."

He looks puzzled. "How can I help you?"

"Joanna Navarro."

He shakes his head.

"Cafeteria worker."

"Oh. Joanna. Long hair?"

"Yes."

"She's in trouble?"

"She's dead."

"Oh, my God. What happened?"

"Traffic fatality. How well did you know her?"

"Not well, just to say hello in here."

"Did you ever go out with her?"

He frowns, puzzled. "Date her? No, why would you think that?" Then worry replaces the puzzlement. "What exactly are you asking me? I barely knew her."

"You never asked her out or talked about going out?"

"No. No, I live with someone. I don't go out with anybody else. Did someone say I went out with Joanna?"

"Did you know she was interested in you?"

"In that way? No. It never occurred to me. She was just friendly. We would joke with each other."

"About what?"

"Her kids. Being busy and tied down. She said she hadn't seen a movie in how long and I told her she needed to change that, fly the coop every once in a while."

"You didn't know she thought that was an offer?"

He collapses with a sigh. "It never occurred to me."

Protected, beautiful, kind, repressed. Joanna didn't understand. Colleen asks Oakes a few more questions just to be sure she has her profile right. She lets him go when she sees Dolan bounding in looking newsy.

"I called the pound while I was looking around. Gray truck was found abandoned—get this—sort of hanging off a corner on Brighton. Right neighborhood. It's been towed. We have to go to the pound."

On the way, she calls the patrol car she's put on the search for the single witness. "Any word on Oliver Moore yet?"

"Haven't found him." Voice thick with guilt.

THE AUTO POUND IS BEHIND the warehouse district in a series of streets that look forbidding and that lead to buildings you'd rather not visit: refuse, recycling. One attractive mauve-and-blue sign in the midst of the grime points you to the auto pound—broken concrete, crooked metal gates, dirt.

The office is a trailer shack on stilts. There's a long ramp that folds back on itself up to the entrance. This is to torture the poor and the lame who can't afford to rescue their rusty buckets.

They park.

There is also a BMW parked outside the shack and an irate man huffing around while a very blond woman looks despairingly at him from the passenger seat of his car.

"Don't bother. They're fucking closed," the angry man tells the detectives.

"Yeah. They are," Dolan says easily. "Hours aren't convenient."

"You're telling me."

"No. What kind of car you looking for?" Dolan asks. On the off chance the man wants a gray truck.

"A Jaguar. Blue. It's mine. This is my girlfriend's."

Dolan says, "I'm pretty sure you can get your car tomorrow about eight A.M." He moves a few steps toward the ramp.

"How come you get in?"

"Police," Dolan says.

He and Colleen climb the ramp without looking back. They hear a car door slam and the BMW zooming away.

They knock. They wait. The officer on duty knows to expect them, but he opens the door to them only after a long bout of fumbling.

About a dozen sheets of 8½-by-11 paper line the walls of the tiny room. Those pages are not exactly yellow, but they're dirty and the tape holding them up is yellow and cracked. A little thrill goes through Colleen. This is perfection of a sort. The answer is—to *whatever* you are asking or hoping for—No!

Wall: *CLOSED Saturday after 12:00. CLOSED Sunday. No CELL PHONES. NO evening hours.*

Window: *NO change given. NO checks accepted.*

Interior door: *NO ADMITTANCE AT ANY TIME. NO PUBLIC RESTROOMS.*

Another wall: *Pay Phone at End of Ramp.* (Handwritten underneath in pen: *It don't work.*) And on the wall, someone has printed a large FUCK YOU. And someone else has filled in all the spaces on the letters so that it's just one giant doodle graffiti and the curse isn't immediately apparent.

"This place is fantastic," Colleen says.

Dolan looks at her as if she's lost her mind.

The officer is slithering through the "No Admittance" door. A moment later he appears behind the smeared glass window flanked by the signs.

"The gray truck, the one pulled from Brighton. We need to look at it," Dolan calls after him.

The officer studies a piece of paper for a long time.

"Learning to read," Dolan mouths.

"Meet me down at the gate. Make sure the door locks behind you."

They descend the steep ramp, knees bent like skiers, and Dolan exclaims, "I don't get why you're calling this place fantastic."

"It just is. Pure."

"Some days I don't get you."

"I know."

Several minutes later, their man appears at the narrow gate. He points them to the gray truck, some fifty yards away. They pass a blue Jag. The gray truck is a Ford. About eight years old. "Don't think so," Dolan says almost immediately.

He stoops down anyway, examining every part of the car. It's not banged up at all. There's a scratch in back, but nothing on front or back that looks as if it hit a human body. No cracked glass anywhere.

"Shit," Colleen mutters.

Dolan smiles largely at her as he plucks the citation from under the windshield wiper. "Evanosky. Who else?"

Evanosky, of no use to anyone, roams the city and signs 80 percent of parking citations. Most people in the city come to hate him at one point or another.

False leads, the meat and potatoes of police work. They head off to Lindo's.

RYAN WAKES UP AT ONE O'CLOCK with the sun in his eyes so blinding that he feels dizzy. When he can manage to shield them from the glare, he looks over and finds Jack is awake, just lying there.

His heart is slowed down. He's not like he was a few hours ago. "Did you get up while I was sleeping?" he asks Jack.

"No."

"You didn't look around this place?"

"No."

"There's some kind of attic. I remember that. They might have something up there we can sell."

Jack sits up, peels off the covers. He looks at the heater that's whirring. "It's hot in here."

As if in agreement, they both get up. Jack feels around the back of the heater until he finds a switch to turn it off.

Before they go downstairs, Jack stops at the bathroom and pulls back the shower curtain on the tub. Ryan looks in the medicine cabinet and announces, "Aspirin. That's it. Let's go take a look at the big bedroom."

The large bed is made up with a quilty tan bedspread. Ryan opens the bureau drawers while Jack looks into the closet, reporting, "A robe for a lady. Another heater. Flannel shirts, pants." Ryan digs into the bureau, holds up a pair of boxers, and laughs.

"You must be feeling okay."

Not okay. But not as jumpy as before. Sleep helps when he can manage it. Then eventually the appetite comes back. He knows his pattern.

They also check out the tiny room, like a nursery, next to the large bedroom. Jack is thinking out loud, saying, "Neil worked in here. Remember? Set up a desk. Right here. All those papers he dragged along."

"He was a complete idiot," Ryan says.

"Yeah, but he's the one who knew about the place. We'd never have got here without him."

The whole time they were there Neil never even got down to the lake. Just worked. Pathetic. They never thought of him as a father. He didn't try to be a father. "Thought he was important because he wrote articles."

Ryan points to a narrow rectangle on one wall. "*That* door," he says, "leads to the attic. We'll check that out later. While there's still daylight. Let's go downstairs."

The living room holds several bookcases, all of them crammed with books. On the floor is a basket with magazines. Four chairs and a big sofa and a little sofa. Every piece of sitting furniture has a table next to it or behind it with a lamp on. The woodsy, musty smell in the air triggers a craving for a cigarette. Ryan fumbles in his pocket and lights up. "Want one?"

"Okay." Jack takes one and sits on the sofa, scanning the room restlessly. "They used to have a radio here. Didn't they? I remember it. I mean, sometimes there's news on the radio. We're going to have to know if they're looking for us. We could use the truck radio if we have to, but I hate to run down the battery. Or . . . use the gas." He gets up abruptly to look in the kitchen. "No. Not in here. No radio. Maybe it broke." Jack just stands in the kitchen, looking around. He touches the table.

Ryan, watching him, goes into the kitchen. "What are we doing here? Huh? How long you think to keep us up here in the boonies?"

"I don't know. It's nice, though, right? Till we get our heads straight and we know what's next. I'm going to open a couple of cans of soup, see if the stove works."

Jack turns a knob on the stove. The burner lets out a hiss of gas, but there is no flame. He turns it off, waits, lights a match, turns it back on, and the flame on the burner flares up high. "Good. We need water to mix in with the soup. The cans are that condensed kind."

"No water. Remember? You tried—"

"Right. Yeah, but . . ." Jack opens the door to the basement. "They have circuit breakers now, used to be fuses, but one of them . . . is marked . . . pump." He flips the switch, looking proud of himself. "Try the faucet now."

Ryan turns on the tap. Nothing comes out, even though there is the sound of the pump motor starting up. Why does Jack think he knows what to do?

"I'm going to the basement. I haven't given up."

Jack disappears for five minutes while Ryan paces and then follows down a few steps to the basement. He sees his brother turning valves, and pretty soon there are new sounds. They go back upstairs, where water coughs and sputters out to the kitchen sink. "Ha," Jack says. He stands watching the water flow more and more steadily, a can opener in hand.

"Great. You're playing house. I'm going to look at that side porchy thing." When Ryan opens the door to the sun porch, he finds the same wicker furniture that was there years ago, but now there are solid windows where there had been only screens; and now there's a television. And a portable radio. Same old radio.

Jack is behind him in moments. "They brought it in here, the radio," Jack says, but first he tries the TV. "It must be unplugged." He feels around for the cord and fits it into an outlet. A crackle of static introduces a fuzzy picture. Soon the sound comes in moderately well, but the picture continues to be no better than shadows moving. "It's some kind of movie. Spies or something." He changes channels. Racing. Baseball. None of it *watchable.* Only *hearable.*

Ryan feels anger flash up his throat. He plugs in the radio and dials around until he finds a station. "There," he says angrily. "You got your radio, too. You want news, you'll get news."

The radio and TV war with each other. Ryan switches back to the channel with auto racing because it comes in better than anything else. That's something I could do, he thinks. Drive fast. Like those drivers squealing around tight turns—exciting. He gets a sudden flash of himself driving last night. His thoughts are leaping around all over the place. Jack watches the race cars with him for a few minutes before leaving him alone.

After a while Jack returns with two bowls of soup.

The smell gags Ryan, so he smokes instead. A silence grows between them again as Jack finishes both bowls of soup, then begins fiddling with the radio tuner.

Ryan tries to ignore him, but the static in between stations drives him up the wall. Nothing feels right. The wicker sofa is hard. His whole body is itchy, as if he has a rash.

"We only have cold water. I'll go find the boiler in a bit," Jack says.

"I'll do it." Ryan jumps up and finds his way down to the basement. Laundry machines, clothesline, vacuum cleaner, brooms, two broken chairs of the outdoor variety near a small workbench. Boiler. With written directions. Jack isn't the only one who can do things. He turns some knobs and, whoosh, the gas comes on.

He bounds up the stairs to find Jack waving him silent, pointing to the radio. He makes himself listen. County executives this and spring festival that. Just junk. Then suddenly: "Police are investigating a traffic fatality that occurred on Pittsburgh's North Side. The victim, Joanna Navarro, was an employee of Allegheny General Hospital and was the mother of two. Anyone with information about a gray truck leaving the area at high speed at around four A.M. is requested to call the police."

"Gray!" Ryan says fiercely. "See that? They ain't ever going to find us. Gray."

COLLEEN WAS STILL AT THE OFFICE on Sunday afternoon when John Potocki came in. She was in the middle of punching in a phone call, but she paused after four digits—area code and one more—to say hello to him. He wasn't on duty, just picking up something from his desk, didn't say what. He looked winded, as if he'd just played a tough game of basketball with his son. "You have something?" he asked.

"Hit-and-run."

"Who's the vic?"

"Young mother."

"How young?"

"Young enough. Two little kids."

"That's what you're on right now?" He gestured to the phone.

"The ex-husband. Artie tried him earlier. I get my turn." She hit another five digits and her finger was poised over the button for the last one.

"I'll let you be."

She held a hand up for him to hang out for a moment. "I have to find out if he's really in New Mexico. Plus, I have to break the news."

Potocki sat and waited with her during the ringing.

"Rico Romez? We've been trying to get you all day. This is Detective Colleen Greer. Pittsburgh Police. Homicide Division."

"I was out. What's up?"

"I'm afraid I have news for you about your ex-wife."

"Joanna?"

"Yes."

"What . . . kind of news?"

"She died early this morning."

"Died?"

"Yes."

"How?"

"It was a traffic fatality."

"Holy—holy Mother of God."

"I'm going to have to ask you a few questions."

"Me?"

"When did you see Joanna last?"

"Man, I don't remember. Like, three years ago."

"Can you be more exact?"

She could hear him muttering, "Summer before, summer before, no, working for . . . summer before that, no. It would have been four years. Summer. July."

Potocki rolled a little closer, gave Colleen a nod of approval.

"What sort of relationship did you have after the divorce?"

"Why would you want to know that? We didn't like each other when we were married. We didn't bother each other after. What's this about?"

"Were you in much contact about the kids?"

"No."

"When did you come to see your kids?"

"Not in a while."

"How long?"

"Year and a half." She wrote this down. Potocki rolled up to read it.

"Sure?"

"No, wait, longer, I think. Why you asking me these things? A bit over two years." She turned the one into a two and made a face at Potocki.

"How did you see them without seeing her?"

"Picked them up."

"You were paying child support?" She made a face. Potocki nodded.

"When I could. When I had it. So she has a car now?"

Asks about car, she wrote down. Either a pure mistake or a lie. "Can you account for your whereabouts last night, early this morning?"

"I'm in fucking New Mexico."

"I know that. Can you account for your whereabouts?"

"Yeah. I was home last night."

"Anybody see you?"

"My wife."

"Where were you at, say, two in the morning your time?"

"In bed."

"What about five in the morning your time?"

"In bed."

"When did someone *other* than your wife see you?"

"Look, I wasn't in Pittsburgh. I'm completely through with Joanna; I don't have anything to do with her."

"Where were you at nine in the morning your time?"

"Went out to get the paper."

"Where did you go for that?"

"Down to the drugstore."

"Anybody see you?"

"I had a conversation with a clerk."

"Give me his name."

"I don't know it."

"Name of the store?"

She shook her head at Potocki and pantomimed putting an X over his name. She'd already determined there were no flights out of Pittsburgh likely to get him home to New Mexico by nine his time. She'd checked Cleveland, too. Plus his name wasn't on any roster. And nobody had rented a pickup truck at either airport. She wanted to cry. There was nothing.

Long shot: He could have hired somebody to off Joanna. But he would have to be very motivated. "Mr. Romez. You understand we have to ask you these questions?"

"What kind of person are you? How can you get your mind to come up with this shit?" He hung up on her.

She winced and held the phone away from her ear.

Potocki gave her a sympathetic smile.

She sighed. "Damn. Not a hint. Not a lead. And the patrolman lost my only witness."

"You sound bushed." Potocki stood. He was looking good, trimmed down and flushed with energy.

"I need some sleep. But I'm planning to stay awake until eleven or my night'll be shot." Before she could edit herself, she said, "So if you don't have anything better to do, you could have dinner with me, keep me awake."

"Uh. Bad timing. Can't. Plans."

Suddenly she felt her face redden. What was she doing? She was crazy with fatigue. "Oh, well, I kind of like these long days. They make me feel needed."

"Take care," he said.

Something with his son, maybe. But then why didn't he say so? Ex-wife?

But a little later, she overheard him telling Dolan he was going to a concert at the Post-Gazette Pavilion—he didn't use the new name of the place—and wanted to catch a nap first because it was going to be a long night out and a long drive back. She looked around for a newspaper to see what concert was in town. Brad Paisley. Potocki taking his teenage son? Not likely.

Christie walked through the outer offices and stopped at her desk. "You look really tired."

Thanks a lot. "I am."

"Anything?"

"No. Waiting for labs. Waiting for people to come forth."

"Why don't you come to our place tonight? We're having some people over. Roast beef, potatoes, veggies, bread, you know, buffet style."

"What's the event?"

"There isn't one. We just got in the mood. Marina saw some nice big roasts and we thought, Why not. If it stays nice out, we'll drift outside."

"Well, it definitely sounds like fun. What time?"

"Seven. Get there whenever. Dolan's coming."

"Oh. Good."

The invitation felt like an afterthought, Dolan already invited; she wrestled with pique for a few minutes. Better to just swallow her pride and go.

She watched Christie walk away toward the elevators. He was good-looking—she thought so. People differed about looks, but mostly people liked symmetrical faces, proportional features and bodies. He'd said once he thought he was utterly ordinary and forgettable. Plain brown hair, going somewhat gray, skin that had a natural olive tint, relatively proportional features. Nice brown eyes. He wasn't startlingly good-looking, but women went for him. They just did. Colleen remembered a woman she'd interviewed once studying a newspaper picture of Tommy Lee Jones. "Not beautiful, but he's hot." The alert body, the intelligence. The renegade moral code behind the eyes.

And she remembered the detectives sitting around one day playing "hot and not." A wicked game, really. Somebody would shout out a name—Margaret Thatcher. Nancy Pelosi. David Letterman. The rest would vote "hot" or "not." Mixed in with the celebrities were other detectives. "Hrznak." "Not." "Nellins." "Not." "Dolan." "Hot." "Littlefield." "Hot." She groaned, but she came out "hot." So did Christie, but he laughed, saying he was hot only because he was there, listening. Potocki was hot. So was Janowski, her pal in Narcotics. But Coleson and McGranahan, two of the senior homicide detectives, were not.

What did it all matter?

McGranahan was sour, but supposedly happily, or at least solidly, married, long-term. Potocki was a sweetheart whose wife didn't want him. Colleen hadn't had a date in two months. Hot didn't necessarily get you laid. What did it matter?

There were some things she was sure of. One. She could live happily ever after with Richard Christie. She knew how to argue with him. She knew his faults. She was herself with him. But unfortunately, he was very married. Two. She was getting old and on her last chances to have a baby. Some people, thank God, still thought she was hot, though she probably had a clock ticking on that, too.

What time did she have to get to know anybody outside of work? She and Potocki had been together twice, to be exact; they couldn't help themselves. But coworkers were supposed to stay away from each other. She'd made a faux pas asking him to have dinner. There he was with a date—which was a good thing, something she had encouraged—and she was left looking desperate.

People, underneath it all, were stupidly romantic, full of illusions. Witness Joanna Navarro thinking because the doc was friendly to her he was interested in her. What did a person do when pheromone attraction went one way but not the other? Nothing. Live with it. It was just nature being inefficient.

She called the labs. "Anything on the Navarro case?"

"We're doing the headlight glass. Probably a Chevy truck, probably ten years old or so, but we're not ready to say. And it looks like the marks we thought were blood, nail polish, lipstick on the vic might be paint. Car paint. Tell you tomorrow."

"So there was something *red* on the truck?"

"I'd say it's more likely *the color* of the truck. But I guess there could be trim of some sort."

"Shit."

"What?"

"We had one eyewitness and he's gone. We put the word out already. Gray."

"I know."

"It was dark—night—but there were streetlights."

"Yeah."

This time she hung up and cursed.

She heaved herself up out of her chair and headed to the park. She combed the streets, looking. When she saw other people who looked as if they slept in the park, she asked about Moore. Finally she went to the Salvation Army and the Light of Life Ministries, but he hadn't checked in that day. She couldn't find him. She drove home.

There were no messages on her machine.

There was no food in her fridge. The freezer had a few goodies, but it meant thawing and cooking.

A long sudsy shower later, her hair washed twice, she studied herself. Circles under her eyes. She put on a pair of pants and a sweater, went to the kitchen, and brewed a short pot, which she waited for with the television news on. Her announcement came on—police looking for a gray truck. Well, if it had to be changed, it had to be changed.

Two cups of coffee got her into her car and on the way to Christie's house.

IN THE SHOWER USING JENSEN'S SUDSY SHAMPOO, Jack examined the gash on his forearm that he got yesterday fixing the old lady's roof. She'd made him sit down and she put antibiotic cream on his arm and bandaged it up. She said she used to work for a doctor. When he left her, he took off the bandage because he didn't want his brother asking where he got such a professional-looking job done. He kept his jacket on most of the time, and Ryan was too wasted to notice.

He could see yard and woods out the bathroom window while he showered. He wished he could just stay here. The old lady told him she'd bought her place for only sixty-five hundred dollars, but, she explained, it was a long, long time ago—and she and her husband did all the work themselves.

He was going to have to go back to her.

He put on a plaid robe he found on the back of the bathroom door, gathered his laundry, and instructed Ryan to hand over his clothes and take a shower. By the time he got up from the basement—another thing he liked about this place was the washing machine and dryer, figuring out how they worked and all that—he found Ryan wearing a woman's robe and sitting with a tall glass and a bottle of whiskey. The glass was about half-full.

"Where did you get that?"

Ryan opened a cabinet built into one of the bookcases. He said, "Look what I found. We're in business. Booze. A bottle and a half and . . . another couple of ounces."

Jack said, "It might be better to stay away from it for a while." Ryan looked at him blankly. "That's not going to last long."

"Well, then we'll need more. Drink a drinky yourself, make you more human." Ryan sounded like their mother. *Have yourself a glass of mead.* That was something their mother used to say for any kind of liquor.

Jack went into the kitchen and got himself a glass. While he was in the kitchen, he started a pot of water boiling. He figured he could boil the little bit of spaghetti there was for supper. Use the chili sauce in a can to put on it.

Ryan was staring at him as he came back into the living room carrying the empty glass. "What took you so long?"

"Uh . . . planning a nice dinner."

Ryan laughed. " 'Swhy I like you, bro, you my bitch, my wife. Take good care of me."

Jack poured himself two fingers.

"That's it? Modest portions?"

"Conserving."

"Good little wife."

He felt himself getting red with anger, but he just sat in the chair opposite his brother and drank down his whiskey in a couple of gulps. The buzz in his arms and legs felt good, like sleep, and it would have been nice except he had too many things he needed to figure out.

"Seven thirty," Ryan said.

"So?"

"Way past dinnertime. I'm hungry. What you waiting for?"

"Conserving," Jack said defiantly.

"Wish Chester was here," Ryan said. "That'd be a good time."

Jack went to the kitchen and checked the water, which was not yet boiling. He heard movement and saw Ryan climbing the stairs to the second floor. He thought he heard him going up to the attic.

There was a bit of daylight yet. They'd decided not to use any of the electric lights at night. He gathered what there was of plain spaghetti and seashell pasta. Not much. If the sauce was no good, they could eat the noodles plain.

Jack felt his jaw tighten. It was hard not to like Chester, but he hated the way Ryan used Chester against him—to prove he was not enough fun, not tough enough, not . . . He heard the noise behind him before he turned around.

"Lookee what I found," Ryan said. He held a rifle in one hand and a box of shells in his left. It was a big, beautiful thing with wooden sides. It had a strap. "How hard could it be? Huh?"

DOLAN WAS STANDING ON THE FRONT PORCH with one of the other detectives, Williamson, and just chatting.

"Hey, partner." He smiled.

Colleen told him about trying to find Oliver Moore again and why.

"Damn. Well, we'll have the labs even if we never find him. When are the labs ready?"

"Tomorrow morning."

"Food is super. You better get in there."

She poured herself a large glass of wine at the side table in the dining room. The table held the end of a roast and several side dishes. People she didn't recognize were drifting to the back porch and the front, to the living room and the kitchen, to talk. It turned out there weren't too many police among the guests.

Christie's wife, Marina, came into the room carrying a platter with a whole roast on it. She wore skinny black pants and a hot pink top and strappy sandals. *Hot.* Nobody in the wide world would vote *not.*

"Hi, Colleen. Glad you could come."

"Thanks. Everything looks wonderful."

"I'll carve you some beef." She put aside the old serving platter that still had some meat on it and replaced it with the new. "This one is just out of the oven."

"Sounds good to me."

"Medium, rare, or well?"

"Rare. Always."

"Me too. Richard likes it well-done. Blows my mind."

"Yeah. What is he thinking?"

"If you want other than wine, we have a bar going in the kitchen. We have most things."

Colleen, if she'd known, would have started with a Scotch. Altogether it looked like a great party, plenty of everything, a generous feel. "Thanks. That's good," she said, referring to the pile of beef Marina had just put on a plate.

Marina handed it over. "I'll let you do the rest. Let me know if you need anything." She went off to the kitchen with the old beef platter.

When Colleen had filled her plate with potatoes, green beans, salad, and thick bread, she took it into the living room and sank into the sofa. Dangerous. The softness was going to put her to sleep. She thought longingly of the Scotch in the kitchen and decided she might have some when the wine was finished. As she put a too big forkful of food into her mouth, a man sat beside her.

"Mind?"

"No. Sorry. I'm chewing."

"That's okay. I'm Steve. Purdy. I live next door."

She swallowed before she was ready to. "Not police, huh?"

"No. Not at all. Closer to criminal."

"Aha. What do you do?"

"Stocks. Investments."

"Oh. Well, I understand the 'criminal,' then."

"You've had bad experiences?"

"I've had no experiences. But please don't try to sell me anything." Some guy had tried to sell her Countrywide two days before it started to topple. "I just need to relax."

"So you're police?"

"Yep."

"I didn't know any police when Richard and Marina moved in. They're fantastic—great neighbors to have."

Colleen wondered how well this Steve Purdy could be doing in his profession. Ethnic Bloomfield was a great neighborhood as far as she was concerned, but it was not typical stockbroker territory.

"I'm going to get myself a drink. Can I get you a refill on the wine?"

"Actually, I'd like a Scotch if you're anywhere near."

"My pleasure."

Christie wandered into the living room. He looked different. He was wearing soft moccasins, a short-sleeved shirt in a coarse weave—he was a man putting work aside. "You doing okay?" he asked.

"Yeah. I'm almost alive again."

"Good." He laughed. "I don't know. You crack me up, Greer."

"Always glad to entertain. Met your neighbor. He's trying to sell me something, I think."

"Himself most likely."

"I thought bonds for my retirement."

"Probably not that."

She wasn't sure how Christie felt about Purdy, so she just made a face and shrugged.

Steve Purdy. Not un-hot, not not. Somewhere in between. Plus, she hated being seen as so obviously in the hunt.

Later, when she heard a couple of the detectives talking about the incredible woman they'd seen Potocki with—"young and leggy and she's a doctor"—Colleen felt a sadness that went beyond logic. She had told him to date, to get over her, hadn't she?

So even later, when Steve Purdy said, having followed her to the backyard during the dessert phase of the party, "Could I call you? Maybe we could catch a movie sometime?" she said yes.

A fantasy ballooned quickly even as she tried to shoo it away. Steve Purdy would reveal untold depths. She would realize one day with a jolt that she was in love with him.

Cripes. Bad as Joanna Navarro.

THREE

MONDAY

THE CHILDREN WERE DRESSED UP in what looked like yesterday's Sunday clothes, and they sat on the sofa with their grandmother between them. They were dressed and ready to go to the funeral home, which, if they were lucky, would happen by tonight. The boy looked to be about seven, the girl about five. Their clothes, clean and well cared for, were not fashionably logoed or styled. There was a whiff of polyester about them, a hint that the family believed coming up in the world depended on looking unwrinkled and, if you were a girl, ruffled. The grandmother wore nylons and heels with a black dress and a black sweater that was knitted wide to look lacy.

The apartment—lace here, figurines there, holy pictures and crosses—was still scrupulously clean and orderly. Today the apartment smelled strongly of oil and pepper. A photograph of Joanna had appeared on the side table. Colleen's eye kept going to it. Faces said a lot—Joanna had been vulnerable, all humility and hopefulness.

The children, Estella and Leo, looked at Colleen with more awe than she liked and a boatload of confusion under the awe. Both of them held their heads at a tilt that promised future emotional upheaval and pain—what was it about that angle suggesting insecurity, a troubled soul? Both were thin children, bony-faced and toothy. When Colleen imagined their lives unfolding, all the strength they would have to summon to get along well in the States, she felt a sag of fatigue for them.

"If their father is not ready to take responsibility for them, are you willing to be their guardian?"

"Yes. They're mine. I wouldn't . . . let him have them."

"I'll send someone from Social Services to work it out. You and your daughter both had jobs. Financially, things will be different now—"

Celia Navarro pulled the lacy sweater more tightly closed. "We can do it. We don't have to leave."

Colleen persisted, speaking as gently as she could. "If you work more hours, you have to find someone to be with the children. You can't leave them alone. I mean, someone will be here to talk to you about this, but I'm giving you a—" She stopped herself from using the slangy "heads-up." "I'm just telling you in advance what you'll have to work out."

Colleen turned to the children. She wanted to see something natural in them, engaged, even hopeful. She smiled and started with a simple question. "Do you go to school near here?"

In unison, they said, "Yes."

Celia nervously interrupted. "She go to kindergarten. He go to second grade."

"You must have some pals at the school. Friends?" Colleen asked them.

They nodded soberly.

"And you're doing well in school, I'll bet?" she asked.

Their grandmother answered again. "They pass. They pass everything so far."

So. Average or below. And not allowed to speak for themselves.

Colleen felt terrible for them. And sorry she hadn't been able to draw them out. She turned to their future guardian. "Do you have friends to spend time with? Are there other people from the Dominican Republic around?"

"We have friends," Celia said cautiously. She appeared to think hanging out with her countrymen was going to get her in trouble.

"It's good to be with people."

Celia looked away.

This was what being afraid was. The family wasn't calling for vengeance because they didn't want to be noticed, deported. They probably told themselves they were kneading the yeast of forgiveness.

"I'll keep checking back." Before she could stand up to leave, her phone rang. She took the call while she was still sitting and could jot down what she heard. It was the labs, with the news she expected. She wrote down certain words as she heard them, a shorthand that she hardly needed; the facts were memorable. *Chevy. Pickup—'94 or '95. Broken front left headlight. Paint compromised. Probably whole truck was red.*

WHEN ARTIE DOLAN ANSWERED HIS PHONE, a patrol cop told him, "We just put a baby on an ambulance, but she's going to be DOA. She was beaten. That's the mother screaming in the background. Her boyfriend was supposed to be watching the baby. He's saying he doesn't know anything about the baby's bruises." The cop's voice caught. He whispered, "Paramedics tried to bring the kid back, but . . ."

"How old?" Dolan asked. His spirits were spiking upward with the idea of this case.

"About a year."

"Jesus. Where's the boyfriend now?"

"He was acting strange, high on something. He might have run by now. There's a back door."

Since he was the secondary on the Navarro case, Artie knew he should hand over the baby case to someone else, but this one had his name on it. Coleson and McGranahan were across the room, immersed in paperwork. He looked around at the other detectives talking among themselves or writing, and he decided to abandon Colleen again to take a crack at the boyfriend. Commander had once compared him to a black Lab when it saw a squirrel or some other small creature moving—dashing toward it before anybody else could even see it. Dolan called Christie to say he was jumping on the case. He winced, waiting for a reprimand.

"Sounds like your kind of thing," Christie said evenly.

"I'll get back to Navarro later today," Dolan promised. "Is Greer there?"

"She was at her computer an hour ago. I don't see her now. Don't worry. Navarro interests me plenty. Let me work with Greer for as long as necessary."

Dolan swatted away a fly. Was it the *case* Christie found interesting or Colleen that drew him in? He'd never seen his boss as distracted by anyone as he was by Colleen. Damn. Marina was a terrific person. It was in Artie's nature to meddle, but he couldn't find a way to say, "Watch it, Boss. Marriage trouble is bad trouble." He said a careful, "Greer's doing okay solo. I'll catch her in a couple of hours."

COLLEEN CALLED THE PATROLMAN from yesterday—Peters—and told him to meet her in the park. When he did, she mapped out quadrants and points to meet up with him again. They had to find Oliver Moore.

"I'll take Cedar and the Aviary. You take everything that borders on North Avenue. Look for him and ask people."

After an hour and a quarter, Peters phoned her even as he came bounding toward her. She was moving away from the Aviary and toward North. "Found him."

"You left him?"

"He's good." Peters pointed and then walked her a hundred yards to where an elderly man was sitting on a bench near the pond, his eyes closed.

The man was black, with closely trimmed gray hair and eyes that, when he opened them at her approach, were full of weariness. He sat up and met her gaze; she thought he looked vaguely familiar, no doubt from her days of running in this park.

"Mr. . . . ? Moore?"

"Yes."

"I'm here about the hit-and-run. You're an important witness."

"Man, I'm your only witness. Felt like I was the only human around."

"Why did you leave?"

"I thought I was supposed to. Your fellow who was here, he dismissed me."

"I'm sorry. That was a misunderstanding. Yes, we definitely want you. You actually saw the accident?" He nodded. "Tell me about the vehicle you saw."

"It was a truck. I told the 911."

"And the police tried to look for it right away. Tell me anything you can about it."

"Gray."

"There are all kinds of trucks," she began, holding off on what she most wanted to ask. She started to draw on her legal pad. He pointed to her crude drawing of a pickup.

"Open in back? Or capped?"

"Open."

"Anything visible?"

He shook his head.

"You didn't catch any part of a license plate?"

"Nobody coulda caught it. They were flying."

Flying sounded about right. "We'll find the guy."

"Guys. Two guys in it, hooting and hollering."

"Two?" This was new. "Are you sure?"

"Seen them before they hit her. They went through the light. They were driving wild."

She silently cursed Peters. Two. And now she had to get the subject around to colors. She'd been at the computer all morning, and she knew what she was aiming for. "You've been very helpful so far," she assured him. "Very. Mind if we take a walk up toward the street? Just to get more exact about this truck—"

They stepped around the duck and goose droppings. The geese had moved on to a different spot in the park, but pigeons and ducks flapped away from them as they walked.

"People don't agree on *colors* and shades, you know. I'll point things out and you describe the color as you see it. Okay?"

He said, "Well, okay."

She pointed to a blue car.

He said, "Blue."

She spied a light green label on a plastic tea bottle. She put her toe on it.

He said, "Neutral. Like green."

Right, she was going to be right; now she needed to move to the yellow to red range. After a moment, she pointed to a discarded bag of chips. "What color, even what shade of gray, are you seeing on the lettering, the name?" She went over to it and put her toe on the orange lettering.

He said, "Light gray."

She pointed to the street. "That car. That little boxy car that just stopped."

He hesitated. "Gray."

"Darker than the bag of chips? Or lighter?"

"Darker gray. Am I doing okay?"

"You're doing great. You're helping."

Just to be sure, she pointed out a few more reds and got a consistent answer: gray.

The truck was red.

It still seemed strange, in spite of the science of it, that any car would contribute paint from an impact with a body, just as it did from an impact with another vehicle. Strange and sad.

Walking Moore back to the bench where she'd found him, she asked, "Do you have a place of residence?"

"I don't want to go to jail. Please."

"No. I'm just asking. How did you end up on the street?"

"Funny how these things happen." When he saw she expected more from him, he added, "Beats some other ways of getting by."

"You sleep inside somewhere in winter?"

"Yes, I do."

"Thank you, Mr. Moore." She dug into her purse and finding no fives, tens, or ones, handed him a twenty. "For you. Get yourself a couple of warm meals."

He looked at the money, folded it with one hand into his palm, and put it in his pocket. After a moment, he said, "Thank you. I will."

"Where can we find you?"

"That's harder. Salvation Army on a rainy day."

When she left him, she called Christie. "Red truck. There is a little red on the vic, no gray, and I can put it together between the labs and the witness. I wanted to find him to be sure. He's colorblind. I tested him."

"You know how to do that?"

"Computer. I read about it all morning. You want the term? Protanopia. One percent of the population has it."

Christie whistled.

"He's good on blues and all that. And he can see green, sort of, if it isn't too yellow. But anything red, orange, and yellow—"

"You're sure?"

"Yep. Red isn't bright to him. In fact, for him, it's very dim. He tends to see black or gray—a range of grays from light to dark. So given the fact that it was at night, given the slight paint deposits on the deceased, we're looking for a red truck. Chevy pickup. Broken headlight. Front left. It's going to be a '94 or maybe a '95."

"Good work. I'll do the news bulletin."

"Thank you."

"What next?"

"Canvasing the park area. The other thing Moore told me is it was *two* guys in the truck, probably young. Somebody might know them."

"I'll come over to the park, help with the canvasing."

"Okay." She didn't want to ask where Dolan was; it wasn't her style to get him in trouble. Still, she had the needling feeling he found ways to avoid their partnership.

"Dolan is nailing a guy he thinks killed a baby."

"Oh. Man. That's big. I'll call him, check in with him."

WHEN JACK WOKE ON MONDAY, Ryan wasn't in the other bed. Then Jack heard a shuffling sound downstairs. The clock on the bedside table sounded like a person; instead of ticking, it gave off a hoarse breathing sound. It was almost noon.

When they were kids on vacation here, they slept later than they wanted and woke despairing that they had missed hours at the lake. They slid down the banister, ate toast or cereal, and ran off. For those few days, it seemed their lives were not so bad. Vacation, they kept saying, vacation. Like other kids have.

By the third day at the lake, their mother was disgusted with

Neil. They could tell she was going to dump him soon. She tired quickly of people, all people. Friends, husbands, even her sons. She'd look at them as if she couldn't remember how they got there or why she had to feed them.

Jack had liked the early years in England—the house they had there and his father, whom he remembered only indistinctly as a person who provided treats, no beatings. Oh, well, it was a long time ago.

And Neil hadn't been that bad.

The one thing Jack could be sure of throughout the changes was that Ryan would always be there, too, rolling with whatever punches came at them. And that Ryan would make fun of their mother or Neil or whatever guy she was seeing and they could have a good laugh. Over the years, the brothers had school friends along the way, but they spent more time together than with anyone else. It had always been that way because they were only a year apart in age. Supposedly they had different fathers. Their mother always told them in anger that Ryan had a more interesting father than Jack did. She usually said it when she was pointing out Jack's faults. Ryan, at least, had personality, she said.

A year after Ryan dropped out of school, he pressured Jack to quit, too. Then the truck became their home. It was their bedroom, dining room, even their bathroom in a pinch—they kept a jar in back.

Now Ryan sprawled at the kitchen table, waiting for him. He had a glass of whiskey going. "Let's go back to Pittsburgh."

"And what? Score drugs?" Jack said. "It's not helping that you're drinking."

"It helps. I can think. I want to go back."

"Okay, but not right away. After we get money and fix the truck."

"There are more body shops in the city."

"Pay them with—what?"

"Something. Nobody's looking for us." He moved up from the table and paced the kitchen space.

"It isn't going to go away, just like that."

"You're always good for the negative, you are. We'll be fine."

"Right. You killed a woman."

"Shut it! What kind of a partner are you?"

"I'm not your partner."

"What are you then, asshole?"

"Your brother."

Ryan didn't hit him. He expected Ryan would, but he didn't. Instead Ryan sat back down at the table and said, "I guess. I guess we had the same mother anyway."

After a while, Jack said, "I'm going to go back down the bottom of the hill, see if I can find the old lady, get some work. Cash would buy us food and gas, anyway."

Ryan studied him. "You worked for the money last time?"

Jack flushed. "Yes."

"Oh, man. Look for the old lady's purse, why don't you? That'd be quicker. If she has enough, we could be out of here."

"Maybe. Maybe."

"I'll come with you."

"No."

"I'll drive."

"We're *not* taking the truck. It should stay hidden— And you need to clean it up. It's a mess."

Ryan didn't say anything, just scowled.

"All right then. Watch TV. I'll clean it later. Just let me go find us something."

Ryan pursed his lips tight. Finally he said, "You need a braver heart."

"Fuck you."

"Where's she live? Your old lady?"

"Bottom of the hill and then . . . to the left, I think. I can walk it. It's only a mile." Again the blood rushed to his face. Ryan could usually tell when he was lying.

"You mean just coming in to Sugar Lake?"

"Yeah."

They stared at each other. Ryan said, "What do you call your old bird? 'Ma'am'? You call her ma'am, I'll bet."

"I don't call her anything."

"I say take her for everything she's got and then some. Bring something home."

"I'll try."

"Trying doesn't cut it. Do it, man. Have some guts for a change." Ryan looked toward the living room, where the empty booze bottles sat on the coffee table. "Wish I had some smoke right about now. . . ."

"Clean up the truck. That's what you can do."

Jack left him and walked down the hill, wondering what he would do if the old lady didn't give him work. She lived halfway down the hill and to the right. He turned around several times to be sure Ryan didn't see where he was going.

ADDIE PUT ON ONE OF HER GAUZY INDIAN SKIRTS, a brown and beige one, and a gold T-shirt and a brown cardigan over that. The sandals she chose allowed her feet to spread out comfortably. She added some colored beads, all colors. She loved fabric, color.

Tom Jensen said something last year about her still having a perfect figure. Hardly. She had the usual damage. It was only that she stood up straight.

She was just fixing on a pair of small hoop earrings when she heard a noise. Then she thought she must have imagined it because when she looked out the window, there was no vehicle in her driveway. But then it came clear—someone calling, "Ma'am? . . . Ma'am?" shouting, "Anybody home?"

HE SAW HER HURRY PARTWAY DOWN the stairwell. "Oh, it's you," she said. She waited, looking at him curiously. "I paid you, right?"

"Thought I'd see about more work."

"Oh. Where's your truck?"

"Um. My mate dropped me off. He'll pick me up later." He looked off to the road, down toward the lake, the opposite direction from where Ryan sat holed up. "He works, too. My friend."

"You don't work together?"

"Not much. You need something done?"

"Oh, let me think what I can manage. Well. You can sand the second-floor windowsills. If you do a good job, you can prime them."

Prime. He could figure out what that was, not that he ever saw sanding or priming up anywhere close.

"I don't have a sander. I use elbow grease. Which is why my shoulder hurts a bit. You don't have tools, do you?"

"No."

"So you're staying up here? With someone?"

He thought she was the kind of person who would know everybody. So he said, "More out on the road on the way to here."

"What are their names?"

"Barnes," he said because he couldn't think. After too long a pause, he added, "Sarah and Peter, friends of my parents." He was breaking out in a cold sweat.

"I don't know them."

"They keep to themselves, mostly." He could feel the lies making telltale red blotches up his neck and throat. Why had he thought she wouldn't get curious? He moved toward the door, wondering what to say about where he was going next.

"Let's start with the windowsill in the bathroom. See how it goes." She came down the stairs a bit more. She was dressed up, possibly going somewhere and didn't want him to know. She was saying, "Last night, I put everything in the hallway outside the bathroom, so I'd be ready for today." She ushered him up the steps ahead of her.

He saw things on a tray: paint, the brushes, a scraper, some sandpaper, a scrub brush. She said, "If there's paint that's chipping but won't come off, you use this. Then you sand it all down smooth. Then use the brush to get all the dust off."

"Where do I dump it?"

"Wastebasket. Call me when you've finished this one. We'll see where to go from there."

He watched her go downstairs. The tools were lined up, and they looked simple enough. He had to try. Soon he heard a radio playing. The idea that the accident might still be on the news sent a shiver through him. Gray truck, gray truck, he told himself. He heard pots and pans clattering. Ten dollars an hour. He could drag it out. Enough for food, if nothing else. It would take a couple of days of work, more, to fix the truck.

He concentrated on the job at hand. He spent twenty minutes working on the bathroom sill. When it looked smooth, he decided to start on places on the outside part of the windowsill that were down to raw splintered wood. The woman hadn't asked for it, but it would buy him time. Once he got started, he began to notice places on the upper window frame that needed work. Weather, years of weather. When people lived in rural places, they left their windows open.

A sugary smell made its way up the steps from the kitchen, making his stomach gnaw itself.

Some minutes later, she came up the steps to check on him. "Still on the same sill?"

"I started doing the outside. And these spots here. Seems like if you're going to do something . . ."

"You're right. 'Do it right.' I agree. That's . . . actually very good. Go on, then, sand the bedroom next and the spare room. Wait and prime everything at once."

"Okay."

"I got myself to the store yesterday. I'm about to make myself an egg sandwich. You want one?"

"Yes, ma'am." He could hear Ryan making fun of him.

"Come on down for the sandwich in, say, ten, fifteen minutes. I don't want to climb the steps again right now."

By the time he finished brushing the bathroom sill and moved his supplies to the bedroom, it was time to go down. He took a quick look around the bedroom—bed, nightstand, two bureaus with all the usual things on top of them. He went down to the kitchen.

The eggs were fluffy between two pieces of bread. His stomach almost ran to meet the food. She said, "Let me guess. I'll bet—" and she came away from the refrigerator, revealing with a flourish a bottle of ketchup. He loved ketchup. She laughed, saying, "Don't tell anyone. I like eggs with ketchup, too."

He wondered if Chester really roughed up old ladies or if it was all talk, all a game. Ryan, the other day, said they were "persuasive." What would a brave heart do—twist her arms behind her back, whisper threats in her ear?

"You want a cup of coffee?"

"That would be . . . Yes. Thank you."

So they ate together.

The sandwich was amazing. What did she *do* to it? And the smell coming out of the oven drove him nuts.

She saw him looking. "I'm making cupcakes for the church bake sale. I always make a few extras, so you can have one when they're iced."

"Thank you."

"Oh, look. I've got a heron in the yard."

She went to the window in the kitchen and looked out on the garden side. He saw a bird with a long beak and long legs. "They usually don't come up here. They stay at the lake. And they're usually not alone. Do you see any others?"

"No." He got up and looked out from behind her, aware of how close he was to her, how easy it would be if he wanted to strangle or pull a knife. He looked as hard as he could. "No. What did you call it?"

"Heron. Some people say egrets, but this is a heron. They like lakes, fish."

"I wish I could live out here permanently," he said, and it was true, but he didn't know why he told her.

"Where are your parents?"

"Oh. Different places."

"I see. England?"

"I always think I sound, you know, American."

"You have traces of English."

They sat down at the table again for the last sips of coffee. Jack felt stuck for speech so he asked her about the soldier in the photograph on the side table in the dining room.

"My husband. He was in the Second World War. In the army."

"My mum said women love a uniform. I told her garbagemen wear a uniform so I might go in for that. She didn't like my humor."

"Mothers worry. It's what they do."

Because he could see she was about to ask him something personal, he headed her off. "Is your husband, is he still around?"

"No. No, he died ten years ago." She sounded sad. Like she wasn't over it.

"Ten years is a long time."

She smiled. "I guess it must seem very long to you. I feel like he was here just . . . last week."

When he went back upstairs he worked for a while in the bedroom, wondering if he could get another day or two's work out of her.

She brought up a cupcake. It was chocolate with chocolate icing. She stood there while he ate; he tried not to gulp it in one bite. "Is everything you make good?"

She laughed. "I never think so. But somehow I've cooked pretty much every day since I was twenty. A lot of it sticks."

He was curious who she cooked for and was about to ask, but she was turning away and taking his plate downstairs.

Later, different sounds filtered up. He realized it was the television. He came to the top of the stairs and saw her lying down on the sofa. She didn't open her eyes or say anything. He went back to sanding and checked back a bit later, and she looked exactly the same.

Slowly, quietly, he opened drawers in the bedroom. A couple of envelopes with papers. Her name was on them, Addie Ward, Adelaide Ward. There wasn't any cash. She kept ancient yellowed books about appliances. In another envelope there were birthday cards. Jewelry, of course, jewelry. His heart quickened. He closed the drawer quietly. Sweaters and tops in another drawer.

He went back to work.

RYAN HAD FORCED HIMSELF TO FILL A BUCKET—actually a white industrial-sized container that once held something called kalamata olives—with dish soap and hot water. He found a scrub brush and some kitchen towels. Then he walked outside to look at the truck. The ripe animal smell from the blood made his stomach quiver.

There was more blood than he'd guessed. He scrubbed and he poured the rusty-looking sudsy water over the ground, but he had to go into the house to make up a fresh bucket.

The truck looked strange with one clean fender panel. He filled the bucket a third time and did what he could find the patience for. Now anyone could see the nicks and dents and dings all over the thing. He stood back and surveyed his work with sadness. The truck didn't seem right, clean.

Hit a deer, hit a deer, hit a deer, he practiced saying until it felt real. He pictured the deer startled, then flying through the air.

For a while he lay down on a dry patch of ground under a tree, pretending he lived here. Jack liked it, but Jack didn't mind being bored. Ryan needed excitement—race car driving or something that made the blood zoom to his head.

He smoked two cigarettes, the last he had, and went back into the house. There was not a drop of liquor left in the bottles.

It was weird, Jack going off on his own, not telling him things. What was he supposed to do with himself out here in the boonies? Pacing back and forth, inside, outside. About four in the afternoon, without deciding exactly, he thrust his hands in his pockets and, leaving the doors to the house open, returned to the truck. It didn't have to stay hidden. That was Jack's idea, not his. He got in and started it up. The familiarity of the action made him feel better.

The road was tree-lined and pretty. What if, after all, Jack had just walked down the road, hitched himself a ride, and gone wherever the driver was going, never looked back? Maybe he wasn't at some old lady's house at all. The utter silence on the road brought back his panicky feeling. He kept turning around to look behind him, stretching up to look ahead.

At the foot of the hill was a square building. It didn't have a name, just a flashing sign that said, IRON CITY. He parked in the lot, went right up the cement steps and in, and when he was inside the place, which was large, he walked straight back and hit the men's room, all the while scoping the joint. There were four customers, laborers in thick shoes, coveralls, and billed caps, sitting at the bar. The bartender was a big load of a guy staring at the TV.

As luck would have it, the place still had a cigarette machine, and it was out in the hallway on the way to the men's room. Ryan pissed a good one and came back to the machine, where he went through a pantomime of putting in a bill and waiting and pulling a knob, hitting the machine, kicking it once, muttering a curse, and doing the whole nine yards until he saw that someone had noticed. He began to slump his way toward the front door.

"What's the matter, kid?" asked a customer.

"Ah, nothing. Used my last bill on the machine and it ate my money."

The bartender frowned. "It don't usually do that."

One of the customers held out a pack to Ryan and said, "Go ahead. Have one on me."

"Thanks." He took it gratefully. And the matches the guy slid over. Lit up.

"You're new around here."

"Just passing through."

"Where to?"

"Eventually New York. The state, not the city."

"What for?"

"Folks are moving."

"From where?"

"Butler."

"You want a drink?"

"Yeah, I do, but I'm outta—"

"On me, I meant. You're of age, aren't you?"

"Heck, yeah." He started to pull out his fake ID, stolen ID is what it was, hardly convincing, saying he was John Kaharchak, forty-three years old.

But the man was winking. He was burly, with a beard. He seemed to like a good joke, Ryan's kind of guy.

"Get this boy a whiskey. Same's mine."

The bartender poured. Ryan looked at it eagerly, a generous

portion. "What brand did you want back there?" The bartender gestured toward the cigarette machine.

"Marlboro."

The merry man laughed. "Not Kool Lights. Not on your life."

Ryan sipped his drink and waited for the cigarettes. This was good. Things he needed coming to him. It gave him an image of being on the road and making it. He was going to be rich one day, he knew that for sure. He needed an idea . . . and a pal with spirit, another Chester to help him break into places, make a little luck.

"Where's your folks now?"

"Visiting friends."

"Passing through, you said."

"People they wanted to see on the way through."

"You didn't want to go along?"

"Spare me."

"What kind of accent is that you're using?"

He paused and said, "Probably you're hearing some Aussie."

"Aussie. That's what I thought."

"That's 'cause I spent some time there."

"When?"

"When I was three to when I was about fifteen. My folks were working there."

"Cool. What at?"

"Oh, they're teachers. I wouldn't call it work."

"You wouldn't?"

"Not honest work."

The merry man laughed up a storm. It earned Ryan a second drink.

"You okay with two drinks?"

"I grew up with whiskey at the nipple. In Australia, the kids are allowed to drink at any age. Warm beer. Whiskey. Whatever. Nobody ever kept it from me."

"I see."

After a while, he thought he'd better go back up the hill before he talked too much and couldn't remember what he said. With reluctance, he left the bar and trudged to his truck. Nobody seemed to be around when he got in and drove up the hill.

But Jack wasn't at the house. His good mood dissipated. He felt panic overtake him—the bird fluttering in his chest.

ABOUT FOUR O'CLOCK, Jack saw from out the bedroom window the old lady carrying what looked like two boxes of cupcakes to her car. She came back in and called up the stairs, "Looks like we have to quit for the day. I need to take these to the bake sale." But she sounded uncertain.

He came to the top of the stairs. "You want me to quit? Or just keep going till you come back?"

"I don't know."

"Well, how long will you be?"

"A couple of hours. Maybe you better come back tomorrow."

"Oh. Hmm." He came the whole way down the steps. "Well, I better get paid for today."

She rummaged in her purse. It was the same one she had yesterday, and it was hanging from her shoulder. "Oh, damn," she said. "I went to the market and I didn't go to the ATM. Can it wait till tomorrow?"

"That's a bit tough."

"Oh." She looked at him curiously. "What time does your friend pick you up?"

"Maybe in an hour or two."

"Well, then you might as well keep working until you have your ride. If I don't make it back in time, could you come back later tonight for the pay?"

"What about the door?"

"I don't lock it. Just pull it shut."

He watched her drive out, and when he was sure she was gone, he put on the kitchen radio. He noted where the station marker was before moving the dial. Advertising, music, music, somebody shouting religion, news—but nothing that sounded like Pittsburgh news. He looked out the living room door to be sure she hadn't come back. He put on the TV. There were tons of channels. That was because of the dish on the roof—which she hated because of how it looked. Movies, cable news. He skipped and skipped around, and even found the local news under way, but there was nothing about the gray truck at all. They'd either said it or they weren't going to. The sports guy came on. Penguins. Pirates.

From the kitchen came voices also talking about the Pirates and the Penguins, but then he heard something like: "In a new development in the search for the hit-and-run driver . . ."

He ran to the kitchen.

". . . a mother of two on Pittsburgh's North Side, the police are now looking for a red truck, a '94 or '95 Chevy pickup with a broken front left headlight. Anybody seeing the truck or having information as to the owner of that vehicle is asked to call the Pittsburgh Police."

For a full minute he didn't move. Then he began to plan. At dark, in the night, they could drive up to Canada—fix the truck or ditch it. If Addie Ward heard the news, would she remember he'd driven here in a red truck on Saturday?

It's almost six o'clock.

Jack bounds upstairs and to the old lady's bedroom, where he goes straight to the jewelry. He can't tell what's real. He pockets earrings and chains. Then he lets out a cry and sits on the edge of her bed. His heart thumps so hard he can feel it in his fingers. He stands, takes everything out of his pockets, shoves the jewelry quickly back into the drawer, and hurries out of the house.

ADDIE SITS BEHIND THE TABLE that holds her pretty cupcakes as well as larger cakes, round ones and square ones, pies, and also boxes of cookies, one of which she recognizes as not home baked—contributed by a worn-out woman with three kids. Addie is tempted to buy them since nobody else will likely want them. She can give them to that boy when she pays him. In her handbag is a hundred and sixty dollars from the ATM. This boy is expensive because he's slow. He's probably going to tell her six hours again, sixty bucks.

Today he looked a bit better than he did the first time he came by. Two days ago his hair was unclean. It's the kind of hair—too long, badly cut—that reminds her of British Isles hoodlums in films. An undernourished look. At least she's given him a couple of meals.

A lone customer comes into the church basement. Addie struggles to remember the woman's name. M something. Mary, Marie, Margie, Martha. Oh, damn. The woman is a permanent resident of the town and a member of the congregation at this church, and they talk most Sundays, but the name won't surface. Marian. No.

The woman, lingering over the poppyseed cake, doesn't notice Addie at first. Then, "Oh, Addie, it's you. I didn't see! I was just—I'm sorry I wasn't looking."

"That's all right. And how are you?"

"Fine. I think. You?"

"Very good."

"I think I'll take this one. It's big, anyway."

Addie boxes the poppyseed cake, saying, "Four dollars. It looks like a good one."

"It does. You look great—springy and pretty."

"Thank you."

"I wish I had your hair and skin."

"Oh, well, I think yours is just fine."

"Nah. My people wrinkle early. What is your secret?"

"Oh . . . I used to use Pond's Cream, but you can't even get it anymore. Now I just buy whatever's on sale." The woman's name continues to play escape games. "What are you doing these days?" Addie tries, hoping the answer will jog some memory. Getting old is really the pits. Ears. Mind. Legs. And who knows when the heart will go?

"I've been spring-cleaning the house, taking things to the garage, you know, things I want to give away. It's such a big job. I don't know that I can do it anymore. Not by myself. My husband won't help. He just doesn't see the need to organize."

"Oh, men are like that. We keep things going, don't we?"

"I'm going to hire someone. My back is killing me. I wonder if there is anyone on the bulletin board who does odd jobs."

Addie considers. Jack with no last name. Probably this woman—Meryl, Mollie, Megan, Melissa, no, none of them—won't want to pay ten an hour. "Well, check the bulletin board. If you don't find anyone, I might have someone you could try."

The woman goes over to the bulletin board and studies it for some time. When she comes back, she says, "Nothing. Guitar lessons. Babysitters. How about the person you mentioned?"

"Well, I just have a very small experience with this boy. You'd have to interview him and work out what you'd be willing to pay."

"What's his name?"

"Jack. Jack something. I don't have a last name. But if you could write down your contact information, I could give it to him, and if he wants the work, he could call you. He's actually sanding and priming some windowsills for me. I don't know anything about his other commitments. I'll be paying him tonight or tomorrow. You could ask."

"Or you could just call me when you find out."

"Right." She taps her head. "Right. Of course."

"Man, those cupcakes look good. The ones with the little twirl on top."

"Oh, those are mine!"

"You should have said."

"They're fifty cents each. I didn't set the prices. Our minister's wife did. What's her name?"

"Dolly."

"Dolly. Right."

"Well, give me four cupcakes, too." The woman pulls out two dollars. And along with it comes a piece of paper. "Shopping list," she says. She appears to think about it and goes back into her purse until she produces a pen. Bending over, she tears off the bottom of the shopping list and writes something. "Oh, my back," she says as she does. "Every time I do physical labor, I pull out my left side and then it hurts to move any which way."

Addie puts the four cupcakes in one of her available boxes. When she hands it over, the woman hands her a piece of paper. She forces herself not to look at it right away.

"Wonderful to see you, as always," the woman says before trotting off with her goods.

Emma. Well, the M is in the middle. A lesson there, whatever it is. Emma. Emma Hopper. British Isles from way back, without the accent, of course. Protestant stock. Skin that wrinkles, like the boy's skin, paper thin.

No customers. Addie digs into the handbag she carries and opens a light paperback copy of *The House of Mirth.* It seems she's been rereading it for the better part of a year in between other things so that she can hardly remember what foolishness Lily has committed from one reading to the next. She can only be sure there will always be foolishness.

BEFORE HE ENTERS THE PATH TO THE JENSEN place, he hears a shot. Very clearly. One shot. He listens. There are no shouts, no voices, nothing else. Jack runs into the house, looking about. "Ryan?" he calls. "Ryan?"

"Out here."

He hurries through the kitchen and out the back door, and there is his brother, aiming the rifle at something.

"Stop. Stop. I could hear that from the road."

His brother drops the rifle. "Yeah. This thing has a hell of a kick. Practically smashed my jaw."

"Put it down."

"You're supposed to brace it. I know that much."

The ground is still damp around the truck, which is all cleaned up.

"Come inside. We have to talk." When Ryan gets up, he stumbles, laughs at himself, and Jack almost has to catch him. In that move, Jack smells liquor. "What's—you found more booze?"

"I went down to the bar. Got it bought for me."

Jack stands stock-still just short of the doorway. "You are joking. Aren't you?"

"No. Big guy bought me two drinks and I cadged me some fags, too. I can make my way. That's one thing I know."

Just to be sure, Jack asks carefully as they go into the kitchen, "You watched TV today? Or not?"

"No."

"Radio?"

"No."

The sun is on the other side of the house, but the kitchen still looks great, welcoming. Jack wishes he never had to leave it. He sits at the long wooden table. "We have to talk. It's serious."

"Oh, boy."

"It was on the radio. The news. They aren't looking for a gray truck anymore. They're looking for red."

"Huh?"

"I heard it. I heard it. Look, you took the truck down the hill? Who saw it? Because it's on the news and we're in deep shit."

"Nobody saw it."

"How could that be?"

"Their noses were in their beers. They weren't looking."

"Was there news on in the bar?"

"No. Golf."

Jack nods. "Okay. The truck needs to stay around back where it is until we . . . actually leave. Tonight. At dark. I have to go back for the money. She didn't have it."

Ryan looks at him incredulously. "Why didn't you take something from her?"

"I did. I put it back."

"Why? She see you?"

"No. It was just—"

"Pussy."

"You know how to sell jewelry?"

Ryan leans across the table, alert now. His eyes are bright. "I want to know all about your old lady. Everything."

And he can't explain it but it's like old times, he can't keep words to himself when Ryan is around, he tells everything—nice old bird, cooks for people, wears jewelry, husband is dead, drives an old station wagon.

"Was there a working phone at her place?"

"Yes."

"Did you call Chester?"

"No."

"Fuck. Did you call anybody?"

"Who? Thought to call Mum, but I didn't know what to tell her. Ask for money again, she'd probably hang up and that's that."

And as he tells the secrets he's kept, he feels the seesaw tip and the power reverse.

COLLEEN RECOGNIZES THE VOICE GRADUALLY, just before he says who he is. Steve Purdy.

"I hope it's okay that I called you at work. Can you talk?"

"It's okay right now."

"You got some sleep?"

"Eight hours. Which is rare. The food—knocked me out."

"I couldn't do twenty-four hours. I'd have to change jobs."

"A person does think of it."

"Well, here's what I was hoping—if you feel up to it—I was hoping we could go to a movie sometime—like maybe Friday night, with dinner before or after? There's an indie at the Harris. Called *The Sweet.* I'm thinking we could eat someplace nearby."

"I'll have to make it a maybe. I have no idea what this case I'm on will be like by then." She doesn't say there's hardly a chance the one slim lead will get her anywhere. "If it's solved, I'm game."

"I'll hope it's solved. How long will you have to stay tonight?"

"I *am* supposed to leave here sometime tonight. I did eighteen hours yesterday, came in early and it's—" It was six thirty.

"Well, then . . . I get how tired you are, but I'm wondering, would you want to have some dinner tonight? I could take you, you wouldn't have to fend for yourself. Mondays are a bad night for restaurants, but I'm sure we could find something."

It does her spirit good to think she is so fetching that he waited only twenty-four hours to call and sounds eager to see her. She tries to picture him but can't be sure she is remembering right. Thin but not emaciated. Tall, doesn't stoop over, clean clothes. Hair light brown. She has the facts without the picture.

She wants to go home to freshen up.

"This doesn't negate Friday. It's just a spur of the moment—"

"That sounds . . . awfully nice."

"Should I look for a restaurant?"

"Any simple restaurant will do."

"Pick you up at seven there?"

She looks at her watch. "Make it seven thirty. I'll take my car home." She gives him the address.

In calculating the time to get home, shower, find something to wear, she's reminded that dating is a lot of work. She's quick. Still, she might be a few minutes late. But before she says so, another call comes through. "Just a minute," she tells Purdy.

"Woman wants to talk about the hit-and-run," the desk sergeant tells her. "Should I put her on?"

"Absolutely." She switches back to Steve. "I have to hang up. I'll call you back, but here's my cell number in case."

Most citizen calls are worthless, but you gotta hope. "Detective Greer," she says. "How can I help you?"

"I . . . might have a tip about the truck that hit the woman."

"Right. Let me have your name."

"Tanya King."

"And your phone number."

The woman gives it. Colleen knows the desk officer probably has it, too, but it's always good to be sure the person is consistent. "All right. What do you know?"

"I know two guys who *have* a red truck."

"And?"

"They're nuts. And I haven't heard from them since the accident."

"You have a relationship with them?"

"It's complicated. They bother my boyfriend all the time and so I see them."

"And they stopped bothering?"

"Well, he's in rehab. They did come here looking for him."

"Two of them?"

"Yes."

"How old?"

"Nineteen, twenty. Brothers."

"When was that?"

"Saturday, pretty late at night. It would have been before the accident."

"Do these brothers use drugs as well?"

"Whenever they can."

"What drugs?"

"Anything. Crack lately."

"Interesting. And what makes you think the truck was theirs?"

"A feeling."

"Okay. Tell me their names and where they live."

"Jack and Ryan."

"Last name?"

"I don't know." As Colleen is counseling herself to remain skeptical, Tanya King says, "And they don't live anywhere. They sleep in the truck. They park it somewhere on the North Side, way up on Federal."

So this is really something.

"How about I come over and talk to you? Get more details?"

"When?"

"Now."

"Okay."

Colleen jots down the address and calls Steve Purdy on the way to her car to nix the dinner. She's starved and planning to grab something on the way. But his phone doesn't answer.

"Call me," she tells his machine. "I'm not going to be able to make a seven thirty anything. I have to go question someone."

Completely desperate, she drives through a McDonald's for a chocolate milkshake. I'm drinking ground plastic, she tells herself, with chocolate syrup mixed in. The concoction quiets her roaring stomach enough to get her to Tanya King's place.

Fifteen minutes later, up on Perrysville, Colleen sits across from Tanya, a tall, lean, dark-skinned African American. She's good looking, probably in her early twenties, but her eyes have a vagueness that suggests if she's not currently using, she has some residual fogginess. Colleen guesses she's pulling herself up by whatever bootstraps she can find. The apartment is clean and neat.

"How well do you know this Jack and Ryan?"

"Not too well."

"You think of a last name?"

"No."

"Your boyfriend would know it?"

"Probably."

"His name?"

"Chester Saunders."

"Tell me about their relationship."

"Well, these two boys were always getting him to do things. I think he was afraid of them. Bad things."

"Bad things like?"

"Break into houses. They're a real bad influence."

"Was your fellow ever arrested?"

"Yes. Once. Possession, but it wasn't anything much and they let him go."

"Were Jack and Ryan ever arrested?"

"I don't know. I never heard they were."

"Where did they live before they started living in the truck?"

"They have a mother somewhere in the area."

"Chester would know?"

"I think so."

"Tell me about the truck."

"It's red."

"Lots of red trucks around. Anything else about it? What style?"

"You know, pickup with a flatbed. They never had a cap or

anything. It was always just open. Chester told me they sleep in the front when it's cold out. In summer, they sleep in the back."

Colleen decides her time will be best served by finding the boyfriend. "You have to tell me where Chester is doing his rehab."

"He's not allowed to talk to anybody yet. I'm not allowed to call or visit."

"This is a homicide. Let me deal with them."

"Yes, okay. He's at North Hills Rehab."

Colleen's phone rings and she sees it's Steve Purdy. "I have to get this," she says, touching the call button.

Into the phone, she says, "Just a minute. Just a sec."

She turns to Tanya. "I'll almost certainly be in touch again. You've been very helpful. Call me if you need to go out of town for anything."

"No, I'm here."

Outside the girl's apartment, she gets back on the phone with Purdy, who says, "I was in the shower when you called. Sorry."

A clean fellow.

"Some things are happening here. I have to go talk to a guy who might know something."

"Oh. Well, I understand. Feel free to call back if you're hungry later. I can do a late dinner. If you want."

"I'm guessing it would be nine o'clock or later. I'd be coming from work. I'm not fancy."

"No need to be."

"I might take you up on it."

THE REHAB PEOPLE WERE having their evening meeting. "I'm sorry," said a prim blonde. "Patients can't be interrupted. For anything."

Colleen had to summon her anger, which was burning only

weakly at the moment. She channeled Dolan on a tough day; she held her badge close to the woman. "This is a homicide investigation. If you interfere with it, you're risking charges against you. Homicide trumps the daily routine, wouldn't you say?"

The woman looked left, right, left, right. There was no one to rescue her. "I don't know how to get him out of there," she whimpered.

"You knock on the door, enter, say his name, say, 'Emergency,' and escort him out. Straight to me. Then you find us a room."

The woman did exactly as she was told. Colleen could see through the door that the group looked energized by the interruption. Twenty people craned their necks, trying to see her. But Chester adapted quickly, made his way out, shone a playful smile at Colleen, and confided, "Thank you, Detective. I've already heard all their stories three times."

Colleen almost laughed. There was something about the kid that belonged onstage. He was a natural comic. He was a little bit George Carlin and a little bit Robin Williams; she liked both. And he was one of those overweight people who carried it well.

"In here," she said, working to get rid of her smile.

The ordinary preliminaries helped. She handed him a legal pad as she took out her own smaller notebook and instructed him to write down his name, address, and phone numbers. He kept looking up, asking, "What's this about?"

When she saw he was finished writing, she said, "Vehicular homicide. We need to ask you some questions."

"I don't own a vehicle. Unfortunately."

She turned her legal pad around to read his name and address and slid it back to him.

"I been in *here.* I been in . . . *meetings* or in a bed for days."

"I know that."

"So what's it about?"

"What have you been on? What landed you in here?"

"A little bit of everything, to answer your first question. Crack, to answer your second."

"I see." She jotted it down in her small notebook.

"Yep. Almost died. They said I did kind of die, but they brought me back."

"Your girlfriend is very worried about you."

"She sent you here?"

"She told me where you were." Chester was at least nonplussed for a moment. Colleen let him stew. "What exactly did you sell to Ryan and Jack?"

"Them? They're in this? What about them?"

"Chester. Try to answer questions, not ask them. Try. What's their last name?"

"Ritter, Rutter, something like that."

"You don't know for sure."

"No. It's one or the other. I think Rutter. But what's going down? You said *vehicular* homicide." He appeared to like the word. "Are they hurt?"

Colleen paused for a long time to let him figure out he was still trying to do the asking. "What drugs did you sell them?"

"None."

"Then where did they get them?"

"I don't know."

"You have to know. You were selling, weren't you?"

"No."

"Then where were you buying? Where were *they* buying?"

"Man, I don't know where they got their shit. I bought from *them* a few times."

She knew from the way his eyes had shifted that it was a lie. She let it sit there.

"Tell me about them."

"What's to say?" She waited him out. It took a twenty-count, during which he began to look longingly toward the door. "I only know them a little."

"Where do they live?"

"Now that's tricky. They seem to be roaming lately. They don't have a place."

"Why aren't they with their mother?"

" 'Cause they won't get jobs."

"What's she like?"

"Kind of wild."

"In what way wild?"

"Kind of hot." Trademark smile beamed. Smile faded. "And she has a big temper."

"She turned them out?"

"I guess. They didn't have anyplace to go."

"So Tanya put them up sometimes?"

He looked surprised. "Yeah. A couple of times."

"Write me down their full names, their mother's address, everything you know about them. Help me find them."

"Are they lost?" He cackled, a cheerful sound.

"Did I tell you this was a homicide investigation?"

"Vehicular," he said, trying out the word again. "Vehicular. With a truck on the end."

She paused. "Okay. Tell me everything you know about the truck."

"I don't know anything. It's red. A Ford. No, a Chevy."

"Write."

He scribbled some. He hesitated over the names.

"What?"

"I don't think the mother's name is the same as theirs."

"You know her name?"

"No."

"Where'd they go to school?"

"They were done with school. Dropped out."

"I didn't ask that. Where'd they go when they went?"

"Up on Perrysville."

Colleen was exhausted, and her milkshake was wearing off. She released him back to his meeting, knowing he'd make a story of her. Standing in the hallway near the front desk, she called the office from her cell and asked them to run the names Ryan and Jack Rutter through every mill they had. If they didn't find anything, they should try Ritter.

The blond woman at the desk pretended to be riveted by something she was reading.

Colleen found a women's room on her own, washed her face with a tiny bar of complexion soap she carried, put on some lipstick, poked her hair this way and that for an attempt at a Meg Ryan coif. Her small efforts would have to do.

ADDIE WAS READING AT THE KITCHEN TABLE at around eight thirty, eating a bowl of soup, with a book propped up in front of her when Jack came for his money. She was very involved in the reading. This wasn't her handbag book, but her downstairs book, another novel. She was also savoring the soup, even though it wasn't homemade—she could do much better.

She finally registered the knocking and his voice. By the time she got up, he had opened the door and entered. She came out to the living room and saw him looking about. At what? The photos again?

"Saw your light," he said. "I figured you didn't hear me knocking."

Her hearing problem was not something she liked to admit. She went to the side cabinet and opened it and took out her handbag. "I'd ask you to work tomorrow, but since you got ahead tonight, I think I can finish up on my own." She wished he were a talker. If he talked, she'd know what to do with him. "If you need work, I have another name for you—a woman I know. Give her a call. I hope it works out. Or you could give me your phone number and I could pass it on."

"Um, okay," he said.

"How many hours today?"

"Four."

She was surprised. She thought he was going to claim six. He must have left soon after she did. She handed him the forty dollars in a twenty and two tens and went to the kitchen to get a piece of paper.

How pale he looked. It couldn't all be hunger, could it? The idea appalled her. She saw the spare cupcake she had saved for herself and the broken cookies she had bought up. Feeling selfish, she kept the cupcake back and took him only the cookies.

"Here you go," she said. "Something I bought for you. Just jot down your name and number."

She watched him do that while she dug in her purse for the other slip of paper, the one from Emma Hopper. "This is the woman who needs a worker. But call first. And I don't know what she's able to pay. It could be a bit less than what I paid you, so maybe you should clear all that straight off. She's very nice." She handed the paper over.

"Where's she live?"

"In town. Cochranton. I'm not sure of the address. You could call her and if you two agree, she'd give you directions."

"Okay."

On the way to the door, she examined his walk. Defeated. What was it about him that tugged at her? She couldn't see the truck or the friend anywhere. "Are you finished with school?" she asked.

"What kind of school?"

"High school. There's some good tutoring down at the church."

"I don't go anymore. I wasn't much of a student."

Young. He was young. "Um. Well. I hope someday you feel like going ba—"

But he was already at the door and gone. He walked out the driveway toward the road. She didn't see him getting into a vehicle and wondered if his mate had dumped him again. But soon enough she saw a truck speed down the road.

She suddenly wanted to call someone, just to talk. The feeling of loneliness grew and her heart ached, but she couldn't say why exactly.

Her soup was cold. She put it back in the saucepan she'd used and heated it a little, staying close to the stove so she wouldn't overheat it. But she missed her moment and now it was too hot again. So she climbed the stairs to look at the work the boy had done.

It was very neat. Careful. Sanded and primed, better than she would have done. She didn't feel so bad about giving him Emma Hopper's name. Thinking she could tackle the actual painting tomorrow, she took off the earrings and necklace she wore because they felt heavy and irritating, as jewelry sometimes did at night. She put them on her bedside table and hurried down to her soup.

On the kitchen table was the boy's phone number. Jack Rigger. No area code. It would probably be an 814 area code. Everybody around here was. She called Emma and left the number on her answering machine.

OUT OF THE CORNER OF HIS EYE, Jack watched Ryan shoving the cookies into his mouth while driving down the hill from the old lady's place. The beans they'd tried to cook had never gotten soft enough, so they turned off the gas and gave up on them. Jack carefully folded the piece of paper Addie Ward had given him and put it in his shirt pocket.

"What's that paper?"

"Somebody who wants work done."

"We're getting out of Sugar Lake. You can toss it out the window. How much money you have?"

"Forty. It isn't much."

"Why only forty?"

"I worked four hours."

"I should have gone in and bashed her on the head for you. You didn't even take the jewels. . . ."

"I don't know how to sell jewels. Do you? Shut it."

"What'd you do, sit and knit together?"

Jack bit down on his anger. "If she found something missing, she'd call the police and we aren't far away."

"But you took the piece of paper and it's in your pocket."

"Yeah. I conserve. You never know what you'll need."

"Little wifey."

"That's getting old, you stupid fuck." He plucked two cookies from the box on Ryan's lap. His heart was still pumping madly from minutes ago when he had to write down his name and didn't know what to write. It ended up he used the name of the friend he had when he was in his first year in school—his last year in England. There was a John Rigger in his class. And he himself was John Rutter. He was called Jack out of school, but the teacher used the more formal "John," so the boys got to be known as Rigger and Rutter. And, of course, people mixed them up. One day the teacher did a whole presentation on their names and what they meant. At the end of the day the kids scattered home with pieces of paper telling them about the derivations of their names.

John Rigger's family came from shipbuilders. From way back. Rigger was happy about that. Other kids were told their people had been chimney sweeps or stonemasons. There were two Pakis in class, three Africans, and three Chinese. The teacher said she didn't know what their names meant, so they didn't get pieces of paper. But Jack's paper said his name went the whole way back to olden times, to Cheshire, and that his family had a coat of arms. Centuries ago, they were in wars and they had money.

At home, when he showed the paper to his mother, she exploded with laughter. "Oh, man, he always said he was a toff. I didn't want to believe it. And I—of course your teacher didn't tell you this—my people, Miner, came from coal workers. Which is why your toffy father and I didn't get along." She directed this to Jack. "They're weak people. So that explains a few things."

They hadn't seen their father in a while by the time Jack was in primary school. He could hardly remember him except as a person who was kind to him. Weak in what way? Jack pointed out to his mother a line on the paper the teacher had given him saying that a lot of the Rutters went to America. "Maybe we have relatives there," he said. He pictured the three of them on a long plane ride finally met by the open arms of people who wanted to take them in. "Where's Barbados?" he asked, because apparently some of the Rutters had gone there.

"Now that wouldn't be a half-bad stop," his mother said. "Sands and beaches. Don't you worry your poor head about it," she said in a tone of relenting. "Those other Rutters don't have a clue we exist."

"I'm not weak," Ryan said.

"No. Your father was a glorious bandit."

Rutter had treated them equally. But they came to understand, as children do, in bits and pieces, that he'd only really fathered Jack. Sometimes the boys speculated about Ryan's father. Once, when Ryan was about twelve, he asked his mother what his father was like. "Clever," she said. "Charmer. Could get around anybody."

"What was his name?"

"One of his names was Botts. It didn't suit him. He was more dashing than Botts." For a while, Jack called his brother Botts. Ryan never found it particularly funny. Eventually Jack dropped it.

The brothers had always looked more or less alike. People thought they did, anyway. They looked like their mother, who said their chins were okay, but then she always added that part about their undistinguished noses. They knew by the age of seven they had missed out on "those big noses Prince Charles and other uppers got."

Now Ryan said, "There's that bar I went to yesterday. We could—"

"Get on the small roads and keep driving north," Jack said levelly. "We need to park where the truck doesn't show itself and we need to get real food."

"Aye-aye, sir, wifey, sir."

The truck bounced over bumps. When they'd passed out of Sugar Lake, Jack asked, "How'd you get served back there?"

"I was clever. Man, I gotta get on a bigger road," Ryan announced. "I need food now. I'm starved."

Jack didn't stop him. Ryan followed his nose and pretty soon they were on Route 19, where they read a few signs and decided on Meadville as large enough for food, gas, and a place to blend in temporarily with a lot of other trucks.

As they drove into the town, Ryan said, "A KFC, a Pizza Hut . . . ?"

But Jack noticed a supermarket that had a gas station. He pointed. "More economical."

Ryan shook his head mockingly, but without slinging the usual insults drove into the gas station.

Jack handed his brother a ten. "That's it, for gas."

"That won't get us across a puddle."

He was afraid to give up all his money at once. "I'm going to the store while you get the gas." He crossed the parking lot and went inside the market.

He picked up one of the already cooked chickens and put it in a cart. His mouth watered. He chose a small package of assorted cold cuts, bread, juice, and soda, adding in his head. Almost twenty bucks. Still, they could get by for a day or two on the food. Well, a day. Ryan was now on the ravenous part of the cycle. No appetite usually, depending on what he took and what mix of it, then suddenly a day later or so, hunger, big hunger.

He looked at the cart of the man in front of him. Milk, fruit, vegetables. He never ate vegetables, but they were okay mucked up with a lot of onions and oil like the old woman, Addie, made the first night. He found himself thinking about her a lot. He liked her. He wasn't supposed to, but he did. When he got to the lot, Ryan had moved the truck and was leaning against somebody's old Toyota sedan like a movie star doing an ad.

"Come on. If we're going, let's go."

"You see cameras, eh?"

"No, but you do. Acting up like a fuck-all jackass. Who are you doing all that show for?"

"Myself. I got bored."

The first thing they did after leaving the supermarket was to park the truck in the back of an insurance office so they could eat. It was past nine thirty by then. They decimated the whole chicken in minutes and made their way through part of the bread. They made it halfway through the juice and halfway through the soda. Ryan looked happy. He said, "How much money is left?"

"Maybe like twelve."

"Sure?"

"Yeah."

"Let me see it."

Jack held it out.

Ryan took it and counted as if he had a bundle instead of a ten and two ones. "This is nothing. We got to get us some more."

"Right. I'd say let's move a little further on, then park the truck."

Ryan looked at the bills thoughtfully, folded them, and put them in his shirt pocket. "One thing leads to another. Spend money to make money. The night is young."

Jack felt a new pang of alarm.

Ryan's gaze went to the street where a man ambled along holding a full plastic bag and wearing a backpack. The man's age was impossible to calculate. He looked old to be a student. He wore a thick beard, and his hair was long enough to be halfway down his back. Before Jack knew it, Ryan was out of the car, following the man.

Was Ryan going to mug the guy? Jack couldn't look. Couldn't not look.

"Mister? Excuse me? Hey, man!" Finally the fellow turned. Ryan started walking along with him, talking, just talking. Jack couldn't hear what they said, but he knew, he got it.

Ryan came back to the truck, saying, "I know where we're going next."

"Don't do this. I'm telling you, don't."

But Ryan had already pulled out and was driving fast.

"Let me out."

"Coward."

"Call me anything you want. I don't intend to go to jail. You want to get caught, you just keep at it."

"We *need* something to make us feel better—booze, weed, something good. We can't keep running scared."

Jack looked over at his brother. Ryan was wearing a flannel shirt he'd found at the Jensen house. Otherwise they both wore leather jackets, jeans. Both had shaggy hair. He felt he was looking at himself, scared, all his life, of one thing or another.

There was a yellow light ahead, turning red. "Slow down. Look at the road."

Ryan screeched to a stop.

The sound shot straight through Jack. People in the next lane turned to look. He said, "I'm not going with you. I'm not in this with you." The words surprised him; they felt unfamiliar in his mouth and they'd come tumbling out.

Ryan snorted, "Oh, I see."

Jack opened the door and got out.

Okay, never mind, get back in. That's what he expected to hear, but it didn't happen.

He began walking. He'd no idea where he was. The roadway was lined with strip malls. Employees were getting into cars, stores were dark, the last gates coming down. The traffic light turned green and he saw, peripherally, the red truck go off. He tried not to look desperate. He pretended to survey familiar surroundings, to be just a guy walking a familiar path. The air was heavy with the prediction of rain. There was a coffee shop in the strip across the road. He didn't have any money, since he'd passed the last of it to his brother, but he thought he could sit in there, watch for his moment, maybe slip something from the tip cup.

COLLEEN LOOKED OUT THE restaurant window to where she'd lucked into street parking downtown in a loading spot. "Hope I don't get towed," she told Purdy.

"I don't think . . . at night. But police don't get towed, right?"

"Yeah, unfortunately we do. Plus, there's a guy named Evanosky—prowls the city. Nobody gets a pass. Where are you parked?"

"Lot." He smiled.

Okay. Careful. A careful man. But— the cloth napkin felt good to her touch. And so did the tablecloth. Yes, it would be good to live it up more often.

"Can you talk about your case?"

"No. It's verboten."

"I figured. But you're thinking about it—"

"Can't help it. Sorry. So. You could tell me about yourself."

"I'm not great at talking about myself."

"Not to worry. I'm good at interrogating. You've been married—"

"Who hasn't?"

"I haven't."

"You're strong, then."

Point for him. He didn't say, *How come a pretty gal like you isn't married?*

"—several times," she added with a challenge.

He laughed. "Yes, I get the interrogation strategy. Two. I don't think that counts as several."

"And you have kids?"

"A daughter from the first. She's eighteen. Asking for lots of money these days. She'll be in college for the next four years."

"Why don't these kids want to be clerks anymore?"

"Are you kidding?"

"Yes. Totally. I am."

He smiled at her. "I come from Indiana, PA."

"Oh. I'm from Altoona." Local, then, both of them.

When her phone vibrated and a waiter approached the table at the same time, she picked up the call and listened. It was Potocki. She covered the mouthpiece and said sotto voce, "Scotch, Johnnie Walker Black, neat," before she got up and took the phone out of the restaurant proper to the space in front of the restrooms.

"Interrogating someone?" Potocki asked.

"No. Eating dinner out. What's up?"

"It's Rutter. The name is Rutter. I got their pictures."

"How do they look?"

"They look right for the job."

"Address?"

"I'll give you what's on the licenses, but I did some checking. The family moved and didn't do a change of address."

"Damn."

"Right. And no priors for your two boys. Unless they did j-time under another name."

"Damn."

"I know."

"They could be anywhere. They apparently live in the truck. And we don't even know for sure they're the right boys." She looked about the restaurant. She could see the waiter getting their drinks from a bartender.

"Your dinner good?"

"I haven't had it yet. Thanks for the info. I'll try the high school tomorrow morning to see if I can trace the address through the mother. She has a different last name."

"Sounds right. I couldn't find any other Rutter. Where's Dolan in all this?"

"He's got something going on that baby case. It's keeping him happy—I guess. I gotta go."

She went back to her table and picked up her Scotch. She lifted it to Purdy and took a sip. Feeling decisive, she said, "In case I get interrupted again and they threaten to stop serving—they must hate staying open on a Monday night—order me the mussels and then the yellowfin."

"Barely cooked, it says." He seemed suddenly older with his glasses on, reading the menu. "That's okay?"

"What the doctor ordered. If they cook it too much, I'm going to be unhappy."

"You like bloody food," he observed. He smiled at her warmly and shook his head. "It's— You don't have to answer this, but do you get scared? Some of the time?"

"Oh, yeah." She sighed. "Everybody does. How about you—getting married all the time?"

"That's the problem. I didn't get scared enough."

That made her smile. It really did seem a scary proposition. Janet Littlefield made marriage work. And so did McGranahan, Dolan, Christie.

In her silence she wondered what went wrong in Purdy's two marriages.

The waiter trotted over, and just then her phone buzzed again. The readout told her it was Christie calling. "Just a sec."

"I have my assignment," Steve Purdy assured her. "Go ahead."

She went back to the hallway, passing people having deep conversations at four tables. Not terribly busy, she registered. She hoped the restaurant made it. "Okay, boss."

"Checking on your progress."

"I followed up a tip. It's a possibility. Two homeless boys, but I don't have a truck registration for them and I don't have their mother's name. So tomorrow early morning I'm going to the school they *might* have attended."

"Which school?"

"Perrysville."

"I can meet you there tomorrow. What time?"

"Seven? How's Dolan doing on the other—"

"His guy flew the coop. He's on a search, wearing his killer eyes."

"I'll bet he is."

"I thought I'd let him go after the guy. You're home now?"

"Downtown. A restaurant."

"Just getting dinner?"

"Yeah. Like practically on Greek time."

"What's that mean?"

"Everybody ate at eleven at night when I was there."

"Is that right?"

"Big meals, too. Under the stars. But very late."

"How do they sleep?"

"Their genes must protect them from acid reflux. I don't know. They seem to have longevity. Also apparently Greeks have some natural protection from tooth decay."

"Are you joking?"

"No, no, really I'm not. They seem to have some secret for health." She winced. Tricky subject with Christie, who had been sick last year but was now in remission.

"You're eating alone?"

"Nope. With your neighbor."

He whistled. "He was speedy on the uptake."

"He's very polite."

"Well, he'd better be. Catch you tomorrow morning."

"Right. Meet you there."

She went back to her seat, saying, "Sorry. I always think I should answer calls. I mean, I *should*. Boss. Checking in."

"You mean Christie? Man, I like that guy."

"He does have the magic."

RYAN ANGLED THE TRUCK toward a parking place that had a banged-up concrete wall to separate the property from the dentist's office next door. He could see kids milling around on the other side of the building, college kids probably. By the time he parked, jockeying back and forth a few times, the truck was positioned to more or less minimize the view of the dent on the driver's-side front bumper. "Here we go," he said. In his pocket was the stolen ID that bore no resemblance to his face or age. He had to hope this was a place where they didn't really look.

What he'd said to the bearded guy on the street was that he was looking for a friend who had a problem with drugs. That was the smart way to ask. Chester taught him that. The guy knew what he was asking and told him where to go. He said a city guy came into Meadville on Mondays to sell. The fact that there was a crowd suggested this was right. So, his luck was back.

The building he walked toward was dilapidated; its neon skipped and skittered. The sound system inside was faulty, pounding out distorted music. He waited until two people were going in, and he got behind them and flashed his card.

The bouncer wasn't big. He was like a small wrestler. "Sorry," he said to Ryan. He thumbed him out to the lot.

"Shit. I just want to get some cigarettes."

"Not here. That's a bum ID."

Ryan shouldered in anyway, and the guy shook his head and didn't stop him. It took him a moment to get his eyes adjusted to the place through the dimness and the smoke. A couple of kids were dancing to the hazy, thrumming music. He finally found what he wanted—a girl standing alone, stretching up to look at the dancers, that fakey look as if pretending to scan the crowd for a friend. She was heavyset and wore a lot of eye makeup.

He laid on the accent thick, gave it an Aussie gloss. "Dance with me? For the time of your life?" *Loife.*

Her eyes widened. She held the plastic glass with her drink away from her body.

"Okay, okay, I'll dance with you, girl," he teased, "if you buy me a drink. Or give me a sippa. I'm about out of cash, see? I know that's a shabby thing to come in here with not enough money to get me home, but I needed a little company."

"Where do you come from?" she asked as he nudged her toward the dance floor. She had a light voice. He could barely hear her.

"Down under," he shouted.

"Really?"

"Afraid so, sheila."

"I'm not Sheila," she shouted back.

"Girl. Girl is sheila, sheila is girl. In my lingo."

She didn't seem to understand. Which was okay with him. She said, "I'm Brittany."

"Okay, Brittany. What are you drinking?"

"Tequila."

"And you're going to share?"

"Here, have it." She said something he was pretty sure was, "I'm not so good at it."

"Not good at tequila, hmm." He downed it and began to dance up close to her.

"I like your accent."

"Nothing I can do to change it. I'm stuck with it."

When he moved her off the dance floor, he said, "Oh, man, I need another of those tequilas. I better see if some bloke will stand me to one. Unless—"

She pretended to think, relent. "I'll get you one."

"If they make doubles? I won't ask you for more. I had a bad day."

She nodded and went off. He looked around at the group. College kids were pathetic. They didn't have bandit charm. He went up to a guy who looked more watchful than the others—the way when he lit a cigarette, he checked who was behind him, beside him. "Who's selling here?" Ryan asked.

The guy gave him a long, calculating look. "Little black guy in an orange shirt."

"How much?"

"I dunno what you want. I'm not speaking for him. You negotiate. He'll deal if you stock up."

"Thanks." He would need more money to add to his twelve. The girl Brittany walked toward him, balancing a drink. He was pretty sure that with a minimum of work, she'd go for him. He wondered if she had her own apartment or if they'd have to resort to the truck.

He downed the drink fast. "Sorry," he said. "I needed that." He wanted to do his trick with the cigarette machine, but he couldn't see a machine anywhere. "Wait for me. I have to hit the can."

"You didn't tell me your name."

"Ryan." He stopped himself. Shouldn't have said. The booze had made him careless.

"Ryan?"

"Nah. That's what everybody's called in my country. It means *guy.* I'm Gregory."

He headed for the lav. On the way, he saw what looked like a girl's wallet with a shoulder strap—just sitting on a stool. He swiped it quickly and kept walking, wrapping the strap around it until it was tidy. He tried to look confident, acting the part of the boyfriend just taking care of his girl's things. When he thought the moment was right, he slipped it under his leather jacket.

Inside the men's room, he took the only stall there was and quickly opened the purse. This was amazing. This was luck if he ever had it. The little wallet was a gold mine. Some kind of pill, three crack cubes, and twenty bucks. A lipstick, a condom. He kept the pill out and fitted everything else but the lipstick in his jeans pockets, side and back, stuffing toilet paper on top of the small items so that nothing would fall out. The purse was a problem. He had an impulse to flush it, but he knew it wouldn't go down. He wrapped it in toilet paper and left it in back of the toilet.

Jack would have been no good on an excursion like this one; Jack was weak, scared. Ryan had to pretend Chester was there, cheering him on.

Ryan studied the pill. It didn't look familiar, no logo on it. But it was in the wallet with other good things, right? In his mind, Chester did a little comical shrug, a *Why not?* Ryan popped one in his mouth and swallowed. It only went partway down, so he had to go out to the sink and scoop water into his mouth. Three guys were in line; two were taking a leak. It felt like all of them watched him. One of the men from the line went into the stall Ryan had been using.

Ryan cut out of there, past the kids milling around, past the bouncer, to the outdoors. He could feel something already. Was it the tequila, the pill, or just fear? He had a little vertigo, a strange sense of the world tipping, as if the pavement moved. . . . His heart was working hard. He shook his head—dog shaking off water—to steady himself. But for a moment he thought he must have missed putting the brake on in his truck, the way it looked to be moving, coming toward him.

But it *wasn't* moving. So he got to it and into it and began to drive. He had to concentrate to make the traffic lights stay still long enough for him to see them. It wasn't the first time he'd exerted his willpower over objects. It worked. He felt good, powerful, magnificently alert. He drove until he saw another bar, the good kind—didn't look fancy. When he pulled in, he forgot to hide the bashed part of the truck. He almost went back, but he decided not to move it. There was nobody hanging around the lot at this place. Nothing bad was going to happen.

In the glove compartment, in the finger of an old glove, he kept the pipe, *stem.* It was a glass tube he'd bought from Chester for only a couple of bucks. Chester had fixed it up, but the steel wool filter was clogged now from use.

Ryan kept a lighter in his pocket and two books of matches in the glove compartment in case of emergency. He slid way down in the seat and put in one of the rocks and ran his lighter back and forth above it. Then he smoked it up. It was . . . good. The girl had bought well.

He felt absolutely great when he pushed open the truck door and went to the entrance of the bar. He liked dinky dives like this. There was no bouncer to worry about.

He bellied up to the bar, which was fairly well populated, mostly older people. The man beside him had two twenties just sitting next to his glass. Ryan reached in his back pocket for the twenty that came from the girl's purse, which he figured ought to get him started on a couple of drinks in this place until somebody bought for him. He put his twenty on the bar and ordered a double whiskey. Got it, drank it down.

He felt good. A little hyper still, but really good. The alcohol would bring him down some, he figured. It had in the past.

"Another," he told the bartender, who never met his eyes.

While it was being poured, he searched for a cigarette machine and, miracle of miracles, this bar hadn't gotten rid of its old thing either. He did his little pantomime, ending by kicking the machine.

When he came back to the bar, he saw the bartender had taken his money and made change. Nobody said anything to him.

"Cigarette machine ate my money."

"It works fine."

"No, it doesn't."

"I'd think twice about that."

He scowled into his drink and took it down. This place was the pits, he decided, not lucky like the last place. It was costing too much, nothing coming to him, nobody buying him anything.

"Another?" the bartender asked.

"Might as well."

The bartender took several dollars from him before pouring. Just then, the man beside him got up to go to the john.

This was it. This was the chance.

Ryan drank fast and reached for the forty on the bar. He was tucking the money into his shirt pocket next to the twelve from his brother when he felt himself being pulled off the stool.

Suddenly there was pain. A knee in his back, his hair pulled—it all hurt, and somehow he was down on the floor with a big heavy guy hitting him in the face.

"Knew what he was the minute he sat down," the big guy said.

The taste of blood and a stinging feeling told him his lip was bleeding.

Somebody pulled the big guy off him. The bartender appeared, looking down at him. "I'd get out of here, I was you."

"My money," the big guy said, reaching into Ryan's shirt pocket and taking everything that was there. "I'm not a sap."

Was the man laughing? He couldn't tell. All he knew was people were moving him and he was light, like wind, he was on a ride, he moved through the room without feet, out the door; it was so easy, being lifted like that. But then he hit the pavement and he felt every inch of the hard gravel and earth beneath him.

He wailed once and hated himself for it. He moved gingerly to be sure he could move. He sat up enough to see he now had holes in his jeans and bloody knees. He thought of his money in the fist of the fat man with the fat friends.

He had nothing left now, not even two dollars.

He stood unsteadily. A couple of the men were at the door looking at him as he wobbled to the truck, climbed in, and started it up. He was shaking so badly, he wasn't sure he could drive. But there were still men at the doorway, looking, wanting to get at him again; he needed to get away, pull over for a while, and get his bearings.

The night was cloudy, and he saw the first sprinkles of rain. He bumped out of the parking lot and on his way. When he saw a street to his right, he turned; when he saw another to his left, he turned again.

COLLEEN SAID, "IT WAS VERY NICE. THANKS." There was no ticket on her car.

"I enjoyed it. You worked the whole time."

"I like work."

"I don't exactly. I just do it."

"Ah, you need a new profession. Live your dream."

"Guitar virtuoso? Oh, for a little talent."

She had to laugh. "Maybe that's not it."

"I know it's late. It's fun talking to you."

"I'm glad to hear that. Sometimes I get snippy. I don't mean to."

He shook his head. "No offense."

She'd heard people talk about working at love. Maybe that was it. She worked at work and always expected love to be a matter of chemistry.

They said good night at her car.

HE KEPT LOOKING BACK TO SEE if he was being followed. When his windshield got hazy with the drizzle, he peered through the drops and kept driving; he kept to the small streets.

He noticed his heart was thumping steadily even though he felt scared. But he also felt down, sad. He could picture Chester shaking his head over the bar incident because things like that didn't happen to him. Nobody ever beat up Chester.

He was on a road that was only a hairsbreadth from being positively rural. Three houses, that was all he could see.

He stopped but left the engine running.

The houses weren't fancy.

The rain was light now.

Chester lived by going into strangers' places, taking what he could, somehow never getting caught—well, except for the time he was caught sleeping. He wondered if he could pull a Chester in one of these houses.

He shut off the engine, then opened the glove compartment. He hadn't bothered to put the stem in the glove last time—not wise. He chose one of the cubes and put it in the pipe and heated it up, using his lighter. He lay down on the seat again and smoked in an attempt to get the mix of things he'd taken tonight just right—he wanted to be high and alert, not depressed, not scared.

The first thing he felt was a knock at his heart, *change* making its way into his blood. Muscles, breathing, all obeyed something bigger than they were. It felt like power making its way through his system.

He knew he could quit the drugs as soon as he put all this shit behind him. He was smart and he had will, strength, and even some charm. He needed to be a boss somewhere, in charge of something big—a casino, a club—where he got to make the decisions.

There were noises outside the truck. The men had followed him after all. If there were a lot of them—

He wasn't going to take another beating. He'd have to drive fast or . . . the gun. He'd forgotten the gun back at the house. The one thing of value and Jack had rushed him out. Scared him.

He forced himself to look out the back window.

There was nobody around except a man walking his dog—an old guy, a little bit stooped, walking like his knees didn't quite work. Ryan felt a new wave of excitement.

Very slowly, almost quietly, he opened the door of the truck as the man was passing. "Hey, buddy, excuse me." His voice was too loud, too angry.

The old man turned around.

Ryan moved toward him. The dog stretched at his leash, trying to get a nose to the bloody knees of the jeans, then the crotch. "You live around here?" he asked the old guy.

"Yeah . . ."

"Well, my truck, you see, broke down. I need to call my brother to come pick me up."

"Call Triple A. They'll take you along with the truck."

"We . . . don't have Triple A."

"Oh. You want me to look at the truck?"

"No, I had a kind of a bad night. I just want my brother to come pick me up. But I need to get to a phone. You have a phone?"

"Yeah. Here, Bossy, you come here. Come on, girl, leave him alone."

The dog left him reluctantly, looking back.

"Could I use it? Your phone?"

"I guess so."

He smiled his best smile. "It sure would be a help. You could bring it outside if you want. I could call from the yard."

"Just . . . that's not it. Is it long distance? Because I have to watch the phone bill."

"Somebody bugs you about it, huh?"

"No, I just have to watch it."

"I'd reimburse you for the call."

"Okay, then, that's fair. What's wrong with the truck, exactly?"

"Distributor cap."

"How do you know that?"

"Well, I knew it was cracked. I was chancing it. You know, it was sputtering and all that. Then when I stopped and needed to start it up, it just went on me."

The man looked down the road, where there was nothing except two mostly darkened houses. "How come you stopped?"

"Stupid. I wanted to look up something in the manual and I didn't want to use up gas. I should've used the gas."

"I'd say."

They walked together to the house. Ryan noticed the man didn't have to unlock the front door, just opened it without a key. Gold mine around here with people like that. But when the man lit up a low-wattage lamp, Ryan saw what he'd got into. This was a poor place.

The man kept his dog on a short leash wrapped around his hand. He looked worried.

Ryan almost left, he almost said, *Fuck off, loser,* but he'd heard people sometimes lived like this and kept thousands under the mattress, so he decided not to give up so quickly. His heart was pounding hard. He had to work to keep his thoughts on track. And the dog kept trying to get at him.

"How come you use a leash? He dangerous?"

"She. She runs wild, kind of. I worry she won't come back."

Ryan laughed. "You talking about your dog or your wife?"

"My dog. I don't appreciate you getting smart with me."

"I'm sorry. I'm sure your wife is a very nice lady."

In the silence that ensued, given the pinched expression on the man's face, Ryan felt sure the wife was dead. Good, that was good. The man was alone.

He began to unleash his dog, saying, "Just hold on a minute." The phone, sitting on an end table, was an old beige thing. The man went to it once the dog was free, picked it up, straightened out the cord, and brought it to Ryan.

The dog was all over him, sniffing at his wounds, his crotch.

Ryan petted the dog a little. She was much too curious about his torn jeans.

"What'd you do to your knees?"

"Got under the car a while back thinking it was something else."

The man's eyes narrowed suspiciously. "Just go on and make your call and get going on your way."

Ryan put the phone down. "Maybe I don't want to make the call right now, huh? Maybe I want to talk a little bit of turkey with you." He looked past the man to the television behind him; it had an antenna. Everything was old, old. "Let's just say I need to know how much money you have in the house."

"Oh, my God. Is that what—I don't have anything here."

"Why should I believe you?"

"Because . . . I don't. I just have my Social Security, and that runs out usually before the end of the month."

"Come off it. Crying poor mouth."

"There's nothing here."

"What's in your pockets?"

The man emptied his pockets. Key. Balled-up tissue. Piece of paper. Dime and two pennies. He was shaking badly. The dog watched them both nervously. "Don't let him hurt me," the man said, looking straight at the dog.

"Nice doggie," Ryan said. "Come here." The dog obeyed him. She was a small mixed-breed terrier of some kind, a nervous, worried dog. He picked her up. "Nice doggie."

"Just leave."

Ryan went to the front door and threw the dog outside and shut the door before she could get back in. The barking started up bigtime.

"Bossy!" the man cried. "I can't leave her out there alone." He flung himself toward the door, but Ryan shoved him away.

"Give me some cash, then I'll leave you alone. Fucking dog. Why does she have to bark like that?"

The man looked interested, as if Bossy might save him from something or other.

"If you have nothing in your pockets, you have it somewhere. Where is it?"

"I wish to God I did. Look, look around."

"You bet I will."

The barking stopped. Suddenly there was a peaceful silence.

"You come with me," Ryan ordered.

He made the man walk in front of him around the house, which was only one story—they moved from living room to kitchen and dining area, past a small bedroom, bathroom, to a slightly larger bedroom. The bedspreads and towels were threadbare.

"Take the mattress off," Ryan commanded in the back bedroom.

When the man hesitated, Ryan shoved him at the bed. Finally the man heaved the mattress off. There was no money between mattress and box spring. "Pick up the box spring." There was nothing tucked between the box spring and the frame.

Together they went to the tiny bedroom. The man was panting hard, real hard. Like maybe he was going to have a heart attack. The second mattress he made the man lift up was on a board, no box spring. There was nothing.

"You go in the bathroom first. Medicine cabinet. Prescriptions. Hand them over."

Fumbling at the bottles, the man handed over two. Another fell in the sink and he grabbed at it. Ryan looked at the two bottles in his hand. One was only Tylenol. Ryan tried to read the prescription bottle.

"That's my thyroid," the man said.

"I think your thyroid is in your throat. What's that you picked up from the sink?"

"I don't remember."

"Hand it over."

The man did.

Oxycodone. Fucking empty. Empty.

Chester said lots of people kept money hidden in their kitchens, in cans and things like that. Ryan threw the pill containers into the sink. "Kitchen next. Get moving."

The dog howled once. Then the barking started up again.

"My friend has some money. I could call him."

"And say what?"

"Just to bring some money over."

There was hardly anything in the kitchen. Dog food. Crackers. Cheese. Couple of cans of things.

Man, can I pick them, Ryan thought. This guy is the biggest loser.

"I'm going to call my friend." Suddenly the man broke away and ran to the phone. Ryan hurried in after him. He watched him dial a nine and then a one. He grabbed the phone away and slammed the man so hard in the chest, the old guy fell down to the floor. "You stupid fucking bastard," he said. This man was every dumb thing he planned never to be. Old and poor and stupid.

"You're a lying piece of shit," the man said. "Get out."

Blood pounded in his ears. "And what? Let you call the police?" The man tried to get up, but Ryan pushed him back down.

The phone squawked an alert that it was off the receiver. Ryan grabbed at the cord and pulled it out of the wall. "No phone calls."

The dog barked wildly outside the door.

"Just go." The man scrambled backward and was halfway up.

"And have you what? Describe me? Describe the truck?"

There was a light in the man's eyes that betrayed him when he said, "I won't tell anybody." Ryan got the cord around the man's neck to stop him, show him who was boss. He had to hold the man's arms still—it was like hugging him. The phone and receiver crashed to the floor. But instead of getting more scared, the man got tough. He kicked, he fell to his knees, he tried to rip at the cord. Ryan started squeezing.

The old man wouldn't *stop.* He tried to fit his thumbs under the wire. He fell back and kicked again.

Ryan cursed; he kept squeezing. The dog barked and the place seemed strange, unreal, in the dim light. Finally the man was quiet.

Maybe faking it—he was a fighter. Ryan backed away, watching. He didn't want to touch the old man again.

He hurried out of the house, shivering off the image of those eyes getting bright, looking at him; he had to block the door with his body as he closed it so the dog couldn't get back in. The rain was starting up again.

"Come on, dog," he said. "Come on. Let's go, girl."

The dog looked uncertain, yapped at him and nipped at his legs, but finally followed him to the truck.

AT ELEVEN FIFTY THE UNMISTAKABLE CLANG of metal on metal, the whoosh of garbage bags, had told Jack he wouldn't have much longer in the shop. He'd pretended to read the local paper, which is what he'd been doing for two hours, all the while watching the two workers, who were about his age—a young man who kept a sluggard's pace and a young woman who whizzed about him unapologetically. She came to Jack's table with a wet rag. "We're going to have to kick you out. Sorry."

"It was nice in here."

"Oh, well." She hesitated. "We have to throw out what didn't get sold. You want a cup? For the road?"

"Sure. That'd be great."

She chose a paper cup, poured, and brought it back to him. She didn't say anything else but went back behind the counter, where whatever she did produced more clanging of metal.

He stood, addressing her. "If possible, could I hit the can before I go?"

"Let him in," she called to the other worker.

The young man who was mopping on his way to the bathrooms looked frustrated but moved aside.

Jack looked around the men's room for anything he might need. Toilet paper as tissue, okay, yes. A few paper towels. That was about it. He wished he had a water bottle to fill, but he didn't. He relieved himself and went back out to the main shop, where he saw through the windows what he had felt coming on—rain. "Oh, shit," he muttered.

The girl watched him. "You have a car here?"

"No."

"How'd you get here?"

Strip malls were car territory. He didn't know what to say. Finally he muttered, "It's a long story."

"You didn't walk?"

"Somebody dropped me off."

"Where do you need to get to?"

"Pittsburgh," he said, surprising himself.

"Whoa," she said. "That isn't too close."

His heart started to race, but he was a person with an anonymous face. The red truck was what they were looking for. Without it, without Ryan . . . The thought made him unsteady. He'd never been apart from Ryan, so he wasn't sure what to do next.

"You hitchhiking?"

"Yeah, I guess."

"I could get you to Seventy-nine if that's what you want. People say it's best to hitch on the ramps going into a highway. I don't know. You hitch often?"

"Never before."

"You musta made some chick really mad," said the guy who had been listening in.

"Yeah," he laughed. "Yeah, I guess I did."

"When they get mad, whoo, I just clear out."

He nodded. "I'll take the ride to Seventy-nine." It felt good to decide. The girl started wiping the counter. He wasn't sure where to wait for her. He studied the display case with the pound cake and sandwiches.

The girl paused in her work. "We're supposed to throw the old ones of these away, too. Bobby usually takes them. Bobby, can you spare a sandwich?"

The kid paused, hands on the mop handle. "Okay. Whatever. Sure."

She didn't ask Bobby which one he wished to give up but grabbed the thickest one and handed it over.

"I'll save it," Jack said. "For later." He stood drinking his coffee and only after it was too late thought to ask, "Sorry. Is there anything I can do to help you guys?"

"We're about ready to roll."

The three of them left together and walked out into the misty rain. He studied the girl's hair on the way to the car. It was curly but kind of limp, maybe from tying it back while she worked. She was not beautiful, but she had an open, friendly face and reminded him of the girls in school who were in the second range of popularity, those who talked to the ones above them and the ones way below. She pulled a sweatshirt hood up over her hair.

Bobby got into a truck that looked a little like the one he and Ryan owned, except that Bobby's was tan. Trucks were everywhere and maybe not very noticeable.

The girl opened the doors of a black VW Bug. Bobby tooted his horn twice and drove off, windshield wipers going too fast for the pace of the rain.

"What's your name? I know his. Bobby."

"Stacy."

"Thank you, Stacy."

"You've had a bad day."

"You could say that."

"So, I'll get you to near Seventy-nine. The rain isn't too bad. At least it isn't cold out. If I had a spare umbrella, I'd give it to you, but I forgot to bring one at all." She turned and looked into the backseat. "No, I don't have anything. Sorry."

"I'm a big boy. I'll survive the wet."

"Where you from? England?"

"Once upon a time."

She put her windshield wipers on the intermittent setting. Jack played the little game of second-guessing the rhythm, wondering when the wipers would next come to life.

"And you've been here how long?"

"Almost thirteen years." It was the truth. He was too tired to think of a lie. But he was also remembering that the way to avoid answering questions was to ask them. "You go to school?"

"Yeah, I do. I go to Thiel."

Where Neil taught. That's all he knew about the school. "Why'd you pick Thiel?"

She laughed a little. "I'm not even Lutheran. I'm not . . . Evangelical. But it's kind of one thing after another. They offered me this big scholarship. It's close to home, so I can still watch my little sisters a lot of the time. And Thiel had my major."

"What's that?"

"Biology. Conservation biology. It's the track I'm aiming for. My parents secretly hope it's going to be pre-med, but I really like the environmental issues."

"You and the politicians, eh?"

She stiffened. "I think it's important."

"It is. I shouldn't be sarcastic. I have to learn to watch my tongue. Gets me in trouble."

"Like earlier tonight."

"About like that. So are you almost graduated?"

"I wish. I only just finished up my sophomore year. I had three finals yesterday and another one today. I didn't think I could make it to work tonight, but I did."

"You didn't even look tired."

"I guess I have energy. My mother always says I do."

"Eatin' right, livin' right—there, I did it again. And I didn't mean to."

"You have a sort of button you push and what comes out is a mild put-down."

He had to think about this for a while.

"You never said your name."

"I didn't, did I? It's Dennis." His father's name. His mother used to say it put her in mind of teeth.

He managed not to answer anything more by talking about the strip malls and businesses and rain until she said, "Well, this is it. My turnoff is here. Will you be all right?"

"Oh, yeah, don't worry about me."

"Be careful."

He got out of the car, holding the sandwich tight to him. Something about her face as she leaned over toward the passenger door made him almost cry.

"Sorry I don't have an umbrella."

"It's okay."

She gave the horn a quick toot and drove off. He waved, but she might not have seen him.

And then . . . nothing. A sandwich and rain and a hope that luck would come his way.

CHRISTIE STANDS AT HIS BACK DOOR, saying, "Rain again."

Marina watches him, wondering if he will stay up watching junk television again. "Do you feel all right?"

"Yeah, yeah. Just restless."

"I can see that."

"Negative ions."

She runs her hands over his back until his shoulders drop, relaxing. "Is everybody okay at work?"

"Oh, sure. Artie and Greer are the only people on new cases right now. Artie is feeling greedy, grabbing whatever there is."

Marina hesitates. "You should get some sleep. Are you worried about him?"

"He's a little funny lately."

"In what way?"

"He needs something big. I've never seen him quite this way."

Her husband has always said Artie Dolan is his best and most reliable detective. "Do you think it's competition—partnering with Greer?"

"Man, I hope not. She's doing her job. She's fine. But you're right. If she gets one beat ahead of him, he's flying off to show his stuff. It surprises me, it really does. And yet . . . he's also doing good work. He's working on that guy who beat his girlfriend's daughter—"

She nods. It's made the news.

"I'd rather have Artie after him than anybody else. It's just the way he needs it that worries me."

Marina would have preferred to hear something negative about Greer. Because Colleen Greer is attractive, she mixes up the sexual chemistry at the office, and nobody is immune. On the other hand, Marina is not naïve enough to think that Greer would be *less* appealing if she were troubled and bad at her job. It could end up quite the opposite, with men trying to rescue her. "I'm going up to bed. It's really late."

"I'll be up in about fifteen."

She kisses his shoulder. He turns from the rain to embrace her. The hug is 80 percent. Eighty isn't terrible. Most people would die for 80. But she's seen better and, like Dolan, she's greedy for the big take.

HE'S WALKED FOR TEN MINUTES and then stood at the ramp for a good twenty minutes, trying for a ride. The rain isn't heavy, but he's wet enough to be uncomfortable and cold. Finally, he starts to walk onto the highway, eating the sandwich for comfort.

How many days would it take to walk to Pittsburgh? he wonders. That'd work up a sweat. He walks for another forty minutes—dangerously, on the wrong side of the road, *with* the flow of traffic, stopping occasionally to stick out his thumb. It's a bust. It must be the shabby way he looks. He keeps going, feeling hopeless. Suddenly he hears a toot and a car pulling off onto the berm, and then he hears the car coming up behind him, really close. Without looking back, he runs ahead a few steps to get away from the nut who is practically running him down. He turns to see through the glare of headlights that it's a truck, not a car, it's—red.

His brother, sticking his head out the driver window, yells, "Hey, buddy, need a ride?"

He hesitates for a moment, walks back, opens the door, and gets in. The heat is on in the truck. His brother is feeding the bread and cold cuts left over from their dinner to a dog.

The dog is sitting in the space between the seats and stops eating long enough to stretch forward, sniffing Jack.

"Where you going, buddy?" Ryan asks, as if he doesn't know him.

"Pittsburgh." It's the way the truck is pointed—south on 79.

"Well, me and my pooch, we're only going as far as our house in a little place called Sugar Lake. Nice beds we got. You're welcome to stop with me if you have a mind to."

Jack shivers, giving a curt nod.

FOUR

TUESDAY

THE MORNING LIGHT has just broken. Addie, stooping down to grab the new weeds, balances carefully. She has to put her coffee cup down on the ground for a moment. The air is still damp from last night's rain. The lettuces, like little babies, are tender and perfect.

She pushes herself up, hands on thighs, and reaches back for the coffee, which she carries to the other side where the main garden patch is, with newly planted tomatoes, squash, spinach, peppers, peas, onions, cucumbers, cauliflower, carrots, broccoli, beets. Asparagus and rhubarb she's had in for years. She can almost taste the tartness of the rhubarb pies she makes every summer.

Doing nicely. Shoots coming up everywhere. Eight-by-twelve and packed full.

Her mind ticks off recipes to use it all.

"What's in your vegetable soup?" Archer asked her the first time she offered to make it for him and he was nervous he might not like it. "Everything," was her answer. "And even some of the kitchen sink."

That's it. She'll make a beef-vegetable soup later today, before the afternoon gets too hot. Oh, it won't be the same as with her own garden produce. She will have to use store-bought carrots and celery and potatoes plus frozen peas and frozen everything else.

She sips some coffee, pulls her robe around her.

She wishes she'd put in potatoes. They're so cheap in the supermarket that she talked herself out of them.

When her children were young, she taught them to garden. They weren't keen at first, but they caught the bug. Same with the grandchildren, Marie and Esther. They're now great gardeners, and they teach their own children.

Except for Martin. Her son doesn't garden anymore. If she worries about anybody, it's Martin, a workaholic, once divorced, and now finally with a new wife.

Oh, Martin *looks* like Archer, but he keeps not *being* like Archer. He didn't inherit the joy. And maybe never got over being angry about it.

Most men—Archer, Tom, others—always lit up when she talked to them. But Martin, impervious to her charms, made her try harder—always a bad idea, trying too hard. She loves him anyway. She'd die for him.

Inside, with a second cup of coffee in hand, she presses herself to go to the mudroom, where she has a new can of white paint. She pulls it up by its handle, finds the new paddle still in its store bag along with the new small brush for tiny spaces. After a few moments, she locates a clean brush and puts everything she will need on the rough wooden worktable in there.

But it's still early. Still coffee time. She moves to the living room and reads for a while. Without thinking about it, she reaches for the remote control. In a split second the eager leaning-forward heads and torsos of newscasters fill the screen. Their voices seem harshly gleeful about financial disasters of various sorts. Pressing the channel button repeatedly, she moves past other newscasters, past muscled people grunting cheerfully through exercises on a beach somewhere and salespeople smiling through demonstrations. Tuesday. Her heart starts up a little rat-a-tat just like that. Suddenly she knows that she will not paint the windowsills today.

ONLY TWO PEOPLE ARE IN the high school office when Colleen arrives. It's still early, but she's already been to Headquarters to pick up the driver's license pictures Potocki left for her. Once more, she takes a quick look at the faces of the boys. Slightly tilted heads, defiant eyes. Fear and victimization in their expressions. Most people's driver photos look like mug shots, but theirs are even muggier than usual. Pale boys, young looking, brown hair, blue eyes. Nothing a Hollywood treatment couldn't cure, but . . .

"I'm investigating a homicide. I need information on two boys, Ryan and Jack Rutter. That's R-u-t-t-e-r." She presents her credentials and the photos to a woman who looks confused and goes to fetch another woman. The second woman comes out to where the file cabinets are. Without being prompted by the pictures at all, the second woman says, "I think I remember them. They both dropped out early. Let me . . . if I guess—" Without introducing herself to Colleen, she puts on the smudged glasses she wears on a chain around her neck and begins looking through one of the file cabinets.

Bad sign for those boys, Colleen thinks, the dropping out. She puts the pictures back in her bag. Nothing to go *to*—that's the usual story. The birth dates indicate one would be nineteen, the other twenty.

"How'd you beat me to it?" she hears behind her—and there is Christie coming into the high school office. "I'm used to being the earliest bird."

"You'll have to watch your back," she teases.

Today he wears the dark blue jacket that is not a blazer but is formally tailored anyway, a putty-colored shirt, and a light blue tie. She is more used to seeing him in clothes like this, not the open clothes he wore at the party at his house. He's said Marina is always outfitting him—she's a good shopper and does it well on a policeman's salary. Of all the jackets he wears, this one is Colleen's favorite.

She's schooled herself not to be in love with him anymore, but man, she misses the feeling, misses dreaming the transgressive dream that he will one day leave his sweet family and walk into her house forever. Without romantic illusions, life is a bit crabbier, a matter of choosing healthy food over dangerous and delicious food. Letting the fantasy go makes her irritable. It also makes her feel old.

"Purdy treat you okay?"

"Very polite. Very generous. We had a good dinner."

"You had a good time?"

"I think I was tired. I don't know. I wasn't fully, you know, conscious. You don't know anything bad about him?"

"No. No, I don't."

The office worker studies a file folder while Colleen opens her bag and hands over the pictures to Christie.

"Promising," he mutters, handing them back.

Then the woman comes toward them, still wearing her unfashionably large glasses. She's heavyset and life is punching at her, but she's punching back. "Here it is. We had two boys, both dropped out in the senior year; the younger one doesn't give a reason except that his older brother dropped out and is doing okay without school. Ryan and John Rutter."

"Could we see the file?" Colleen asks. She feels Christie nudge her, and she knows it means, *Right, gotta try.*

"Sorry. We're not allowed—privacy laws. But I'll cooperate as best I can. What can I look up?"

"Mother's name and address. Also, I'd want to know about any behavior problems with the boys. And any other contacts. The father's info if you have it."

"No father in the picture. Discipline problems, yes. Disrupting the classroom. Tardy. Unexcused absence . . ."

"Over what period?" Christie prompts.

"Junior year. Ryan."

"How long ago?"

"Three years."

"And the brother?"

"Left two years ago." The woman reads and they wait. "Tardy, absent, a hallway fight. Disciplinary action."

A few kids must have arrived at the school grounds because shouting teenage voices filter into the office. Kids may hate school, but you can feel them coming at it, in waves.

Colleen never likes it when Christie horns in as if she can't ask her own questions. She says simply, "We know their mother went by a different name. We have to find her. I'd like to apologize, by the way. I didn't have a chance to ask your name earlier on."

"It's Mrs. Major." The woman looks uncomfortable. "I don't know if I'm allowed to give that out about the mother."

"Well, *part of* why I have to find the boys' mother is really for their own safety. If you could just tell me where she was last?"

Major looks through the folder and relents. "Not far, actually. Defoe Street. Name is Rita Black." Colleen and Christie both take out notebooks and wait patiently; she tells them the house number.

On the way out to the car, Christie says, "Let's hope the boys went to Mama. You have cuffs?"

"Yes."

She has her phone out and is about to call the office when Christie interrupts her. "Might as well call Potocki and have him look up the truck registration under Black—eh? You tried that last night under Rutter?"

"Sure did. Potocki's not on until four."

"Right. Littlefield can look it up, then. We want to know if Rita Black bought a red Chevy pickup."

"I know. Are you—? Do you think I'm not on top of this? I was about to make that very call."

"Sorry, Greer. I'm sorry. Just being an ass."

"No. No."

"I sometimes am."

They get into separate cars and drive to the address in the Perrysville area. While she drives, Colleen asks Littlefield to start a DMV check for cars registered to Rita Black, Defoe Street.

The short, stout man who comes to the door on Defoe wearing sweatpants and a tank, carrying his large coffee mug with him, says he bought the house from a Rita *Miner* a year back and that she was moving out of it to move somewhere nearby but he doesn't know where.

"Did you keep in touch?"

"No. No reason to."

"Mail forwarding, packages?"

"It never come up. Anything come for her looked like junk mail. I tossed it."

"Anything with the name Rita Black?"

"Couple of things. Also for a guy named something Black."

"You know *anything* at all about where she went?"

"Uh-uh. Never asked. She never said."

"Ever see her sons?"

"Heard from them. They come banging on this door the other night, looking for her."

"They didn't know she'd moved?"

"Didn't seem to."

"What night?"

He pauses, figuring. "Saturday."

"If those boys come back, I'd appreciate it if you'd call me right away. Right away," Colleen says, handing over a card.

Walking back to their cars, Colleen says, "Saturday. Could have been before the accident." She calls Littlefield back. "Try also under Rita Miner. My bet is that's the maiden name resumed."

Littlefield says, "Looking like a good lead?"

"Oh, yeah. Hollywood casting. But you never know."

Christie is watching Colleen. She's aware he's working to hold his tongue, rein himself in. It makes her laugh. "Post office in the meantime," she says. "Quick way to the address."

"Right. Correct."

RITA MINER IS GETTING DRESSED FOR WORK when the knocking on her door starts. She has just managed to get on panty hose, which she detests but has to wear because her boss, a proper older woman, insists. Puh. Dumb. She's just slipped on the skirt she likes—*Oh, dear, isn't that too short?* the old bird will say, all the while trying to smile at Rita. But there's the knocking at the door, then the doorbell. Rita doesn't yet have on a shirt or shoes.

The doorbell rings a couple of times while she pulls out three shimmery, soft blouses. Unable to decide, she throws on a short robe and goes to the door, ready to tell the Jehovahs where to stuff it. But there they are, the real shirts, and stuffed at that.

Cops. She should have smelled them. What'd I do this time? she thinks. But so far, knock wood, she hasn't been arrested for anything, only stopped, questioned, given traffic tickets.

"Of course. Come in," she says. "Be aware I do have to get to work."

"In case we should ever need to contact you again, where's that?" the woman asks.

"Work?" She doesn't like the woman detective, who is . . . Colleen Greer, according to her card. Rita frowns and addresses the man. "I work at Bobby Rahal."

"The car place? North of the city?" he asks.

"In Wexford. All the ads? Bobbyrahal.com."

"What do you do there?" he asks, smiling.

"Meet and greet. I'm the receptionist." In her mind she hears her own best voice, accent ironed out mostly, calling out to Mr. Vemko, Mr. McCall, Mr. Goldstein, saying, *Mr. X is here to drive the Cadillac.* Or the Mercedes or the Jaguar. Mostly she has to look good and not get her phone calls mixed up. She was hired by men, but the woman who told her she had to wear hose is the one who orders everyone around while pretending not to.

"You weren't born in this country?"

"No. England. Jolly old."

"Citizenship?"

"Oh, I have all that. Thanks to a man I married."

"When was that?"

"Long time ago. Twelve years." Surely it's not about that. Old Neil Schlager, useful for citizenship.

"We'd like to talk to your sons," the woman detective says. Definitely not as friendly as the guy.

"Oh, well, so would I. I don't know where you can contact them. They moved out, they have lives of their own. They probably live with girlfriends—I don't know. They don't call their mama."

"You have no contact with your sons?"

"No. Not for a while. Is this about them, then?"

"Yes."

"What'd they do?" Some version of theft, surely, she thinks, easiest way to a buck, and one of them has it in his genes.

"When did you last see them?"

"You aren't going to tell me what they did?"

"We only want to question them. They might know something about an incident we're investigating," the man says mildly.

"So it's just questioning?"

"That's all it is."

Believe that, you could sell her Manhattan all over again.

"When did you last see them?" he asks.

"A year, maybe. Possibly a little more."

"That's a long time. According to the post office, you moved here almost a year ago. Do they know this address?"

"No, they don't. I need to tell the people who bought my last place so they can find me. It's on my list of things to do."

"Give me just a little history," the man says—Christie. Richard Christie. He has also put his card on the coffee table. "You moved here from the Perrysville place, Defoe? Guy who bought from you says he sometimes got junk mail for a fellow named Black. Your husband?"

"Yes. That is correct. Stanley Black."

"And you got citizenship through the marriage?"

"No, that was someone else."

"Is Mr. Black here, then?"

"No. We split—it would be two years ago. He moved out."

"Are your boys in touch with him?"

"I doubt it. They never liked him."

"Where is he now?"

"No idea. When I'm done with someone, I'm done."

"Would they be in touch with the husband you mentioned from twelve years ago?"

"No way that I can imagine. I think he went to live in Florida."

"His name?'

"Neil Schlager."

"We'll need for you to jot these things down. Names. Addresses. Marriages, that kind of thing."

"Cripes." She looks at her watch. "I get in trouble when I'm late."

"We'll be happy to explain to your bosses."

"That's all I need. I'd rather tell them I got a run in my hose. So what'd my boys *do*?"

"We don't know that they did anything. Or that both of them did anything. Perhaps one."

"You aren't going to tell me?"

The man smiles a little, but she reads the smile more carefully now, thinking, Why did I figure I was getting around him? He doesn't like me.

The woman interrupts. "When did you buy the red Chevy truck?"

"Truck?" she answers, surprised.

"Yes."

"Couple of years ago. Believe me, before I started working at Bobby Rahal." Now she gets to drive a pint-sized Caddy. From the used lot.

"We have to find your sons. Any ideas?"

"Call me what you want, a bad mother, whatever. I don't know where they are. Maybe they were just being, you know, boys."

But slowly, she's waking up. The day's coming in on her. She reads the two cards on the table again. Homicide detectives. Homicide.

Now the man takes a turn again. "Can you tell us about places they like? Who their friends are? We need to locate them."

"They hang together, used to. Anybody else—I don't know."

"They got into trouble in school—"

"They were never meant to be cooped up six hours a day."

"Which one of them caused the most trouble?"

"Oh. Well, Jack. He's the younger. Has a bit of crazy in him."

"Jack," he says, and scribbles something down.

Let it be Jack, she thinks.

"SHE WOULDN'T EVEN ACKNOWLEDGE ME," Colleen gripes.

"She did at the end. She thought she was getting around me. You can see it's how she operates."

"Yeah, her clothes were half off. What a piece of work."

"Greer. I've never seen you like this, showing your inner little old lady."

"That woman sets women back fifty years."

"Except for washing her hands of her kids. That's pretty contemporary."

"I guess. No myth of maternal love there."

One reason Christie likes working with Colleen is that she doesn't hide disapproval or irritation and she doesn't play up to him. "What's next?" he asks, reigning himself in. She's got her dander up today. And she's just about past needing a mentor. She's ready to be on her own.

"Check on priors for Rita Miner. Back for another crack at Chester Saunders. Find the ex—they might be tight with him in spite of what she said. Miner paid the truck registration fourteen months ago, but not since. The truck is driving around without a sticker. If it's driving." She pauses, leaning on her car. "Put it on the news? Their pictures and all we know?"

"The downside of that?"

"They burn the truck. They destroy all evidence. We know they did it, but we can't pin it."

"Upside?"

"Somebody comes forward before they fix the truck or burn it. We get them."

"Right. But it's already been on the news. Some of it, what you knew early on. We haven't revealed we know about the boys. We *could* keep that close. It's a hard call."

She opens her car door, thinking about her choices. "When in doubt, do nothing," she murmurs. "All right, Boss, what would you do?"

"I'd back off the news. I'd allow those boys to be comfortable if that's possible. But that's a gamble. It might not be right."

"Okay. I'll back off for a while."

"You want me to come with you to see the friend, Chester?"

"You must be bored."

"I don't know when you'll have Dolan back. He's having trouble cracking his man."

"He's not used to having trouble."

"I know it." Artie could usually get them weeping and confessing in five minutes.

They move off to their two separate cars—inefficient police guzzling more gas than they have to. He watches Greer move quickly, check her watch, her phone.

THE V-NECK SWEATER, CHECK. Tom Jensen folds and packs the new ragg wool sweater from Patricia because there are going to be some cold nights still. The new boxers from Janice—the oldest and the practical daughter notices worn elastic on his old underwear when she does his laundry or picks through his drawers. He adds to the suitcase a couple of new T-shirts, also from Janice. Then he begins to put in the summer clothing that he ended up bringing home to wear into the hot Indian summer last fall. Three sport shirts—the blue plaid, the off white, the white—and seven or eight polo shirts, the style he chooses to wear most days.

His wife, Marian, got all the summer things ready before she died. On her deathbed, she insisted he hire the woman down the street, Elaine, for weekly cleaning and general upkeep, and she made him promise he would keep employing her. If she could, Marian would materialize in ghostly fashion to check if the breakfast dishes are in the dishwasher or not. It's a sad and ironic truth that he's way better at keeping up than he was when she was alive. He supposes, like most men, he has a lazy streak that just comes naturally.

Neither of his daughters wants to inherit the place at Sugar Lake. He's been banging his head against that particular wall for several years. Janice, who lives nearby, wants him to sell it. She and her husband have a long list of other places they hope to vacation in. Patricia lives in Santa Fe with her new husband; she says rural Pennsylvania can't compare with the beauty of the West. Apples and oranges, but she doesn't want to hear it.

So there it is, a place of memories, and they don't want it. Neither do the grandchildren in New York, Savannah, and Delaware. Marian's funeral was the last time he saw all of those grandchildren and great-grandchildren together. Will it ever happen again? Probably not. Why kid himself about how things are? Youth is the busy bee season. Playing, winning, losing, getting hearts broken, repairing them. *He* might find it sad that they don't have to go to the lake to watch the fish, that they can tune in fish swimming or gorillas mating right on some little box. But to them, it's happiness.

He's glad he had Sugar Lake as a boy. He can remember the smell of summer up there—what fragrances wafted in on the air when he first woke up each morning. He can remember being older and listening to the war news and his father fretting that he'd get called up while he secretly wanted to go. And then it happened; he *did* get called, but he didn't see action because they put him in the intelligence office, working on codes. He lost a couple of friends in the war, but he survived because he had a decent head for math and an ability to persevere. Luck. That's all it was. Then the war was over and he came home, got married to his high school girlfriend, had his kids. So goes a life.

He steps from his room to the spare room, looking for a pair of slippers he wants. On the bureau in the spare room are some dozen photos of his wife that his daughters gathered for the funeral. There she is, Marian at all ages, smiling faintly at him. In high school, when he first laid eyes on her, Marian was a thin girl with regular blond hair that waved nicely. He'd loved her hair, her friendliness toward him, and the sense he had that she knew what she was doing in every setting.

Tom studies the pictures. Her hair got blonder for a while until she gave in and let it go gray. He feels tenderness when he looks at the most recent photo. He loved her. He took care of her. But he lost the in-love feeling not long after he got married. It just went away; it just packed a suitcase and left.

Before she died, Marian said—and she didn't say it meanly—"You always loved Addie."

"No, no," he protested.

"It doesn't matter," she said. "You were good to me. You stuck with me."

"Of course I did."

"It's okay," she said. "I just wanted you to know I knew."

Now why would she say all that? To make him feel guilty? Okay, accomplished.

He puts in one sport jacket in case he wants to go to church. Or out to dinner up in Erie one day. If they serve dinner early enough, that is. He can't see worth a damn at night. Tomorrow he's off.

He goes down to attack the breakfast dishes.

CHESTER'S GOT HIMSELF A FULL PLATE of eggs and bacon.

Seven to eight o'clock each day, they are supposed to pray and contemplate; breakfast is from eight to nine. Then they have the nine o'clock meeting. Chester has gotten to know everybody except the new guy, the youngest, who came in only last night, a goofy-looking pale white guy. Two older guys and the new guy gravitate to Chester's table. Got my magnet on, he thinks.

"What happened to you?" Chester asks the new guy after they've helloed and chewed for a while.

"I got caught buying my pipe," the kid says. "It was like a sting thing. Parents got called."

Sean, an older guy, sort of good-looking, skinny, with dreads, assesses the boy. "What'd you ask for?"

"I asked for a crack pipe."

"There's your mistake. You supposed to ask for an incense burner. They can't get you if you only want to burn some smells."

The second older man, Philip, says, "Best ones are those giftie things—looks like a little flower in a piece of glass. Ask for them, you be okay." This man does not look healthy. His head is shaved.

Chester bides his time, letting them have their say—where to buy rose tubes, how gross it is to use a converted highlighter, whatever they can murmur under their breaths.

"You know about all this?" one of the boys asks Chester.

"I sure do. Believe me. I wrote the book," he says. "My first smoke, they gave me a made-up thing. I don't know what it was. My suppliers were using Coke cans and car antennas. I didn't want to smoke anything skanky. So I borrowed a stem, one of those nice ones with the roses, and I was like, This is what I want. So one day, I hear this one guy complaining that he keeps losing the spark plugs to his motorcycle because people use them to make pipes."

"Yeah, I know about them. They good," says the bald man.

"But, no, wait a minute. I'm thinking, Okay, maybe I'll see where he parks, try messing with one of his spark plugs. But. This guy," says Chester, warming up to his role, "is aching to keep his spark plugs intact. Right? So he goes out and buys a bunch of crack pipes, the little rose tubes—twenty-something of them. And he tapes them to his bike with a note: 'Need one, go ahead.' So, well, I come along, and if I need one, I figure, why don't I need twenty, twenty-two. So I bag the lot and I take the spark plugs, too. Sold everything. Little business. Lunch money, anyway."

"That's not true."

"It is!" Well, half-true. "I heard later the guy was real mad. He was roaming the hood yelling, 'I had a good idea. I was generous.' I was like, 'Yeah, man, but so did I. You had socialism. I had capitalism. Who wins, huh?' "

"You told him that?"

"Nah. I told the walls. I don't like a physical fight." The guys laugh on cue. "Just picture him going into some convenience store asking for twenty crack pipes—probably what he asked for."

They continue laughing over their eggs. They like him. He's ready to tell them his "just chilling" story when one of the workers comes over to him to say the police want to talk to him.

He winks. "There's a female detective took a serious liking to me. Be right back."

When he gets to the outer office, there are two of them, the woman, Detective Greer, and now a guy with her. The guy is Commander Christie. Chester can tell this is important because Christie's the one who's always the spokesperson when the police are on the television news.

They all go into the conference room.

The woman speaks first—Greer. "You heard from your friends at all?"

"No. We don't hear from anyone in here. We're . . . protected."

"I know sometimes word gets through. Anything on the Rutters?"

"No, ma'am."

She looks cross today. "Tell me this—were they on mostly crack or other things?"

"Whatever they could get. Pills, crack, liquor."

"Hmm," says the commander. "They didn't bother with weed?"

"Oh, sure, weed." Chester smiles to show he is cooperating. "Oh, yeah, most everybody who is on anything is on weed. It's basic."

"Where did you guys buy?" Detective Greer asks.

Like he's going to give that up. "Just on the street."

"Where on the street?"

"Back side of the Giant Eagle." Not true. He tries to look worried.

The Greer woman says, "Don't worry. I'm not interested in the dealers."

"Okay, then. Back side of the Giant Eagle. On Cedar. One of the workers on the loading dock—takes in the lettuce and fruits and stuff."

"Okay. I just want to find your pals." She hesitates. "Before something happens to them. They're in a very vulnerable position now."

Chester's concerned nod says, *I see. I'm helping.* He flashes a smile at her. The story is forming in his mind, how he got some poor innocent lettuce handler type in trouble and sent the detectives chasing wild geese. Already he can tell he's the center of everything at the rehab center because everybody needs a good time. Everybody.

AT THE BACK OF THE GIANT EAGLE, Colleen stands around watching the workers, then asking questions and showing the pictures of the boys. The smell of lettuce lingers in the air. Other smells hit her. Squashed onions. Cantaloupe that is too ripe. Fuel from the big rigs delivering.

Chester is a complete bullshitter—of course, she knows that much. She told Christie after they left the rehab place that she found Chester likable. Christie said, "Oh, spare me." But the truth is the kid was born with natural joy. People want to laugh when they're with him. It's a gift.

She and Christie go inside the store to take a quick look at the clientele and the cashiers for any suspicious activity. There is no sign of the Rutter boys about. She could put a detective on it, but she knows it's a waste of time.

She is surprised to see Christie buy a single doughnut from the bakery and take it outside the store with a paper cup of coffee in hand.

Tempting. But she backtracks and buys an apple, congratulating herself for her strength against addiction.

Next they drive to the new address for the guy they are calling "Rita's ex." His name is Stan Black, and to their surprise he is home.

"Police," Colleen says. "We need to ask you some questions about a couple of people you know. May we come in?"

"Sure." He opens the door and lets them in. He is so deeply tanned and muscled, he must spend all his time at it. He has coarse curly dark hair, trimmed neatly; he's done a close shave; his shirt, opened to the breastbone, is crisply laundered; and he wears a gold chain. Not surprisingly he's perfumed with cologne or aftershave.

"Are you on your way to work?" she asks.

"No. Not till later."

"Where is work?"

"Club One. I'm a trainer."

"Have you been there long?"

"Couple of years. What's this about? Somebody from there?"

"No. Not from there," Colleen answers. "We're interested to know the whereabouts of John and Ryan Rutter. You were or are married to their mother."

"Was. That's in the past."

"How long?"

"A year formal divorce. We were separated before that."

"She had your name."

"For a while. She went back to her maiden name. I insisted because of credit cards and that sort of thing."

Colleen writes it all down, partly to show her boss how orderly she's being. Her memory would cough up the details, no problem. "You don't see her at all?"

"Not since we split."

"How about the boys?"

"Jack and Ryan? Not at all. Hardly at all when I was with her. I have to say, I could see they were looking for trouble."

"Maybe they found it. So, they haven't called you?"

"No."

"Okay, another kind of question: They and their mother had full citizenship?"

"Yes. She was married before."

"How about . . . accents? Their mother has a bit of one."

He thinks. "Sometimes. Like they could turn it off and on a bit. Not much of an accent, I'd say."

"Hm. What was the home life like?"

"They were gone a lot of the time, like I said. They'd stay out all night, stay with friends. I have to say, Rita was not my idea of a good mother. She was just as glad to be rid of them. I suspected they slept in the truck. Why would she let them do that?"

"The red Chevy."

"That was what we bought."

Colleen pretends to look around his living room. When a silence settles, she says, "We'd like to find them. Can you help us figure out where they would go? If not to their mother or you, where?" Black looks perplexed. "We only want to talk to them. They might know something about an accident. Where could we look for them? Take your time."

Stan Black pounds his head like a guy on a game show. "With friends? I don't know."

"Names of their friends?"

It's clear that if he could win a million for it, he couldn't come up with the names of their friends.

What he does come up with, as he thinks, is a muddled realization. "I think I saw something in the paper about an accident. A woman."

Colleen nods.

The man gets wide-eyed.

"Just a few more questions. How long were you with their mother?"

"The better part of two years."

"And Jack was the bad influence? Would you say?"

"I would have guessed it went the other way. I mean, both of them were surly with me. They were civil if I got them something. Like I helped with the truck. I test-drove it and gave it the okay. Their mother bought it for them."

"To live in," Christie says.

Black turns to Christie once he's spoken. "She thought it would keep them busy, happy."

"You ever been arrested? Ever been in trouble?" Christie asks then.

"I had two DUIs."

"That's cleared up?"

"Yes. I don't drink anymore. I use pomegranate juice instead. I'm completely turned around."

"Any other arrests?"

"I was tossed in one night for getting into a fight. Long time ago."

"What was the fight about?"

"I was young. I . . . hit on some guy's woman. I thought she was alone. I mean, I thought he'd dumped her. She responded. Then the guy came out of the can and he responded."

"It was a setup?"

"I think it was. It was a game they played. There are a lot of crazy people out there." He bristles. His chest hairs bristle. He is a nervous boy, a mama's boy, and always will be, no matter that he's already crossed forty and no matter where his mama is.

"Where'd you get the tan?" Colleen asks. "It's a good one."

"Florida."

"You got out of work?"

"Ten days' vacation."

"You ever think of working at the new casino?"

"Funny you should say that. I have thought of it. Why?"

Because he sure looks like a dandified croupier.

Christie is laughing behind his eyes. She can tell he's read her thought.

She scrambles to say, "Oh, I always heard it was good money. And I think they'd be looking for trainer types, you know, tanned. Makes people think they're on vacation. That kind of thing." She hands one of her cards to Stan Black. "If those boys should call you . . ."

"I can't imagine they would call me."

"Would you get in touch with me right away?"

"Absolutely."

"You never know. They might need someone. If they do call, find out where they are."

"Okay."

The would-be croupier sees them out.

"Heavy on the aftershave," Christie says.

"Heavy on the 'I am a studly guy.'"

They're walking fast to their cars. Christie says, "You don't take breaks, do you? You're allowed to stop for lunch. It's noon."

"I was thinking a soup and a sandwich. But real fast. You game?"

"Yes."

WHEN JACK COMES INTO THE KITCHEN, Ryan is sitting at the table, tapping his foot. The dog is in the basement, barking. The sounds are terrible—yips followed by a sore-throated hammering.

"Should you let the dog up—stop that racket?"

"It keeps jumping on me."

"You going to tell me where you got it?"

"Maybe," Ryan says, "if you tell me where you went last night. You weren't walking the highway the whole time, were you?" When Jack doesn't answer, Ryan gets up and slams around the kitchen, slamming down a glass so hard on the counter, Jack thinks it's going to break. "I thought we were a team. Brothers. Now it's nothing but secrets."

"Okay. I met a girl. She was nice to me. Gave me a sandwich. Where'd you get the damn dog?"

"I just did. I met a dog on the street. She was nice to me."

"You're nuts."

The dog yips and pauses, as if listening.

"Speaking of. See this cut?" Ryan pointed to his forehead. "Guy who did this took fifty-two bucks from me."

"And the torn jeans?"

"Nothing to say about that."

"So . . . where'd you get that much money?"

"Not making roofs and shit like you. You want to do something, go back to the old lady. Or the other woman who wants to hire you. Get us some dough or else I will."

"We shouldn't have had the truck out last night."

"You agreed. It was your idea."

"Well, I changed my mind. This is our best bet," Jack says. "Holing up here. No drugs. No booze. Just quiet."

"Yeah, well, I like a bed all right. I wouldn't mind some heat. And a few other things."

"We have beans." They laugh a little. The dog has begun barking loudly again.

"Shit. Beans."

"I'll start them up again." He puts on the gas. The beans are still hard from last night, like pebbles.

"I'm not going to like them any more today than I did yesterday."

"So you have any more of whatever you had last night?"

"If I did, I wouldn't be standing here. Had the last of it before I picked you up. And I don't want a sermon." Ryan turns abruptly and goes out the back door.

Jack holds his head in his hands. Last night his big brother looked cross-eyed and roughed up and riding high. Didn't care who saw the truck. Or him. Today he's jumpy. And what is the deal with the dog? Jack stands at the kitchen window, watching his brother out back. Ryan is leaping around outside, hurling stones so hard he's taking the bark off a few trees. He looks like he did at seven, eight.

The unwelcome thought edges in that separating Ryan and

drugs is not going to solve anything. Ryan has always been moody and crazy and looking for something he thought was going to make everything better. A truck, a fight, a friend, something. Anything.

Jack can't catch a full breath.

It's the drugs, he wants to tell himself. But it isn't just that.

He finds hot sauce and salt to help them through a couple of beans meals. He stirs the beans, losing heart. He doesn't want them, either.

How long do they have before it all comes down?

Outside the window, he sees Ryan now has the gun in his hands. He never saw him fetch it. It must have been left on the back stoop last night. He holds his breath as Ryan practices aiming it. Without shooting. For now.

The kitchen fills with steam. When the beans are slightly soft, he scoops some out, hits them hard with salt and hot sauce, and carries a bowl of them out to his brother. He puts them down on a rock. Ryan looks at the beans, then paces the damp yard.

"Where'd you get the dog?"

"I don't remember."

"It belongs to somebody."

"Us now."

"Somebody might hear the barking."

"She's not really used to us. She'll get used to us."

She. "She have a name?"

"Bossy, I heard her called."

Jack stands still for a moment. "I'd like to get us to Canada. Eventually. When the time is right."

"What's that song?" For a moment, he's wistful and dreamy, a Ryan that Jack hardly ever sees. "Canad*ah*."

"Just stay put today."

"So are you the boss now?"

"Yes." Jack nods, goes back inside.

The dog sounds hurt, as if someone is hurting her. When Jack opens the basement door, the dog jumps on him. He knows what Ryan means—it's frightening. "Easy, girl, easy." Let her out for a bit? Before he has the front door fully open, the dog streaks through it, across the driveway, and down the rough path toward the road.

"Hey, girl, come back," he tries halfheartedly, but he can't bring himself to raise his voice or call out "Bossy" because he doesn't want to tangle with Ryan over this. He starts down the road, sure he will see the dog and be able to bring her back, but everywhere he looks, left and right, as he walks, the dog is gone.

In time, he's past the old lady's property and beyond—and not long after that, he's down on the main road. He sees the lake in the distance. Herons and people.

No dog. Give it up. The dog is gone.

He passes the bar his brother talked about. Without deciding, he's on the road to Cochranton. It's not the kind of road people walk on, so he tries to look more casual than he feels.

His heart jumps when he hears a car pulling alongside him. It jumps even more when he realizes it's a truck, and red, and then suddenly that it *isn't* his, but someone else's. A big, burly man says, "Okay, was that cigarette machine really broken? Thought I recognized y— No. I'm wrong. I thought you were somebody else. You look a lot like another guy. You need a lift?"

He shakes his head.

"You have a twin hereabouts?"

He shakes his head.

"Parents still visiting friends over in Cochranton?"

He can't catch up to all the questions, though he can figure out what the man's confusion is about. He hesitates for too long, shrugs and nods.

"Okay. I just want to know one thing: You *want* to be walking? You don't need help or anything?"

"I'm fine." He says this slowly, trying to erase any accent.

"Okay, then." The man drives off, shaking his head.

Twenty minutes later he's offered another ride, and this time he's tired enough to take it. The paneled beige van the guy is driving has small print saying, "Jim Brandy, Electrician."

"Where you headed?" the man asks.

"Cochranton."

"Couple of minutes. You live there?"

"No, just visiting."

"What you doing on the road, then? Broke down?"

"No, I wanted to see the lake."

"You walked? Most kids these days aren't walkers."

"I am."

"Good for you. Where you want to be left off in town?"

"Just at the market."

"Right you are." The man looks over at him nervously. "Some people say never pick up a hitchhiker. I can't live like that. I believe in 'Do unto others.' You know what I mean?"

"Yes."

They get into town and Jack gets out of the truck, wondering where to go next.

" 'Thank you' is okay. I'll take that."

"Sorry. Thank you."

"Right."

He goes into the market because it's expected of him. The aisles seem to be filled with people wearing logoed aprons. Tempting as everything looks, he walks out without filching any of it.

WHEN ADDIE'S PHONE RINGS, she is happy to hear her friend Betty's voice, until she hears something else in it, a catch in the "Hope I'm not bothering you at a bad time."

"Oh, no, you didn't get me doing much of anything, just making soup—I don't know why, it's a winter meal."

"What kind of soup?"

"Vegetable."

"Ummm."

They talk about this and that, Pete's battle with atrial fib and the meds he's on. Betty is a generation younger than Addie, but the medical issues have begun.

"And when are you coming up to see me?" Addie asks.

"Oh, not until late summer, probably." There it is, something funny in Betty's voice again.

"I'll look forward to that." Addie notices an antic dog dancing around the edges of her property, one she doesn't remember seeing around before. She hopes it's not a rabid stray.

"I probably should go pay bills," Betty says. "I'm behind on everything."

"I've got a container of soup for you and a pile of books whenever you can get here. Sooner if possible."

"Tempting, tempting."

They hang up, and Addie goes out to see about the dog.

She can't get rid of the sound of that catch in her friend's voice. Was it because . . . Addie calculates the date—the one test every doctor uses to find out if your mind is leaving you. Yes, right, damn, today is the day. Betty lost her son twenty years ago in a car crash. He was only eighteen and a brilliant prospect for scholarships, medical school. He had everything going for him, including the enormous love of his family; he was a boy living a perfect life until a drunk truck driver crossed the road and ended it. A terrible thing. Terrible. And it happened in the spring season.

Betty called today to keep herself going. An image of the young, handsome boy comes to Addie in a quick flash, and she is crying. They say that when you get old, you cry at the drop of your baseball cap—labile, it's called. She's more prone than others since she always cried easily.

Addie tries to shake off the sorrow. She'll be no help to Betty this way.

She walks toward where she saw the dog dancing, but it's gone.

She chokes back tears, concentrates on the wildflowers at the edge of her property—because aren't they beautiful? Texas bluebonnets and foxglove and bishop's flower, chicory, and daisies, plenty of daisies.

Addie goes back into the house, where she searches for her glasses, then for the little phone book she keeps on her kitchen counter.

When Betty answers the phone it is only too apparent that Addie was right. Betty's been crying, too.

"Oh, Betty, it's me," Addie says. "I . . . just realized."

"Today is the day."

"I know. I figured it out."

"Why is the grief so terrible still? I don't want to be a burden to people."

"Oh, you're not a burden. It's just . . . the normal course of grief."

"It doesn't go away."

"I know."

"Nothing escapes you."

"I think plenty does these days. I'm not the same."

"You're perfect."

"No, definitely not that." Isn't there some Eastern philosophy that would say she is highly imperfect, signaled by her still being here, and that Betty's son, taken early, had achieved perfection? "I still wish you were here so I could hug you."

"Maybe next week. Are you lonely?"

"No. Maybe just a little pokey from being on my own."

"I'll think about next week. Pete would want to come, too. We don't do much apart these days."

"That's fine. Pete is welcome."

Betty's voice catches again, and Addie's eyes tear up in sympathy just as the dog appears, whimpers, and disappears once more.

JACK FINALLY COLLAPSES ON THE GROUNDS of a building that seems to be a library. Ryan doesn't want him to, but he's going to call their mother. As soon as he figures out how and from where.

The ground is wet. The moisture seeps into his jeans and he has to stand to dry himself out. That's when he notices schoolkids have begun galumphing down the street. Two girls talk intently. Behind them five boys yell and shove one another. One of them is making a.call on a cell phone.

He's got to borrow the phone. He doesn't have coins for a pay phone even if he could find one. He starts toward the group. Signals. The kid looks at him.

"Hey, buddy . . . yeah, you. With the phone. Let me use your phone, would you?"

"What for?"

"I have an emergency."

All the boys stop. The one with the phone scrutinizes him, head to toe. "You're not hurt?"

"Well, no, but somebody I know is."

"Go to the emergency room. That's what it's for." Little shit.

"It isn't that kind of emergency. It's somebody who needs to know something before he does this thing that will lose him . . . a lot of money."

"How much?"

"A hundred thousand."

"Oh, man. You're kidding. I mean, what would you tell him?"

"Never mind. If you won't let me use your phone, I'll find someone else."

The kid hands over the phone. Jack begins to walk away with it so that they can't hear what he says, but the owner of the phone follows him. Jack kicks toward the kid. "You have to let me be. I'll give it back." The kid slinks backward, suspicious looking, while Jack dials 411 and asks for Rita Miner.

The operator puts him through. It turns out the number is her old number, the one he knew, so she didn't move far. But he only gets an answering machine. "Mum. It's me, Jack. I have to talk to you. We need your help. Ryan did something . . . he's in trouble. I guess I'll try to call later. It's complicated. I'll call back."

Scowling, he hands the phone back to the angry boy.

"You could, like, say thank you," the boy says, mimicking a parent—maybe, Jack thinks giddily, the guy in the electrician's truck.

Unavailable is what his mum is and usually was, so there's nothing new there, but in his fantasy, before he called, she was home today, she missed him, she suddenly even liked him. She said, *You did right to call. You're a good kid. Smart. I'll give you my car and some money till this all blows over.* She even said, *I'll help you get Ryan under control.*

The little boys lope down the street, the angry one looking back from time to time.

Jack walks the back alleys until his pants dry out, while he allows himself to consider that slip of paper in his pocket. Risky, but if he could make another, say, sixty . . . When it's getting on to three in the afternoon, he takes out the paper. Name and phone number. No address.

If he can borrow another phone, he'll call the woman. Walking the back alleys again, he's trying to figure out how to proceed when he becomes aware of a woman, way ahead, parked in the back of her house and carrying large bags of groceries into the house. Food. Purposefully he slows his pace. He can hear her call out to someone in the house, "Ben? . . . Ben! Where are you? I could use some help." Her car door is hanging open. He can grab a bag of food, and if he's caught, he'll say he saw her struggling and was wanting to help out.

He approaches the car. A quick look to the house tells him she's not yet in sight.

She's left her handbag. Looking toward the house again, he feels around inside it. Wallet, yes, a big, bulky thing. Phone! He starts moving, slowly at first, innocent looking, then turning back and seeing no one, at a good clip, all the while stuffing the wallet and phone into his pants pockets.

He keeps going, his heart slamming the whole way up to his ears. The alley empties onto a street with cars going by, so he doesn't dare look at what he's got. Man, there is no place to hide in this little town, no back lots, no ghetto alleys. Up ahead he sees the French Creek Café. They'd have a bathroom.

He can't tell if people notice him when he enters the café. They don't seem to. He passes the waitress and gets himself into the men's room. And even in his hurry as he passes the mirror, he sees, man, he looks bad. Pale. Then, leaning against the locked door of a stall, he opens the wallet. Fifteen dollars and several credit cards and lots of other kinds of cards. Photos of people. Various pieces of paper.

Chester's and Ryan's voices set up a chatter. *You did it. Good going! Keep the money. Dump that other stuff. Keep the credit cards, in case.* The voices become gradually more negative. *It's hard to use cards without getting caught. Fifteen bucks'll get you through one day, maybe.*

He can hardly breathe. His hand stills his heart, which is flip-flopping all over the place. *Not much of a haul,* Ryan says.

Chester asked once, "How come you want your brother's approval? You ain't ever going to get it."

As his breathing slows, he takes out the cell phone and the slip of paper the old lady gave him. He presses in the numbers of the woman who needs to have some work done, guessing at the 814. An answering machine says, "You've reached Emma and Ben. Please leave a me—"

"Hello, hello," a frantic woman says.

His brain kicks in. Something. Something. Ben? He looks more closely at the paper in his hand and hangs up, panting. Slowly he pulls the credit cards out of his pocket. Emma Hopper. Of course. Who in the world is less lucky than he is? A phone he can't use and a job lost, all in one move.

He stumbles out to the dining room, where he slumps in a chair at one of the tables.

"Menu?"

"Yes. Um. Yes."

There are signs all over the walls. One says, EAT IN OR TAKE OUT. Another gives a list of specials: MONDAY: BACON-CHEESEBURGER CASSEROLE. TUESDAY: CHICKEN AND BISCUITS. WEDNESDAY: SAUERKRAUT AND KIELBASA. SATURDAY: BARBECUE RIBS. Medals and awards fill the back wall. He reads from a distance—the awards are for cows or pigs that got raised locally.

"I have fifteen dollars. Will it get me two of the chicken and biscuits to take out? I mean with tax and all?"

"You'll make it. Just barely. Nothing left over for drinks. Did you want drinks?"

"I'll have to do without."

"You will. Unless you take the dishwasher job," she jokes. "You want to be a dishwasher?"

"Not really."

"Nobody does. But man, they need somebody back there." The waitress is old, scrawny, and sour looking, but when she smiles she doesn't seem unfriendly at all.

He notices the sign then among all the others: DISHWASHER WANTED.

"So two takeouts?" she asks, all business again.

"When does the dishwash job start?"

"Uh . . . anytime."

"You mean, like today?"

"Yeah. You serious?"

"Might be. How long would I work?"

"We close at eight. Open up in the morning at five thirty, but workers come in at five. You interested?"

"I think, maybe yeah. For now then, just, just one chicken and biscuits."

Suddenly a light wind-chimey sound begins to emanate from his pants pocket. "Somebody calling you," the waitress observes.

He nods and walks outside to pretend to take the call. When it stops ringing, he opens it to see what he knows he will see. The phone number he just called has called back to the cell phone. She's trying to find her phone. He powers it off.

Playing chicken, they call this. How long till he's caught? Will he get his sit-down meal? Will he make it to eight tonight, with a little cash in his pocket and food to take home?

How long can he keep going?

And . . . if he makes it, he has to walk the whole way home. . . . Home, he just thought, *home*—the Jensen place.

"Boss says fill this out."

The paper is a handwritten list that asks for his name, address, telephone number, Social Security number.

He writes, "Jack Rigger. Route 173." He makes up a post office box number: "P.O. Box 28." He makes up a phone number starting with the area code he just called. Then a Social Security number.

Nobody asks anything else of him.

He eats chicken and biscuits and the salad and beans that come with the meal. It's delicious, almost as good as the food the old lady fed him. Then they take him back to the kitchen.

RYAN WANDERS THE HOUSE, back and forth. Every time he gets to the kitchen cabinets, he kicks at one of them. It feels so good that he kicks at the front door on the other end of his pacing. He starts to kick at the chairs, too, in moves that make him feel like some martial arts Jet Li type. Arms outstretched, swing of the leg. Pow. Twist and kick. Where the fuck is Jack?

Finally Ryan collapses on one of the kitchen chairs, catching his breath. One cabinet door is coming off its hinges. Good. He did that.

He goes out to the truck and looks in the glove compartment. No. Nothing. He wishes he could talk to Chester about last night. He forces himself to put on the radio, and it takes forever to find news. Nothing about an old guy. Okay. The guy lived. Right? Lived and hopefully shut his face.

He goes into the house and switches on the television, wondering if there will be any afternoon news, but all he can find are soap operas—concerned voices, a woman getting a pelvic exam—all seen through a haze of electric snow.

The pill he had last night—was it because he had it with smoke or was it the pill itself?—made him feel like cars on the road had animal life, coming at him, yawning with mouths open, ready to eat him. It must have been the pill that did it.

Be positive, man, Chester says. *One step at a time. Like, hey, you found the gun. Anything else?* Up out of his chair, he starts for the second floor, realizes he hasn't heard the dog barking in a while, but finds his body moving on to the small room with the crooked small staircase that gets him to the attic. This time he won't rush. On Sunday, he moved clothing aside, looked quickly into boxes, hurried to the shelves and the corners to see what he could sell. He found the gun, then located the ammo, and that was that.

Now he methodically goes through the pockets of the clothing hanging up there, using gestures as if he's frisking the person wearing the clothes. Amazing. He finds a dollar in one pocket and a quarter in another. By the time he has exhausted the clothing and looked through every box of kitchen appliances and mismatched dishes, he still has only the dollar twenty-five.

Junk. It's all junk. Stupid people keep all this shit.

At the bottom of a pile of boxes that hold salt shakers and such, he finds a carton of papers.

He drags that box to the window, where he has more light. Outside it's a cloudy day, still damp from yesterday, not too hot, not too cold, but gray, everything grayed out. The first things he takes up are bills. Heating oil. Lumber. Electric bill. Water bill. Then more electric and water bills. Thomas Jensen. It's him all right. Same fucker. All of this is in a gift box in the larger box. Nobody sane would keep this kind of shit.

What's under the box of bills is more interesting. Photos. There is Jensen, looking like Mr. All Right with his hand on the door and another shading his eyes. Picture of the house. Picture of the yard. Picture of the lady that sat out in the car while Jensen told them they were worthless. There she is looking up from putting food on the table, with that expression like, *Oh? Me? Oh, don't take my picture!*

Ryan keeps looking, digging, as if it's his own family photo stash. As he digs, the Jensens get younger and lots more people come into the pictures. There's nothing written on the backs of them. Just people. Swimsuits. Everybody smiling all the time in that way people do with the camera on them. Disgusting. Because it's all fakery. Surely somebody in this pile was pissed off one day or another. Some pictures are so old, he isn't sure who he's looking at. Is it Jensen and his wife or some other couple or their kids? He can't tell. All he knows is the photos don't look contemporary and neither do the clothes.

There is one he stares at for a long time, an outdoor photo, like a picnic or something. Must be twenty people in it. He counts them. Twenty-two. Everybody except one person is smiling.

He carries the box down the steep little stairs with him, leaving the smaller box with the bills behind.

He opens the basement door to call to the dog. She doesn't answer. He tiptoes downstairs, thinking she might be dead. He looks around. Gone. Escaped somehow. He goes outside and begins to circle the house, kicking at whatever his feet will reach—the corners of the building, the woodpile. After a while he carries in a few small logs and the few sticks he can find to the fireplace in the main room. He arranges them just right and lights a match. When the fire threatens not to catch, he looks around, rips up a magazine, and watches the colors fold and glow. Even so, the fire is not quite picking up, so he tries one of the photographs, laughing. It burns well enough. He tries another. He watches the people's faces light with alarm and collapse inward.

COLLEEN HAD SPENT THE WHOLE AFTERNOON on the street, running photos of the boys made from their driver's licenses, but at the end of the day, she had nothing to show for it. She slogged back to the office, disgusted. Dolan was there, looking punch-drunk. "What happened?" she asked.

"Got him."

"He confessed?"

"Yeah."

"You sure he did it?"

"I'm sure."

"What did you have to say?"

"That neighbor kids were hanging at the window, that they saw him doing it. That they told me he was out of his mind. That an insanity plea would be his best bet."

"Were there any kids?"

"No."

"But he didn't doubt it?"

"No. He was ready."

"Remorse?"

"None I could see. How you doing at finding the boys?"

"They didn't have many friends or acquaintances. I can't find anybody to tell me where those two would go except Chester Saunders, who won't cough it up."

"Put it out on the news?"

"I want to. Boss thought it would warn them and they'd burn the truck."

Dolan appeared to think about this. "Could be." He sighed. "I don't always agree with the boss. I'm all yours tomorrow. Right now I need to clean out my head."

"I understand."

"Who's been helping you?"

"Boss has."

"Ah." He looked at her curiously. "You done all you can do for today?"

"Probably. No new ideas."

"I'm going home, then. You call me if you need me. What about the Navarro funeral?"

"It's tomorrow. It's going to be quiet. I helped them keep it off the news—Could you do the funeral with me? And if I can't make it, instead of me?"

He wagged his head thoughtfully. "Sure. Wow, I'm whacked." He stood and started to move off. Just as he got to the door, Potocki came in.

Colleen could hear Potocki ask, "What happened?"

"I got him."

"Congratulations. You're cooking. And your hit-and-run?"

"Greer's still on it. She doesn't have anything new."

She turned in to her desk, but she felt Potocki come up behind her. Soon she was getting a shoulder massage, not something she was in a hurry to stop. "Poor kid," Potocki said. "Nothing happening. You done for the day?"

"I don't know," she grumbled. "I could go back to the mother. I want her phone records, but I can't imagine she would give me consent. And I don't have probable cause. Oh, man, that massage feels good."

"Let's go get some dinner."

"You just came in. It's kind of early."

"Did that ever stop you? I didn't get any lunch today."

She wheeled around in her seat. He looked good. Upbeat and healthy. His new life was agreeing with him.

Christie for lunch, Potocki for dinner, neither of them hers, both looking good. She was born to be challenged. She stood up. "Let's go, then."

"Good decision. I know head against the wall when I see it."

As they walked to the fleet cars, he asked, "Why aren't we blasting the news with all of this?"

"Boss didn't want to. Actually he seemed to go kind of vague when I brought it up."

"He does that when he can't make up his mind. He lists the options."

"That's what he did."

"He's not always right."

"No. Believe me, I know that."

"Where to?" Potocki asked.

"Something simple. Not too expensive."

They walked to the parking lot. "Where'd you eat last night?"

"Six Penn."

"Fancy. Was it good?"

"It was good."

"Boss told me he's a broker, your date."

"Jeez, is nothing private in this family?"

"Not much."

"Well, you should know the legs of your new squeeze are also the subject of gossip." Colleen felt her face get red. She always got mad at herself when she struck back without thinking.

Potocki held up his hands. "I didn't start any of that. It didn't come from me."

"Okay. Okay."

Then they got into one of the cars, Potocki driving. "So where would you like to eat?"

"Atria's. Again. I have a coupon."

"I'd be happy to treat you."

"It's okay. I have a coupon for twenty-five dollars."

And so, once more in their work together, they drove past West Park, where Colleen had spent part of the afternoon questioning people, and toward Atria's, which was not far from where Potocki now lived in his bachelor pad, a reduction from the big house he'd shared with his wife, Judy, until only a year ago.

"How's Judy being?" Colleen asked.

"More steady. For a while she didn't want me to come back home, but didn't want to divorce me either. Talk about messing up the mind."

"Yeah. I'll bet."

"It was good for me in the long run. I gave it a good long look from every angle, and then I was sure I didn't want to patch it up. She saw that and it solidified her, and so now . . . we're proceeding nicely. I don't mean it isn't sad."

Colleen couldn't imagine it as anything short of devastating.

"All those years," he said. "If you'd asked us early on if we could even imagine separating, I don't think either one of us could have said yes."

"No place to park," she commented after a while.

He didn't seem to care, but continued to pass occupied meters without cursing. He made a left toward the Warhol Museum and wound around back streets. Colleen watched him drive slowly, as if they were on a tour of the city. He pulled up in front of the Warhol to a spot with a yellow line.

"I wouldn't chance it."

"No, I'm just thinking. I should go to the Warhol sometime. I should do normal things." Then he started up again.

Warhol as normal. Good.

He'd clearly been working out. He tended to weight gain because he had good hearty Eastern European genes, but he was trim now, stomach almost tucked in and face thinner. He was controlling himself, whatever that meant.

He wound around a few more side streets. Without seeming to notice, he passed an available meter only to tool around for another few minutes. At the end of it, he passed in front of Atria's just as a meter opened up.

"Parking mojo. Always had it."

"I can provide quarters."

"We only need one. It's five thirty. So. Couple of drinks before dinner?"

"Amen."

CHRISTIE WAS WATCHING THE NEWS, but he was doing it standing in the living room, as if he might move off to the kitchen at any moment or go upstairs or outdoors. Weight on the balls of his feet, he was poised for movement, but he didn't move. He became aware of the Lexus pulling in next door. Without moving, he tried to see if Steve Purdy came in alone. He couldn't see, but he heard only one car door slam.

Dating too rapidly—not a good idea. Also not his business, as long as she did her work.

Marina came into the living room and sat, trying to see the news he had on. "Sit? I can't see around you," she said irritably.

"Oh." He sat.

"Worried about something?"

"I might have given bad advice to Greer on her case. I was trying to be a mentor and I knee-jerked to give her the opposite of where she was going. I feel sort of shabby."

"You must be angry with her."

He thought about this. The comment itself made him angry because of its smack of truth. He had no good reason to be angry with Greer.

"What did you work on today?"

"Mostly . . . the hit-and-run. We questioned people in the vicinity of the accident. Didn't lead to anything."

"Where was Dolan?"

"Busy."

For a while they didn't say anything.

"Greer went out with Purdy?"

"Apparently yes, last night."

"Did she like him?"

"I can't tell."

"I'm going to bet it doesn't take. I think she needs a little incest. Not much, just a jot, just a jot."

Christie felt his face furrow with surprise. He knew what Marina meant—not literal incest, but something forbidden. Damn, Marina was scary sometimes. He'd never told her Colleen had been attacked by a predatory uncle and was probably scarred by it.

"I really can't watch this." She hated CNN. She took the remote and switched to the PBS station. Bill Moyers suppressed a sigh and faced the camera straight on.

They both watched in silence for a while.

"What incest would you prescribe?" he asked.

"I'm not prescribing. I'm nervous. There you are working right along with her, and I know what she needs. She needs to break some code. Some boundary."

"I think . . . I think you're right. But she's not a bad person. She's not mean-spirited. She works hard. She takes everything seriously.

She's getting older and I guess she's lonely. Maybe Steve Purdy will surprise us all."

"I wish. I worry about you worrying about her. What's happening with Potocki? I thought he was gone on her."

"I steered them away from each other. It's the advice I'm *supposed* to give. It might have been a mistake. I don't know. But he seems to be fixed up with someone else now."

"If I joined the force . . . if I went against your advice and went into training, I'd be part of the problem, incest, because I'd want to be on Homicide. There we'd be on the same squad. What would happen to us?"

"I'd be nervous about your safety. It would be on my mind constantly."

"Do you think we'd split? Or would we make it?"

He looked at her. Her eyes were moist, her face open, not angry.

She always bugged him about his inclination to play God, seer, sheriff. Now she was asking for a prediction. He looked into the future and imagined all kinds of things—arguments, her successes, her failures, other men drawn to her, his difficulties managing her as an employee.

"We'd make it," he said.

AFTER TEN O'CLOCK ON TUESDAY NIGHT, Jack finally sits across from Ryan. He's gulping in breaths because he walked the whole way back from Cochranton, and in no way is he used to that much physical activity.

"I thought you weren't coming back."

"For a while there, I thought so, too. I still can't breathe. You like that?" He indicates the takeout meal.

"It's cold."

"I could probably put it in the oven."

"I'd fight you for taking it out of my hands. Yeah, I like it. So, you keep working, we get food, is that the idea?"

"I guess."

"Did people ask you where you came from?"

"A little bit." He doesn't tell Ryan about the man in the truck who thought he *was* Ryan or about the phone he stole that was now in a garbage can, disabled, battery out. He wiped it as well as he could, but it still probably holds his fingerprints. If they can get fingerprints off paper, they can get them off a phone.

"What am I supposed to do here while you're out being regular Joe?"

"It's just for a couple of days. I'm due at five in the morning."

"I'll drive you then," Ryan says more kindly.

"It's tempting, but—"

"No, no, I'll go early. I'll let you out away from the restaurant."

"Okay, all right." Jack reaches into his plastic bag. "I took three rolls. They were going to throw them out. You know. People didn't eat them and so—but they were clean. It ought to get you through tomorrow until night."

Ryan looks at the rolls dismissively. "You should have lifted some meatballs with them."

"Wish I could have."

"And they fed you?"

"They fed me. I had the chicken like yours in the afternoon and a burger with fries before I left."

"So, where's the money? They paid you, right?"

"Not yet. I get paid end of the week. Unless I say I'm quitting . . . like if we decide to drive away." He looks at the smears of grease on the table. "If I let you drive me in, you'll come right back with the truck, right?"

"Yes."

"You built a fire today? I can smell it."

"I burnt all the guy's pictures today."

Jack waits to understand what that means. He looks up at the walls. There are still the same things hanging there, a picture of some guy, a picture somebody drew of the lake.

"Family pictures, photos, a whole box of them. Someday he'll look for them and think he lost his mind."

"I . . . I'm not sure I get the point of that."

"If you don't, I can't help you."

The assembled pile of food garbage in front of Ryan—bones and paper napkins—reminds Jack of something, but he doesn't know what. "I wish to hell we could go back to last Friday."

"What was last Friday?"

Before the woman froze in her tracks. She couldn't decide which way to move. Jack knows what that feels like.

"What do you think? Night of fine TV, early to bed, early to work tomorrow?" Ryan cackles.

Jack laughs in spite of himself.

ADDIE SITS ON THE EDGE OF HER BED Tuesday night to kick off her sandals. She idly takes off the earrings and necklace she wore today—same ones as yesterday because they were sitting right there on her nightstand. She gets up to put them away in her bureau.

Funny, she thinks, what did I— Nothing is in the right place. Her spirits sink. The boy Jack must have opened her bureau. She's willing to think the worst of him—she's not a cream puff—but she hates what the realization has done to her: thumping heart, shortness of breath, everything a little out of focus. Damn him, then. She pulls herself together and looks methodically at the contents of the drawer. It's strange. Nothing is missing, at least nothing she can immediately think of. And most of what's in there, except for a few pieces—one ring, two good gold chains, one pair of earrings with diamonds—is costume jewelry, not worth anything much except her peace of mind.

She would like to think she messed it up herself, but she doesn't think so. A quick check of the other drawers tells her nothing. On the other hand, what would he do with her clothes?

She goes downstairs to check her handbag. Everything is there.

Puzzling. He looked but didn't take? If the boy comes back, she might question him, find a way to learn more about him—where he actually lives. It's eleven, too late to call Emma Hopper to find out if she hired him and if it worked out.

That night, she does two things that give her grief. She locks her doors and carries her handbag upstairs with her.

IT'S JUST AFTER ELEVEN, and Colleen's still at the office, piddling with paperwork because the drinks she had with Potocki hit her right in the knees. The wobbly feeling lasted until about nine and she didn't want to drive home in that condition, and then she just kind of stayed. For once she's found it relaxing doing her reports. She should do them on a couple of Scotches more often.

She drank freely at dinner because she thought Potocki was going to blow off work and say, *Come on back to my place. I don't want the woman with the gams, I want you with your thighs you fret about.* And she was thinking that without a little liquid folly she would not be able to take him up on it. But he didn't ask. All through dinner, she thought he was on the verge of asking, but he didn't. Instead they took a long dinner and they came back to work and she logged in another good four hours, which was accumulating to a very nice overtime vacation, compliments of the boys who did the hit-and-run.

Earlier, she had some coffee at the office, only a cup because she couldn't afford to be up all night. At one point she called Joanna's mother to ask how they were all doing and to report they had a line on two boys who might have hit her daughter but that the boys were hard to find.

Now it's after eleven and she's still just a tad wobbly, but if she hangs till midnight, Potocki will take that as an invitation, and a desperate one at that. They've done well at staying on the abstinence wagon. He's got his doctor with the gams, and she's got Steve Purdy. Well, maybe.

So instead of hanging for any longer, she gives Potocki a fake punch and goes to her car and goes home alone.

WHEN CHRISTIE HITS THE SACK, he's spooning with Marina, a position that relaxes both of them and gets them to sleep. He's aware that he's breathing into her neck and that if it were the other way around, he would find the breath irritating, but she doesn't seem to mind.

She's kind, she's beautiful, she's smart—he's not tired of talking to her *or* looking at her. It's just that Greer . . . distracts him.

Distracts. That's it, in a word. But it doesn't mean he wants to dump Marina.

He catalogs the problem like a detective. Colleen has told him secrets. That makes for intimacy. Her hair always looks a little tousled—the bed-head look. It conjures thoughts. She's horny and she can't hide it. His natural inclination is to help people out, so he has to keep at a constant running monologue about how he wouldn't, couldn't.

When he heard she and Potocki got a little mixed up one night about a year ago—he thinks it was twice, actually, but she never admitted to a second time—he separated them as partners so they wouldn't do damage to the workplace. But in his heart, he's not sure he was thinking about the workplace. Because he felt a pang of jealousy then and again today when she admitted she'd taken a date with Steve Purdy, a nice enough guy, but not . . . not good enough for her.

He tosses away from the spoon position. Marina reaches a hand back to touch his thigh. So, she's not asleep either.

He squeezes her hand.

Marriage is a real funny thing. Certainty is not an aphrodisiac.

He closes his eyes tight against the hall light, attempting to do Marina's theater casting trick—picturing people together, seeing what happens visually, in terms of voices, energies, sounds; projecting scenes between them, imagining. Because he can't sleep, he's figuring Colleen's ideal match, the type of person she *should* be with. She has too much people-energy to be alone. So he works on the problem until it puts him to sleep.

FIVE

WEDNESDAY

JENSEN'S WINDUP ALARM CLOCK rings at four thirty, and Jack springs to life. He's never had to get up in the dark to go someplace. He almost likes it. "Ryan." He shakes his brother. "Hey, man. If I walk it now, I'm late."

His brother groans and opens his eyes. "There is no coffee in this place."

"I know."

"You're going to have coffee where you work, you lucky fuck."

"When I get paid, I'll buy coffee. There's a pot here. I saw it." He tries to figure out a way he could slip a cup of restaurant coffee to his brother, but it's too dangerous. Somebody might see the truck coming in close. Or see his brother sneaking up to the back door of the restaurant for a Styrofoam container. It just won't work. "Look," he says, "just get up, okay?"

Ryan sits up, then puts his legs over the side of the single bed. "It's dark out."

"Well, yeah." He leaves the room while Ryan dresses. His brother has taken to wearing one of Jensen's old flannel shirts, but Jack isn't wearing any of the owner's clothes himself.

Downstairs on the way out to the truck, when they pass the pathetic bag of rolls he's brought his brother, he wishes he'd filched some ham or cheese.

It's damp and cool. There are still stars visible, and something from the woods smells fantastic. The truck is wet with dew.

Ryan grunts as he starts up the engine.

Nobody passes them on the road until they leave Sugar Lake. When a car finally does go by in the other direction, the driver doesn't look. "Leave me off pretty soon, edge of town, and then get back up there right away."

"You're telling me you don't want me to nick coffee and a brekky from the Country Store?"

"That's what I mean." He points up ahead a block. "See that building? Yellow brick? If I get in trouble or I can't walk it, if I don't get home tonight, when it's dark enough, come look for me there. In the back."

"What is that place?"

"Library. We need a pickup spot. You know a better one?"

"No."

"So if for whatever reason I can't get home—"

"Like what? Since you're so keen on keeping the truck hidden?"

Like . . . police after him because of the wallet and cell phone. Though he wonders, too, if he can make the whole trek again. "Make sure you keep the truck around back."

Ryan lets him off.

He starts walking toward the café and after a moment turns to be sure his brother is heading back to the house.

ADDIE WAKES AT FIVE, a bit before her usual time. Some mornings she reads a little in bed, getting her bearings. But this morning, there's too much on her mind. Her jewelry drawer. Jack. She will call Emma as soon as it's late enough. And Tom Jensen is on her mind, too. Today is when he said he would come up to Sugar Lake, barring difficulty.

She gets up, shaking off the usual aches. She'll tell Tom about the messed-up jewelry drawer. There's a comfort in that—having Tom around, knowing. The more Addie thinks about it, the more the facts don't stack in Jack's favor. The boy just appeared one day, Saturday. Then he was supposedly dropped off another time—Monday—by someone he said he didn't get along with. And then on Monday night, whoever waited for him stayed out on the road. Something isn't quite right, but he could be nothing more than a mixed-up boy.

She puts on her robe and slippers, trying to move fast. Down the stairs and all is well. She does two things quickly—flips on the living room light and unlocks the front door—and in just those moments a truck starts into the yard, suddenly stops, reverses, and peels out. The boy's truck? It all happens fast and it's not light enough to know for sure, but it has to be, right?

She stands at the door, trying to see. She can almost hear the truck going up the road, but that's imagination because her hearing isn't keen enough. She wanted, after all, to trust him. Now that's ruined.

While she brews a pot of coffee, she wanders her own house, checking things. Everything is there. From time to time, she peers out the door, wary.

The clock inches along slowly—how can it not be six o'clock yet? Then it is. How can it not be *seven*?

She drinks coffee, standing at the doorway, and eventually eats cereal standing there, until her old easiness comes back to her and she feels almost free of fear.

At ten minutes to eight, she dials Emma Hopper. "Emma?"

"Addie."

"You knew my voice?"

"Any day. I'd always know your voice."

"Were you awake?"

"Oh, goodness, yes."

"Well, I . . . was calling about the reference I gave you for a worker, a boy who—"

"Oh, I thought you were calling because you heard."

"What?"

"My terrible day yesterday. My wallet was stolen. And my cell phone."

"Oh, no. Where?"

"From my car. I stupidly left them in the car. I took the ice cream and frozen things into the house first, you know, to get them into the freezer and . . . I left the other things in the car."

"Was the person caught?"

"No. Nothing found so far. I spent all night canceling my bank and credit cards. I called my phone, but nothing happ— It's a nightmare."

"Oh, how terrible. How . . . just awful."

"It is. All I got from my husband was, 'Why'd you leave them in the car?' I told him because things like that don't happen here."

"Listen. Did you ever hear from that young worker I told you about?"

"No. He never called. And I didn't call him. I didn't have the time to think about it. And now I don't want to bother."

"Well, here's a worrisome thought. I never wrote down your address, just the phone number. But maybe he looked it up in the phone book. Maybe it was this kid, Jack, who stole your things."

"We're not listed."

"Not in the phone book?"

"No. We were getting crank calls a while back, so no."

Addie feels a rush of relief. So the boy *couldn't* have found her that way, then. She feels so much better.

"I was worried. I felt responsible. You see, well, it's just that I saw a truck, it might have been his, coming onto my property at something like five this morning. And then it turned around and left. That can't be anything good. And I don't really know anything much about the kid. So I wanted to undo my recommendation."

"You'd better call the police. Talling helped me yesterday. He's a good guy. You want me to contact him for you?"

"No, no, I can do it."

"What is going on with the world, huh? You can't live a simple life anymore."

"Oh, I know." But it seems like the oldest story there is. People are always going to have things that other people want. That simple.

It's only just eight o'clock.

THE DENTIST'S ASSISTANT WORKS AWAY at dislodging plaque while Jensen sits, impatient, itchy to get on the road. This is his last task to check off in Pittsburgh. His car is packed and ready to take off for Sugar Lake.

But the assistant, Rose, keeps jabbing at one particular tooth.

"Wha-i-i-?" he asks.

"Loose filling, I think. Dr. Meier has to say."

"Oh, 'amn."

"Got you. He has time today. It could be a quickie."

Damn, he thinks to himself.

Dr. Meier confirms the diagnosis of a loose filling. He's smiling broadly, perhaps to show off his very white teeth. "Today or next week?" he asks. "It's not a big job."

"Today."

"Okay. We're going to give you some Novocain. I have to drill the old one out. It'll be worth it. The new one will be much prettier."

Just do it, he thinks, without the sales pitch. Just do it. He sits back in the chair to take what is coming to him. Novocain has always had a bad effect on him.

"I have another appointment, but I can do it right after that." Dr. Meier is already numbing the spot that will take the needle. Once Jensen gets the needle, he'll have the sensation of being caffeined up almost to the level of a panic attack for a day afterward. Novocain jumps his heart, and it's a matter not of fear or ideation, but of plain chemistry. The drug is known to give some people rapid heart flutters.

Does he want to try to do without it, maybe? But when the needle comes at him, he allows it to go in. Sometimes other people are in charge. Sometimes it's that simple.

How do dentists tolerate all day long that horrible sound of drilling, like living around construction? Of course they're rumored to be depressed and suicidal—like that case in the paper of a supposedly nice dentist who offed his wife and himself. Something to do with *debt.*

Two hours later, the smiling Dr. Meier and a somewhat less joyful Rose show him in a mirror that his tooth is now secure and that it looks better, too. He can't quite feel his face. His heart is beating in what feels like an erratic manner. He signs off on some insurance papers and makes small talk with the staff, mainly the beautiful Annie Calderazzo at the front desk, swinging her long hair as she takes his money, and Rose, who waits to see him out. "Feeling okay?"

"I'm fine." He doesn't tell her the Novocain has done its usual, making him feel he can hardly breathe. It'll pass, it'll pass.

"Beautiful day," Rose says. "What will you be doing? Are you a golfing man?"

He shakes his head.

"You look like a golfing man."

Whatever that is. Clean, he supposes. The polo shirt under the sport jacket. "Going up to my place at Sugar Lake."

"Oh, that sounds fun. What do you do up there?"

"Nothing much. Watch the sky."

"Amazing."

"It is, sort of."

"Have a good time."

"I will. I will."

His taste buds are asking for a cup of coffee, but his body can't handle even a trace of caffeine now. That's sad. It's one of the major pleasures.

"When will I feel my face again?"

"Two more hours. After twelve, in time for lunch. Don't try to chew just yet. You can drink. Are you hungry?"

"No, no, I'm fine. Well, a little hungry."

"I myself use every excuse to get a milkshake," Rose tells him conspiratorially as she sees him out.

He's in his car, he's on his way, finally; but before he gets out of Mount Lebanon, he stops at Scoops for a milkshake. It's almost ten thirty. He thinks about asking for the men's room, but he'd rather get on the road, drink his milkshake while he drives, and just get there.

IT'S ABOUT ELEVEN IN THE MORNING when Officer Talling taps on Addie's door. He's officially Cochranton police, but she called him instead of the county office because she, like Emma Hopper, knows him a little from church. "Oh, my God, the smell!" he says.

She's just iced the cake with chocolate icing, careful not to get any of it on her clothes. She can be dangerous that way. She wears one of her favorite skirts, blue and purple mostly, with a blue dress T-shirt. She's chosen a decorative pair of pink and blue beads that blend but add that dash of something extra. Otherwise, she's wearing silvery earrings and silver bangles; she's dressed and ready for the day.

"Oh, I can't cut into it. I . . . was going to give it to someone."

"You've only broken my heart, Addie! No, I'm joking. Really. Listen, are you okay?"

"I'm fine."

She feels very foolish. She went through her jewelry drawer again and everything was there.

Officer Talling is not tall, not short, but of average height and portly. He's neither young nor old, but in the middle. He smiles a lot and doesn't seem to mind his job or find it stressful. Not like the police on television who slam suspects against walls and step through blood. His job is easier, probably. A few domestic disturbances, cars blocking driveways, school safety, a few old folks dying in houses because nobody knew they were there, petty thefts—some shoplifting at the market. Now, of course, Emma Hopper's wallet and cell. And Addie's little problem.

"So what is this thing you wanted to report?"

"Wanted to . . . Hmm. More that I felt I should. . . ."

"Okay."

"It's a simple thing. A boy came by asking for work. He had no experience, I could see that right off, but he worked hard. He did a good enough job, actually. I paid him. He went off. Yesterday I noticed my jewelry drawer was messed up. But I couldn't find anything missing. Today, this morning, early, I was opening the front door and it looked for all the world like this boy's truck coming into my yard. But then the driver just backed up and drove away."

"He used it as a turnaround?"

"I don't know. I don't think so."

"Why?"

"Seemed more like a change of mind."

"Okay. Tell me his name and address. I'll look into it."

"I only have his name and a phone number. He wanted other work. I gave his name to Emma Hopper in Cochranton. And I just found out that she—"

"Uh-oh. I see."

"But I never gave him her address and she isn't listed in the book *and* she never tried to call him. So . . . I'm being foolish, right?"

"I don't think so. The kid could be working the area. What kind of truck?"

"Regular pickup. Red. Like every other truck around here."

"Okay."

"Let me make you something to eat. Scrambled eggs? Nice toast?"

"I can't. I've already had two breakfasts."

"Two. That sounds like a happy morning in my book."

"How, my dear, do you keep your girlish figure?"

"I don't know. I never stint on anything much."

"Well, maybe that's the secret. It works for you. Are you pretty certain nothing is missing here?"

"Nothing I can see."

"Well, let me have the name. I'll check it out."

"Can you copy it from this?" She hands over the piece of paper the boy wrote on and waits while he pulls out a notebook and pen.

"How's your garden this year?" he asks as he writes.

"Glorious. Thank you for asking." She only wishes she'd made two cakes; there is always a need.

COLLEEN HAS TO WAIT IN LINE while everybody at Headquarters, it seems, needs to see Christie. She wants to put an argument to him about going public with what they have.

Dolan's just called from the funeral: "Eight Dominicans in attendance, looking nervous, only five people from the hospital—not Jason Oakes—and then Celia Navarro and the two kids. That's it. Small. It's going to be quick, too, that's my prediction. The priest is about to start in. You talk to Christie yet?"

"No. You still agree with me?"

"Yeah. We're nowhere otherwise," Dolan says.

So when Christie finally finishes with two other detectives and the D.A., she knocks, goes into his office, and begins, "I want to move this case forward."

"What? How?"

"I want to go aggressively after the two boys. Call them persons of interest. Get the public involved. Let the boys clear themselves if they're innocent. It's all we have."

He hardly even pauses. "Okay."

She's surprised. She was ready to argue harder. "You're okaying it?"

"Yes."

"I thought you were against it."

"These are all judgment calls. I agree we're nowhere. Okay. Let's do it."

"I'll start it, then."

First she gets it on the police bulletin. Finally she manages to get hold of two news teams to pick up her statement.

"Happy to shoot you," the WTAE reporter tells her on the phone.

"More important to put up the two photos of the boys. I just need to make sure the phrasing is right."

"You have the photos?"

"I have them on a CD. I could jpeg them to you."

"Do that. I'll come by anyway for a statement from you."

KDKA takes it by phone and computer. WPXI promises her a callback. She has to hope the radio stations will also pick up her revised statement.

RYAN'S OUT OF HIS MIND WITH BOREDOM, and it's only noon. It's taking everything he has to sit tight. Why did the old bat have to come to her door? She was supposed to be asleep.

Open door, money in her purse—that's how Jack described her. But Jack is a fuckup.

Hide the truck, hide the truck, that's all Jack can say.

He has other ideas. He can think. One way, when he decides to make a run, is to use the old lady's car. That would buy them a little time. Another choice is simply switching plates. That would buy possibly even more time because she might not notice it for a while. *He* doesn't look at his own plate, ever.

With luck they could be three days away from here before anybody figures it out. More.

So his mind drifts to where to go—small towns, where it's cheaper, Jack says. But as soon as the truck is sold or dumped or repainted, Ryan wants to go back to Pittsburgh.

Whatever. From now on he wants a bed. And food and booze and a real television and, whenever he can get it under control, the occasional high. And conversations with Chester.

When did he start letting Jack boss him around? A sudden fury hits him, and he's up and moving.

He picks up the rifle from where it is propped in the corner of the sun porch. Probably would fetch a hundred or two.

The kind of people who have these summer houses—they don't leave much around, just the furniture. They use up their food and lock up the place and go. The tiny bit left in tins is because they're afraid of rats, mice. Vermin. Chester never worked this part out, the skimpy rewards to be had in a country place.

The only thing Jack is likely to bring home is food.

For a while Ryan scrapes the rifle along the floor, watching it scratch the surface. He takes a roll from the bag his brother left for him, though it isn't wise to use what little bit there is too early. He slams the refrigerator door and the cupboards open, closed, looking. There is nothing to put on the bread, not even a dab of jelly.

He drags back to the sun porch, where he kicks once at the

television before he props the gun once again in its place. Then he sloughs off up the stairs to the WC, taking his time, wondering what to do with himself for a long, long day.

He hears a sound that might be a car.

JENSEN PULLS UP, GRABS TWO GROCERY BAGS, and rushes toward the house with his keys outstretched. Something is wrong. He can smell something has been burning. He has to take a leak so badly, he doesn't spend time looking about outdoors.

The key turns with no resistance. Was the door unlocked?

His heart, still racing, thumps crazily. Before he pushes the door open, he thinks, maybe . . . did Addie walk up to greet him? Then he enters and it's clear in an instant it's not something good, like Addie. Someone has camped out here. He's heard of this kind of thing, winter squatters. The place is a mess—a cardboard box in the living room, things askew, cigarette butts in soup bowls. The place is dirty. There are bits of unburned logs in the fireplace. His heart bangs against his chest even harder now.

And the floor is scratched. And, oh, his wife's robe is balled up on the couch. He creeps toward the kitchen with his two grocery bags. He has time only to see glasses and dishes on the counter and in the sink. And that they broke some of the cabinets.

What a homecoming. He's got to get to a phone in order to get his own phone turned back on. Every year, he suspends service from Sprint when he's away, calls to put it back on. He's going to be with the police all day, just as soon as he pulls himself together and deals with his bursting bladder. He hurries up the stairs.

He has no cell phone. How he wishes he'd listened to his daughters about carrying a cell.

Jensen's hands are shaking so badly, he can't get his zipper down. He manages finally and lets out a stream of urine that seems as if it will never end. Then the bathroom window shows him what he didn't see from the front yard or notice from the kitchen, a truck parked out back.

Oh my God, he thinks, oh my God. Someone is still around. There's nothing he can do now except talk calmly to the intruder, get him to leave, then get himself down to Addie's place, make sure she is okay, and then call the police from there.

He hears footsteps. He closes the bathroom door for a second, pulling himself together, then opens it.

Suddenly he's face-to-face with a kid. A bum. A kid who stands there with his hands in his pockets.

"Oho. Grandpa."

Jensen pushes past him to the stairs. "Come downstairs," he says, feeling ridiculous. "We need to talk."

He hears the boy come down the stairs behind him.

Why does the boy look familiar to him? Does he belong to one of the neighbors?

At the foot of the stairs the kid leaves him and walks toward the sun porch. Jensen stops, wondering what to do. In only seconds the boy returns. This time he's holding a rifle—and it's Jensen's own rifle from here at the house. For a moment they look at each other.

"Put down the gun, why don't you?"

"Not just yet."

"Where . . . where were you when I came in?"

"Your attic."

"What do you want?" Jensen looks steadily at the kid, trying to meet his eyes.

"Couple of things."

"You've been staying here," he says simply. Oddly, as he speaks, he can feel the nerves coming alive in his cheek. It's both numb and tingly, that in-between stage.

"Waiting for you, pops. Let's go into the kitchen and see what kind of supplies you brought us. I saw from the window you were bringing in some stuff. We'll have a little something together. Go on. Move."

Jensen turns to the kitchen. Nothing seems quite real. Nothing. He takes in things he only half noticed before—a pot on the stove, crumbs on the floor. And those cabinets, the one off its hinges, several others looking beaten up—dirty and nicked. How long has the kid been here, ruining his place?

The kid is peering into one of the bags. "Take two slices of bread. Make a sandwich. Meat, cheese, mayo, whatever you have here, mustard. I want it all. Understand?"

"Yes." Slowly he takes off his sport coat and drapes it on the back of a chair.

"What do you understand?"

"You're hungry. You want me to feed you. Do I know you?"

"Oh, yes."

"You belong to someone around here?"

"No. You think back, you'll figure it out."

He works to control the shaking of his hands as he takes out two slices of wheat bread. Animals, when afraid, lie down and offer the neck. He . . . he isn't quite ready to chance that. This young man is both slow and fast, all nervous activity beneath the fake calm.

"And make one for yourself, old man. We'll have a sit-down together."

"I'm not hungry."

"Took your appetite away, did I?"

He's thinking about the voice. The voice. "I'd have to say so. How did you get in?"

"That's simple enough. You didn't barricade the doors with steel."

"You don't need the gun." His Garand.

"I like it."

"Who are you?" But the knowledge is creeping up on him.

"You still want easy answers."

Jensen remembers where he's seen this boy, where he's heard this accent: the people he had to kick out because they were trashing his place. From England, the mother was. A terrible woman with a mouth on her that unsettled him.

"You remember now."

"How many of you are there?"

"Me and my bro. We been wanting to see you for a long time."

"I don't understand."

"Two weeks of fun you still owe us. We keep very close books."

"I . . . paid you back. I gave your mother her money back."

The kid laughs. "And you think that did it?"

Jensen feels a great itchy rash creep over his neck and face. This is something different going on here, something he can't catch—

"So here we are."

WHEN THE WTAE MEN CAME BY a little bit after noon, one on camera, one on microphone, they went into the conference room to record her statement. She got an irritating case of butterflies as the camera whirred on her, but she faced it down and took her time speaking distinctly: "We are now seeking two persons of interest in the hit-and-run fatality that took the life of Joanna Navarro of the North Side. The police have reason to believe that two youths, Ryan and John Rutter, formerly of the Perrysville area of the North Side, may have important information regarding the incident. Joanna Navarro, a mother of two, was killed late Saturday night when she was hit by a red pickup truck we believe to be a '94 or '95 Chevy. Anyone seeing the truck, license number PLW 2421, or the young men pictured in these driver's license photos is asked to call us at Pittsburgh Police immediately." When the man on mike clicked it off, she asked, "You'll put up the phone numbers? I didn't dictate them."

"I promise. Nicely done, by the way. Ought to get you something in the way of witnesses."

"People always come forward. It's a matter of sorting the good tips."

"We wish you luck. We'll get this on the five o'clock show."

She'd struggled with whether she should say the boys had an accent, and she'd decided not to.

"Your head honcho usually does the news bites. How is he? Is he okay?" The rumor mills had spread the news of his illness last year. It was harder to spread news of wellness.

"He's fine. Just very busy. And he said he wanted me to get used to being on camera."

"You don't like it?"

She paused. "Not much."

She bade the reporter and the cameraman good-bye in the conference room and went upstairs, where all she could do was pace. Something was going to happen now. She and Dolan had to be ready.

THE BOY HOLDS THE GUN ACROSS HIS LAP while he eats a sandwich, his second.

Hunger. Jensen can understand how awful it would be to be hungry, how it could make a person crazy. He's trying to think what to say to calm the situation.

"What else is in the bags?" the boy asks.

"Food. Various kinds. Cereal. Milk."

"Yeah, I saw that. I'll have some milk."

Jensen lifts the carton from the bag on the floor and puts it on the table. The kid looks at him for a long time before he takes the plastic quart bottle and snaps off the security lid. He drinks from the bottle.

"You can have the food."

"Yes, I can. I decided that on my own."

"Why don't you take it and go?"

"Maybe I want my two weeks here."

"Is that what you want? Really?"

"*You* still want easy answers. Maybe the short of it is I don't like you or your kind."

"I'm going to put the food away." Jensen reaches into one of the bags.

The boy jumps. "What's that sound?"

"Ice . . . I brought containers of ice because I wanted to keep things cold on the way. I also have to turn up the setting on the fridge."

"I see. Well, be done with it."

Jensen lifts butter and cheese and places them in their containers in the refrigerator. The solid squareness of things in his hands helps him focus and he doesn't feel as much fear when he has ordinary tasks to do. But. Two weeks? Two weeks more? Is that what the boy wants, with him playing servant? Well, it won't happen.

He eyes the gun.

He doesn't know if it's loaded. He never loaded it. If it's just for show, there is nothing to keep him from going out to his car and driving to the police.

"Where did you find that?" he asks. "It's an old thing. I kept it because it belonged to a friend of mine who died in the war."

"What war?"

"World War Two."

"Still shoots good."

"Does it?"

"Yeah. Is that what you wanted to know?"

Jensen's spirits take a long slide downward. "Have you hurt anyone with it?"

"Your trees out back. I gave them a hard time."

Jensen continues to put food away. Lettuce. Carrots. Celery. Mayonnaise and mustard. He puts down the packages of rice and pasta in his hands, trying to gauge the expression of the boy. Then he drains the excess water from the Tupperware that holds ice cubes and puts the containers in the freezer. "I have more food in the car," he says. "I'll go get it."

"Whoa. That sounds like a lie if ever I heard one." The kid plunks down the milk container. "Empty your pockets."

"You want my wallet? Is that what you're asking?"

"Everything. All the keys, everything."

Taking a deep breath, he takes from his pockets wallet, handkerchief, keys. "Tell me what you need. I want the best outcome here."

"Do you?"

"Yes. You were hungry. You must need money."

"Let's go get the other groceries." The boy points with the gun and raises it to shooting position.

They start toward the front door. But Jensen has a secret. When he travels he always carries an extra car key because of one time when his main set of keys got locked in the car. He keeps the single extra key in his back pocket. That's the way out. Eventually. When he finds his moment.

"How much more do you have to bring in?" the boy asks.

"There is one more bag in the backseat—breads, crackers. And the large suitcase with my stuff."

"Stuff?"

"Clothes."

"Clothes."

He can't have Addie coming over to check on him. She'd do that. She might do that.

The boy follows him out, close behind him, frisking him as they go. "What's this, what's this? Holding out on me. Not wise. Not the least bit smart. Hold still. It's . . . a car key!"

"We don't need it. The car's open," he says quickly.

"Don't bullshit me. I know why you kept it. I know how you think, see?"

"I wasn't thinking about—"

"Open the trunk."

In one quick move, he turns and swings at the boy, a fist to the jaw meant to surprise him. And it does. Soon they are on the ground, and he's kicking, but so is the kid. Tom yelps as a pain shoots through his knee and another through his hip. And the next minute it's *his* shirt collar being pulled and he feels like a puppet, being lifted up like that.

"You're a stupid old man, aren't you?"

He limps to the car to hold on. His hip hurts badly. The boy picks up the gun. "Open the trunk."

Jensen opens it, knowing the box of liquor in there spells trouble.

The boy, holding the rifle carefully, as if he might shoot it, says, "Well, lucky for me, *init*? I finally get something to cheer up this place. Let's get that box inside, old friend."

"What's . . . what's your name?"

"You don't remember?"

Jensen shakes his head.

"Ryan."

And he has a brother somewhere. Two against one. He tries to think what he can do against two.

"Come on, pick up the box."

He lifts it and carries it, all the while limping, into the house. His hip is sending shots of pain that take his breath away. And his knee keeps threatening to give way; something about the way his foot hits the ground feels soft, grayed out.

"Keep going, grandpa," the boy says.

"You need to put down the gun and . . . let's talk. Okay, Ryan?" He speaks the name carefully. "Let's talk about what you need."

"Not on your life. We're going to get supplies in and put on the TV—which is worse than shitty, by the way—and I'm going to have a few drinks while I wait for reinforcements."

CHRISTIE HAS PULLED AT THE STRANDS of thought since Colleen left. Is going public right? The boys, in trouble all their lives, okay, disaffected, disenchanted, all that. No mother-love to get them up out of the muck. They are probably not worth saving. Why does he want to know for sure?

Young equals reckless. And still out there, and now scared, too.

That's it. And it's not that Colleen doesn't know it, too. She does.

The Young and the Reckless, the TV program should have been called. He stares out his window.

THE OLD MAN IS LIMPING PRETTY BADLY as Ryan herds him and the box of liquor to the sun porch at the side of the house. "Sit. We're going to keep company for a while."

Jensen sits.

Ryan paces back and forth to be sure there is nothing in easy reach that the old man might grab or throw or otherwise use as a weapon. The old man sits in one of the wicker chairs, waiting. Jack isn't going to be back for hours. Ryan puts down the rifle so that he can open one of the bottles of liquor. All the while he keeps a close eye on his captive. "I'm going to have some of your hospitality."

"Look, why don't you let me help you."

"In what way?"

"Money, a place to stay."

"Okay. I'm going to let you help me. As soon as my partner gets here."

"Your brother . . ."

"We'll see what you can do. For one thing, you didn't load up your wallet. Thirty-two bucks, I see. What's that all about? We're going to need more cash."

"We could go for it now."

"Broad daylight. Me with a gun in your back. I don't think so. You want a drink?"

"I think I do."

"Well, then I'm going to march you to the kitchen, let you get us two glasses."

Jensen gets up, stepping gingerly on his right leg. But his eyes are alert; he's scanning the place. "What are you looking at?" Ryan asks as they pass into and through the living room.

"Trying to figure out what you were doing. What's all that?"

"That box? The pictures that were in there . . . I burnt up."

"Pictures?" Jensen turns around in the kitchen doorway.

"Family pictures."

The old man grabs on to the back of one of the chairs at the long table.

"Hey, hands off everything. Just do what I tell you. You're going to get us two glasses. You hear me?"

"I hear you." The old man's voice is shaky, but Ryan can see he still has some fight in him. Jensen tries to support himself without touching anything. Good. He's wounded, at least, slowed down. He says, "Whatever you want . . . it isn't going to help to threaten me, to mess with that gun. All it does is keep us from figuring out what to do."

"Two glasses."

Jensen, limping, has to grab on to a chair, then the counter, to get to the cabinet, where he manages to reach two glasses. Without much warning, he turns and suddenly lurches out of the kitchen and back toward the sun porch with Ryan following. Just as suddenly, he turns, and before Ryan knows it, the glasses are flying and the old man has put an elbow to his ribs.

Bent over with the surprise of it, Ryan manages to turn the gun around; grabbing it by the barrel, he slams the old guy hard in the hip with the butt of it. Jensen tries to grab hold of a living room chair, but he goes down with the hit.

"You son of a bitch, you asked for it. This is what you asked for." Ryan hits him again. The old man's face recoils with pain.

"Down to the basement," Ryan orders. "Come on. No, don't pick up the glasses. Just start moving. Move. Down to the basement."

"Don't do this."

"Do what?"

"Make it worse. Just leave."

"As if you know everything."

So they go down to the basement with Jensen hobbling ahead of him, and he makes the old guy pick up a long stretch of thin rope that's coiled around a peg on the wall at the foot of the stairs. Keep him still, keep him *down here,* he thinks at first. But Ryan feels frightened to leave the old guy where he can't see him. "Let's take that rope upstairs." He makes Jensen climb up way ahead of him so he can't pull that trick of falling back on the stairs.

A wiry fellow. Cords in his neck muscles, funny walk. *I don't ever want to be old,* Ryan reminds himself. "To the kitchen. Pick up one of those chairs and take it to the television room."

Jensen obeys.

"Now tie that rope around your wrist—your left wrist. Tight. And I mean tight." The first time Jensen does it, Ryan can get his finger under the rope. He makes the old guy unknot the rope using his teeth and his free hand and then tie it again. "Hands behind your back," he says then. He ties the two hands together and makes Jensen sit back in the chair. He pulls the rope down to Jensen's feet and ties the feet together. He's never had to do this before, and it's not easy to work and keep the gun handy the whole time. For a while he has the gun across his lap and it keeps bumping into the old guy—it scares him, anyway. Jensen has stopped fighting him.

Ryan ties and pulls at the ropes, concentrating.

"You made me do this," he says. He feels depleted, exhausted. What is it with these old people, wanting to fight?

Jensen doesn't say anything.

"Well, I need a drink."

He opens a bottle of liquor. This stuff is more expensive than what he generally gets. This is Jack Daniel's. He drinks from the bottle, not bothering to go back to the living room where the two glasses lie on the floor somewhere. He's got to get hold of himself. There are hours to go until Jack gets back.

He puts on the television.

Chester can charm his way into and around anybody. It's too late to pull a Chester. They've got beyond that.

Jack Daniel's is pretty good stuff, he notes. Someday, when all this is over, he will have good things of all sorts.

The old man isn't crying, only looking straight ahead, as if at the television, but not.

WHEN TALLING LEFT ADDIE this morning, he thought about getting old, and he hoped he got old gracefully. He'd told Addie to start locking her door, just in case there was something funny with this Rigger boy, but he admired her freedom of spirit. He had to hope she wasn't losing it—the classic way. They always thought something was missing or that something of theirs had been invaded. He'd put two or three elderly people in nursing homes when the paranoia just got too bad. One was his grandmother, one was his aunt, and the third was a neighbor who had nobody to care for her. It was a sad state of affairs, getting old, and it was nothing he relished. But one thing was sure—they always thought possessions were missing, first sign when they started to go wonky.

At the bottom of the hill, he made a drive around the lake, just to see if anything looked amiss. He was pretty used to the local vehicles and didn't see anything unusual.

Yep, pretty soon the summer people were going to be here. There'd be some teenage drinking at some point that'd seep down to Cochranton and that he'd be called in about. But, hey, it was a job. If nobody acted up, he'd be out of work.

When he got back to Cochranton, to the nice new Municipal

Building, he sat back at his desk and looked at the number for Jack Rigger. He decided it couldn't hurt to talk to the kid, give him a little scare.

No area code. He tried calling it with an 814 and didn't get anything more than a machine telling him he had reached Marissa and Pete and that they would get back to him. He left a message. He tried it with a 724 start and got a Verizon message that the number was not in service. Frowning, he gave it a 412 prefix. This time he got a grumpy man growling hello, and his spirits went up.

"I'm calling to talk to Jack Rigger."

"You got a wrong number."

"Don't hang up. This is the Cochranton police. I need to locate Jack Rigger."

"No Jack Rigger here. This is the Ellises. We don't have Jack anybody here and definitely not Rigger. You got a wrong number."

"Have you had this number for a long time?"

"Forever. Somebody's pulling your chain."

"Sorry for the trouble."

He hung up, putting his hopes on Marissa and Pete. He had other work to do, and he was going to have to get to it. He paced around and looked for a Coke in the fridge. Found one. He ate the two sandwiches his wife had packed him, paced some more, then sat down and made some other calls he needed to make. The whole time, in the back of his mind, he was doing mental preparations for the class he needed to teach later—he'd be filling in for his chief at the Allegheny County Police Academy late this afternoon. His chief was having some vascular surgery just about now. Today's lesson was supposed to be on how to administer the Breathalyzer.

The whole teaching thing made him nervous. He liked people fine, he just didn't like them in numbers. His stomach was all queasy with worrying about the class.

THE WOMAN WHO RAN THE KITCHEN SAID, "You're a good worker, John Rigger. You better not quit on us. You have dishpan hands yet? All wrinkled?"

"Yeah."

The cook and server was what his mother called "stringy." Not much of a body. His mother always scoffed, *Those nervous types. Spare me. Arms always moving. Who do they think is chasing them?* This one had brown hair pulled back in a rubber band, but she also wore a kerchief over it. Her clothes, a polo shirt and pants, were baggy, as if anything that restricted movement drove her crazy. She reminded him of a refugee. "Take a break, kid. You didn't even have lunch yet."

"I had pastries for breakfast."

"Just stop with the dishes. You need to eat. What do you want?"

"The special. . . ."

"Cabbage and ham. You like cabbage and ham?"

He shrugged. "Never had it." He'd been smelling it all day, and by now he did crave it. "It's not what's on the sign."

"Nah. I mix it up sometimes." She ladled him out a big plate of food. "Here you go. I wish you'd smile once or twice."

"I didn't realize I didn't."

"You got a heavy look about you. What's that little accent you have?"

"Australian," he said.

"I thought you were going to say North England. I like accents. I really like them in movies."

"People do." He ate so hungrily that about the only thing he was sure of was that there were potatoes along with the meat and cabbage.

"I shouldn't make you talk while you're eating."

"It's okay."

"I'm getting you bread to sop it up. With the bread it will hold you till dinnertime."

"I might want to ditto this for dinner."

"There won't be any left. It's going like hotcakes."

Jack planned to lift whatever he could, but most things were in containers or one of the refrigerators, and Penny—her name was Penny—never left.

"You go to college?"

After a moment, he said, "Going to be starting at Thiel."

"In what?"

"Biology. Environmental."

"You must be smart."

"I guess."

"You smoke?" she asked, eyebrows way up.

"When I have it."

"Be my guest. Let's go out back and have us one. I'm going to get you to smile somehow, some way. I set that as my goal."

"You have kids?"

"I have a grandkid almost your age already. I started young, let's just say. *Real* young."

"How did you make a living?"

"I was always a doer. Always. I mean, the boy married me. But I always worked. Lugged the babies here and there. That's how I was."

"How old were you when you started?"

"Sixteen. I'm not recommending it, mind you. Don't try to copy me."

"I won't."

Outside the back door, smoking, he felt on edge that somebody was going to see him. When a police car went up the street, his whole body went weak with fear.

IT'S ONE THIRTY, so Colleen is about to fetch her lunch makings from the refrigerators, but Dolan is just back and he's pulled up a rolling desk chair to her station. She tells him the development: "The photos of the boys will make it to the five o'clock TV news and into the paper tomorrow morning. We'll be on the radio anytime now."

He wheels back and forth a little, holding on to her desk. "I'm ready. You look nervous."

She's got copies of the license photos taped up in her cubicle. One smiling, one not. "I keep calling them boys. . . ."

"Boys, young men, punks . . . ," Dolan says. "Whatever they are, we're going to find out."

Eager. Dolan is eager to hunt. She cautions him, "I could get broiled on this one. Tanya King's tip plus the simple existence of a red truck in Miner's family is all we have."

Dolan chews on it for a while. "It is slim."

When her phone rings, she brightens. "Maybe it begins."

It takes only a split second to recognize the voice this time. Purdy. "Colleen. I know I'm calling you at work. I was wondering, did you have lunch yet?" he asks lightly.

"Um, yes," she says since it's close to true; she has bread, turkey breast, and yogurt in the office refrigerator.

"Just thought I'd offer. I'm in my car about to stop for something."

"We don't usually stop for lunch or . . . go out, you know, sit."

"If you want to, I'm available. I realize you can't take a lot of time."

Dolan is watching her, smiling knowingly. He mouths, "Go!"

"I know I sound like a complete drudge."

"No. I understand."

Dolan is wagging his head and making impossible to ignore faces that suggest she's making a mistake.

"Listen. Okay. My partner is telling me to *take a break* and get out of the office. I could probably get to someplace local like, say, Legends, so long as I keep it really brief." She'd have her phone with her. Why is it so hard to budge?

"I can either pick you up or meet you at Legends in five minutes."

"Meet you there, then. Five minutes." She hangs up.

Dolan says, "You don't like him very much."

"He's perfectly fine. I just . . . I'm trying to get my head around going out with a stockbroker. I never dated anybody corporate before." Feeling around in her handbag for her phone, she says, "I really won't be long, and I do have to eat."

"I'm here. Not going anywhere."

"Call me right away if anything comes in."

"Maybe."

"You shit." She slings her heavy handbag over her arm. "Why are you in such a good mood? You just came from a funeral." The truth is, she can't bear funerals and sent Dolan just to avoid the sadness.

"True." He pauses and his face changes.

She took his phone reports but never asked anything else. Now she senses both she and Dolan need to come down off their nervous high. "Was the funeral sad?"

"Bad sad. Those little kids are nowhere near having anybody who can help them process this."

"Oh."

Dolan pats her hand. "You go break another heart, honey."

PURDY IS WEARING A SUIT—A NICE ONE, in navy with a pale stripe, all very subtle. She orders pasta with shrimp. "Shouldn't take too long."

He looks worried. "I hope they're quick in the kitchen."

"Please don't be insulted if I suddenly have to grab a takeout. The bread and olive oil are almost enough."

"Umm. Oh, yes. I wanted to tell you, *The Sweet* isn't showing anymore. We'll have to find another movie, in case Friday works out."

"Right. Okay." She has no idea what's playing around town. She really has to quit living in a tunnel, learn what's going on outside the station. "Tell me about your daughter," she says. "She lives here?" She allows a brief fantasy of herself as stepmother—arguing, shopping, watching movies on TV.

"She and her mother just moved to Chicago."

"Ah. Do you have a picture of her?"

He lifts his butt off the seat and takes out a wallet from his back pants pocket. Colleen finds this interesting. Most men in suits use an inside breast pocket. He flips past his driver's license and credit cards to a photo of a woman and a girl. "This is recent," he says, handing over the whole wallet. The leather is smooth, the wallet weighty. "That's her mother with her."

The daughter looks a lot like her mother—and in the photo, his ex and his daughter hug each other as if to say, *We don't need you, see we're tight, we're fine.* Both of them are pretty, the daughter especially well coiffed and confident looking, probably 75 percent bravado.

Colleen realizes that if she grew her own hair out, *she* might look a lot like the ex-wife. Is that what Purdy sees in her? "Thanks." She hands back the wallet. "You miss your daughter?"

"A lot."

"Did her mother remarry?"

"No," he says, sounding relieved.

How interesting. To carry a torch through another, second marriage. "You don't carry around pictures of your second wife?"

"No. No." He blushes. "Why?"

"Oh, I don't know. I always admire divorced people who make

their way through it all as friends. You don't have to answer me. Really. I can be a pain sometimes."

"I'm not friendly with Brenda. It was rough. She was . . . we didn't really take."

"Oh, I'm sorry I asked, then."

When Steve Purdy puts away his wallet, she watches the way he moves. She can picture him at home, showering, being careful about his clothing, working at his computer, paying all his bills, calling his daughter. He's sad, doing his best to keep up with life.

"I'm glad you're asking me questions," he says. "It helps. I can get bottled up."

She laughs. "I was just telling myself to quit prying. Okay. How did you meet your first wife?"

"The usual way. We were college sweethearts. Got married. Waited three years. Had a kid. Nothing unusual. Her name is Diana."

"Your daughter?"

"No, my wife. My daughter's name is Jessica, like half the girls her age. She hates her name. She wants to be called something exotic, but it's too late. Plus she doesn't look exotic."

"No, she looks pretty all-American."

"We had to call her Mina and Mitra for a while. We finally figured out there was an Iranian boy in the picture. Afsoun. When he left the country—"

"You ran him out?"

"I thought about it. No, his parents took him. He was a good kid, but she was too swacked. Anyway, after about a month, she was Jessie again."

"You and your wife must have had to talk about that some."

"We were on the phone quite a lot over Afsoun. Brenda and I were separated at that point."

Colleen can guess the next. "Did you work with Brenda? Meet her at work?"

Steve Purdy looks a little surprised. "Yes."

Brenda is probably dark-haired, peppy, sexually adventurous—a cliché. "It happens."

She suspects Diana never forgave him for something, maybe for taking up with Brenda; if it happened in that order, Diana might still be working through it, in which case she sent her picture along with her daughter's to torture him.

Does she, Colleen, want to jump into this? That's a question she leaves unanswered when lunch is finished.

After Purdy drives off, she sits in her car outside Legends and calls Dolan. "Anything?"

"Not yet. Waiting is the hardest. You have to trick it, like what you do with weather, you know, take an umbrella so it won't rain."

She drives to the Navarro residence, looks up at the building, then gets out of the car. Is the after-funeral meal finished? She takes a deep breath and taps on the door.

"Who is it?" Celia's voice comes through nervously.

"Detective Greer."

The door opens. "You learn something?"

"Nothing for sure. But I wanted to tell you— You might see on the news that we put two pictures out there—for TV and newspapers."

"Pictures?"

"They're boys who *might* have been the ones. Might have been. We don't know for sure. We only want to talk to them." All the while she speaks, she eyes the kids, who are watching TV. They're eating cake out of bowls and half the time hitting each other and laughing.

"How are they doing?" She gestures toward the kids.

Celia makes a face. "I don't know. Glad to get out of school. They don't—" She points to her head.

"They don't comprehend?"

"They don't want to think about it. They want to call their friends."

"I'm going to give you some names. Places to take them to talk about what happened. It's called grief counseling. It's important. So they don't . . . you know . . . pretend it never happened. They should remember their mother, be able to talk about her."

Should.

All those children in war-torn countries lose parents, and yet they carry water the next day, dig through rubble, go out to the fields to work.

People move on, one way or another.

She stands at the living room door, feeling helpless. "I didn't want you to be shocked when you see the news. Or too hopeful. It's just a lead. I know this is a tough day."

"Okay. Thank you for telling."

The kids don't even turn around or look up at the sound of Colleen's voice or the door opening to let her out.

ADDIE, DRIVING INTO TOWN for a bottle of cooking oil, all the while thinks she might see Jensen on the way. In her mind, she toots her cranky old horn, waves to him, and he waves back. Or he'll be driving the road behind her just as she's coming back. Then he'll pull in at her place on the way to his. They'll have some of the cake she made, several cups of tea.

A dog trotting in the middle of the road about a half mile from her place interrupts this fantasy. Yes, it's that mixed-breed terrier she saw yesterday moving restlessly at the edge of her property. It looks back at her, pauses, then moves over to the side of the road.

She continues on her mission, buys the oil, and starts back to her place, and there is the dog again, several hundred yards closer to town.

She pulls over as far as she can without going into a ditch and gets out of her car. "How're you doing?" she asks. "Are you lost?"

The dog trots toward her. It—he or she—isn't mangy. Its coat, while not glossy, has been brushed and its collar is worn but once held an owner's tag. She. A girl. The dog gives a little whimper and cries into her palm.

"Oh! I'll keep you," she says. "No, no, somebody misses you, I think." The dog looks at her curiously. If she can get it to come home with her, she can call the Humane Society and insist they find the owner.

"Come. Come on, girl," she tries, walking toward the car.

The dog comes a step closer.

"I have half a mind to drive you myself," she says. She looks at her watch. The dog waits. Meadville, she thinks, should I? She really *ought* to stay around in case Jensen calls her. "Come on. Into the car." She taps her thigh and the dog gets in.

Once she's home, she leaves the dog in the car until she finds a bit of rope to make a leash. The dog is very well behaved. She ties the rope and there is hardly a protest. After she leads the dog to her porch, she fastens the rope to one of the banisters. "Yes, yes, I'm going to feed you," she says. Luckily there's a bit of vegetable soup she hasn't frozen, with good chunks of beef in it. "I hope you're not vegetarian." A few minutes later, she brings the soup and a bowl of water to the porch. The dog eats and drinks hungrily. "Poor thing," she says. She goes inside to make her call to the Humane Society. The man who answers says he can pick up the dog in about an hour.

Addie reads a little outdoors, where she can watch the dog and the road for the Humane Society man. The dog also watches her. Dogwood blossoms drift on the breeze like snow, and she has the illusion of moving backward in the seasons.

She fetches her scissors and cuts irises and keeps waiting. Much more than an hour passes with no word or appearance from the Humane Society worker. Somehow she feels held up, irritable. She decides after a bit to put on a pot of spaghetti sauce—her everything-plus-meatballs sauce. It's always a winner. She has the ingredients handy. It'll be a good thing to have around. Tom will probably want supper. And there is plenty of room in the freezer to hold another couple of containers of it. Start it now, all will be well.

TALLING KNOWS PERFECTLY WELL how to stop an erratic driver and what questions to ask and how to do the test, which he's done thousands of times. He knows if they're old and can't walk a straight line, it might have more to do with the whole balance system in the body than alcohol. On the other hand, there might be some sedative or something interrupting concentration. He knows to tell all this to the trainees, especially: Don't, don't, *don't* slam your man to the ground and put a knee on his neck or you could end up with a case like the infamous one in Pittsburgh—the suspect guilty of nothing and very dead and the policemen with lives that might as well be spent in hell. Err on the side of caution, he will say, and on the side of respect. You just need to get the drunk driver *off the road.* But the ideas are coming at him every which way.

He checks his watch, twitchy to go, but if he goes now, he'll be there early, and early has a bad effect, makes him feel too eager. So he sits at the computer and does a reverse phone search with the number he has hopes for, Marissa and Pete.

It comes up. Marissa and Pete Studicki. Well, there are only about fifty explanations for why there's no Rigger listed. He decides to get at it later. But he tries Rigger just for the heck of it. There's only Riggins and Riggs and Rigby, no Rigger. Humph, he says to himself, little puzzle to occupy me tomorrow.

Soon after that, he takes a phone call and it's good news. A careful garbage collector has found Emma Hopper's cell phone and wallet in a city garbage can. He sends one of his men to fetch it and print it, and then he calls Emma to tell her. "The cash is gone, of course, but your photos are there. Credit cards are gone, but if the guy tries to use them, we've got him." He explains she can't have the things back until they've been photographed and printed. She's awfully upset that someone touched her things, more freaked out than she was yesterday when the things were missing. He gives her as much time as he can and promises to see her tomorrow.

Then he clears the space in front of him on his desk and keeps going over and over the points he wants to make to the class of police recruits. Chief says always narrow a lesson to three points to pound it into their heads in a way they'll never forget, but there are about ten or twelve things he has to say. Get them down to three? How? He dials his wife, who is a nurse working over in Meadville. "Can you talk?"

"For about thirty seconds."

"How would you get the whole Breathalyzer lesson down to three points? There's like twelve points."

She says, "One. Be safe. Safety for police and suspects." He grabs a tablet and starts to write. She says, "Then you can say everything about pulling the person over, how to treat them, who might pass out from the Breathalyzer, checking for weapons, everything."

He writes furiously.

She says, "Two. How and when the test works."

"Aha," he says. "Here's where I tell about old people who can't walk straight."

"Right-o. Three. Keep it legal: how to book a DUI. Does that help?"

"It helps."

"You won't be home for dinner."

"Yeah, I will. Academy is four to six thirty."

"I was going to do clam linguine."

"Great."

"I gotta go. We have a guy having trouble breathing here. Bye."

Man, she's sharp. Man-she-is-sharp.

A faint memory of school—outline form—spurs him to make notes. It's getting on to three o'clock. It occurs to him that if he'd called his wife earlier, he could have gone to the French Creek Café to see if they had any chocolate cake. Addie's cake put the craving into his head, and he's not going to stop thinking about chocolate cake until he has a couple of pieces.

ANNE MARIE LENNOX is just getting off work at three—she does the early supermarket shift in Meadville—and she's trying to figure out whether to get her hair cut today or keep growing it. There's a shop about a mile away that doesn't require appointments. To make this decision, she pulls down the visor on the driver's side to study her hair. People have been telling her she looks better with it longer. It's more trouble for sure. She can't ask her guy, Bill Guinnert, because men always want women's hair to be longer, as if fearing they'll get the genders mixed up. Anne Marie once had a really short sexy cut and no trouble attracting men, but now, of course, she's older.

She decides not to get her hair cut today, so she does the seat belt, ignition, radio ritual that she doesn't have to think about. She punches through a few stations on the car radio and starts for home and a bath, a hair wash, a glass of wine before dinner. A pound-and-a-half block of ground meat is defrosting in her fridge. With a little effort, it becomes meat loaf; if she's not in the mood, it's cheeseburgers tonight, two big ones for Bill and one medium large for her. He's a big eater, a big guy. And jolly, that's what she likes, because there's not enough joking in the world.

She's driving along, not paying particular attention to the radio, when the halting voice of the newscast announcer, a woman who often stumbles over words, breaks into her awareness.

"Pittsburgh Police are seeking two persons of interest in the . . . hits . . . hit-and-run fatality of Joanna Navarro, last Saturday night. They believe two young men, Ryan Rut . . . Rutter, twenty, and John Rutter, nineteen, may have pertinent information about the death. Anyone knowing the whereabouts of the young men should contact Pittsburgh Police. The police are also seeking a red Chevy pickup truck with the license plate PLW 2421, in connection with the killing."

Funny. Bill drives a red truck. Even funnier, he, Bill, was just telling her the other day about an underage kid in a bar, con artist type. Then Bill told her—was it just yesterday?—he was driving down the road and sees the kid again, *thinks* he does, and the kid doesn't recognize him, and after he drives off he thinks either he is no longer a memorable guy, alas, or the kid is a different kid, a look-alike.

But it's a Pittsburgh case in the news.

She switches to a different station with music.

After a while, almost home, she calls Bill's cell. When he answers, she hears the television and voices that tell her he's in a bar, stopped for a few.

"Bill?"

"Hi, babe. What's up?"

"There was an item on the news . . ."

"I can hardly hear you."

"Where are you?"

"The joint in Sugar Lake."

"Did the kid in the bar there—the con artist you told me about—did he have a red pickup truck?"

"I didn't see any kind of truck. Why?"

"Something on the news about two brothers and a pickup truck being wanted in some case in Pittsburgh—a woman got killed in a hit-and-run."

Bill isn't paying attention. She can tell he isn't. There are just bar sounds and him saying, "Hmmm. Interesting."

But then she hears, "Hey, guys. You know that punk who was in here the other day, looking for freebies? Any of you see what he was driving?"

There is a long wait while the men joke and piss around. Anne Marie comes very close to hanging up.

But Bill gets back to the phone, saying, "Nobody saw any truck. Or any vehicle at all."

"Oh. When will you be home?"

"Five. Five-ish."

"Bad day, good day?"

"Same kind of day as usual, medium shitty," he says cheerfully.

"WHY, THERE, YOU SMILED," Penny says. "Let's go out and have another cig. We deserve it."

He nods curtly, aware that she wants more than a nod and a smile.

They go outside. He tries to turn his back to the street as much as possible, but he doesn't want to look suspicious.

"How often does the owner pay wages?" he asks.

"Saturdays. Why? Oh. Of course. You're short of cash. Don't even have a pack of smokes to your name. I'm going to give you a full pack, just a little gift."

"You don't have to."

"No, I want to. I like having a smoke buddy."

"Um. Thank you. So . . ." He tries to think how people talk to each other. "How are your kids?"

"They're doing real well. They're employed. I count that as a blessing. Where are your folks these days? Still in England or what?"

"Nah. They live in the U.S. now."

"They kick you out of the house?" she asks, eyes narrowing. "I bet they did."

"Yeah."

"Where you staying?"

"With a friend."

"Thank God for friends, huh. Your friend puts you up?"

"Yeah."

"What did you get yourself kicked out for?" She laughs. "Let me guess. Drinking?"

"No," he answers, but only because he can't think. "Yes" would have been a good answer.

"Pot. Smoking pot," she tries.

"Yes."

"Most kids do."

"They're very strict."

"I wasn't strict with my kids. I knew they were going to act up. I talked with a smart woman once, very smart, about how I tried to let my kids just be kids and how they turned out perfectly all right in the long run. She said what I did was 'benign neglect.' You know what benign means."

"Sort of."

"I hate afternoons when it slows down."

Not much of the benign, he thinks, in the neglect he had, but he doesn't say. This woman is going to keep asking him questions, and he has to keep track of what he's said: Jack Rigger, biology major, about to go to Thiel next year, tossed out by his parents for smoking pot, living with a friend.

"Your friend live with his folks or on his own?"

"On his own."

"You take food to him?"

"Um, yeah, if I can."

"Want me to help you pick over the stuff people throw away—perfectly good rolls, all that? Of course it isn't legal, but I always used to take things home. Put them in the oven, heat them up, kill the germs, you do better than the jokers who waste everything, you know?"

"I know."

"Come on, kid. Anything that gets thrown, I'll help you pack it. I understand."

A sick feeling comes over him suddenly with the memory of a dream he had last night, probably from all the dishwashing he was doing; in the dream, he was eating a big helping of mashed potatoes and chicken out of a large rectangular garbage can.

"McGUIGAN SENT ME," he tells the old woman, slamming his car door shut. "I'm Sid Kickle. You Mrs. Ward?"

"Yes, I am."

"The van is in use. McGuigan couldn't come. He's who you talked to. We got dogs running loose everywhere, it seems."

"It's an epidemic," she says.

He's pretty sure that's a joke. She seems amused by it, anyway. "I'll just take him in my car."

"You're sure you're from the Humane Society?"

"Yeah." He feels a mite resentful, but he pulls out his wallet and extracts a card.

"Take good care of her. Find her owner."

"You have any idea whose she is?"

"No. I know most of the people around here. No, I don't. She's acting lost. You know, mournful."

"Well, we'll list her. We need to say where you found her."

"On the road about half a mile down, almost to the lake."

He takes out a small notebook and writes down *Sugar Lake.* "It's nice around here."

"Thank you. If you can't find her owner . . . or someone to take her . . . let me know."

"You want her?"

"I don't want her to be killed. You'll let me know?"

"Do my best."

He fastens a leash to the dog's collar, but as soon as he gets the creature in his car, she starts barking nonstop. "Easy, girl," he says.

The sound is giving him a headache. He rolls the window down only a crack on the passenger side, and immediately she's trying to put her nose out.

"It's okay. Take it easy, girl," he keeps telling the dog. She listens for a while, gets agitated looking at the road, and starts barking again.

McGuigan makes it to Meadville, having squired the anxious dog without a safety cage. He's thirty years old and finally found something he can do. He stretches, rubs his aching temples, and grabs the leash, but as soon as he opens the driver door, the dog leaps up and somehow climbs right over his back and shoulder. "Ow. Wait." To protect his face, he lets go of the leash, trying to bat her off.

It's too late. She's gone. Dragging the damn leash and running like a crazy thing.

Oh, man.

Some days you just want to shoot yourself.

He drives around for nearly an hour trying to find her, but she's gone, he's lost her. People shake their heads in answer to his inquiries. With his head hanging, he goes back to the compound to report his failure.

RYAN WATCHES THROUGH ELECTRIC SNOW Dr. Phil and Oprah telling people how to be. Get it together. Be an adult. Right. Sure.

The old guy . . . isn't really watching. He's working to figure things out. "Where is your mother?" he asks finally.

"I don't know."

"You're estranged?"

"You could say that."

"She doesn't support you?"

"We flew the coop a long time ago."

"So . . . you're up here with your brother?" Ryan doesn't answer. "You chose this place in particular." Ryan doesn't answer. "Because of me."

"I remembered you."

"You said I owed you. What do you figure I owe you? Time here?"

Ryan doesn't want to answer anything ever again. Five o'clock comes, and the news comes with it. He stares at the television with half a mind to change the channel, but he has a good buzz going now and doesn't want to get up. It's okay. It's going to be okay once Jack gets here.

For a while the old man closes his eyes. Dead, maybe. That would be a relief. Ryan keeps drinking and tries in his mind to be Chester, easy.

There is nothing on the news about the pathetic old guy in Meadville. Good. That's good.

Then he hears his name. Just like that. And Jack's . . . "John," they say on the news, "Ryan and John Rutter." He can see two rectangles where supposedly their pictures are, *pictures of them* on the news. Just like that. Names, pictures, description of the truck, and even the license number.

The old guy's eyes open. He's not asleep or dead.

COLLEEN HAS MADE IT BACK TO THE OFFICE and is pacing when the first call comes in.

A man with a gravelly voice says, "I seen on the news you people are looking for these two guys. I seen the one guy a couple days back."

"Where?"

"Put me on with a detective."

"I am a detective. This is Detective Greer, Homicide. How do you know it was the person we want to talk to?"

"I seen his face in my bar. Believe me, I remember him. He tried to lift money from a guy he was sitting next to. Got himself into a fight. Drove off in a red truck," the man says triumphantly.

"All right. I'd like to come talk to you."

"You're a detective or what?"

"Detective, yes, Homicide."

"Okay."

"Tell me your name and your location." She looks at her watch. It's getting on to five thirty.

Dolan stands. He can tell this is a good tip.

As she writes, Potocki walks past and waves at her; Christie comes out of his office and takes up a conversation with Potocki.

Colleen watches them and keeps writing. She gets down, *J. T. Knoerdle, owner of a bar in Meadville, not a tall thinker . . .*

She checks her watch against the wall clock, calculates. "Will you be there at your place in an hour and a half, no, let's say two?"

"I'm not going anywhere."

"Okay, Mr. Knoerdle. We'll be there very soon. Do you have any idea where the person we're looking for might have gone?"

"Up north. Running from something, they go north."

"We're going to Meadville," she tells Dolan.

"Where Casey went to bat?"

"That was Mudville."

"What's up?" Christie asks, coming over to them.

"Sighting of one of the suspects in Meadville. We're going to talk to the locals."

"Persons of interest," Dolan corrects her with a wily smile.

"We'll go with them," Christie says to Potocki.

"Do we need," Colleen begins irritably, "all of us?" But even as she speaks, she realizes she has what everybody wants and she needs to share.

"Mudville," Dolan is saying to himself. "I had to memorize that poem in high school. 'There is no joy in Mudville. Mighty Casey at the bat.' "

"I don't think that's how it goes," Colleen tells him.

JENSEN THOUGHT FOR A LONG TIME about the incident ten years ago. He could remember the moment when he'd walked into the house then—it was similar to the jolt he got this time. Things looked wrong. Furniture and figurines and the prints hanging on the walls were out of place, and there were towels everywhere and sand, what looked like wet sand, on the floors and carpets.

They'd thought it was going to be a happy event—they'd driven up for a party at Addie's—a big cookout, and they were going to stay overnight and then drive back. They thought all they were doing was paying a courtesy visit to their tenants.

Marian had gone to the front door first, seen the place in bad shape through the screen, knocked, and gotten no answer. That had rattled her. She got back in the car to tell Jensen they had a bad situation. Then he went up, knocked, waited, and finally went in, and that's when he found towels draped everywhere on the floors and furniture and the pictures all skewed, as if the people crashed into the walls as they moved about. He found the renter, a Rita Miner, in a bathing suit with some kind of gauzy cover-up, staring him down. She was smoking up a storm, and he minded the smell—he'd stopped years ago. Slowly he took in the rest of the damage. Food on the coffee and end tables. Muddy fishing gear on a chair.

"Excuse me," he said. "We knocked."

"Well, we didn't feel like answering. This place is not available. We're here for two weeks."

"I . . . I own it."

"What are you doing here? You rented it out, eh?"

"I did."

"So it isn't yours, not right now. Maybe this counts as trespassing."

Her voice and accent were new to him. Her husband had made the arrangements by phone—he had a different last name, but Jensen couldn't remember it. The check had come to him from a Rita Miner. This was Rita. She sounded English. Liverpool or maybe some other town to the north of London. "I have to say I don't like what I'm seeing."

"Me?"

"The mess."

"It's a vacation house, right?"

"Yes. It's on the rugged side, but—"

"You coming here to police us? That doesn't swim, see?"

"Wet things will ruin the chairs and the floor. That's why we have clotheslines outside. And the food . . . you can't leave food around. It will attract insects, mice. Once you get an infestation, it's hard to get rid of it." There were flies buzzing around his head as he spoke.

Then the husband appeared from the upstairs. Glasses, untrimmed scraggly beard, unkempt hair. He didn't seem to go with the woman. She was overtly, even brazenly, sexual. He looked as if he didn't know he had a body. "Who's the visitor?" the man said, puzzled.

"He says he's the owner."

"Of course I am. I'm Jensen. You sent your check to me."

"So. What's the problem?" the man asked.

"He doesn't like how we're keeping up his place." Her tone was the mocking childish tone of playground fights.

And, as if—he actually laughed about it later—as if he needed to amp up the nightmare one more notch, two boys came into the house dragging nets, mud, towels, and throwing everything on the sofa.

"There's some lady sitting in a car outside," one boy said.

"She even came to the front door," their mother said. "Checking on us. Who do you people think you are? You rent out a place, you stay out of it, right?"

Jensen said, "I didn't come here to get into an argument. All I'm asking is you take better care of things." He remembered other people telling him he should have gotten a security deposit.

He must have made a face of some sort because the woman said, "Is that face for us? That you're-shit-and-you-know-it look? We're definitely not like you and we're proud of it."

He told her levelly, "We came by to see if everything was working okay, if you needed anything."

"We need for you to go, asshole."

Her husband said, "Hey, ease up, Rita."

Her eyes shone. She clearly wanted a fight. He thought, belatedly, she'd been drinking.

"Look, okay, this was a mistake. We shouldn't have rented the place out. It's always just been—"

"Not to riffraff, anyway, right?" She *wouldn't* let up. She turned to her kids. "We're not good enough for his place. See?"

"Let's go," the husband said. "Let's just leave. I can't work here. I'd rather leave."

The woman exploded. "Are you kidding me? We paid for this place. It was my check. I paid two weeks. I can't lose that."

"I want to go. Tell your boys to pack up."

One of the boys pushed the husband, saying, "Coward."

Jensen dug into his pocket. He produced the rent check, which he'd never cashed. "I'd refund it, your two weeks."

"That's a deal," the husband said. "Take it."

The woman laughed. "You wouldn't know a deal if it bit you on the ass." Then she said, "Okay, give us cash for that and we'll go. We'd need cash on the road."

"There's a bank. I'll be back in an hour."

"Why do we have to go? Because Neil wants to?" the older kid asked.

"He changed his mind," the husband said. "He needs the place for himself. I can't work here anyway, so we're going."

Jensen left them to their argument. He went to the car and explained to Marian that the two of them had a job ahead of them—they were going to be cleaning. They'd be lucky if they got over to Addie's at all. "Get to sleep in our own beds, though," he said to cheer her.

"We shouldn't have rented it."

"We have to go to the bank. This is going to cost us. Maybe a lot."

He'd thought, What a story we'll have to tell Addie if we make it to the party.

ADDIE IS READING IN THE YARD AGAIN, hoping the clouds pass.

All afternoon she's expected Tom Jensen to drive into her yard. It puzzles her that he hasn't—and that he hasn't called. It isn't like him. On the other hand, she knows he suspends phone service at Sugar Lake when he leaves in the fall and activates it when he gets here, so maybe he hasn't bothered to start it up again yet. Still, it's more like him to call from home or the road if he decided not to come or got delayed. After puzzling over this for a while, she goes inside and tries his Pittsburgh number.

There is no answer.

Trouble on the road.

The spaghetti sauce smells wonderful. Even though it's a little early, she's in the mood to eat now. With a little pique, she thinks, she never made him an invitation to dinner; it's simply tradition and familiarity dictating this unsaid invitation. She starts the water boiling.

It's amazing how irritable she feels. She examines the feeling, turning it this way and that. When she's just about outdoors again, heading for her book, which is facedown on the lawn chair, her phone rings. Aha, finally. She hurries back to it. The voice that greets her is not Tom Jensen's but her daughter's.

"Linda!"

"Hi. Just checking on you."

"I'm still here."

"What's up?"

"I've just made a huge pot of spaghetti sauce."

She turns off the water so that it doesn't boil down before she's ready for it, and she walks outside with the phone.

"Thinking of coming up on the weekend. Just to see you."

"Not to stay?"

"I'd come up Saturday and stay one night. I miss you, Mum."

"I miss you, too. Of course. Yes. Come. That would be wonderful."

"What just happened? You got quiet."

"Nothing, nothing. I was just getting settled in my chair in the yard. Reading."

"Any books you want me to bring you?"

"Yes. Anything new. I'm game."

"Oh, and I want to have your car checked out. I'm worried it's not safe."

Oh dear.

When the call is ended she puts the phone down in her lap and tries to read. It hits her that if Tom got to Sugar Lake and felt ill or had a heart problem and she didn't check on him, she would never forgive herself.

Take the pot of spaghetti sauce and a package of pasta up there? Too complicated. Leave it on the stove, invite him down?

Has he taken offense at something she said or didn't say? She sounded not very welcoming in their last phone call. She must make it right.

She goes in and has only a quick piece of bread dipped in a little of her delicious sauce before going out to her car.

BRITTANY IS DIGGING IN THE FREEZER for something that might make a dinner, something either her mother or her roommate's mother gave them. Stuffed cabbage. Oh, well. Okay, stuffed cabbage.

Her roommate comes in from work, dumps everything on the living room floor, and flicks on the TV, which means she's not much in the mood to talk to Brittany. They don't get along. They know they need to find other living arrangements, but they haven't dealt with which one of them will leave and where the new roommate will come from. Brittany thinks Elissa is stuck-up and full of herself. Elissa thinks Brittany eats too much and is naturally unhappy—or that's what Brittany thinks Elissa thinks. How can she be naturally happy when her own roommate hardly talks to her?

She's got the freezer container in hand when she walks to the living room to see Elissa headed for the bathroom. "Have to pee," Elissa says, "and glad you're not in there."

Brittany stares forlornly at Elissa's handbag, tote, jacket, and something else in a Rite Aid bag. "You going out tonight?" she shouts toward the bathroom. "I wouldn't mind going to a club again."

There is no answer.

And then she sees *him* on TV along with another boy, as plain as anything, the boy she almost went with the other night, the one who disappeared on her. She scrambles to turn up the volume.

Elissa calls out finally, "I have plans tonight."

"Quiet."

"Why?"

"I'm trying to hear—"

"What did you say?"

Ryan Rutter. Not Gregory. He was funny. He had a dash of charm, but it was possibly mainly the accent that got to her. He's *wanted* for something.

Now, just when she needs to listen, Elissa comes back, shouting over the TV, "The bars are dull in the middle of the week. I made other plans. I had a lousy day."

Finger to her lips. She doesn't look back at Elissa. She hears the part about the red truck and she gets the license number, which she moves to a magazine to write down. She didn't hear what he did. Robbery, maybe. With that other guy who looks like him. Or maybe drugs. He was *very* interested in scoring some.

She switches channels.

"What is up?"

"I know him. I want to get the story."

"The criminal?" When Brittany nods, Elissa whistles in what sounds like a compliment.

"He was Australian. He had a whole different way of talking."

"What'd he do?"

"I'm trying to find out."

Unfortunately it's politics and sports and weather everywhere she looks.

Finally Elissa picks up her laptop, which has been sitting on an end table. "What's his name? I'm pulling up WTAE. This thing better have power."

"Ryan. Rutter."

Soon Elissa says, "Here it is. Brothers." She paused, reading. "Hit-and-run."

"Oh."

"Looks like they killed a woman."

"On purpose?"

"I don't know. Here, you read it." Brittany tilts the laptop screen to read the article. Elissa is already dialing the phone. She's saying, "I need the detectives on the hit-and-run case." She's *telling*. Grabbing even that for herself.

ADDIE SIGHS, DIGGING OUT HER KEYS, so rarely used. After a lifetime coming to Sugar Lake and feeling no fear, today she locks her doors, both of them, before going to her car.

There is just the faintest smack of cool dampness in the air. It's good weather for sleeping, just enough that she'll want the old wool blanket, the kind you can't find in the stores anymore, thick wool with a satin binding. She owns four of them for the lake house alone, not a one with moth holes, which is some sort of luck.

As she drives, she thinks, Lazy me, I could have walked, given myself some decent exercise. It's only a mile altogether, up the road and back.

Her station wagon *does* make a rattly sound all right, but that sound is, oh, twenty years old and nothing seems to come of it. The springs of the seats are completely worn; she's had to put pillows over them not to get poked in the butt. The upholstery has burst in places on the backs of the seats too, so there are towels draped over. All right, it's a bit hilarious looking, but it runs, and Archer rode in it many times. You could probably still scrape off skin samples, get his DNA. Maybe there is enough of Archer in the car to clone him.

Her car is just the right thing for the rough roads up here.

She rounds the bend just before Tom Jensen's place, thinking that surely she will learn later today that his trip was delayed because he got a cold or one of his daughters needed something or he sprained an ankle. In her mind, she is already comforting him for those things when she sees up ahead through the trees into his driveway that his car—yes, that's his car—is there.

Something jumps in her chest, a small electrical jab to her heart. She finds herself driving past his place, to give herself time to sort things out. Why wouldn't he call? Aha, maybe he came up with one of his kids or grandkids, with whom he's in a heavy conversation. Which means she should just turn around and go back home.

Her hands are shaking a little. What she takes in, peripherally, are the more isolated places up the road—larger tracts of land owned by people who can afford it. Some of them will sell in time when they need the money. Eventually Sugar Lake will be overdeveloped. And speaking of—she comes upon a construction tractor, a backhoe. She slows down to look. A foundation is going in.

Is Tom Jensen miffed? She must make it right. Even if he's with someone, she can poke her head in; she can offer a spaghetti dinner.

So she turns the car around in a dirt path that will one day be a gravel driveway. She drives back down the road more purposefully. Her heart is beating hard, but she can't let that stop her. She drives into his yard and parks behind his car. He still has pretty good hearing, so she fully expects to see him come to the door. But he doesn't. Nothing happens. He could be ill, needing her . . . an accident, a fall . . . These thoughts make her hurry toward the front door. It's ajar the smallest bit.

And she's right. She can hear a groan. She can also hear the television going.

"Tom? . . . Tom? It's Addie. I'm here."

It sounds like, "Go away."

"Tom? Are you all right?"

A whimper.

When she opens the door fully, several things happen in quick succession. The door slams behind her. That boy, Jack, appears before her, but he's not Jack after all; he's someone else. Jensen is calling loudly, "We have some trouble here. Go away, Addie. Let her go. Listen, she's nothing to do with this." The boy is pulling her hard through the living room. The place is all wrong, messy. Her keys fall out of her hand, to the floor. She's trying to see the boy, who looks like— He's the mate. He's not Jack.

Then he steps aside and ushers her into the sun porch, and there's the chair and Tom tied up in it.

"No. No. Untie him. You can't do this," she blurts.

The boy laughs. "You give the orders, do you?"

"I know what's going to get you in trouble. You're the one Jack calls his mate, his pal, I can figure that much. Where's Jack?"

"I don't answer the questions. See? That's how it is."

"You're hurting my arm."

"Good."

"Let her go," Tom groans.

"Are you kidding? She came in here. I didn't ask her to come. She walked right in. So we're going to let her keep you company."

"Please don't."

Addie's heart is setting up a racket, and she can't breathe right. She knows she must calm down physically to be able to help Tom. Working to fill her lungs, she lets the boy grab hold of her. This time he pulls her to the kitchen.

"Pick up a chair," he says. "Carry it back to that other room."

He's been drinking. He smells of booze and sweat and fear. Hand to her chest, she works to keep breathing. She grabs the chair firmly in the middle by the back slats so that she can swing it, hit him. . . .

"Oh, no, you don't." He jerks her hand away from the chair. "Should have used the gun with you. Didn't know you'd be such a fighter. I'll take the chair in, I'll do that for you." He pulls her around hard—it's almost a dancing move, a tango clutch, except that he slams a kitchen chair against her back and yanks them both to the sun porch, saying, "You two are a lotta lotta trouble."

"Let's talk money again," Jensen says.

"Let's not. Sit," he orders her.

She sits. "Run," Jensen mouths. The boy is tying a rope to the chair. Must he bind her? Crying out won't help. There is no one around yet. Quickly, the boy wraps the rope around her several times. "Please don't do this," she says. She's seen Jensen's arms are behind him, but the boy doesn't ask her to put hers behind, just keeps winding the rope around her body, then her legs. When he's done, it doesn't much matter; because of the kind of kitchen chair she's in, her arms are down at her sides, useless.

She's tried to take care of herself, hoping that one day, when it's time, a long time from now, she would die, quietly and without fuss, in her sleep. She never guessed at violence.

THE DETECTIVES HAD SIGNED OUT TWO CARS for Meadville, and they got on the road pretty quickly, Christie and Potocki in one car, Colleen and Dolan in the other. It was Dolan's turn to drive. Traffic was snarky at first. To entertain himself, Dolan spent time on the phone with Christie grumbling about this and that, including the traffic. The radio played snatches of song and talk as Colleen hit the search button. Her bulletin, if it was getting airtime, and she hoped it was, kept being out of sync with her search.

They took Route 79 to 322 to Meadville.

On the way, after Dolan got finished shooting the shit with Christie, he settled down and talked about his kids. They were heavy into dating, and he had a lot of worries. His daughter thought she was in love. Colleen was reminded of Purdy's woes.

"What did you say to her?"

"I tortured her some."

"How?"

"Joking. You know, 'I raised you to only be in love with your father until you were thirty. Where did I go wrong?' "

"I bet she was very receptive to that. Jeez, now that I think of it, McGranahan was telling me somewhat the same thing last year. You guys are really bad about your daughters." She looked to see if Dolan felt any pain at being compared with McGranahan, but it went right over his head.

"Right," he sighed. "Potocki's son's in love, too. He's not happy about it."

She knew about that. Potocki had mentioned it. "What about Boss's kids?" she asked.

"Still too young. But we've got him sweating it. So what do we have? Up in Meadville? Let's get serious."

"One of our boys went to this bar. He tried to steal money. There was a fight. He crawled off. This was two days ago. Meadville isn't big, but it isn't small. Probably they have somebody sheltering them. A friend. A relative. We probably still have to depend on the public."

"Call the mother?"

"I don't get the impression she's dying to help us. On the other hand she doesn't seem to be dying to help her boys either." Colleen looked through her notes and found the numbers for Rita Miner. When she looked up, she saw they were about to pass Wexford where Miner worked, so she called the work number first, hoping.

A man who answered with a stuffed-up nose said, "She went home at five. She's not doing the late shift tonight. Is there anything I can show you?"

"Not today."

"Are you sure?"

"Positive."

"What are you driving now, if I may ask?"

"A police car. Most days."

He stammered for a moment, looking for a way to transition to a sales pitch, but she said, "Sorry," and hung up.

She tried the home number for Miner. After a few rings, Miner picked up. And only after a pause, she said a careful hello. This in itself was interesting.

Colleen identified herself.

"I hear you put my boys on the telly."

"I had to. They may have information we need."

"I don't think it sounds quite like that. You better be sure you have something. Lawsuits are made of less than that."

"What I did is legal." Colleen was glad she sounded strong; she knew she was skating. Christie had told her as much. "Are your sons the ones who alerted you?"

"What do you mean?"

"Your boys. Are they complaining about their pictures on TV?"

"I wouldn't know."

"Have they been calling you?"

"No, and I don't have to tell you anyway."

"Well, you do actually have to." She made a face at Dolan, who could read the other half of the conversation easily. He smiled encouragement as she added, "There are charges for obstructing an investigation."

"I'm not obstructing anything." The connection went dead.

"She practically told me she knows something. I don't have enough to get her phone records. Yet. Christie is getting really strict."

"He's on a purity kick."

"Why?"

"In some kind of trouble, I guess. He didn't like the way I went after the baby killer, either."

"Well, with Miner . . . If we don't get anywhere in Meadville, I want you to finagle her phone records out of her. Also, make a go at her answering machine. Anything you can get."

"Why not you?"

"You're the sweet talker. She already hates me."

They passed Wexford, Portersville, Butler, Slippery Rock. "I never come up this way," she mused. "I hear about it all the time."

"It's nice up here. People can afford to buy a lot of land. Boss said he'd live up here if he didn't have to live in the city."

"You're kidding."

"That's what he said. About fifteen minutes ago."

"I think of him as a city boy."

"He likes his muskrats and groundhogs and all that, too."

"No fooling?"

After another half hour, Colleen got a phone call from Littlefield, who was on duty. "Another tip. Some girl apparently saw one of the boys. In a place called the Hi-Lite Café in Meadville. Her roommate called."

"Which boy?"

"Ryan."

"Where's she calling *from?*"

"Grove City."

"Ah. Good. That's pretty near Meadville."

"Yeah, it is."

"Give me the number. I'm ready."

She wrote down the number, then turned in the passenger seat to Dolan. "One boy was definitely up here roaming. We already have a second interview."

"Almost two hours from Pittsburgh—just irritating enough," Dolan said. "I wonder how much we're going to be back and forth before it's over. Some guys pack an overnight bag."

"We'll be awhile tonight, anyway," she thought aloud. She wanted her own bed, even if she got to it at two or three.

"Also," he warned as she dialed up her second witness, "we have to tangle with the local police up there. Always fun."

Territorial squabbles. Sand in the gears. Another long, long day.

CHRISTIE SAT IN THE PASSENGER SEAT, relaxed, looking at signs for rocking chairs, homemade Amish products, all kinds of country goods. Then there were the cows. "I like cows," he said. "They're peaceful. They just look around. Chew. Look around some more."

Potocki made a couple of faces that pretty much said he didn't know what to say.

"Marina would hate it. My kids would hate it. Maybe . . . maybe even I would hate it in time. I need the rush; well, I always thought I did. People surprise themselves. The ones you think could never retire do it and they do fine. The ones you think will do fine go seriously crazy and get senile quicker."

Potocki said, "It is peaceful up here. I can see that. My pace is changed already."

"You ever think about whether you'll get married again?"

"I expect I will."

Christie had pretty much decided not to ask his next question; then, as if he had no control over his mouth, it came out anyway. "Is the woman you're seeing—isn't she a doctor or some . . . ?"

"Yeah, she's a doctor. General practice."

"You think she's the one?"

"I don't know. Too early to say."

"Did I step hard on something between you and our Greer?"

Potocki blushed. He said, "I don't know what you did."

"I just said it was to be handled carefully, and I separated you as partners in case you did get involved or . . . stay involved. I don't mean to pry." *What a lie,* Marina would say. *Prying is what you do.* And she'd be right.

"Greer lost interest in checking it out."

"Oh."

"She told me to move on. I did. She said—this was funny—she said no man knows what he's doing after a divorce. He needs at least two or three years of desperate dating before he knows who he is again."

"Women will say anything."

"They will. Especially when they need to punch out your ego."

"But she likes you. I know that. She likes you a lot. Respects you, too."

"Good. I think so. We're pals."

"Good. So if I had to switch assignments ever again, you'd be okay working with her."

"Oh . . . yeah."

"I'll ask her, too." Christie's phone rang. It was Colleen, updating him about the Grove City girls.

"She's moving the pieces," Christie said after hanging up. "She's got a second witness in the area." He looked over at Potocki. "Ever since the first case with us, she worries she's too impulsive. She's always checking herself not to be reckless."

Potocki said, "She's not. She's smart. Good instincts."

"I know."

Cows. Horses. Old barns. Beautiful. Very inviting. Christie studied each successive scene, pretending he'd changed his life and lived out here full-time.

HE'D BEEN STANDING ON HIS FEET ALL DAY. He'd worked nineteen hours altogether over the two days and had a hundred fourteen dollars in his pocket because Penny told the boss he needed the money right away. She also gave him takeout containers and a plastic bag to carry the leftovers she'd saved up for him.

He heard a snatch of popular radio music from somewhere. A couple of people were out in their yards. He walked briskly, with a sense of purpose, toward the road that took him in the opposite direction of Sugar Lake—in case anyone was watching him. Throw them off. He'd turn around in a little bit. Or . . . did he want to hitch a ride to Pittsburgh after all? Get away from Ryan?

He felt lost to think it.

When he got off the streets to a rural road, he eyed an old barn that was falling apart, painted a dark, almost grayish red. He slowed his pace until he was sure there was no one driving by and he went around behind it. Man, he just needed to stop for a while. "Standing will kill you," Penny said. "Young and old, it gets the legs. Only cure is to lie down, prop them up."

It's after eight o'clock now. He can't quite remember how he'd managed the two-hour walk last night. His fatigue is so great, he decides to hang out here at the barn for another hour, then go sit in back at the library until Ryan realizes he needs help and comes to pick him up. It'll be ten, eleven at night by then, maybe later.

He sits on a concrete block behind the barn and opens the bag. Several rolls. Butter. Applesauce. Half a ham-and-cheese sandwich. Meat loaf dinner, completely new and untouched. Couple of pieces of cheese. The meat loaf dinner smells good, but he saves it for Ryan.

RYAN STANDS OR PACES behind the two old ones, studying the backs of their heads. He's still holding the gun, even though it's a big bother. They obey the power of the gun.

He notices the color of gray their hair is—not the same for each of them. Hers is whitish, his is grayish. Also, the guy's is getting thin. Man, old is . . . hopeless. Can't move fast, can't think.

All day he's been trying to get rid of flashes of the other old man. Sometimes he thinks the man lived. Other times not. Which is worse, which is worse? He paces out of the sun porch into the living room and to the front door. There's nothing good, ever, to looking back. Think what's next. Look ahead. He has a choice of vehicles now and keys to all of them.

Feeling wobbly with drink, he bends over to look at the tumblers that fell when he got into it with Jensen. Neither glass broke. He plunks them on the coffee table and goes back to the sun porch to fetch his bottle. Empty, save for two drops.

"Liquor goes fast in this place," he says, mimicking his mother, who used to quote some movie. There are several more bottles in the carton, but some of it is just wine.

"What are you going to do?" Jensen asks.

"I guess you'd like to know."

"I'm thinking, wouldn't it be better to let me drive you to someplace way off? You could lie down on the backseat. I could drive all night."

"You think you could stay awake for a long drive?"

"Yes."

"Maybe. There are two of us."

"Two of you could fit in the backseat. With blankets you could be out of sight . . . especially at night."

Ryan thinks about this. He stoops at the carton of liquor, deciding. Wine—two white, two red. Some kind of labels he can't read, French or something. He chooses instead the bottle of vodka. He opens it, pours a little into a glass, and looks up at Jensen.

"What do I do with her if we go?"

"Leave her here."

Ryan looks at her blue eyes studying him. "You want some vodka, lady?"

"I wouldn't mind a sip."

"You kidding?"

"No, I like vodka now and then."

"Way to go, grandma." He pours another splash into the glass he's using. The question on his face is, *How do you do it without hands?*

She says simply, "Just bring it to me, I'll catch a sip." Her eyes are still fixed on him.

"Here. Have some." He tips the glass, a little of it spills, but she gets two sips. "Don't waste," he says. "You, too, old boy?"

"Yes."

"What is it with you two, huh? You like the sauce." He gives Jensen a sip. "The rest is for me. And my brother."

Jensen says, "Think about my offer."

"I'd want you both to go, of course. Sitting up front where we can watch you."

"No—"

"It's all right," the old lady says. "I'd go. I'm a good driver."

"Are you really?" Ryan asks.

"Yes. I drove across the country just two years ago."

"In that trap you drive?"

"No. I used a different car."

"Where were you going?" Ryan slugs the rest of the glassful.

"I always wanted to see the Grand Canyon. And I did. I went to Reno and Santa Fe. I crossed over the country in the South, across

Texas. I was glad I did it, the trip. It's . . . worth seeing other parts of the—"

"Shut it. I can't think with you talking."

She doesn't say anything more.

Ryan goes into the living room and drinks, just sits and drinks until he falls asleep.

"IT'S QUIET," JENSEN SAYS in an almost whisper. Because the television is still on, he's not sure Addie can hear him, but she's looking at him to read his lips. He repeats himself with more volume.

She says, "Maybe he went out. Did you hear a door?"

"No."

"I tried to pay attention," she says ruefully.

"We have to get you out of this. If I get him to agree to the drive . . . *don't come.* I'll get someone to come back for you. I'll do something."

She doesn't answer for a long time. Then she says, "I'm not sure they're going to let you go. In the long run, with two of us, maybe we can think of something."

"I don't want you in that situation," he says as loudly and clearly as he dares.

"I wonder what's going to happen when his brother comes. He . . . he didn't seem this tough. Maybe I can't judge character anymore. Do you think he's listening to us?"

"I don't know."

"Can you move at all? How tight are your bindings?"

"Bad. My hands feel numb. I can't move." What he doesn't say because the boy may be listening is that he's been trying to work his hands loose and that he has hope he might manage it in time.

After a while of waiting for sound from the other room, she asks a little more loudly, "How did it happen? All this? They were camped out here?"

"It would have been since the hit-and-run. In Pittsburgh." He can see she didn't know. "A woman was killed."

"Oh. Oh. I saw—they did that?"

He speaks carefully, as quietly as he can. "I didn't put it together at first, but just before you got here, it was on the news—their names and pictures."

"Oh, that was a terrible thing. She had children. She was young."

"People are looking for them. That's our . . . hope," he finishes quietly.

They wait again to listen for evidence that he's heard them. There isn't a sound.

"Why here?"

"Remember the summer we rented? The family we kicked out? I guess when the boys got in trouble, they remembered enough to come up here."

Addie says, "I'm pretty sure this one . . . drove into my yard the other morning. A truck drove in, then zoomed away. Can you hear anything now?"

"No." After a silence, he says, "I promise. I'll do something."

"We have to. We have to."

Almost mouthing the words, he says, "Broken glass would work to cut the ropes. I keep looking around. The window. Or a drinking glass. But how to get to a piece of glass . . ."

"Believe me, I'm thinking," she says, "all of that."

"I wanted to see you, but I came up here first. He had the gun and then he fought me."

Another silence goes by. He listens carefully and without raising his voice much says, "The kid burned my photos he found in the attic. Pictures of the family."

Her face shows she's concentrating and got it. "Why would he do that?"

There is a crash from the other room. They freeze and stay quiet for a long time. The kid smashed something? Why is it quiet now? Jensen can't tell what the sound was. He listens for more, tries to pick up what else there is beyond the voices and sounds coming from the television.

There is nothing.

JACK SLIPS AROUND TO THE BACK OF THE LIBRARY, and looking around, feels no one has followed, so he curls up on a slab of pavement. After a while, he positions himself so that he can better look out into the street. When he sees a police car go by, then another, he realizes it could be a simple thing that ruins them—Ryan driving down the hill recklessly or a policeman arresting him for loitering.

Ryan isn't here, that's for sure. Jack indulges in a fantasy. Break into the building. Wash up. Inside there would be better places to sleep—wooden floors, probably. Sleep, then go to work at five in the morning. He gets up from his cement pallet to try the doors and windows of the library. Nothing doing, it's locked up tight. He curls up again on the concrete.

When they are out of this, he needs to get away from Ryan. But right now, what he wants most is the red truck and his big brother taking him to the next step, whatever it is.

J. T. KNOERDLE COULDN'T GIVE THEM ANYTHING more than what he reported on the phone: A punk kid came in and got into a fight. Left in a red truck. That was it.

Christie and Dolan are hanging back at the bar to question customers and to contact the local police to keep it all aboveboard, while Potocki and Greer have been sent to question the college girls.

Potocki is driving, Greer navigating.

"Boss says he might partner us again. I'm okay with it," Potocki says. "Whatever."

"Me too. Absolutely."

They find the three-story apartment complex in Grove City and are buzzed in immediately. They walk up to the second floor.

One girl opens the apartment door, and another girl quickly appears behind her. The place is classic student living—beige furniture and potato chips. One girl is miserable looking, heavyset and hiding behind makeup; the other, the one who answered the door, is energetic, trim and shapely, but she's overly proud of her butt, which she sticks out every chance she gets. She indicates that the police may have the best seats, the sofa.

The pretty one does the talking. "I didn't know the guy. I didn't see him. When Brittany told me she'd met him, I made the call to you guys. It's important, right?"

"Very," Colleen says. She addresses the chubby girl. "Did he by any chance have an accent?"

"Oh, yes, he was Australian."

"Take a look at these two pictures. Can you say which one it was?"

Brittany looks for a moment and chooses Ryan. She whispers, "Did he kill that woman—the hit-and-run?"

"Right now he's simply a person of interest who could tell us more."

Brittany says, "Oh, good."

The other girl makes a face that indicates she is not as naïve as Brittany is.

Colleen and Potocki in silent agreement ignore her and turn to Brittany. Colleen says, "Tell us about him. Anything he said."

Brittany pauses, working up an answer.

Elissa twitches in her seat. "She liked him."

"He was pleasant to you?" Colleen asks.

"He was funny. You know, joking. He told me he didn't have any money. I believed him. He dug into his pockets and nothing."

"Was he on something? High?"

"I don't know for sure."

"Did he ask about drugs?"

Brittany looks nervous.

"Answer," says Elissa.

"He was interested in anything going, I think," Brittany finally says.

"He specifically asked for crack," Elissa tells them.

Brittany looks miserable.

"Did he say who he was staying with or where he was staying?"

"No."

"Did you see the red truck?"

"No. I wasn't outside at all."

"What time was all this?"

"Ten thirty, eleven. More like eleven or later."

"I need for you to write down the address of the bar," Colleen tells Brittany.

Elissa takes the legal pad from Colleen and hands it over to Brittany, who begins to print the name and address carefully.

"And definitely call me if you think of anything else. Did you give your address or phone number?"

"No."

"Anything *I* can do?" Elissa asks.

Potocki smiles. "Not that I can think of."

When they're out the door, Colleen says to Potocki, "We could hit the place, see if there's another witness. I think the incident at J.T.'s bar happened second, later in the evening."

"Right. Right. Sounds that way." They get into the car; he starts it up. "To think, these are the girls who are going to be after my son in a couple of years."

"I feel bad for the big one. The little one keeps trying to squelch her."

"I feel bad for both."

Colleen's phone rings as she's buckling up. "You two eating somewhere?" Dolan asks.

"Not yet."

"We're at a place in Meadville. We're about to order their giant burgers and fries. Should we order for you?"

"You want a burger?" she asks Potocki.

"Absolutely," Potocki says. "I almost ate Brittany's potato chips."

"We were just about to check out the other bar our boy went to," she tells Dolan.

A muffled conversation ensues. Dolan says, "Boss says to hold off. Boss is thinking to organize some cooperation with the locals, keep them happy. He's doing his thing. So come here first."

"Burger first," she tells Potocki. "Orders." She looks over at Potocki driving, and maybe it's only because he's fixed up lately, but he seems so . . . calm, steady. She has to resist reaching over, back of the hand against his chest, familiar.

"How are things with your new woman?" she asks.

He draws back a little in surprise. "Okay . . . people say I'm lucky."

"You are."

"She's hauling my ass into the better restaurants. She took me to a symphony—she already had the tickets. I took her to a country music concert. Made her eat ribs. We're stretching each other. She's smart, not just about medicine." He added, "You're upscale dating too."

"We haven't gone anywhere yet except restaurants. I may get to an art house film this weekend."

"Maybe we should introduce them to each other," Potocki says, laughing.

"Mebbe." She's pretty sure Steve Purdy is still hung up on wife number one and simply extending his period of desperate dating. By the time they get to the restaurant where Christie and Dolan are waiting, she has the beginning of a nasty hunger headache.

Dolan has two beer bottles on the table in front of him.

Potocki orders a beer and she orders a Scotch first, then a beer to follow. The waitress who takes their orders says that the burgers and fries are ready and waiting and she'll bring them right out. Altogether it's a pretty efficient stop.

Christie is saying, "I called a few guys I know of up here. I'm keeping this friendly. What happened with your witness?"

"The girl fingered the older boy as the one who is roaming the town. He must have friends up here. If only the mother would cooperate . . ."

"The mother," Christie says, grunting.

"Well, Boss, I've been wanting Artie to give it a go. And he could try Chester again now that we have a geographical area to quiz him about."

"Good idea. I agree. Artie would do a fantastic job with Chester. He's a slippery kid." When Dolan frowns, he adds, "We'll all probably be going back to the 'burgh tonight. We're not abandoning you. We can come back up here again tomorrow morning."

The waitress brings the burgers. Potocki puts his fries, or a good portion of them, on his burger. Colleen follows suit; she likes them this way, Pittsburgh style.

Christie smiles benignly at her. She guesses that means he doesn't mind the Scotch, which she downs quickly.

IT'S PAST TEN THIRTY when Ryan wakes up from his vodka sleep. He stumbles out of the room and hurries into the sun porch, where he finds the two old folks talking quietly.

"My daughter . . . ," the old man is saying.

"Shut your yaps. What time is it?"

"From what's on TV, I'd guess not yet eleven," says Jensen. "There's a clock in the kitchen."

Ryan shakes his head, trying to focus. "Anybody come in here?"

"Nobody."

Ryan holds on to furniture on his way to the kitchen, and even so, his legs are giving him a fight, wobbly. Okay. Ten forty. He splashes his face with water from the sink and takes a long drink of it before collapsing into a kitchen chair. So where's his fucking brother? Think, think.

Somebody saw the news and has taken Jack in for questioning.

Jack saw the news and ran.

How can he deal with two people on his own? He gets up and splashes more water on his face and sinks back down. He's going to have to get out of this place in one of the cars. His heart knocks out a message of fear. He's still sitting, staring at the gas stove, and it's staring back at him. Didn't Jack say without matches, you get nothing but gas? Well then, it's one of his options.

Then he remembers—wasn't there something about the back of a schoolhouse or library?

The keys to the two vehicles owned by the old people are in the living room. He leans on the sink and pours a glass of water.

Both sets of car keys are on the side table in the living room, where he'd put them. He takes both.

Jack had better be there.

The old lady's station wagon is closest to the road. It's rusty and doesn't look too reliable. But he sees something in the backseat that attracts him—a big old brimmed hat. The rear door is stuck. He gets in front and reaches around for the hat so that driving down the road, he'll look like the old biddy bird. Putting the hat on lifts his spirits. He's going to get out of this yet.

The car, however, keeps veering to the right where the ditches are. He sticks to the center of the road, figuring he can edge over if somebody comes the other way. As luck would have it, nobody does. He makes it to the bottom of the hill and turns to drive the seven miles toward town. The car continues to drift to the right.

He's not the whole way into town yet when he sees the ragged ragamuffin that is his dim brother trudging along the road toward him. He starts to pick up speed to give Jack a scare when he remembers what started all this.

He slows down, toots the horn, and comes to a stop. He reaches over and opens the passenger door. "Hop in. Old lady offering you a ride." He waits for Jack to laugh. "No. It's a disguise, see?"

Jack gets in. Ryan turns the car around in what might be somebody's driveway. "How'd you get this car? Take the fucking hat off. How'd you get it?"

"Took it."

"Shit. Shit. What are you doing? We have to take it back. Did she see you take it?"

"Nope."

"How do you know?"

"I know."

"My God. You're cracked. Now you stole a car." After a pause, Jack says, "I have money now. We could be going." He seems to know nothing of what is going on.

"Not wise. Good thing I'm the brains," Ryan says.

"Why do you have this car?"

"You haven't seen a TV, have you?"

"No . . ."

"We're on the news. Nobody tell you?" Jack shakes his head. "They got our pictures now. Our names. They got everything."

"On the news?"

"Everything. Even our license number. It's probably on the eleven o'clock news right now."

"Then . . . then it's all over. Isn't it?"

"It's complicated. I'm considering what they call a hostage situation."

"Oh, my God," Jack says, staring at him. "Slow down. Tell me what you did."

AT FIRST IT'S DARK except for the television. Then a glaring ceiling light comes on and the boy Jack is before her.

"Don't touch the ropes," the other one, Ryan, says. "And get the fucking light off."

The light goes off. Jack seems to be speaking to her. "We're going to go soon. My brother needs to get to someplace safe."

Suddenly Jack is hauled away physically. She can't even see him anymore, but she can hear the scuffling and cursing and the other one saying, "Whose side are you on, stupid cunt-ass-motherfucker?"

Jensen says, "I can't see what's happening."

She can't see either and she can hear only the occasional thump, but she knows. "Jack is getting beat up," she says.

Jensen calls out, "Let him go. Just come back here where we can work on this. Let us talk to both of you."

They can't hear what the boys are saying. They hear noises, furniture scraping, and the sounds of bitter conversation. After a silence, both boys appear before them. "Offer of money, I know," Ryan says. "Believe me, we'll take your money. I have your thirty-two bucks."

"I can drive you out of town. We can go to a bank machine."

"Think we're dumb, huh," Ryan says. "Bank machines have cameras. We don't need any cameras."

Addie studies them. Jack is wearing the same cotton T-shirt he had on when he came to work for her. Ryan is wearing one of Jensen's old flannel shirts. "Where'd you go all day?" she asks Jack. "Did you take the job with Emma Hopper?"

"No."

Ryan pushes at Jack, poking him in the chest. "Why did you answer her?"

Jack says, "I have money. Over a hundred. Let's go."

"Man, are you stupid. What, just go?"

"Yeah."

"Leave them to talk?"

"We'd be gone. Long gone."

Ryan chews on the thought, wets his lips.

"I need water," Addie says. "If you leave, just let us have some water we can get to."

"What? Lap it up like dogs?"

"If necessary," she says. "Also. I'd like to be untied for a moment, so I can go up to the bathroom. You can guard me. Even in prisons, they let a prisoner go to the john. You should give each of us a chance. There are two of you. We could go one at a time."

"Why'd we do that?" Ryan asks.

"In case you ever get taken in. If it happens that way, it'll go better with you if you treated us with decency."

Ryan stiffens. "I don't plan to be taken in."

"Of course not. It's a gamble."

"Oh, fucking let her go to the john," Jack says.

"Thank you," she almost whispers. "It might take a while for me to get my arms and legs moving. I'll do it as fast as I can."

"Well, let's just do it, then," Jack says.

"I'm pretty numb."

"Numb*skull,*" Ryan mutters.

"We'll be all right if we just have a little water," she tells him. "Maybe put a table between us with some bowls of water. Or put us in the kitchen. We don't expect anyone to come by for several days." Saturday. That's four days.

Ryan nods almost imperceptibly, reaches for the gun, and holds it at the ready while Jack studies the ropes on the old lady and begins to untie them.

At the sight of the gun, Addie has to force herself to talk. "People can be without food for a pretty long time. Not without water. I guess you know that."

Ryan rolls his eyes. Jack fumbles roughly with the ropes. When she feels them loosen, she flexes her arms and feet.

"This will take a minute," she warns, standing and getting her bearings. "I'm okay. Just stiffer than usual."

The idea of moving again—God, how wonderful, like a cripple being given a cure by Jesus. Gratitude fills her. She shifts her weight from leg to leg, preparing to climb the stairs. She can't even think about being tied up again.

"Okay. I believe I can do it." She reaches over and touches Tom's face. His eyes have tears in them. "I'm fine," she tells him.

Ryan hangs behind for a moment with Tom Jensen, but then she hears him coming up behind her and muttering to Jack, "Watch her."

"I'm watching her," Jack says.

"Go in the bathroom with her."

"Okay. I will."

Jack comes into the bathroom with her, shuts the door partway. "Sorry about this," he barks.

She had hoped to slip a razor blade into her waistband. Even a small glass that she could break—but there is no hope of that with Jack here.

She tilts her wrist. Her watch tells her it's twenty minutes till twelve. He turns away from her as she lifts her skirt.

She thinks, These may be my last moments. She looks out the window at the night. "Stars," she says, because she knows the kind of thing Jack likes. "They're more three-dimensional out here in the country. They're clear tonight. That means good weather tomorrow. Maybe you'll be on the road by then."

"You watching her?" Ryan calls.

"Yeah." A lie.

She looks at Jack, turned away. But there is nothing to grab hold of, nothing at all to use.

"Who was driving the truck last week? When that woman was killed?" she asks in a voice so low, she isn't sure he hears her.

The boy doesn't answer.

"I don't think it was you. I think you're protecting him. He's not like you."

"What's she yapping about?"

"Nothing."

"Don't be stupid. Watch her."

Jack turns to her as she's pulling up her drawers. He sees her old-lady body. "We're all made the same," she says. "We're—"

"Piss and shit levels us. I know about that."

"I knew you could finish it for me. You'll want me to go out ahead of you. Thank you for this break. It meant a lot."

"Well, it's the last one."

"I understand."

Ryan is standing at the bottom of the stairs with the rifle pointed up at her. Fury fills her that she will end like this. She descends the steps, noting how her body moves, looking at her feet, at her hand on the banister, not at Ryan. If he's going to do it, she doesn't want to give it her last bit of attention. Without sentiment, she thanks her muscles for working, her heart for not tossing an attack.

When she reaches the foot of the stairs, Ryan orders, "Take her to the kitchen."

"Why?"

"Just do it."

She walks erectly, expecting a shot. Her eyes cast over the mess of the kitchen, looking for something, an idea.

"What are you looking at?" Ryan is suddenly in front of her with the gun in one hand. She looks at him, unflinching. He slaps at her face hard. She can feel her hearing aid slip out. She tries to catch it but misses. At first it's only a foot away on the floor. She reaches toward it, but he kicks it out of the way and shoves at her with the gun. Then he yanks her violently down to the chair. "Get her rope from the front room," he commands his brother. "Let's get this biddy tied down."

Jack leaves and comes back with the rope.

She slips forward by a quarter inch or so and arches her back. If he doesn't notice, the bindings will have some slack.

"Tie her like I did. Arms to her sides, each leg to a leg of the chair."

Jack proceeds to tie her. At first his movements are rough, then not so rough. He doesn't ask her to sit back in the chair. She's not sure how much room she's given herself, maybe hardly any at all.

"Let's give the old guy his last piss and bring him in here."

Last. She heard that. If only she could talk to Jack instead of Ryan.

Both boys leave the kitchen. Testing briefly, she finds she has a little movement, not much, but she leans back now to hide the fact. She waits. God, God, don't let Tom do or say the wrong thing. Don't let him get himself shot.

It seems forever until she can make out the noises of them coming into the kitchen. They put Tom across the table from her. She can tell the way he's looking around, he wants to try something. She shakes her head slightly, hoping he'll see. *Don't. The one with the gun is dangerous. Don't.*

Tom groans as Jack ties him. He works the same way, arms at the sides, each leg wrapped to a chair leg. We can move, she thinks. We can scrape forward in the chair, get to the cabinets, pick up a knife with our teeth. I have not given up.

Jack puts two bowls of water on the table between them. The kitchen clock shows it's ten minutes to twelve.

"Get more rope. Tie the chairs to the table," Ryan says.

Oh God, oh God.

"I don't know if they can reach the water, you know, to drink."

"It doesn't matter. We should burn the truck."

"That'd bring somebody too quick."

"Right, right. Look at them, listening to us."

THE FOUR PITTSBURGH DETECTIVES have been sitting in the station in Meadville, facing Tom Senteros, the Meadville chief, and now three other guys come in and take their seats. There is an uneasy edge—the unspoken, *If it's a good case, don't take it from us. If it's our territory, let us do it our way.*

Senteros is fresh-faced and young looking, though he is about forty-five; he wears round glasses that give him a bookish, innocent look.

Christie introduces his team to the new guys. Potocki, Colleen, and Dolan nod in turn as he says their names.

Tom Senteros, pointing to a plainclothes fellow who looks sleepy, adds, "This is Collins. He's ours, Meadville."

The one state trooper, tipping back his hat, says tightly, extending his hand, "Seeger." The other says, "Wilkes," no hand extended, but a friendlier sound.

Christie gives the impression they have all the time in the world by presenting the case in an easy, thoughtful manner. "Your offices have always been helpful in the past. I hate barging into somebody else's territory, especially getting on to midnight, but we had these calls earlier this evening and we wanted to move fast, see what we have. It's complicated in this way: The persons of interest are young. Maybe stupid. Probably scared. Probably reckless. It's tricky."

"You have positive ID on them? Killing that woman?" Senteros asks.

"Last Saturday night," Collins murmurs, catching up.

"We have a tip," is all Christie says, for they have no proof at all that these were the boys who actually killed Navarro. "We're just about to leave town tonight, but we wanted to alert you. We're able to come back early tomorrow morning, see if there is anything else we can do. I'm wanting us to work together on this."

"What are you asking from us?"

"Just that you help us look for the Chevy pickup in this area. Red—a '94 or '95. The boys might still be here."

Collins puts up a hand. "I can help with that. I know Meadville."

At that point, Colleen's phone rings. She reads the ID, says, "It's our desk," and makes a move to excuse herself. A flicker of irritation goes through the others.

"You have the particulars handy?" Senteros asks.

Potocki at the ready hands over a sheet of paper with everything printed out neatly. "They probably changed the license plate by now."

"Surely," Senteros grumbles, "if they have a brain."

"We don't like 'em too smart back home," Dolan says.

They all laugh briefly.

"So . . . what, they know somebody up here? Go to college up here?"

"Explain what's next," Christie orders Dolan.

"Okay. They didn't make it out of high school. They didn't run with a college crowd. Something drove them up here. In a bit, I'm going back to the 'burgh to work on the mother and one of the friends, see if we can find that out."

Senteros nods toward a wall clock. It's a few minutes before midnight. "You going to wake folks up?"

"Gonna try."

Colleen comes back into the room. "Two sightings," she says. "And they match. One of the boys, the younger brother, works in the kitchen in a café in Cochranton. The cook there saw the eleven o'clock news. She liked him fine. It might be why she took a little time to make up her mind to call. She's willing to meet us at the café. We can do a quick print of the place. The good news is he's due back at work at five in the morning. The other is a Bill Guinnert, who ran into two boys who looked alike—different times—and they match the pictures. And he mentioned the accent as 'fake Australian.' The café worker is the big lead."

"Cochranton has their own police," Christie says cheerfully. "You have their number?"

Senteros says, "I do. Are we getting to the point of overkill?"

"There's room for everybody," Christie says, "and I will be real glad when we know if we've got the right guys. Everybody's invited to Cochranton. Let's keep our eye out for the truck the whole way."

"Somebody's garage," Collins mutters.

"You got it," Dolan says. "Or over a hillside or burnt up. Somebody's going to see it sooner or later."

Senteros's phone rings. They all watch him while he listens, grunting. When he hangs up, he says, "Nuisance call. Dog that won't stop barking. I'll dispatch someone."

IN THE LIVING ROOM OF THE JENSEN PLACE, Jack takes his brother by the shoulders and shakes him hard. He has just got his brother to put down the gun. "You aren't thinking, man. You aren't thinking at all."

"Yeah, I am. You're a pussy, that's all."

"The other was an accident. This is—"

"Shut it."

"No, no, no, the old man has a point. Let them do the driving while we make sure they get us out of town. Oh, man, why didn't you just get out when the old man came home?" Jack's heart is going a hundred miles an hour.

"I can't think." Ryan sits down. His eyes are flashing craziness.

"Leave the gun behind. Wipe the prints off."

"I want the gun."

"Too bad." Jack tries to steady his own thoughts. Everything is going so fast now, he can't catch up to it. "We have to buy time. I . . . I think we take the truck and one car down the road, put the truck in the old lady's garage, close the door to the garage, then come back and each of us go in a different car—meet up on the road a bit later, dump one of the cars."

"That's bullshit."

"They're looking for two of us together. It gives each of us a fighting chance. We only need twenty-four hours to get real far away. Pick a direction. Not north. If we started north, they'll keep looking north. We should just go—"

"Bullshit, bullshit."

"No gun, no noise, no burning the truck, no fire. We drive for twenty-four hours. I'll drive the old lady's car. I'll dump it after six hours. Which direction you want? East, west, south?"

"Fuck this. How will I know where you are?"

"You won't lose me. I'll be behind you on the road. Pick a direction."

"South."

"South. That's Route Seventy-nine. Take it the whole way to West Virginia. Wherever Seventy-nine ends. There'll be a gas station or something. You'll see 'End of Highway' or some such sign, that's where you find me—if I lose you, which I won't. It's going to work out."

"Why'm I listening to you? I been dragging you along all my life, retarded little brother—"

Jack is hauling Ryan up off the couch. He swings with both hands, wildly, until he lands one good punch on the jaw. He's shocked at the feeling of his fist against the bones in his brother's jaw. The surprise almost stops him from the push and shove he does next.

Moments later, Ryan lies sprawled on the floor.

Jack says, "You were the one driving the truck. I stuck with you this long. Listen to me or else."

Ryan stands up unsteadily and shuffles toward the door. He digs in his pockets and tosses two keys to Jack, hardly looking at him.

Without a word, he goes out, gets into the truck, and waits for Jack to move Jensen's car and the old station wagon out of the way.

Jack moves as fast as he can, first angling Jensen's Nissan sloppily and then getting into the old lady's station wagon and backing out.

Both of them know not to put on lights; they drive down the road slowly at midnight. There are towels on the back of his seat to cover the old upholstery and cushions beneath him—the stuff feels like it's grabbing at him. He can almost smell something pleasant, like perfume or shampoo, very faint, along with the fumes of exhaust. He thinks, Better drive with the window open, but when he tries, he finds the handle is broken. He reaches over and winds down the passenger window.

Why would she not get a better car?

The truck is moving oddly. Jack realizes Ryan is reaching for the glove compartment while he drives, taking something, putting it in his pants pocket. The stem. Ryan will buy crack again as soon as he can. Hopeless. Why does he keep hoping? When they get to the path that leads to the old lady's place, Jack pulls in, leaving room for Ryan, who drives the truck straight into the open garage, putting on the parking lights for only a second, then switching them off. He emerges, his walk still unsteady, and pulls hard at a rope over his head to close the garage door. He fumbles with the handle, back and forth.

By then Jack is out of the station wagon.

"It won't lock," Ryan mutters.

"Give it up. She told me she doesn't believe in locks."

"Think there's more money in the house?"

"I don't know."

"Let's look."

"I saw you take the pipe out of the glove compartment."

"I might cadge something down the road. Let's go in there." Ryan points to the house.

Jack doesn't stop Ryan, just says, "Be quick. Real quick. We have to get going."

Ryan tries the front door and a moment later grabs at the set of keys in Jack's hand. "So she doesn't believe in locks, but today for whatever reason . . ." Ryan jiggles the key impatiently and finally gets the door open. "Smells good in here," he says.

Something she was cooking, chili or something. "If she has any money, it's going to be in that dining room cabinet. I watched her. That's where she keeps it."

Ryan begins searching the cabinet.

Jack goes to the kitchen. In the moonlight he can see the box of spaghetti on the counter and a big pot with water on the stove next to a pot that holds sauce. He doesn't put on a light. Instead he lets Ryan rattle around in the other room, looking for money. He dips a finger in the sauce and tastes. Then he uses a big spoon that's sitting on the stove and scoops some. It's thick with meatballs and things, definitely the best sauce he ever tasted.

Another smell hits him. He traces it to a large rectangle with foil on top at the far end of the counter. A cake. A whole cake. The pungent chocolate rises to greet him. He feels around in cabinets until he finds a plastic container with a lid. He scoops as much sauce as he can into the container and has another mouthful before going back to his brother. "Any money?"

"No. Found a purse under a pillow in the living room. Nothing in it. We should go upstairs."

"No. We're getting out. Get moving. You're losing time."

Ryan looks at him. "What is that you took? You already have all that stuff from the restaurant."

"Something she cooked. You can have all the restaurant stuff."

"I'm not hungry. I had Jensen's food."

"And his liquor."

"You bet."

They get into the old lady's car and drive back up the road

together. Partway there, Ryan takes out the pipe and looks defiantly at Jack. "You're afraid of everything," he says.

"ARE YOU OKAY?"

"I'm . . . okay. I lost my hearing aid. Sorry I can't hear much."

"They were fighting. They left a bit ago," he says loudly. "But I think it sounded like they're coming back."

"Going upstairs—it gave me hope."

All the while he was up, climbing the stairs, he should have *grabbed* something—a towel. Hit out. But he was afraid Ryan would use the gun. Possible survival versus almost certain death. The story of the Jews and the Nazis. And he'd always thought he would fight rather than succumb.

How long until someone finds them? How will his children be told? He can imagine his obituary, respectful, the people of Sugar Lake and Pittsburgh mulling over the words in the paper, police keeping a watch on the Sugar Lake house so funeral raiders don't snag whatever the boy left behind. He sees the newscaster's face reporting the shooting. He sees his body in a coffin. It's real to him, imagined without sentiment. He sees his daughters arguing about who should have taken better care of him and then turning their minds to selling the place. He can picture people like the boy's mother, come to buy the place for a song, then living there, tough people who aren't spooked by the idea of a double murder.

He can't move. He can't do anything.

Addie says, "I'm going to get my hand free in time. I don't want them to see."

His spirits lift again. "Hurry," he says. "Can you hear me?"

"I'm trying to move this— The one boy, I should have talked to him more. I believe in talking and I didn't say the right things."

"They're going to be back," he shouts. "Are you making any headway?"

"I don't have it yet. My shoulder hurts. I have to move my whole arm to get my hand free. I'll do it. Don't give up."

"Watch me," he orders. She looks up from her concentration on the ropes. "If I can talk them into the drive, you stay here."

"No, both of us. If we could move, we'd do *something*."

"Shhh. Quiet." He wants to weep. If they creep back quietly and hear her, there's going to be no hope at all.

Then he's sure. "I hear them," he practically shouts. "Don't talk now. They're here."

"Are you sure?"

"Yes."

"What's happening?"

He listens. "They're moving around. I can't tell."

Jack comes into the kitchen and looks at them. He's clearly agitated.

"Would you be able to move the water a little closer? I can't reach it," she says.

He brings the bowl to her lips and lets her drink. His face is angry, scowling. He puts the bowl closer to her on the table and angles her chair a little differently. Jensen watches without asking anything for himself. He can hear the thump, thump, thump that must be the windows being closed. It means they're going to shoot. They want to mute the sound.

He urges Jack, "Talk to your brother. I could get you into Canada by morning. Nobody is going to be looking for my car."

Ryan enters the kitchen. "Still blabbing. Get going," he says to his brother. "Go on."

Ryan checks the windows and closes the one that's open while Jack leaves the room. Ryan, too, is scowling. He looks uncertain, but at least he doesn't have the rifle in hand.

The next thing Jensen knows is that Ryan is pulling at the kitchen door that leads to the living room. It's a swinging door that's almost never been closed in all these years, so it's stubborn; it budges finally and swings shut. Then Ryan opens the oven door and turns the knob. A hissing sound begins. Tom looks at Addie. She understands.

"Please, no," she says. "Just let us be."

Ryan leaves the kitchen, the swinging door making a draft as it closes again.

Jensen forces himself to concentrate, listening. "Both our cars. They're taking both." The gas smell comes at them, sharper with each second. It's no use shouting; there is no one to hear.

THE WOMAN NAMED PENNY WHITE is bright-eyed and buzzing; she likes the excitement she's stirred at the French Creek Café, where the detectives crowd into the kitchen. "I tell you he worked right there." She points. "I would talk to him, and at first he didn't answer—but I warmed him up. He was hungry. Like a hungry dog or something that's been in the woods and don't trust anybody. I ended up liking him."

"Why?" the trooper asks.

"I don't know. He did his work."

"He didn't talk to you about where he was living?" Senteros asks, clearly hoping that the answer will be Meadville.

"He was real close about that, and I didn't push. He said he had a friend in the college."

"Which college?" Senteros presses.

"Thiel."

Christie thinks whimsically, That means Greenville Police, Thiel College Police—let them all come!

"Did you believe it?" Senteros asks, deflated.

"Well, I did. We shared a couple of smokes. He never did mention Pittsburgh or anything like that." She hesitates, then says, "He wanted to take food at the end of the day. I figured it was for some pal."

Christie nods to Colleen and Potocki—the brother.

"Do you know anything else about him?" Christie asks in a mild voice.

"No. Good worker."

"What vehicle did he drive?"

"Never saw a vehicle. He always seemed to be walking."

The door to the kitchen bursts open. The friendly looking man who comes in says, "Sorry. I came as fast as I could." He looks like a kid who's fallen asleep watching television and is trying to pretend he's fully awake. Christie, looking closer, is pretty sure he sees the flushed face and disorientation that suggest a Cialis evening interrupted.

"I'm Ned Talling. Cochranton Police. When we have what we need from our good Penny here, we can meet over at my office. I have phones and computers and such," he offers with a genuine smile.

Nice. Some people are plain nice, and they carry it with them.

Some ten minutes later, Talling has ushered them into the Cochranton Police station, saying, "Welcome, welcome," and Christie privately marvels at the man, because policemen *hate* being invaded.

The little room is full with Meadville and state and Cochranton Police—and Pittsburgh, of course. Dolan has just started back to the city to wake up Miner and Saunders or there'd be one more squeezed into the room. Yet Talling is saying, "I think we should call in Wayne Township Police, too."

Christie catches Colleen and Potocki suppressing smiles. "Why Wayne Township?" he asks mildly.

"Well, I talked to a real nice lady the other day. From Sugar Lake. She called me because I know her from some church business where she's active. She *should* have called Wayne Township, but she called me and I went because I like her. She said there was a red truck came into her yard, a worker she had hired, and it just turned around and left, rude."

Christie feels a welcome charge of excitement. "I'd sure like to talk to her."

Colleen and Potocki rustle in their seats, ready to go.

"I just have to give Wayne Township a quick call—"

Christie taps his foot, trying to contain his impatience with procedure. It's a quarter to one.

"What's her name?" Christie asks while Talling dials his number.

"Addie Ward. She's everybody's honey."

They're all moving. Three Pittsburghers, Meadville, Cochranton, state. A phalanx of cars, everybody eager to get in on the action.

"BREATHE," ADDIE TELLS HIM, "while there is still oxygen in the air. Before the place is filled up."

Already he feels very bad. A headache throbs. But he rocks his chair toward the stove with an idea and is surprised that it moves a little. He tries—three moves, six, nine, twelve, but he isn't there. Addie watches him, eyes hopeful. She keeps trying to free her hand.

Oh, Addie, Addie, why did she have to be hurt too? Ten more minutes go by. Dizziness begins to take hold of him, and he has a bad bout of coughing. In the glaze of moonlight that illuminates the table, he can see the rope is cutting Addie's wrists as she tries to free herself and can't.

He turns to the stove again. He's stretching every muscle to move the chair a few inches, to incline his body just inches toward the hissing noise. It doesn't seem possible. Minutes click by on the clock. He's afraid to look at the clock again to see how much. He's sick and dizzy, more faint by the minute, but if he can use his mouth on the oven knob . . . His head drops toward a cabinet. He hears her cry. "Knife," she's saying. "Knife."

THE BROTHERS MADE IT PAST COCHRANTON at a quarter to one, and then they made it to Route 79 and nothing happened. It was smart, taking these other cars. He, it turns out, is the smart one.

A hollow carves itself out of his gut. The feeling is like hunger, gnawing. If the old girl and Jensen can reach the water, they'll live for a while. He left a little room when he tied the chairs to the table so they could angle themselves to the water . . . should have left some food. He looks to the passenger seat where he has the takeout from the French Creek Café next to the old lady's sauce.

It's going to be all over anyway, when they're found. The old folks will talk, and he will be trying to keep Ryan hidden somewhere, maybe some small town. Ryan will do something crazy. And that will be that.

When they were children, Ryan took care of him, showed him how to do things—play video games, climb trees, ring doorbells and run. They hid together when their parents fought. Their father would emerge from a fight and rescue them, take them out for some treat. After the time his mother cried for Ryan's real father, who died in prison, their parents had a terrible row, and their mother kicked their father out. They didn't see him after that.

Then there was Neil, and that didn't take. And Stanley, and that didn't take. She doesn't like people. Except she liked Ryan; she always took his side. Ryan didn't care. He hated her anyway.

Ahead, the Nissan drifts to the right and jumps jerkily back into the lane. Shit, Jack thinks. He's still messed up.

In another thirty miles, the station wagon could run out of gas. The Nissan should probably be fueled up, too.

WHEN THE POLICE CARS finally pull into the yard of the woman Talling talked about at a bit after one, no lights go on in the house. That's the first sign.

Christie lets Talling tap on the door. There is no answer. Talling opens the door and goes in. They all follow, switching on lights.

Christie immediately sees the handbag on the sofa, and in a quick move to the kitchen, he sees the food sitting out, the open cabinet door, the foil poked up on one end of the cake. He comes back and opens the handbag. "No wallet." He bounds upstairs. Neat beds, nothing amiss.

He finds the wallet with money in it in the bedside cabinet.

He peers into the bathroom. Empty. He descends the stairs and looks around. "Something happened here, but I don't know what."

"Left her door open," the state man says, shaking his head.

"Oh, yeah. I told her not to. Old school," Talling explains.

The others walk around curiously.

"She left in a hurry," Colleen says quietly.

Talling almost whispers, "Oh, man. I'm never going to forgive myself if she's hurt."

A new police vehicle streaks into the yard. It's the Wayne Township car, catching up. Most of the assembled company leaves the house for the yard, following Talling, who had the last contact with the Ward woman.

"I know this good fellow. This is Willy Kramer," Talling says as Kramer exits his car, making a half salute, half wave.

Christie hopes Colleen can manage all these people, but if she can't, he's butting in.

Colleen *does* take over in the next seconds. She begins a quick round of introductions, but Christie ducks out of the niceties and walks to the garage. He tries the handle. It wobbles back and forth too easily. He lifts the door.

Ha. There it is. He moves in to look at the front fender. This is the evidence they needed. He almost shouts out his relief. The boys are now officially suspects.

"Talling," he calls.

Talling comes across the yard and up to him. "Wow."

"Yep."

The whole group in the yard and on the porch becomes aware

the truck has been found. They start toward the garage. Christie says hurriedly to Talling, "Here's what you can do for us. Explain all this to your Wayne Township man . . . why we need to get our Pittsburgh forensics people here. Tell him I *have* to take the truck. I'm going to need complex lab work on this one." Christie lowers his voice. "We have a rookie on the force—" He tips his head toward Colleen. "This case is her baby. She started it; she needs the credit. Let them know." Shameless, the way he uses her, the way he banks on half of these guys falling for Colleen's open, hopeful look. "Talk your Township man out of holding this up, huh?"

Talling scratches his head. "Do my best. That's all?"

They're all listening now as the two men emerge from the garage. "That and help us find the old lady."

Talling takes Willy Kramer aside. A second later, Christie is on the phone with the Pittsburgh dispatcher, requesting a mobile crime unit and a towing unit for the truck.

"The whole way out in where?" the dispatcher asks.

"Sugar Lake. Sugar Lake."

"Sugar Lake," she repeats. "Is that in Pennsylvania?"

"It sure is."

In the center of the group in the yard, Potocki leans over and speaks something into Colleen's ear. She looks surprised, taken off guard. Aha, Christie thinks. It begins to work.

COLLEEN THINKS MAYBE POTOCKI SAID, "You're beautiful." It sounded like that, but there was enough squawking of radios and phones that she isn't sure. Maybe he said "dutiful." But Christie is gesturing to her to hurry up and really *take over.*

She addresses the assembled group. "We need to make a *unified* effort to find the woman who lives here."

"Addie. Adelaide Ward," Talling tells the others.

Colleen asks, "Does she have a car?"

"Yes. It's missing. A station wagon. A Buick. It must be a 1970. It's a relic. She won't give it up."

"Do you know her license plate?"

"No," says Talling.

"Not to worry. We'll have it in a minute," Colleen says smoothly. She points to Potocki, who is already on the phone for that information.

A state trooper—Seeger—asks Talling in a loud voice, "Why is she doing the talking?"

Talling puts up a hand. "Her case. One at a time. Everybody gets a piece."

Seeger is not happy. Colleen continues, pretending to be unfazed by the interruption. "We need to scour the grounds around this house. This could be a hostage situation. That's the good scenario."

Talling tells the assembly, "There's a whole town won't forgive any of us if she turns up murdered."

"We'll need to clear some other possibilities. Where might she have gone if she left on her own?"

"Back to Pittsburgh, where she has a house," says Talling. "But I want to call Emma Hopper for a start. Addie recommended the worker to her. Rutter. Called himself Rigger. Emma might know something." Talling's phone rings before he can make his call. He answers, "Can't talk, babe. Won't forget. Impossible." He flushes again and hangs up.

Christie ends his own phone call. "Greer. How do you want us to split up the search?"

"Okay. Talling is calling some locals. Who knows the lake properties best?"

"I do," Willy Kramer says. "I could drive this lake road in my sleep."

"If you would drive house to house looking for Addie Ward's car, or any suspicious activity, anything, that would be most helpful." He nods. "And if you, Talling, would do that for Cochranton—because you know it best—then the state troopers and Potocki and I could cover the grounds here. Meanwhile we'll call any phone number you can get us that's a contact for her. We can start with notes she has in the house, personal phone directories, as well as her number in Pittsburgh." Potocki points to his notebook and the phone at his ear.

"Detective Potocki has the license number for you."

Everybody grabs a notebook and they stop to write down the number Potocki dictates.

"I want each of you to take one of my cards," Colleen says. She hands them around. "Call me with anything."

Talling says, "Addie Ward is friends with the Jensens, who have a property up here. They come up the middle of June. You should look for their Pittsburgh number in her phone book."

"Potocki, call the Jensens," Colleen orders. "Meanwhile, you'll go by the Jensen property?" she asks Willy Kramer.

He says he will.

"Okay. Disperse. Keep phone contact." It's getting on to one thirty. "Call me often."

Seeger starts off into the woods on his own. Potocki blows Colleen a kiss and goes toward the house. Christie comes up to her, murmuring, "You forgot Senteros. He's antsy. You'll want to deal with him. I'm staying with the truck." Christie heads for the garage.

Huh, who's really in charge?

The second state trooper, Wilkes, politely holds a flashlight for Colleen. He's wanting to cooperate and work the woods with her. "I have a big lantern," Wilkes tells her.

"You sure do. Just a sec. I have to talk with Senteros. I might have him help us with the grounds."

As she approaches the Meadville chief, his phone rings and he answers. He holds her off with a gesture suggesting he's hearing something important. A feeling ripples through the group. Everybody stops where they are, waiting.

"I'm outta here," Senteros announces. "We got a homicide of our own up in Meadville."

TOM HAD UNDERSTOOD. He got a drawer open with his mouth and then managed to lift a knife with his mouth and fling it toward Addie. It landed on the table close to her. She had to pull it to her with *her* mouth. The problem was only one hand was loosened under the ropes, but her arms were still bound too tightly to move the hand. She had to drop the knife to where her hand could get it. If she missed, if it fell to the floor, it was all for nothing, everything Tom had managed.

She dropped it straight down. It didn't fall on the floor, but the angle was wrong for her hand. With her legs still tight together, she twisted and twisted them until the knife ended up slipping around enough that her right hand might reach it. She stretched every muscle. *Have to,* she kept saying to herself. There was no choice. However her hand hurt or ripped on the rope, she had to get the knife. When she was finally able to hold it, she began to work on the ropes, but they were not at all easy to cut. At first it seemed nothing was happening. Then she saw a little fraying. She had to keep going. Had to. It took a long time; she saw that Tom had gone back to working the knob with his mouth. She couldn't see if he was able to turn it or not. Her eyes stung and her head already ached badly. She could hardly afford to breathe in at all now. After the first cut, the ropes started to give. But they seemed almost alive, like snakes, clinging pets, children. They wouldn't move away from her body enough for her to— As she was working the ropes, she saw Tom collapse.

"Tom!" she cried out, struggling. "Tom. Hang on."

Then she tried not to breathe at all. Her head throbbed. Finally she loosened a part of the rope around her knee, and a minute later she could pull her feet out. She was tangled, numb. When she tried to stand, she couldn't hold her balance. She held on to the kitchen table and let herself drop to the floor so she could crawl, dragging her body to the back door.

Then she had to pull herself partway up again. She tugged and opened the back door. There was a screen on it. She gulped at the air; she'd be no good to Tom if she passed out. When she felt a little steadier, she pulled herself up the rest of the way and moved back into the room. She fumbled with the gas knob on the stove. Tom, bless Tom, he'd managed to turn it off before he collapsed. She pulled at his chair—there was no time to cut him loose now—she tugged him with all her might toward the door.

She maneuvered the heavy weight of him and the chair out through the frame and to the outside and finally worked to tip the chair so that he was lying on his back. "Come on, come on," she urged. She slapped at his cheeks. She started to breathe into his mouth, holding his nose, but to do it right, to free his lungs, she had to get him into a better position. She went inside for the knife and began to cut him loose. "Come on, Tom," she said. "Hear me."

He stirred.

"That's the way. Come on, now. You're okay."

By the time she cut enough rope to get his hands free, he opened his eyes.

"Breathe, Tom, that's your job. Just keep breathing."

"Where are they?" he gasped.

"Gone."

"Where are . . . ?" She went close so he could speak without straining. "Where are we?"

"Out back. I'm cutting the rope."

"How—?"

"Don't try to talk. Just take it easy. You need your energy." She put a hand lightly on his mouth and then went back to cutting the ropes.

"No, wait, quiet . . . quiet," he said after a few moments. They both went still. "Oh, my God." He grabbed at her arm.

"What?"

"They've come back. They're back."

WILLY KRAMER WANTED TO FIND those two boys. He wanted to be the one who faced them alone and brought them in. His breathing was excited. If he'd thought about the narrative playing in his mind, he would have realized that he was already telling a story of a long search, already deciding that the first place he looked couldn't be the right one. This was why he'd stopped only briefly at the dark Jensen house, playing his headlights on the driveway, where he could see nothing happening, no cars around, and then moving on, thinking only briefly of the other night when he saw a small light there. Something on a timer, he told himself.

It saddened him that the old lady's station wagon was so identifiable that someone else might find it before he did. But he didn't give up hope easily. In his mind, he pictured the old car snuggled up against some tree. People do have to sleep, after all. Did they have the old lady hostage? And when he saved her, how exactly was he going to do it?

Perfect aim. He shoots both guys in the legs, boom, boom, in quick succession. They fall before they can shoot back. He wrestles weapons away from them.

Not going to be easy.

Should he call for help if he sees the station wagon or the truck? Probably. Probably should.

First assess the situation. Go in alone if he can.

He went up, up the road to where there was new construction under way. There was some kind of a—not a station wagon, an SUV, and it was just pulled up right next to a backhoe. Could be significant. Criminals switched cars all the time.

A head popped up at the sound of his tires. He started his

flashing light going. He got out of the car and shouted, "Please exit your vehicle."

"We didn't do anything," a male voice shouted back.

"Please exit your vehicle. All of you," he added.

"I can't," came a woman's voice. "Just, just give me a minute."

She sounded too young to be the old lady he was looking for. He was pretty sure she was going to turn out to be young and naked. He moved up to the window to see. Sure enough, a buxom one, with good breasts. She covered each breast with a hand.

"This is private property," he said.

"My dad owns it," said the boy with her. He was pulling on his pants. "We didn't do anything wrong."

Shit, thought Willy Kramer. Ten minutes to two! Time lost. And I make two more people hate me. "Let me see some ID," he says firmly. "If your ID is okay, I'll let you go."

The boy scrambles out of the car and hands over a wallet.

Mostly, Kramer hardly studies the wallet. He's thinking about preserving the dignity of the law for about a good ninety seconds and then getting back to his real work of driving deeper into undeveloped territory to capture the Rutter boys.

BOTH OF THEM HAD BEEN AFRAID TO MOVE. "What, what?" she whispered, almost without sound. He shook his head for her to be quiet. He was right. A light from the road had played briefly toward the house. He went utterly still, listening.

"What's happening?"

"Wait."

"Is it—?"

"I heard . . . it was the sound of tires and then . . . then the car went away, I think. Why would they . . . go away?" Tom looked weak, dazed, as if the effort to speak wiped out any strength he had left.

She understood. It had been someone else. And they'd missed it. They should have been calling out. Tom needed help. She started to cry but forced herself to concentrate on the way the rope frayed slightly, then more, then more before it broke.

She had never been more aware of breathing. Air. Oxygen. The miracle of it.

Finally he was able to move, and she was able to pry the chair away from him.

"Lie down," she said. "Just keep breathing."

"We have to get out of here." He tried to raise himself up, but he winced with pain.

"Stay still for a minute. You're bleeding a little. You hit your head against something. Let me look around."

Standing stiffly, she began the walk around the outside of the house; she stepped carefully over twigs and muddy ground; she got the whole way to the front of the house and saw nothing to help them. Not a vehicle in the yard. Not a person in sight.

When she made her way back to him, he was trying again to stand.

"You can't," she said. "Let me get you fixed up. Then I have to walk down to my place for a phone."

"I'll go with you."

"Absolutely not. You need to be still."

In the house she found the bowl on the table. She filled it to the top with water and reached into a drawer she remembered from all the years visiting this house as the one that held dish towels. She grabbed several and went outside.

She washed his head with plain water and tied a clean towel around it. "You look like a Turk. I did as well as I could in the dark. Something happened to your leg or hip," she said. "I think it's your hip. Do you have a flashlight?"

"The right-most kitchen drawer."

She went back in for it and came back out. "Loosen your belt."

"I thought you'd never ask."

She was glad he could joke. It took some effort to adjust his clothes so she could see. There was a big ugly purple bruise on his right hip.

"How did you ever walk up the stairs?" she asked. "I don't see how you did it."

"I'm not sure either."

He grimaced as she felt around to his back and down the length of his hip. "I don't think there's a fracture, but there might be. You need a doctor."

"I'm going with you down the hill."

Men were so impossible. Didn't he understand he was holding her back? "No! I need to move fast, and I *know* about these things. Either you agree not to come or I won't go. I'm getting you a bag of ice for this. If there is ice."

"There's a little. In Tupperware in the freezer."

She goes back into the house. The freezer is empty. There's open Tupperware in the sink, but there isn't any ice. A gas smell lingers in the air. She opens a kitchen window. Her hearing aid is somewhere on the floor, but she can't take the time to look for it.

When she is back outside, she tells Tom, "It will take me ten minutes to walk down the road. Fifteen at most. I'll call an ambulance. I'll let the medics bring me back up. You have your watch. It's one fifty. If nobody comes back by two thirty, you can come down the road. Grit your teeth for forty minutes."

"Did they take the gun?"

"Surely."

"If they didn't, you take it."

"No. No, Tom."

"I want it, then."

Biting her tongue, she goes to the house and uses the flashlight to look. Just to approach the sun porch where she was first tied up makes her feel vulnerable, panicked. But there it is, to her surprise, the gun, propped against the wall between the rooms.

She lifts it by the handle, gingerly for all its weight, and takes it out to Tom. "I'm going. I'll be okay. Don't do anything foolish. I can't have you dying after all we've been through."

Before he can protest, she starts off, using the flashlight to light her to the road. In the moonlight, in her gauzy skirt with her hair wild, she must look absolutely mad.

The moon is only at half. The stars are sharply visible tonight. It's cool—maybe about fifty-eight degrees. Her skin feels chilled, but she is sweating as she moves rapidly, playing the flashlight only when she needs to.

Her breath catches as she moves faster than usual and as words and images come to her in skipping fashion.

My daughter. My son. I'll see them again.

Alive. A miracle.

TWO O'CLOCK. The troopers continue to comb the grounds, though they've been over it a couple of times. *If the old lady's dead, this is our homicide, not yours.* That's what they're surely thinking, all of them, except maybe Senteros, who ran off to his own case.

Colleen walks back into Addie Ward's kitchen through the back door, studying the place—food on the stove and counter. Pasta about to be made, a wonderful-smelling sauce. A chocolate cake, too. She goes into the living room, where Potocki is making his phone calls.

"There was no answer at her Pittsburgh house. I called the daughter next and terrified her. Daughter gave the same advice we already had, to call Jensen in Pittsburgh. I called that number. No answer. She also told me about a friend, Frank McCauley. I tracked him down, woke him up, too. He said he visited Addie Ward the other day and she had him check out the work one of the Rutter boys did for her. McCauley is upset—wants to come and help look for her." Potocki stops, looks around. "What is this place saying? She left her money. She left her food. Did they take her hostage, make her drive them?"

"Something like that. She's an orderly type, it looks like, not a person to leave dinner. . . . We'll have to print the place."

She moves into the dining room, where she lifts a photo from a sideboard—can't tell how old it is—a woman clearly a senior citizen, full head of wavy gray hair, the white sort of gray, not silver, wind blowing her skirt, which she is holding down Marilyn Monroe fashion. The woman in the photo looks spirited, and she is also very good looking. Recent? Ten years ago? Twenty? Locals said she was in her eighties. Colleen studies her. "Man, I hope I age this way."

"You probably will."

"You think so?"

Potocki looks thoughtful. "Yeah, I do."

Colleen hates the look of the aging movie stars who come out of hiding to go on Larry King—stiff and artificial. This woman is completely natural. She puts down the photo.

She paces Addie Ward's living room. She's responsible for heading up this case, but there is nothing she can do right now except wait for various phone calls to come in.

Potocki comes over and kisses her. Just like that. It's not a long kiss, but it's definitely . . . a kiss.

This isn't like Potocki. When he works . . . he works.

"I couldn't help myself. You look tired and worried and . . . nice."

"You like the circles under my eyes?"

"I kind of do. You look very fucked, very fuckable."

"That would be a change."

"It's how your life should be."

Up all night having pleasure. It's been a long time. "Are you offering?"

He shoots her a seductive smile. "I'd like to close the gap on this two-year moratorium."

"But . . ." What about the leggy gorgeous doctor in his life? What about Christie and their jobs?

Potocki says, "I know. You're being hotly pursued by a new guy. With money."

She stops moving. She never lies to Potocki. For some reason, she just doesn't. "I shrinked him the other day. At lunch." Potocki's eyebrows rise in curiosity. "He's in love with his first wife. I remind him of her."

"The question is—"

Just then there's an excited voice in the yard, then a shout. "Something's happening out there." She runs to the front door and out, Potocki behind her.

In the yard is the woman in the photo. Unmistakably so. The lights of the cruisers sweep over her in their revolutions and show her tapping her chest, catching her breath. She is wearing only light clothing, no sweater.

Colleen runs to her but is cut off by Talling, who gets there first and is hugging her. "Addie, Addie," he's saying. "What a sight for sore eyes."

"Please. Oh—how did you know to be here? My friend is hurt, up the hill. I need an ambulance."

"Can you do that?" Christie asks Talling.

Talling is quickly pressing numbers into his phone.

"Mrs. Ward," Colleen says, and when she has her attention, "is this to do with the Rutter boys?"

"Oh, yes."

"Do you know where they are?"

"Well . . . somewhere. They took our cars. To get away. Is there someone here could take me back to my friend?"

Christie already has his car door open, so Colleen leads Addie to the front passenger side, saying, "Mrs. Ward? We'll need for you to tell us everything while we go up there."

Potocki comes forward to help Addie Ward into the car.

The troopers, both on phones, look frustrated by the fact that Christie and his crew have captured her so quickly.

"Oh, I need ice for my friend. Whatever I have in my freezer."

With an assent from Christie, Colleen runs to the house and grabs at ice trays, a bowl, a bag of peas, and where, where, where—she finds a plastic grocery bag. She hurries back out to the car, showing the woman the supplies as she runs. She jumps into the backseat.

The other cars are trying to edge past Christie's car to the road.

Mrs. Ward says, "Oh, and let me call out to him when we get there. Because they could come back, you see, so he's got a gun . . . because he can't move. Make sure they know." She points to the other police cars.

Christie signals the other drivers. Potocki and Colleen each hang out a door, calling out to explain about the gun before they return themselves to the backseat and start out up the hill.

Somehow—and this fascinates her—Christie has used this fuss and angled his car to be first on the road. "Tell me where to go," Christie says to Addie Ward. "And tell us everything you can."

She says, "Oh, I couldn't tell you everything. (It's just a short way up the hill here.) We were tied up. They tried to gas us—one of them did—with the stove and leave us for dead. Tom is hurt because, well, before that, he tried to fight and he got the worst of it."

"You've had quite a scare, Mrs. Ward," Colleen says. She works at getting the ice cubes out of the trays and into the plastic bag.

Potocki reaches over and squeezes Colleen's hand.

"Oh, I couldn't begin to tell— Oh, here. Where you see that bush sticking out up ahead. There's a drive, well, more like a path beyond that."

"I'll give him an alert," Christie assures her. Just before he drives onto the property, he puts on the siren for a few seconds. "Your friend will hear that. Go on, now, call."

"Tom!" Addie calls out. "It's okay. It's safe. I've brought help."

She gets out of the car at the same time Colleen does, and she reaches for the bag of ice. "For his hip. It might be broken. Tom! Tom! We're coming."

There's a lot of noise all at once. Car doors and voices. The trooper and Talling are both on phones again. "Tom?"

"Addie. I'm still back here."

"Is an ambulance coming?" she asks the men on phones. "I'm worried. He lost consciousness for a little while. He'll need oxygen."

"Yes, ma'am. They're coming."

"Good," she tells them. She moves briskly toward the back of the house, and they all follow.

That's who I want to be, Colleen thinks.

JACK LOOKS AT THE GAS GAUGE, which seems not to have moved at all. A car this old, the gauge could be broken. He toots lightly, passes Ryan, and soon pulls off at a service station. He hears his brother pull in behind him.

"Right," Ryan says, coming up to him. "We're using a lot of gas, two cars. This is a good place—around here—to dump yours in a couple of miles."

A strong case of nerves hits Jack's stomach. "For now, just get some gas. Use the money you have."

"We should change the plates on the Nissan soon," Ryan urges.

"Maybe. I'm thinking."

"Come on, man. Anybody'd notice that old thing you're driving. Let's just find a place, dump it. Spell each other with the driving."

"Okay. Get your gas. I'll just put a couple dollars in after you're gone. We shouldn't go in there together. Pay first."

He watches as Ryan goes in, pays, and comes back to start filling his tank. Then he walks over to him and watches the numbers jumping up. "I hope they're okay."

"You what?"

"The oldies. I hope they can reach the water."

Ryan makes a sound that Jack can't understand. Snort, choke. "They're okay. They don't need the water. Never need water again. Something to be said for that, not needing anything." He makes a face that says, *Guessing game time, wanna play?*

"What'd you do?"

"What do you think?"

"I didn't hear a shot. . . . You didn't . . . ?" A shot couldn't have been muffled that much, could it?

Ryan looks irritable. "I put on the stove. I mean the gas. The oven."

For a moment he hopes this is one of Ryan's jokes. "You didn't, eh? Not really, huh?"

"Don't be a little girl now after all we've been through."

Jack makes himself be still for a long time. "There's a cop, I think, watching us. Get on the road. Take any road you want. Mix it up. I'll follow behind in a couple of minutes. If I lose you, and I won't, I'll meet you at the end of Seventy-nine. Wait for me there."

"That's a long way off."

"Just keep driving. Just move it."

"You sure?"

"Positive."

"I kinda wanted your company, asshole."

"Later. You'll have it later. Go."

Ryan drives off. Jack doesn't put gas in the old lady's car. He pretends to be going toward the convenience store to pay, but as soon as Ryan is out of sight, he leaps into the station wagon and starts back to Sugar Lake. Hopeless. There is probably nothing he can do. He helped close the windows—he thought Ryan wanted them closed so nobody would hear the old folks if they called out.

In his head, Ryan is calling him names—pigeon, wuss, girlie, cunt, wife—over and over. He feels himself crying, but he keeps driving.

He'd thought, Get Ryan away, far enough away. Make a phone call so somebody goes to free them.

The night, the road lights, and the other cars seem unreal. The station wagon makes its rattling noises. Otherwise, he is alone, without anything, maybe more alone than he has ever been in his life, and it feels as if he is floating above something real, but not living it, like a dead man watching himself being dead.

THEY MUST BE LOVERS, Colleen thinks, the way she tends him, the gentleness. Jensen tries to shift his position, which clearly produces pain. "Are you okay?" Addie asks.

"I have a hell of a pain in my leg, but I'm clearer in the head, anyway."

She smiles encouragingly.

The police have asked a few questions more, have got a pretty good picture of what went on in the house.

From a distance they can hear another siren, an ambulance coming. "But no clue at all about where they were going?" Colleen asks both of them again.

"No," Tom says, "no."

Addie Ward looks at her, frustrated. "I'm sorry. Without my hearing aid . . . I lost it when they put me in the kitchen chair."

"I'll find it for you," Potocki says, and he goes into the house.

The sound of the ambulance is closer now.

"Oh, and the one boy burnt Tom's pictures. They were in that cardboard box in the living room, I think. . . ."

"What kind of pictures?" Colleen asks both of them.

Jensen answers, "Family pictures. Photographs."

"Which boy? Ryan?"

"Yes. Ryan."

"Why did he do that?"

Potocki comes back with the hearing aid in his handkerchief. "The hanky is clean," he says.

They wait while she puts in the hearing aid. Even while she's fitting it in, Colleen asks, "Jack is the one who worked for you, right?"

"The younger one. Jack."

"What'd they use for phones?"

"I never saw either one with a phone."

"The mother told us the younger son is the bad apple."

"Oh, no, no," Addie is saying over the sound of the ambulance—very close now. "It's the other way. The young one has a bit of a heart. Oh, no."

The ambulance comes into the yard. Soon there are men with a stretcher trotting toward Jensen.

Addie stands. "There now. They'll take care of you."

"Ma'am," says the EMT fellow who is carefully moving Jensen, "you're coming with us, too."

"I'd . . . rather go home."

"Your breathing has been compromised. And look at your wrists. . . ."

"I have to call my daughter. If this hits the news—"

"I just called her," Potocki says. "I had to use her cell number the second time. She must have jumped in her car right away because she's already driving up here with her husband."

"Did you tell her I'm all right?"

"I did, but she's coming anyway. We'll let you call her from the ambulance."

The EMT says, "No police in the ambulance. I'll give her a phone. You can follow behind."

Christie takes Colleen and Potocki aside. It's very late. It'll be morning before they know it, and they're still at it. They might need to find a motel after all, he says. There's figuring to do. The Pittsburgh police are down to one car since Dolan took the other.

While the three of them walk to the car and the EMTs work to arrange Jensen and Ward in the ambulance, Christie says, "I need to get back to the truck just now to meet up with the mobile unit. You can drop me on your way to the hospital." He gets into the backseat.

Talling comes up to them, speaking quickly. "The motels are going to be full with college graduation events. If you don't find anything, I'm sure my wife wouldn't mind—"

"I'm sure we'll be fine. We'll probably stay up and then go back home."

Potocki starts up the car because the ambulance is leaving.

"Let me know. And if you need another car, I'll get you a car."

"Very good of you," Christie calls back. "I might have to take you up on that one."

Talling says, "Whatever you need." He looks worried as they drive off, following the ambulance.

The ambulance goes as fast as it can over the rutted roads. It's two thirty, and Potocki bounces over the potholes to catch up to it, stopping only long enough to let Christie off at Addie's house.

WHEN AN ABASHED WILLY KRAMER GETS BACK to the Ward place, he explains to the others all the places he's looked and how dark the Jensen place was.

Christie, waiting for the mobile unit, listens in.

Seeger tells Kramer, "You have a bunch of good stuff. You have breaking and entering, you have vandalism—but damn, you have attempted murder. This is a big case."

"I want to see those two boys fry," Kramer says stiffly.

"Lots of people want that. They made those old people drink out of bowls like dogs. There was even a bowl of water in the basement on the floor. Christ."

Attempted murder is big all right. With abusive behavior

thrown in. On the other hand, the Pittsburgh detectives have manslaughter, homicide. Hit-and-run. They're going to be drawing and quartering those boys, everybody trying to get a piece of them.

Christie also has questions.

He stands at the garage, taking in the night. He wonders who these boys are and what they did exactly on Saturday night, not to mention up here in the country, and what moves them and whether they have guilt, remorse. But then he wonders that about everybody.

The stars are bright, beautiful, and he thinks again about living where people look at things like trees, sky.

BY THE TIME JACK HAS REVERSED DIRECTION and is coming up the road, there is no other traffic, but when he approaches the path to the old lady's house, he sees police cars there with flashing lights.

He must be too late. Something has happened. His muscles go slack. His whole body signals defeat. But he keeps going up the hill to the Jensen place. He's hardly breathing when he pulls into the rough path. Here, too, are flashing lights. He brings the car to a stop.

Okay. It's over. Done. He's face-to-face with a cop car.

A trooper is coming toward him, gun drawn. Another trooper is on his phone. Jack turns off the ignition. He tries to breathe in, but he can't.

The trooper shouts at him, "Out of the car. Hands on the roof of the car. Out of the car. Hands on the roof."

"Okay. Okay." His legs don't want to work, but he climbs out, stumbling. He puts his hands on the roof of the old lady's station wagon, becoming aware of baked-in grit, a broken antenna.

"Come back to do more mischief, huh? Couldn't get enough of it."

"I came back—"

"Which one are you? Which Rutter are you?"

"John. Jack."

"What'd you want, coming back here?"

It doesn't occur to him that he's not supposed to answer questions. "To see if there's anything I can do. Are they . . . are they dead?"

"Why do you ask that? You left them for dead. Why do you ask?"

"My brother told me he put on the gas. I didn't know. I thought maybe—" The trooper pulls down his arms and with jerky movements gets them behind him and a pair of cuffs on him.

"Maybe what?"

"I could get a window open before—"

"You're telling me you wanted to help them?"

"Yeah."

"And you think I'll believe you?"

He doesn't say anything. Nobody will believe him. And Ryan will get away or lie.

The other trooper approaches and says, "That Pittsburgh commander is on his way. Any minute."

Jack doesn't move. He's like the old folks, being tied up, not fighting it anymore. Did they die? Did they somehow . . . not die? His hands, cuffed behind him, are useless. If he runs to the house to see for himself what's happened, the trooper will shoot. He waits for the next thing, whatever it is.

The troopers talk, but he can't make anything out, just names batted back and forth. Kramer, Greer, Christie, Talling. All about who called whom.

"What's this on the seat?" the first trooper asks him. "In the plastic?"

"Spaghetti sauce."

"You stole the old lady's food, too?"

He'll never be able to explain it.

"Christ."

Two cars zoom into the yard. A middle-aged man without a uniform gets out of the one, saying lightly, "What a night, huh?"

"He came back," says the trooper.

"I see that."

All the police confer for a few minutes, and then the man approaches him. "I'm Commander Christie with the Pittsburgh Police. Homicide Division. I'm going to have to take you into custody—for your involvement in the vehicular murder of Joanna Navarro. I must warn you that anything you say may be used as evidence against you."

Joanna Navarro. The man didn't say anything about the old folks. Maybe they got away. Maybe . . . He tries to ask the question, but he gets only partway before he starts to cry.

"What?" says the homicide detective. "What is it?" He does not seem unkind.

"I wanted to know if they were okay." He inclines his head toward the house. "Are they?"

"You can't ask questions," says the trooper.

Christie ignores the trooper and looks searchingly at Jack for a long time. He puts a hand on Jack's shoulder. He says, "They're probably going to make it."

The trooper lets out a gasp.

Jack nods, sobbing.

NURSES KEEP BUZZING into the cubicle where Addie lies on a cot. Her wrists are bandaged. The effect of the activity around her while she lies still, able to do nothing, is to make her aware of how close she came to death. She's made a Houdini escape.

"It's my friend who needs the attention," she tells the young nurse who pokes her head in.

"Don't you worry about him. We're taking care of him. He's in X-ray now."

“I think he might still need oxygen because of the—”

“We’ve given him oxygen. A couple of police are chomping at the bit to get your story. You feel able to talk to them?”

What more can they want to know? She and Tom were tied up, made to drink water from bowls like animals, made to fear they would soil themselves, gassed, and left for dead. Shamed. Terrorized and shamed.

In come two of the detectives, the one who brought the ice cubes and the fellow who found her hearing aid. Colleen Greer and John Potocki, their cards say. Addie looks over the cards as if they say something serious.

“I’m sorry,” Detective Greer begins. “Just a few more questions. Did they talk about the hit-and-run accident?”

“No. Not . . . well, I don’t think so, and Tom didn’t say. The older one watched it on the news.”

“You feel the young one was *not* the instigator?”

“Jack. I thought I had him. I mean, when he came asking for work, I could see he was ragged. I knew he was needy. I gave him a chance. He didn’t know how to talk. Some people, you know, get stuck. When he got back to the house and found us there . . . tied to chairs . . . I could tell he wasn’t happy about it. But he let us up, he untied us, and let us go up to the bathroom. I think . . . I think he even tied us so we could move a little.”

“What did the other one do when he was tying you?”

“Held the gun.”

She looks at her partner. He’s taking the notes. She asks, “Which one put on the gas?”

“The older one.”

“And what did the young one say? Jack?”

“He wasn’t— I don’t know if he was there. Tom might know. I didn’t hear anything from him. He could have been behind me, I suppose.”

“Is it *possible* he didn’t know about the gas *at the time?*”

"Oh . . ." She tries to remember how it was. "It could be."

"Well, you see, he's been found. He's been arrested. But the circumstances are a little odd. He was driving your car. With your spaghetti sauce in a container on the seat. And he came back to the Jensen place. Can you help us figure that out?"

Addie thinks about it, trying to imagine a sequence. "Did he have a weapon?"

"Only your spaghetti sauce," Potocki teases. When he sees she can laugh at herself, he adds, "The smell about drove me crazy. What do you put in that stuff?"

"Sausage, chicken, meatballs. Everything. Learned it from a Polish woman back home."

"No," Potocki says, "the boy didn't have a weapon. He *did* have your car, though. What do you think he was doing?"

"I don't know. What does he say?"

"That he was coming back to see if you were all right."

"Oh. Well, then, I'd say there's a chance he didn't know about the gas. Wouldn't you?"

"There's a chance," Colleen says. "We're trying to figure it all out."

DOLAN HAS WAKENED RITA MINER from a heavy sleep, and she is none too happy to let him in the door at three thirty. "You can't just bother a person in the middle of the night," she says.

"Afraid I can when it's a police matter. Why don't we sit down?"

She sits, pulling a robe around her. "There must be a law about this."

"There is. It's called accessory after the fact. It's called not obstructing an investigation."

"That's a lot of threat."

"It's true. I need to know when you last heard from your sons."

"I don't know. Didn't I say? A couple of years."

"That has to be hard."

"Why?"

"Didn't you miss them?"

"I didn't miss them begging me for money."

"So they were a burden."

"Believe me."

"They didn't come by here in the last couple of days?"

She shakes her head.

"Maybe you could make us some coffee."

"It's the middle of the night."

"Which is why I could use some. I've been chasing after your boys. They were hanging around in Meadville. Cochranton. Sugar Lake."

Her eyes flicker with interest. She looks away from him. "Okay, I'll see if I can make a pot of coffee."

Dolan does a quick scan of the room as soon as she leaves. He sees a phone answering machine on a shelving system. It's against the law to touch it. It's also completely irresistible. When there's some clanging in the kitchen, he presses the play button, and when a voice sounds, he hurries to lower the volume, nervously watching the kitchen. The call is something about her work schedule. He's about to shut off the machine when a second voice comes on. It's one of the boys, asking his mother for help. Dolan listens hungrily but shuts off the machine before he hears everything because the kitchen is getting quiet. He hurries back to his seat.

"Be ready in a little bit," she says.

"Well, sit. Let's go over this, figure what you need to do not to be charged."

"Charged?"

"Accessory."

"How do you figure that?"

"See, we put a scan on the phone your son was using, and we know he called you. I'm trying to get you to come clean here. By covering up, that makes you an accomplice. It makes you a principal. You don't cooperate, you'll be on TV, you'll need money for lawyers."

Her face changes rapidly from merely put out to seethingly angry. "Why didn't you say what you had when you first came in? You're breaking all kinds of laws. And I'm going to fry you for it."

Dolan stays steady. "Of course you're upset. It's natural to try to protect a child. I would. But the thing is, it's in our best interests and theirs and yours to find them. And you're our link."

She glowers at him.

He smiles. "Really, I'm on your side." His phone rings. He apologizes. "I have to take this."

It's Christie, saying they've got one of the boys. The younger one.

Rita Miner studies him as he listens, so he frames his replies carefully. "That's good. Good. I'll tell her." He pauses. "Jack turned himself in," he says.

"Figures."

"You said if one of them was the driver, it was probably your younger son, Jack. You want to change that now?"

"No."

"Hmmm. How's the coffee?"

"I'll go look."

He thinks about the message on the machine. He imagines himself lifting the tape, knowing full well he can't get away with it.

When she comes back and puts down the tray with two mugs, he says, "Thanks. Now, we still need to find Ryan—"

She sits and faces him. "Why's that if Jack turned himself in?"

"Ryan is the one who was driving."

"How do you know this?"

"Witness," he says blithely.

"That wasn't on the news."

"We withhold some facts on purpose. We need to know, how can we contact their father?"

An expression crosses her face. "Fat chance."

"Do you have an address?"

"No."

"We'll keep trying. Rutter's an unusual enough name."

"Sounds like rotter, doesn't it. I would tell him maybe all the toffs were really rotters and that's how they got named. He gave me all this rigmarole about a coat of arms."

Dolan gets an idea, nothing to go on but his experience in the trade, and he tries it on her. "You liked Ryan's father better."

She stares at him for a while. "I like an interesting man better than a nose in the air. Who doesn't?"

"Where is this interesting man right now?"

"He died in prison. And you're a son of a bitch."

He sighs. "I'd like to find someone who might be interested in the boys' welfare, because the way it looks, Ryan is going to do a lot of serious time and Jack will get some."

"No such thing as courts in this country?"

"We got 'em. Sometimes they're even too lenient." He takes another sip of coffee. She looks at him as if she's pulled something over on him, as if she's recorded every ill-advised word.

He finishes up the coffee and gets out of there.

Before he's even in his car, he calls Christie to report. "Boss, I listened to her answering machine when she was in the kitchen making coffee. We can't use it, but . . . one son called her. On the machine—he was scared, he wanted help—money, I think. He was saying something like, 'Ryan's in trouble.' She doesn't favor the young one, see, she favors the older one because she thinks the younger one's father is uppity or something. She liked the father of her first kid. I find things out, don't I?"

"You always do. You sound pretty lively."

"Just had a cup of coffee. What's up on your end?"

"Truck's about to be towed," Christie says. "Several of us have tried to get from the little brother where his big brother is, but he's not saying. I'm letting them have Jack for a while because they're going to let us have him in the morning. So now I'm going to horn in on Senteros's new case. I just talked a trooper into driving me up to Meadville." Christie tries to stifle a yawn, but it comes through the phone.

"You're tired. Go home, Boss. Or find a bed."

"I'm okay."

Something's up. Dolan can't figure out what it is. "What's Senteros's case?"

"Guy strangled with a phone cord, I hear. Apparent attempted robbery."

"You're thinking something."

"I'll just poke around a bit. You talked to Chester?"

"I'm on my way to rehab—"

"Keep it honest."

Oh. As if Christie's not happy about the answering machine. Which on any given day, Christie would do himself.

SIX

THURSDAY

THEY'RE STANDING OUTSIDE THE HOSPITAL, waiting for Addie's daughter, Linda, and her husband, Hank, to bring the car around from the parking lot. Addie is sitting in the requisite wheelchair.

Colleen moves Potocki aside to confer. "I tried the motels, then Talling offered again, but it's okay. It's going to be morning soon, might as well just keep going."

"But you're going on twenty-four hours."

True. It's almost five. She had gotten up at six. "Eh. Boss sure doesn't want to head home; he's hot on Senteros's tail, looking for excitement." Colleen stifles a yawn and tells Potocki, "We can sleep in the car."

"I've done that before."

Addie waves them to attention. "Are you saying you don't have any place to stay? Because I have room."

"Oh, no, your daughter's staying with you, plus—"

"I have three bedrooms, and there are sleeping bags and cots aplenty because of grandchildren and great-grandchildren," she says. "And a sofa. Whatever you'd like."

Colleen looks at Potocki. Tempting. All they need is a quick nap, a lie-down in their clothes.

Potocki says, "Good idea. We can keep an eye on Mrs. Ward that way, don't you think, Greer? It makes sense."

And so they put Addie in her daughter's car, and they follow. The streets have a brisk, damp smell. They wind into Sugar Lake and into Addie's yard, where the Wayne Township man, standing a kind of guard duty, nods that all is safe. Colleen watches as the daughter and her husband, one on each side of Addie, put their arms through hers and walk her into her house.

Potocki asks Greer, "Have everything?"

She's half-asleep, sitting there. She pulls at her heavy handbag, which contains everything—notebooks, gun—and says, "Got it."

As they enter the house, Addie Ward is saying, "I need to get this spaghetti sauce in the fridge."

Her daughter exclaims, "You have to pitch it, Mom. They say three hours for meat."

"Oh," Addie frets. "I think people are much too fussy about things like that."

"I'm tossing it," her daughter says. "Save you from yourself. Now let's get you to bed."

But Addie stands at the refrigerator, holding her pot of sauce. She tells her daughter, "Show these folks where the children's bedroom is."

"Mum, don't you want to go to bed?" Hank asks.

"Sure I do. But I'm a bit hungry. I haven't eaten much all day. The glucose drip didn't quite do it."

Hank moves over to Addie. "Linda can show them the upstairs. Let me make you toast," he offers. He taps the rectangle of foil. "What's this?"

"That's Tom Jensen's cake. We could cut it, I guess. . . ."

"Let it be," Linda says. "Toast is fine."

"Aren't the rest of you hungry?" Addie asks.

Colleen pauses, knowing she should set up a polite protest. By now she's crazy for the sauce, the cake, the toast, anything. She forces out a weak, "That's very sweet of you, but we're fine."

However, Addie, looking in the fridge, sliding in her pot of sauce, announces, "I have everything we need for French toast. That would be just the thing. It's quick. Does everybody like French toast?"

"Yes! I love it," Colleen says. "Tell me how to help. I'm really good in other people's kitchens."

"Just get out a few plates." Addie is already bringing a bowl to the countertop and taking out eggs. "And Linda can find the syrup. And napkins."

Pretty soon everybody's working, figuring out what needs to be done. When two frying pans are going and Addie is dipping bread in egg batter, she tells her daughter again, "Show them the upstairs. See if there are sheets on. I think there are. Show them where the towels are." To Colleen, she says, "Feel free to have a shower. There's shampoo, everything. I put some of those airline toothbrushes someplace up there. I've had them around for twenty years or so, but they're still in their wrappers. See if you can find them. And," she adds lightly, "there's also the downstairs sofa if you want separate quarters."

"We've slept in our clothes on the floor when we're on a case," Potocki explains. "You don't need to worry about us."

Colleen and Potocki follow Linda obediently upstairs to look at the room. Colleen stifles a laugh when Linda shows them there are two cots and four sleeping bags in the closet in addition to the more obvious choices: the two bunk beds and one double bed in the room.

Linda checks the sheets on the bottom bunk bed and on the

double bed. She's a bit more prudish than her mother is. "Yes," she says. "The beds are made up."

Potocki winks.

Every possibility.

And the smell of French toast drifting up the stairs.

CHRISTIE IS ONE OF FOUR DETECTIVES looking at Ed Hodel, who lies strangled on his living room floor; they note the scratches at his neck, that his eyes are open, and that his body is in complete rigor.

"What would you say? Two days?" Christie prompts Senteros.

"About that."

"You need my labs, I'm willing to lend them."

Senteros grimaces. "We'll be okay."

"Good. Good. Any idea who did it?"

"No. Look around the place. It was a robbery. Things are out of place, mattresses not put back right on the beds, that kind of thing. Be my guest if it interests you."

Christie sees that Senteros's eyes are not quite as welcoming as his word. "Just professional curiosity," Christie says. "Can't help myself. The only *puzzle* we've had back home for weeks is the Navarro case."

"Lean times."

"Yeah." Christie walks around the small house. He sees what Senteros saw. Robbery mess. He comes back to the living room. "Who called it in?"

"The neighbor lady. The guy's dog wouldn't stop barking. That was all she knew. The barking was driving her nuts. When my man got here, he tried to calm the dog, tapped on the door, found it open, looked—and this is what he saw. Of course, the dog went crazy."

"Door was closed?"

"Closed, not locked."

"How'd the dog get out?"

"I don't know. Must have *been* out."

Curious. Skin-prickling curious. "What's the neighbor say?"

"Not a lot. She says she didn't *hate* the dog, but it made too much noise. She took it in an hour or so ago to feed it something."

"Nice dog? My kids want a dog."

"Not my type. I like the big shaggy ones."

"Me too. You wouldn't be upset, would you, if I talked to your neighbor? I know you questioned her. I just have the curse of curiosity."

"By now, I'd think you'd be sick of the whole business."

"Homicide investigation? Some days, yes. Other days, no. I'm wired up tonight, waiting to hear something about the second Rutter boy. And my people are hanging out up here, working with the Cochranton team. They're going to take Jack back to Pittsburgh tomorrow."

"You're booking him for Navarro?"

"For involvement."

"They did plenty of damage in Sugar Lake."

"Talling and Wayne Township let us have him. Very cooperative."

Senteros makes a face again. He could pass for twenty-five; it might bother him that he'll always look like a kid.

Christie uses the excuse of an incoming phone call to walk out the front door.

It's Dolan saying, "Chester's not here. Voluntary exit. And man, they didn't want to cough that up right away. Anyway. He checked himself out by agreeing to do outpatient work and went home with his girlfriend. I'm almost at their place now. Ready to say good morning to them."

"Keep me posted."

"You're all staying up in Meadville?"

"Well. Greer couldn't get a room. Hotels are busy, this and that, then Mrs. Ward—she's a nice woman, isn't she?—said they could stay at her place. Apparently she has an extra bedroom."

"Potocki and Greer get another chance to think about it. Tell you, I'd have a mighty hard time sleeping next to Greer."

Christie says, yawning again, "Hope you shake something out of Chester."

"What about you? Talling's place?"

"I'm just staying up."

He drifts down the road to a house that looks as poor as Ed Hodel's. The woman who lives there is still awake and introduces herself through a battered screen door as Irene Mamajek. She looks haunted, dark circles under her eyes. That look has been there, not just from tonight.

Christie introduces himself. A clicking sound gets his attention. It's the dog coming out of the back room and to the door.

"You're from Pittsburgh?" she asks.

"Yes."

She whistles. "They're getting fancy around here."

"No, I'm just . . . it's only professional courtesy I'm extending. I'm in the area. I'm curious about the case. So, may I come in?"

"Okay. The place is a mess." She opens the door.

The dog noses Christie and follows him to the sofa, where he sits, sinking far in. "I won't keep you long. Do you have the patience to tell me what you told the other detectives?"

"My sleep is all screwed up lately. It's the damn dog. She barks. She wants to run, then she wants to get back in the house. And whatever it is she wants when she wants it makes her bark."

"And they told me you heard something two nights ago?"

"I was sleeping. Early. Pretty soon I'm awake from this terrible barking. I put cotton in my ears and tried to go to sleep. The barking would stop, then it would start up again. It was making me go nuts. Then it stopped. For the night. And I didn't hear the dog again until tonight. And tonight it was the worst ever. Finally, I called the police."

"Hmm." It fits. "Did you get up, look out the window?"

"No, I didn't. The other guy asked me that."

"So you didn't see anything or anybody?"

"No."

"Hmm. What did you think of Ed Hodel?"

"A nice guy. Very quiet, kept to himself a lot. But nice." She looks as if she will cry.

Christie is scratching the dog's ear, and the dog is allowing it. "What's the dog's name?"

"Bossy. He called her Bossy."

"It sounds like you like her?"

"Ah. I don't know. Is Ed Hodel really gone?"

"Yes. Do you know anybody who had anything against him?"

"No. He was just trying to make do. He had a lot of pride."

"What time of night did he usually walk Bossy?"

"Ten, eleven, midnight. Anytime."

"Are there other dog walkers in the area?"

"Not that I know of."

Fibers. He has to make sure Senteros gets prints and fibers.

The dog knows something. Christie does, too, but his knowledge is practically voodoo, nothing he can act on yet. If he's right and if Senteros figures it out before he does, the strangling will trump the hit-and-run. They'll lose the boys.

He yawns, excusing himself and thanking Irene Mamajek. "Would you keep the dog for a while until I talk to my family about her? Call me if you can't keep her for any reason." He goes back up to Hodel's house, carefully capturing dog hairs from his hand into a clean white handkerchief.

RYAN KNOWS FOR SURE something went wrong. It's past six in the morning, closer to seven, and things started to go bad hours ago. He'd kept thinking he'd see the station wagon creeping up on him somewhere on Route 79. But it never happened. So he panicked.

At nearly three thirty, he'd pulled off in Pittsburgh to get new plates. He'd expected to be quick about it, but he passed North Avenue and drove to a small deserted street. The familiar streets made him feel so much at home, he didn't want to leave. He switched plates with a Focus, but he couldn't seem to make himself get into the car and drive away. So he'd counted the coins in his pockets and roamed around until he found a pay phone.

Tanya answered and said, "You are *all* over the news, buddy, your ass is fried, so don't be coming to us. He's sleeping, besides. He don't want to speak to you."

Chester was *there.* "Why don't I come—"

When she hung up on him, he thought he was going to throw up. He didn't have any more coins. He started banging his head against the brick wall next to the phone. The pay phone began to ring. He looked at it for a while, then answered. Chester said, "You're in bad trouble. Go somewhere. Get away."

"I am going. I'm driving down Seventy-nine to where it ends in West Virginia. I'm going to meet Jack there, but . . . we're going to need some money. Also we need you, man. You can think through these things better than anybody. I could pick you up, take you with us until—"

"Whoa, whoa, where are you now?"

"Pittsburgh. Not far from your place."

"I thought you said you were on the road. Get going. Get out."

Chester hung up, or Tanya did. He waited to see if the phone would ring again, but it didn't. It was stupid to call. Chester was right. He had to get far away, that was the only solution. He went back to Jensen's car and got on the road, thinking maybe by now Jack had passed up Pittsburgh. He drove a little faster than he wanted, looking for the old station wagon.

He didn't see it.

He had nothing to calm him down.

He drove for about an hour, fast, making good time. Still no Jack.

Restless, he pulled off short of the cutoff to Morgantown and went into a truck stop. He was afraid to spend the little bit he had left from the old guy's wallet. He bought a Coke. It would juice him up a bit; he was flagging.

He never should have let Jack go off on his own. Cursing softly, he paced around the rest stop and finally approached a man clerking the convenience store part of the shop. "How far does Seventy-nine go?" he asked. "How many more miles?"

"Where you headed?"

"Just driving. Seeing what's on Seventy-nine."

"It goes to Charleston. West Virginia, that is."

"So how far is that?"

"One hundred seventy-three miles."

"You know that *exactly*?"

"I do. People ask me all the time."

"That's like three hours, I guess."

"Two and a half. You'll be there before breakfast time. You get there, have breakfast in Mollie's Home Cooked Restaurant."

"It sounds like Mollie is cooking the restaurant."

"You're right, it does."

He had a little laugh with the man; it made him feel better; he got back on the road. He had to stay awake now.

How far it seemed to the end of 79. Somehow it felt like the longest drive of his life. Two and a half hours of road and nothing to do but worry.

And now he's at the end of 79. And before him is Mollie's Home Cooked Restaurant.

How long will he have to wait for Jack?

He stands by the car, shivering. He gets back in and drives from parking lot to parking lot, checking all the places at the end of the road. When he's seen them all several times over, he goes back to Mollie's and parks and gets out again. And waits.

There are mostly trucks pulling into the lot.

He paces. Jack had more cash than he does and never gave him any. Why was that? Gas, the Coke. After breakfast, he'll be down to nothing again.

A man hails him. "Going to Mollie's?"

"Yeah."

"You been here before?"

"No. Heard about it." He's aware suddenly of several men coming up behind him.

The man in front of him says, "Ryan Rutter, you are under arrest."

"What the fuck for?" He turns to run, but two others slam him against old man Jensen's car, and even though he tries to slip out of their grasp, they're slick, and before he knows it, he's handcuffed and in the back of a car.

"Thanks," says a trim black guy to a big white guy.

"Anytime. Glad to be of help. Tell Commander hello from me."

"Definitely will."

Then they're all talking at once, and one of them is saying that whole thing about "anything you say may be used in evidence against you."

They've said other things, too, but he's not sure which are the charges. Now they seem to be working out something about the cars. "I could always send somebody down here to print and drive the Nissan," the black guy says.

"We can do that for you," says another.

The black man who seems to be in charge says, "Boss always wants us to do our own. Prints and fibers. If you could lend me a driver, though, I could sit in back with our boy. I promise to get your man back home to you midmorning."

One of the other guys—state troopers wearing those dumb hats—puts up a hand and volunteers to drive.

Another trooper says, "I'll drive behind you, bring our man home. You don't need to worry about it."

So they're talking, talking, figuring out cars and rides, and Ryan yells out, "Why me? What'd I do?"

"Know anything about a hit-and-run that killed a woman?"

"My brother's the one you're looking for."

"We'll have to find him, then, won't we?"

"Damn straight."

The black man gets into the backseat next to him and the other guy with the hat and the West Virginia badge gets in front. They start moving, but he doesn't know what they're doing with him, so he just concentrates on what he can see outside the car window. Signs. Other vehicles. Signs.

COLLEEN INDULGED IN A SHOWER at Addie's place—leaving her about forty-five minutes to sleep. The sugar rush from the French toast would become a sugar crash in about ten minutes, so maybe sleep would come. It was good French toast, worth it.

When she toweled herself off, she put on a borrowed nightgown and robe from Mrs. Ward.

Potocki was lying on the double bed with his clothes on but his shoes off. His eyes were closed. "I can take the bunk bed, you can have this bed. Or I could sleep on top of the covers while you get underneath—a sort of Amish boarding."

"That's fine," Colleen said, even though it was constricting to have a big guy on top of the covers while she was underneath. Still, she climbed in, robe and all.

"Good shower?"

"Yes."

He leaned over and kissed her good night—on the lips, not chastely, but not in a prolonged challenging way either. "Vying with—what's his name—Steve Purdy here," he said.

"I do not intend to vie with a leggy doctor. She wins."

She waited for Potocki to say something wonderful about the leggy doctor not winning, but he didn't. Maybe he'd fallen asleep. Finally he said, "You have some problems."

"I'm not sure what you think they are."

"You don't know what's what." He sounded sleepy, slurry.

Impulsively she raised her upper body—and it wasn't easy, short-sheeted as she was—and kissed him. This one was a little longer.

"What are you doing?"

"Seeing if I want to do it again."

"Do you?"

"Yes. Yes, I do."

"You want me under the covers?"

"Not yet."

"I agree."

"You do?"

"We might be doing things backwards, but who's to say that isn't the right way?"

She could hear little sounds in the house, friendly sounds, thumping of shoes, water running. The trooper was still outside. She hoped the older brother didn't come back.

She let herself drift off, welcoming sleep.

FOR THE FIRST HOUR, DOLAN HELD HIS TONGUE and let Ryan Rutter stew. The troopers were breaking speeding laws just as Dolan had on the way down here; Dolan was happy to see he would have the kid in a small interrogation room by ten. "You okay?" he asked in his kindest voice when they were over a third of the way back.

"I'm pissed. My brother's the one that drove the truck and killed that woman."

"It's going to be your word against his, then?"

"Yeah. It is."

"You get along with him?"

"No."

"Because you had different fathers?"

"What are you talking about?"

"What your mother said about you having no father to take care of you. About how yours was the guy died in jail."

Ryan looked about crazily, as if he might get help from the driver. "So? What does that have to do with anything?"

"Maybe you wanted to be like him?"

"I don't know what you're on about."

But Dolan knew he'd knocked the kid off his pins. He allowed a silence to pass again. Thirty miles, sixty miles. He called Christie but got no answer. He combed his mind for details about the younger boy, anything Christie said last night.

After a long time, he said, "You're lucky. See, we *have* your little brother. That's to your advantage. I'm trying to help you here."

"You don't have him."

"My colleagues have him. He told us you hit Joanna Navarro."

"Nope, he was driving."

"You want to stick to that?"

"Yes."

"You getting hungry? I could call ahead and have some breakfast for you when we get in."

"That's good, because I don't have any money."

"You stole a car. You didn't steal anything else?"

"No."

"Unusual. Huh." Dolan called the office and ordered a breakfast to be sent in to one of the interrogation rooms.

Then it wasn't long before they pulled into Pittsburgh and not much longer before he had the kid locked in a room and fed. Ten fifteen.

He washed his face and went in. "Well, we have some developments. The labs are already testing the evidence." This was not true, but the boy seemed to buy it. "Whoever was in the passenger seat slid forward, hit somewhere on the upper torso, and bled. Jack has a wound—that's what my report says; we have the blood. So that's going to tell us something."

"That doesn't mean anything. We were back and forth in that truck all the time. Switched seats."

"The facts fit his story."

"I don't believe you. He's shitting you. Anyway that wound he got from working on some roof or shit."

"Mrs. Ward's roof. I know. He had the bandage off and hit it again."

"I don't know any Mrs. Ward."

Dolan laughed. "You kinda do. You were a bit rough with her. Your brother seems more concerned about people. He went back to check on the old folks—which is lucky for you."

Ryan appeared to sort through this new information. "I don't know what you're talking about—old folks. Maybe somebody he knows."

"See, here's how it is. The courts might go easy on vehicular homicide. Your brother going back to help the old folks makes a good statement. You have luck on your side, man. I don't know why you do, but you do. It turns out it's only attempted murder with the old folks because they didn't die." Ryan was breathing heavily. Dolan said, "Of course we have to finagle the minor charges—breaking and entering, assault, theft—but let's leave those aside for the moment. That's a lot of complication. You just need to explain, see, very simply, how the first thing, the thing with Joanna Navarro, was an *accident* and you didn't know how to handle it. You didn't know what to do, so you ran. You drove off. That's called leaving the scene of an accident. I understand how you felt. You started feeling safe up in Sugar Lake. You'd think about turning yourself in, but then you'd think, Why bother. The thing was done, right? I get it, I really do. Then these old folks show up and see who you are, and all this safety just . . . flies out the window. So you panicked. People understand panic. You just need to *explain* it."

There was a long pause. Dolan waited. "I have some paper for you. You could just take your time, write it down."

Ryan's face turned wily. Dolan had miscalculated. It wasn't time to close.

"My side? My version? About how Jack did it?"

"Jack didn't do it."

"Well, I'm not going to write down your fucking version."

"I guess I should go. You're making me tired with your stubbornness. You've had a shitty upbringing, no father to speak of, no money, no education, didn't know your ass from your big toe, didn't know how to handle the accident, panicked. Roughed up some old people. We have enough to book you. The lie detector will do the rest."

"Should I have a lawyer?"

"You want one, I'll get you one. Write it down. Do yourself a favor. You're not a bad kid. I'm going to go take a break. I promised I'd call your pal Chester. He was worried about you."

"Chester? You talked to Chester?"

"Chester has some smarts. He told us where to find you at the end of Seventy-nine. He's going to be mighty sad to hear how dumb you are."

Ryan's face squeezed in rage. "That's bullshit, bullshit. He never told you. He wouldn't."

"He sure did."

Dolan went into the hall. He was about to punch in the number for Christie—still up in Meadville, he figured—when he came face-to-face with the man himself. "You're back!"

Christie looked terrible. He never looked good when he hadn't slept. "Yep. Hitched a ride in with one of the troopers."

"No redeeming qualities," Dolan said, tipping a nod toward the interrogation room. "Stupid and doesn't see beyond his nose. Hopeless."

"I was watching. You broke a couple of laws in there."

"I know. If he caves, we're okay."

"And the camera is turned off."

"Oops."

"You're tired," Christie said. "You've been driving all night, after all." Christie was handing him an excuse, much as Dolan had handed one to Ryan Rutter.

Dolan didn't know what to say. He hated it when Christie acted holy. When you had a bad one, you used what you could, however you could. Dolan had a couple of crack cubes in his pocket. On impulse he reached in and showed them—four—to Christie. "I was going to try this next. Not give them. Just promise."

Christie shook his head. "Go home, catch a nap. Come back, use your other weapons."

"Which?"

"Charm."

"I can't be that far off. Didn't Jack Rutter say *some* of the things I said he said?"

"Maybe some." Christie looked thoughtful. "The younger one is bad without being exactly hopeless. Or should I say hopeless without being exactly bad. You wonder in a case like his what'll happen. Speaking of fathers, I'd like to get hold of Jack's. There might be a possible relationship there. I'll put Potocki on it."

"He's back in town, too?"

"On the way. Greer and Potocki foot-dragged a bit about leaving what they're calling the Ward Bed and Breakfast. But they hauled the kid to a magistrate, and they got clearance to bring him to us. They ought to be here noon or later."

"Are they . . . you know?"

"I think it's cooking. I think it's on the burner. Why don't you go home and sleep?"

They went to the window and watched Ryan writing. He wrote furiously and rapidly, so they figured he was writing lies.

ADDIE HAD SLEPT FOR ONLY AN HOUR—she couldn't help it; her body wanted to wake with the sun.

She felt a little dazed, but not terrible. In fact, her arthritis wasn't as bad as usual, and she wondered if sleep deprivation might be a cure. She'd made some quick bacon and toast for the police detectives, hoping the smell didn't wake Linda and Hank, and it hadn't. They didn't budge. Pretty soon the police were gone. They even let the trooper leave her yard, because apparently both boys had been found. She got her spaghetti sauce into containers and into the freezer. Then there she was, feeling like herself, in her yard drinking her coffee and looking at the buds on the hydrangeas.

"What are those?" Jack had asked the second day.

She told him florist hydrangeas. She pointed out the broad leaves. He had seemed interested.

When nine o'clock came around, she heard sound in the house, and soon after that Linda and Hank came out wearing jeans and sweatshirts and carrying mugs of coffee. "You didn't get much sleep," she told her daughter.

"You got less."

"Oh, but I'll sleep this afternoon."

"After breakfast, we'll help you pack up; we'll take you back to our house for a while."

"Oh. No. There's no need for me to leave now. The detectives had a call. They got the second boy."

"Did they?"

"So I can stay here."

"But, Mother, think what you've just been through. You can't just go back to regular life."

I can't? She didn't say it aloud. Instead she tested one of the stems of the irises. It was bent, but it didn't seem to be broken. Her eyes began to smart. She knew if she tried to speak, her voice would catch, so instead she concentrated on the pink, blue, and purple irises.

"Mom?"

Addie shook her head.

Hank said, "Linda. Let her be for a moment."

"Why?"

"It's like her meditation time out here. Let her be."

Bless Hank. With them gone indoors, she could think. She would need to bring Tom from the hospital if they released him. If they didn't, she would visit him there. She couldn't just leave him. Linda and Hank would get frustrated eventually waiting for her. They'd want to get back to their own lives. If she kept to the things she needed to do, she could wear them down.

RYAN LOOKS UP, SURPRISED, when Christie walks into the room and shows his ID. He asks, "Where's the other guy?"

"Doing other jobs."

"Well, I wrote what he wanted."

"Let's have a look." Christie reads for a long time, tears off the pages, folds them a couple of times, and shakes his head.

"What?"

"Lies get you in worse trouble. You'll want to be sure you say things you can hang your hat on."

"Jack did it. That's what I mean to say. He can say the opposite. I'm sure he will."

"Don't be too sure of anything. It's a prescription for disaster."

"You sound like Dr. Phil."

"You want to tell me about Ed Hodel?"

"Who's that?"

"Nice old fellow lives in Meadville. You roughed him up some. He's complaining."

"So? He gave me a hard time about parking on his street."

A thrill goes through Christie's whole body. He has to force himself to continue in the same even tone. "And you'd been drinking—so we hear. Kind of in your cups."

"Okay. Yeah, I was drinking."

"Neighbors saw you getting into an argument with him about the truck."

"Oh, yeah?"

"Then you took his dog. Why would you do that to him?"

Ryan goes silent for a while. "I probably should have a lawyer. I thought I was in here about something else. This is getting a bit thick."

"I'll make sure you have a lawyer if you want one."

"I do. Just not the kind that costs."

"Right." Christie shakes his head and makes to get up. "Okay. I don't understand why you took the dog, though, the only thing the poor guy had."

"I was just taking care of it." Christie sits back down. Ryan stops, uncertain.

"The dog barks a lot. That's what I hear."

"You're telling me."

"All last night, she's back at Hodel's place barking up a storm."

"So?" Recognition dawns.

"So. A dead man can't open the door."

Ryan's face goes white. He looks at the ceiling, the floor; he starts shaking his head.

"You probably should write down everything. Your prints are all over the house. You don't want to say your brother was there because we have your prints, not his. You want decent treatment, you're going to have to come clean."

Ryan throws the pen, then the legal pad, across the room. He beats the table with his fists and kicks at the table legs.

Christie picks up the legal pad and pen and tosses them back. "Write what you did to Hodel. Start with that. We'll talk again later." He leaves the room.

Dolan has not gone home after all. He's been watching. "We're tarred with the same brush," he says.

"Unfortunately."

"You got him. You're getting him. That's what counts."

"How do I keep him once Senteros figures it out?"

"You'll find a way," says Dolan. "That thing about possession being nine-tenths. We've got Navarro. To keep him here."

COLLEEN DRIVES WHILE POTOCKI sits in back with Jack, who's shackled, though he doesn't look as if he'd try to use his hands now even if he could. It's eleven in the morning.

"We have to make one little stop before we're on our way," she tells Jack, half turning in her seat.

Potocki is on the phone with Littlefield, giving her instructions about a people search in England. Boss asked for it. She wishes she'd thought of it before he did.

"Dennis Epson Rutter," Potocki says into the phone. Colleen watches Jack in the rearview mirror. He's alert, listening.

They drive the now familiar road that leads to the old lady's house and later Jensen's. Potocki puts a hand over the mouthpiece of his phone. "They're checking." And then he's back to the phone. "Ibstock. Keep at it. Get back to me."

Colleen explains to Jack, "We're stopping at Mrs. Ward's place. Just briefly. We need to thank her. She took good care of us. She made us French toast."

"Best I ever tasted," Potocki says quietly.

"Did she ever feed you? She apparently likes to feed people."

"Yeh." A short sound, almost nonexistent.

"I mean beyond the spaghetti sauce."

"That was just sitting, going to waste. I . . . took it. The other stuff . . . she gave me."

"What was that?"

"Cookies and a cake; a fish dinner; an egg sandwich."

"That was nice of her."

"Yeh."

"Hm. It's pretty around here." She tells Potocki, "Boss has a point. There is another way to live, that's for sure. I haven't planted anything in a long time, but Mrs. Ward's gardens make me want to. Next time I'm off work, I'm putting in flowers."

"That's next week if you want it," Potocki observes.

Right. She's done five days around the clock.

She says, "You helped with the garden, Jack? Didn't you?" She angles the rearview mirror to look at him better.

"Neh."

"Oh, I thought you did. Addie Ward said you were a big help."

"I did the roof, painting. I did my best not to run down her flowers."

"I guess that's what she meant. She said you were helpful. If Ibstock works out, if that's where your father is, I don't know, it sounds pretty rural. He'd have to want to take you on, of course. But it might be nice there."

Jack shakes his head.

"What?"

"He doesn't care anymore. Besides, I'm going to jail."

They pull into the driveway of Addie Ward's place. She's on her phone in her yard, and although her daughter is not in sight, her daughter's car is still there.

"We'll only be a minute," she tells Jack.

But as soon as she's out of the car, Colleen's phone rings, too. She listens for a very long time as Christie tells her how the Hodel case is part of the Navarro-Jensen-Ward case. She listens carefully until she understands what she's supposed to do.

"What?" Potocki asks.

She motions to Addie Ward to wait and takes Potocki aside to explain that there's a second homicide, more intentional than the first.

Potocki sighs. "So much for eventually getting the kid to his father in Ibstock."

"Could be all Ryan. Boss thinks so. Let's hope." Colleen motions another delay to Addie, who seems to understand. She and Potocki go back to the car and open the back door. They lean in. After a silence, Colleen says, "You want to tell us anything about the dog you boys had for a day?"

"I don't know much. My brother got her somewhere. Said her name was Bossy. It was my fault she ran away."

"Where'd he get her?"

"On the street, he said."

"Weren't you together when he got the dog?"

"No."

"Where were you?"

"In a coffee shop off the highway. After that I was hitchhiking."

"Anybody see you?"

"A couple people at the shop. Then Ryan did. I was walking. He picked me up."

"And then he found the dog?"

"No, he already had the dog."

"Did he tell you the truth about where he got it?"

"He just said on the street. I didn't exactly believe it."

"Why is it you weren't with him?"

"We fought earlier. I left."

"Can you explain?"

"We were in the truck. I got out. I was going to try to make it on my own. It didn't work out."

"Why not?"

"I had no money, no place to go. I was trying to hitch a ride back to Pittsburgh when he saw me. He was acting crazy. It was late at night and I gave up."

"Did he ever tell you the dog belonged to a man named Ed Hodel?"

"No. Nothing about where he got it. I'd give it back if I could. I tried to find it."

"The dog's been found. She led the police to her owner—Ed Hodel. He's dead. You sure you never heard of him?"

"No." He begins to rock his body back and forth. "Oh, my God . . ."

"Jack."

How will this kid make it through hearings and jail time and whatever Ryan will try to pull? How will he break away?

"Jack, you've been taking care of your brother, but he's not a person who takes to kindness. Without Ryan in your life . . . people might be pretty nice to you. Did you ever think that? Do you understand that?"

"Just tell me straight out. Are you saying he . . . hurt the dog's owner?"

"Yes."

Jack lets out a sound so painful, it chills Colleen. She and Potocki look at each other. "Will you talk to us? Tell us everything you know?"

He nods, sobbing.

Potocki's phone rings. He listens. He says, "Rutter. Ibstock Brick Company. Got it." He puts a notebook on the roof of the car and starts writing. When he hangs up, he tells both Jack and Colleen, "If we can get your father in here for the trial, it might help."

They haven't noticed Addie Ward coming up to the car until she's there. "Oh, my," she says to Jack. "Well, you definitely shook things up around here." With a bit of tissue she wipes at her own eyes. "These things are hard," she says, "when there's liking mixed up with all kinds of other feelings." She tells the detectives, "I liked him. That's what I mean." She looks into the car. "You're a good worker. You remember that. Work opens doors to other things."

Colleen says, "We just came to thank you for last night."

Addie searches the three of them with her amazing blue eyes and says, "It was nothing. Let me know what's happening with the boy if you would."

"I will."

Colleen hopes Jack will look up before they leave. He's still weeping quietly, turned away. Addie steps back. Colleen and Potocki get into the car. Colleen backs up to turn around.

Addie moves forward a step, and finally the boy looks up.